# UNRAVEL

## THE SPIRIT RUNES BOOK TWO

## CJ WALLINGSFORD

Unravel
Book Two of The Spirit Runes
Copyright © {2021} Courtney J Wallingsford

For more information, address: cjwallingsford@outlook.com

First edition 2021
ISBN: 978-1-954426-04-7
Cover design by Storywrappers.
https://storywrappers.com
Editing by KillingItWrite.
https://www.killingitwrite.com
Cjwallingsford.com

*For my two loves, Eric and Bee*

# TRIGGER WARNING

This is a **dark**, romantic fantasy story.
Physical abuse
Mental abuse
Violence
Adult language
Non-consent

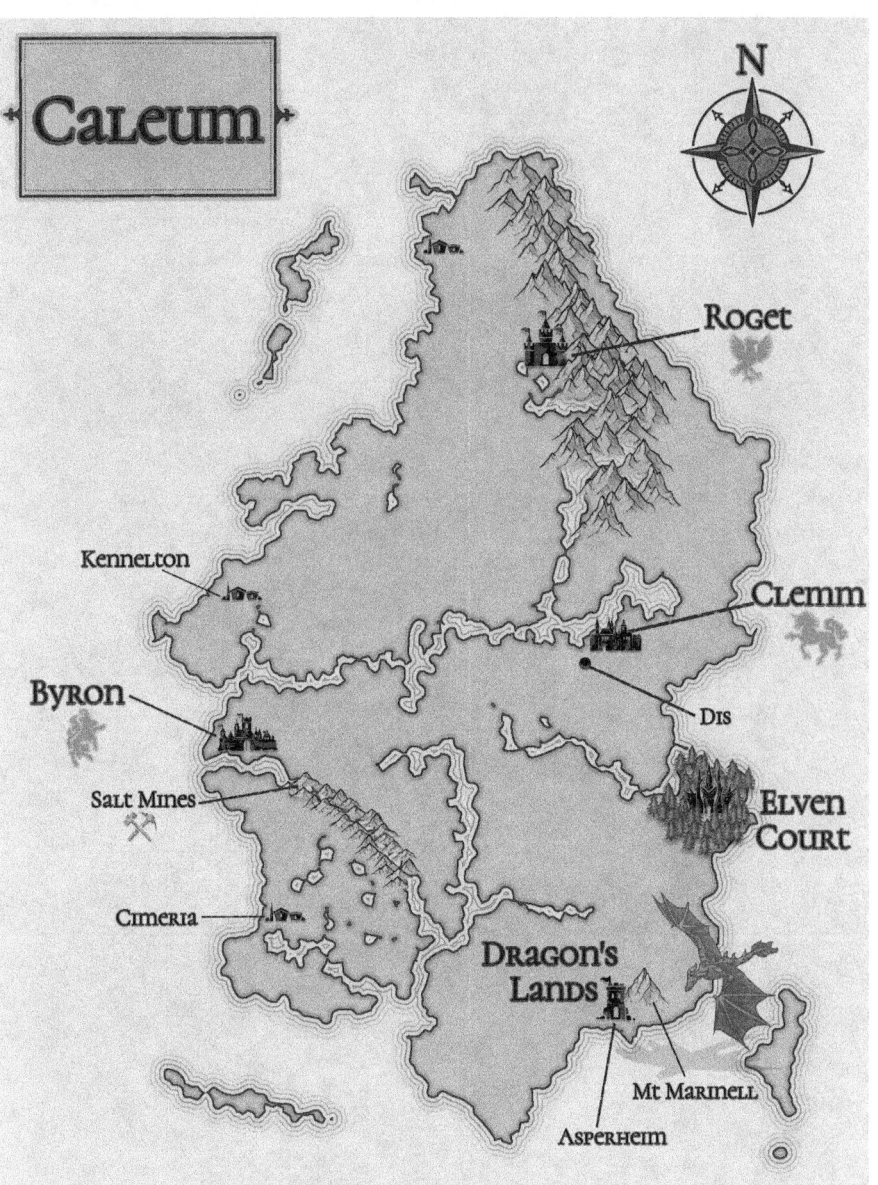

**Caleum**

N

Roget

Kennelton

Clemm

Dis

Byron

Salt Mines

Elven
Court

Cimeria

Dragon's
Lands

Mt Marinell

Asperheim

"My father is gone, but I worry for how long. I fought so hard, and even though I am queen, I still don't feel like I have control. Everything is starting to come apart, including me."
Morella Rowena Annabelle Byron

# CHAPTER 1

*I* see the blade twisting in my skin. The way my flesh peels back from the edge is like soft butter being cleaved from a brick. I cannot look away, cannot register what is being said. There is a voice, a woman asking me something. All I comprehend is pain. I gaze transfixed as the knife carves along bone toward—

*"It's okay, you're alright."*

I hear Declan in my mind. He was not here when I went to sleep. I do not know if he is here now. Our bond, the mental link we share, means he could be anywhere in Caleum. I need him here. I need him to chase this horror away.

*"I'm here."*

His arms wrap around me, pulling me in close to his strong and warm body.

Unshed tears build under my lids, clinging to my lashes. He says it is okay, but I cannot believe him. There are deep scars and sickening memories of my past that do not seem to want to fade.

The nighttime terrors weigh heavy on me, pulling me into torment each time I sleep, like reliving the duchess' torture.

When I close my eyes, the inevitable comes, and then I wake, left to blubber, and sniffle my way into the morning.

*"He's dead. Viktor. Your father. The king. That fucking monster."* Declan's muscles tense as he presses me harder against him. *"That prick is gone."*

My nose nuzzles against a stiff shirt. A dress shirt, I surmise as I bump against a button. The solid build and scent of him below the fabric soothes me. I existed under Viktor's thumb for revolutions—my entire life. He controlled me, tried beating me into submission. The dozens of overlaying scars on my back stand as proof.

Still, I fought, earning freedom in an inking from the Redcrosse monks after near nineteen revolutions of torment. Even when I could ignore his commands, he was still present, blackmailing me, using Marcus, my favorite sibling, to force my actions.

Enough was enough when Viktor had Marcus tortured. I barged into his office without a plan only to find he was not alone, and spirit runes burned into his flesh. It was kill or be killed, and I thought that both would be ideal.

I survived, but Viktor's body was never found. Desperate, I combed through rubble, looking for even the tiniest shred of flesh or bone to confirm he was dead.

"Calm down." Declan's firm lips press against my temple.

My lashes flutter as I crack open salt-crusted eyes. My vision is hazy, as tears have welled and stuck in stubborn fashion to my lids. I sit up, rubbing my face. My eyes dart around.

Blue moonlight illuminates my bedroom. I breathe easy, everything as it should be. I look down at my right leg, rubbing my hand over the thick scar on my thigh with an absent mind. My sheets and blanket are shoved to the foot of my bed and half strewn onto the floor.

"You were kicking." His voice is deep, gruff with exhaustion.

My eyes slide over him laid out on his side. Long bronze hair hangs about his lean face. The tips fall before his eyes and against the bridge of his thin nose, which he brushes away with a heavily inked arm. His head is propped on an equally marred second arm, and he lifts his eyebrows. "It's been half a revolution now."

Trepidation quells within us, the fear mine alone. The skin on my collarbone scarred by the spirit rune burns. The mark is named the Vitale rune, known to give the spirits the power of life. I roll my neck and shoulders, wincing as I stretch. The skin pulls, causing the inflamed marking to sear more vividly.

Declan sits, reaching toward me. I try to protest, but his hand slides over the rune, cold against my shoulder. The spirits are beings in Medius, the dimension above ours. Each being wears a set of runes that provide power. I was never meant to wear this rune, and it is becoming torturous. The cool touch of Declan's hand brings a respite as he pulls energy out of me, the streaming hum lulling me into a tranquil state.

He grunts, pulling back, the cherry-red skin and a blackened print of the rune splayed across his palm. Guilt washes through me.

"Lover," he chuckles. "I'll go through hell into the inferno for you without a second thought."

I groan. "Seriously, Dec, I might be crowned as monarch, but you're the one the court respects. They look to you as king, to fix all the problems Viktor left behind."

Declan lies on his side and pats the space in front of him. "Come on, this conversation doesn't need to happen right now."

I snuggle into him. "This conversation shouldn't need to happen at all," I grumble under my breath, getting comfortable. "I shouldn't have to tell you that the court takes precedence over me."

One arm slips under my neck, and beneath the pillows, his other hand rests on my hip. He nuzzles my neck. "We've had this conversation a hundred times. I'm tired of it. I'm tired in general," his lips whisper against me. "I spent all evening with Leo and Dante going over the legislature of Viktor's taxes and levies."

"Leonard Wyndam, Legia's dad?"

"Yes, and Dante, the Duke of Medicci." Delcan's voice is irritated by my inquisition, having mentioned to me about the meeting. "Wyatt and Chase were there, as well as Daphine."

I hum, not paying attention, glad to be curled into him.

"You need to be more involved in court politics. Even Wyatt asked why I was there in your stead."

"That's because he doesn't like you."

Dec releases a deep breath of annoyance. "You're fully healed, and you're the crown of Byron."

I roll to bury my face in his chest. "We've had this conversation a hundred times."

He squeezes me to him. "You are the queen. You..."

*Shouldn't be*, I think, only half heeding his words. He says something about duty and obligation being rightfully mine.

"Dec," I sigh, "I know, but Wyatt is only one who prefers to deal with me over you. Even Seth agrees with your politics more than mine. You are methodical about your actions, and you are logical in your decision making. I don't think that way."

His lips curve against my neck. *She's right. She isn't the one to make a hard decision, and she doesn't plan well. She does better spending time in the city, helping the elementals in desperate need. I know she's feeding them, probably the only thing sustaining the city.*

I giggle, wriggling into him to be as close as possible. Lately, it is hard to discern where he ends and where I begin. Sometimes we are so at odds, while at other times, our thoughts are parallel. I inhale the scent of him, the smell of fresh rain and something tangy. I grin, thrilled to have him here.

# CHAPTER 2

*W*hen the morning comes, I am alone.

*Typical.*

I check the time and grimace. I missed the court session.

*Again.*

After washing and dressing, I braid my long auburn hair staring at nothing. I grab my book off the low table centered between the couch and chairs, dropping in my window seat to stare out across the City of Cato budding against the Byron castle walls.

I rest the book in my lap, but my attention is claimed by something on the other side of the windowpane. The view spans over the palace gardens and city out to the white walls of Salt Canyon. The ravine is darkened, the oasis of lush green at the base hiding the river from my sight.

There was another collapse in the mines yesterday. I heard the shouts and talk in the city streets, the women crying, and the men grumbling. The caverns are overworked without precaution, leading to hazardous situations.

My heart rolls over in a lazy fashion.

Gordon Pymn was responsible for the mines. He served my

father, the king for revolutions. Cave-ins were rare. Injuries were unheard of.

*Until I killed him—sawed his head off and dropped it at Viktor's feet for amusement. Petty revenge, more like.*

I sigh and shove fingers through my hair. Birds fly across the scene, and my heart yearns to follow them, to chase the clouds, and learn if I can reach the soul star.

"Thinking of running away again?" Declan chuckles. I glance over and beam at him.

*Fuck, she's beautiful.*

I roll my eyes at his thought. He steps forward, lifting my feet and sliding onto the bench. He grabs one bare foot and begins to massage the aching muscles.

I hum at him. My eyes slip closed, and my head falls against the wall. "Not when you do that."

He laughs as he drags his thumb along my arch. "I'm surprised to find you here."

I point to the book in my lap, not bothering to lift my head or open my eyes. I do not have to say anything. He knows. Our mental link formed through his bite as a shade, the venom in his saliva able to force a blood bond, unites our souls.

"Which you aren't even reading."

I open one eye. He is smirking at me with light gray irises, his eyes transitioning lighter with the elevation in his mood. "Jerk." I close my eye.

He pushes hard on the ball of my foot.

I twitch. "Ow."

His smirk turns to a full grin. "It's a knot. It'll feel better in a minute."

"I don't want it to feel better in a minute. I want it to feel better now." I try to pull my foot back, and he lets up.

"You have no patience," he teases with a chuckle.

I frown, not bothering to open my eyes. "Maybe it's a low tolerance for pain."

He scoffs. "Not with as much as you've taken."

Focusing on staying relaxed, I hum. In my extensive experience, I learned fighting against pain only makes it worse. "I know I can take it, but I have zero desire to."

"Even if it means things hurt less after?"

I lift my head and glower. "Everything hurts less after it hurts more."

Declan snickers as the knot releases, the sharp sensation subsiding. "You're cute."

I roll my eyes then contort my face.

"Still cute."

I giggle, closing the book with a grin. "I am not cute."

He switches feet. "With these tiny toes and that giggle? You're so fucking cute it hurts."

I laugh harder. "Dec, you are ridiculous."

"No, I'm fabulous." His lips twist to one side, and he wiggles his eyebrows.

"That's pretty accurate."

He snorts through his nose. We sit there, grinning like fools for no reason at all as he rubs my feet.

"I want to hurt something, break someone," he admits in a low voice, moving his hands to my calf. The massage stays firm but easy, his fingers digging into muscles with ginger care.

"Well, you have my leg, and I supposedly have this high pain tolerance, so..." I hum with indifference.

His movements cease. His eyes narrow on me. "Not you." He reaches out, clasping the back of my neck. I let him pull me forward, and he rests his forehead on mine. "Never you."

"It would be a release."

"Lover, if I get a release from you, it's going to be of a different kind." His eyes crinkle at the corners as his silver orbs dance.

I grin with my tongue between my teeth. "Well..." I wave a

hand toward my bedroom. The book in my lap dissolves to ash, and I frown. "Fuck."

He sighs at me. "Oh well, that's the least of things."

"It was from the library."

"Which you own."

"That makes it worse," I whine.

His face is drawn with a serious fever as he says, "I'm terrified one day you're going to wave your hand, and it's going to be me that dissolves to ash."

My ribcage constricts around my heart. "No."

He kisses the tip of my nose. "So, if it was me or that dusty, boring, old history book? No great loss."

"It was old, but it wasn't dusty—"

"You sneezed every time you turned the page."

"—Or boring."

He lifts an eyebrow at me. "I've been listening to you read that book over the last cycle, and every time you start, I have an urge to headbutt the nearest wall to knock myself out and make that dreadful monologue cease."

I draw my mouth down and to one side. "It wasn't that bad."

"It was, and I'm glad it's gone. How about a fight? You could stand to burn out some energy, and I want to punch something."

I smirk. "I thought you didn't want to hurt me?"

"I won't. You are pretty good at keeping me from landing blows."

"Only because I cheat."

He shakes his head, his hands switching to my other calf. "It's not cheating for you to use magic. You have it. Use it." He shrugs. "Without it, I'd rip you to pieces. Well—" he gives me a half-smirk "—not really, but I could."

"You almost enjoyed that thought."

"Almost, but not if it is you."

"You're always saying you're so different. I don't think you are." I reach out and brush the tips of hair away from his nose. "I think you just don't hide it anymore."

He smirks as he cups my jaw, his eyes brilliant gray. His tongue glides against mine as he kisses me, deep and slow. My toes curl, but he pulls back, resting his forehead against mine with eyes still closed. "I love you."

My chest swells, and it makes it hard to breathe. "Dec."

He grins and kisses me again. "Come on." He pats my leg. "I really need to swing at something." He gives me a skeptical look. "I'm swinging hard."

"So, in other words, don't let you hit me."

"Not even a little bit."

I shrug. "I think I can manage that. Half speed, though."

He looks at me with a pathetic pout. "What if I don't swing that hard?"

"How about three-quarter speed, and you dial back?"

"Half speed, full swing it is." He sighs. "You need to change."

"I thought you liked it when I wear dresses."

His fingers trail along my thigh. I squirm. "I do, but they're not good for fighting."

I hook a finger under the collar of his shirt and tug. "Neither are dress shirts."

He smirks. "I hate these damned things, and if I rip this one, I'll feel better inside."

"Not very king-like."

The left side of his lips tug to one side. "I'm not a king."

I roll my eyes. "We might not be married yet, but you are the king." I smile. "My king." He gives me a dirty look. I lift my eyebrows. "King of my heart?"

He lets out a bark of laughter. "Alright, don't make me beg."

I gasp with a hand to my chest. "You? Beg?"

He grabs me to him, claiming my mouth once more. When

he breaks free, his eyes are bright silver. "You make everything better."

I close my eyes, willing the elements to change. When I open them again, we are dressed in black, grunge clothing. "Ready?"

"Yes."

I dissipate us to the practice field. "Give me a minute." I dance away from a full swing. "Cripes, Dec, some of us need to warm up."

"That was."

I shake my head but grin. "Let me stretch." I move through positions and then stand and roll my shoulders. "Alright."

He steps toward me, reaching out through our link. *"I'm not holding back."*

*"I know."*

*"Don't let me hurt you."*

*"I'll do my best."*

He relaxes, the tension melting echoing through our bond. He steps, I dodge the swing. He smirks, upping the game, moving faster. I can only last so long before I cave, using magic to block and shield. I use the elements to add force to my own swings trying to match his strength. If not for the bond, I would think it had zero effect, but I know he feels it.

I evade and dodge, focusing on keeping him from connecting with any part of my body. My knee is screaming in agony. Although healed, the blasted joint has never been the same. I resort to flips and twirls to stay out of reach, using magic as a shield at times to give him the benefit of solid contact. His speed is increasing, and I am out of breath, my reactions barely fast enough.

I stand, getting in close, slamming an elbow into his side. He grunts, stepping back and swinging in a blur of motion. He is moving faster than my eyes can follow, but I know retaliation is coming, and I get a shield between us in the nick of time. The force of his blow pushes me a few feet away from him. He's on me in the blink of an eye, raining punch after punch against my shield as a vague, hazy figure.

The ferocity shakes my confidence, and the shield breaks. His fist comes toward my face as his eyes stretch wide. I duck, my scalp tingling from the proximity of his attack. In a panic, I blast a force wave at him. His body sails across the field.

"Oh shit," I whisper as I start to run after him, more skipping as my injured leg protests in nasty pulses of burning spikes.

I collide with him in the middle of the field. He wraps me in his arms, my heart racing. He is panting and crushing me against his body, pinning me beneath him in the dirt.

"Fuck," he growls.

"I'm sorry."

He lifts enough to stare down at me. "I almost broke your face."

"Again." I giggle.

He lets out an exasperated noise and kisses me. I struggle but get my arms free, running my hands over his sculpted chest as he ravishes my mouth.

*"Are you okay?"*

*"Fine. Worried about you. I forgot. I got caught up."*

*"You got fast."*

*"I know. Fuck, it felt good, though."*

He pulls back. *"Are you sure you're okay?"*

"You didn't even touch me." I run my hands down his chest and abdomen, perspiration causing his shirt to be damp. "I hit you harder than I meant to."

He laughs and rubs his nose against mine. "Honestly, I barely felt it. I was so focused on nearly hitting you."

Laughter sounds behind us. "You two make me throw up in my mouth."

We both glance up. Declan's brother Seth is standing nearby with arms crossed. He is taller and beefier than Declan, with a frizzy mop of brown hair on his head. Declan eyes his younger brother, with thoughts swirling around the idea of someone to beat on with flesh against flesh contact and an ability to inflict pain.

I grin, knowing the Bard brothers can beat on each other for hours. As shades, they are unmatched by fae in speed and strength, and for any infliction Declan doles out on his brother, Seth will heal within minutes. "Go for it."

Declan's eyes flicker to me with a melancholy tinge. He does not want to leave me, to relinquish my attention. I nudge him. *"Go, have some fun."*

*"I am having fun."*

*"Go beat something. Come find me when you're done."*

I dissipate to my room and make sure the door is closed and locked. I head for the bathroom, tugging my hair free and working fingers through the long sweat-soaked strands. I start the shower and pull my shirt off.

Getting the fabric over my head, I find Declan standing in front of me. "Done already?"

He shrugs. "I got a few full swings."

*"Poor Seth."*

Declan laughs and tugs me to him. "He's bigger than I am. He can take it."

I snicker. "He's bigger, not tougher." I force the elements to reform his dress shirt.

He glances down at it. "Real—"

I rip it open, buttons flinging every which way. "Better? You destroyed it."

He walks me back against the cool glass door of the shower, pressing my skin against it. I shiver.

"No, you destroyed it."

I am in a dress again. I laugh, but he smothers it with his mouth. His fingers grip the back of my thighs, lifting me against him, encouraging me to wrap my legs around his hips. He drags his mouth from mine along my jaw to my neck.

"Dec..."

His teeth sink down into the thin, sensitive skin of my neck, and I arch into him, wanting to feel him, for him to have what he wants, needs.

He makes a guttural noise in the back of his throat. *Mine.*

*"Yes."*

He pulls back, lapping at my neck, drawing a shudder from me. *I hate hurting her.*

I snort. "It doesn't hurt."

"You're bleeding."

I kiss him, tasting the metallic lingering on his tongue. "Still doesn't hurt."

I feel him in my skull. Strong. Warm. Bright. Ambrosia. It is like he is trying to burst free of my head, overwhelming and full, his love and desire for me.

Declan rips the shower door open and shoves us inside.

"Dec!" I shriek with laughter.

I dissipate the clothes to be gone, so there is nothing between our flesh. Warm water streams over our skin as he forces me against the wall and grabs my face, holding and tilting it to allow him to have his way with my mouth. I cling to him and squeeze with my legs, trying to get closer somehow.

He starts bucking his hips against mine, and I grin into his open mouth hovering over mine. "Fuck, lover," he pants. "You make this whole shit show worth it." He slides one hand down my body, caressing my hip and leg halfway around his body. "You're the only fucking thing worth a damn in this fucked world." His eyes meet mine, glittering black with craving and lust. "And you're mine."

I grin at him through the misting spray of water off his shoulders. "I couldn't do this without you, any of it."

He chokes on a laugh. "I do it for you, but right now, I'm okay with that."

I know he means me naked and wet, pressed against, and wrapped around him. "Me too," I tease.

He is grinning and laughing as he kisses me, moving his body against mine. I groan, squirming, and writhing for more. He takes control, giving me what I want, making my eyes roll back in my head, and my toes curl in pleasure until the water is cold.

# CHAPTER 3

*I* wake to the toll of bells. I count and then squeeze my eyes shut and groan. Session is starting soon. I cannot miss it again, not after Declan made that jab about doing everything for me.

Showered and dressed, I slither forth out of the safety of my chambers. I proceed through the servant tunnels toward the kitchens.

*"You shouldn't be in those tunnels. They are for servants. You are queen, act like it. Stop hiding."*

*"I'm hungry, and this is the quickest route."*

*"If you want something, send a servant."*

*"I'm more than capable of getting it myself rather than ordering a servant about."*

*"You can request a servant politely to bring you something as a compromise."*

I start singing a song in my mind rather than answering him.

In turn, he starts growling and grumbling. *"You're going to be late for session."*

I slide out of the passage into a warm room built of stone. Well-worn and nicked wood tables are in abundance around the space, one wall taken by fire brick ovens. My eyes catch sight of a few trays of turnovers.

The crust radiates warmth, no doubt freshly baked and left to cool.

"Ella?"

I turn with a pastry halfway to my gaping mouth. A young man, fae, with long pointed ears and angular features, is watching me with a face of amusement. What stands out are his brilliant purple eyes. My own violet eyes grow wide at the sight of him.

No longer is he a thin, scraggly boy, but nearly as tall as Declan now. He is still scrappy and slender, but not sick or malnourished.

"Dean?" I gape at him.

A jovial grin spreads across his face as he bows. "Your Majesty."

I roll my eyes. "Seriously, don't, kid, or I'll send you back to the streets."

He laughs, rumpling his hair. Flour smears along the ridge of his forehead. "What is the queen doing in the kitchens?"

I hold my tart aloft. "I'm hungry."

"You could have had it brought to you." I sigh, and he gives me a funny look. His face scrunches on one side, and he tilts his head. "I never understood why you pulled me out of the city."

I take a bite of the pastry. "You needed help."

"You really are different."

I grin, finishing my breakfast. Declan's growling in the back of my mind, but Dean's words spark something. "Can I ask you something?"

"Anything," he answers. He holds his arms away from his sides. "I owe you everything."

"Debatable. I distinctly remember saying I owe you a favor for coming along." We both grin. "Can you tell me about your parents?"

The skin of his forehead furrows as his face tilts down. He shakes his head. "I have never known who my parents are. I can tell you about Arun." He glances at me with more light in his expression. "She's the woman who took me in."

"You don't know who your parents are?" My heart skips a beat, and the tip of my tongue wets my lips in anticipation.

"Arun found me in an alley."

*Like me*, I think. *Exactly like me.*

*"Yes, he's the only other one with purple eyes, and he was found like trash in the gutter just like you."* Declan snaps in my skull, *"You're late."*

"Does this have something to do with my eyes?" I drag my focus back to Dean. "Everyone makes a fuss about my eyes being like yours."

I nod. "Yes."

*"Yes, you're different. You have purple eyes. You also have your father's blood and have killed since the age of eight. I don't care. You should be here with me."*

*"Back off, Dec. I'll be there."* I roll my eyes, and his irritation ceases. Aloud I answer Dean. "Yes, this is about your eyes. They are like mine." I point toward my face. "I have to go, but we should talk more later."

I dissipate to the throne room. The young couple in the middle of the room go slack-jawed. I cross my legs and drop down on the cushion next to Declan. From the corner of my eye, I catch sight of his nostrils flaring.

There is no feeling of annoyance seeping through me, so I know he has closed our link. The unfair advantage he has, being the dominant one in our bond. I shake my head but focus on the commoners before us.

"Please, go on." I wave my hand, catching sight of Declan's flinch.

The man bows to me. "Majesty! You are by far the kindest we've ever known. Perhaps you may—"

"The decision is final. The request for a child is being denied."

The back of my neck tingles and prickles crawl along my forearm. My eyes cut to Declan. I want to ask what is going on, but my earlier sassy response has gotten me blocked.

I clench my fists in my lap, disappointed with myself. I have no idea what is going on. Without proper knowledge, if I contradict Declan, it will only look bad. We need to provide a unified front, and I will not bicker with him in front of the court.

"Please," the woman whispers, her words shredded by the restriction in her throat. She latches onto her husband's arm, almost cowering behind him. Her wide eyes are riveted on me, full of vulnerable despair, magnified through welling tears. "Please grant this to us."

I look away from her to face Declan. His jaw is clenched, which does nothing to reassure me. I dig my thumbnail into the tip of my index finger. I do not understand why Declan is refusing such a thing, which only makes me further repugnant with myself.

The sapphire pulses against my breastbone, the jewel a powerful multiplier of energy, and the Vitale rune flames to a steady burn.

I try to inhale slow, cautious breaths to prevent an outburst. *I need to remain calm. Panic will only make things worse.* Clearing my throat draws his dark gray eyes. I stare into them for a moment before swiveling my gaze back to the man and woman. My chest aches with empathy at their wide-eyed gapes and breathless begging.

"Perhaps—" I begin.

*"Morella,"* Declan growls in my mind.

I refrain from rolling my eyes, then flex and straighten the fingers of one hand, the other pinching the skin between forefinger and thumb with all the strength I can manage.

I pick up where I left off. "This is something we can revisit at a later day. For now, a decision has been made, and I believe it will give the court something considerable to weigh on." I take a deep breath in, waiting.

The woman splinters before my eyes. Her grip on the man drags down his arm as her knees buckle. "No, please," she cries. "Please, Majesty, have mercy! I'll be a good mother, a kind mother."

My hands start to shake in my lap, both curling in tight, my nails pressing as sharp pins against my palms. Her distress echoes inside of me. I fight to stay calm. My eyes drop to my clenched fists. I relax them, flex my fingers straight, only to clench them again.

The hiss of release in my ears is like a whistle of air through a small opening—the reverberating strum through my chest as if my internal organs are all vibrating. I wince before the explosion even goes off.

The boom explodes in the center of the room, a wave of force streaking out across the space. Then comes the crackling fire, burning and churning in the air. I reach out a hand with shaking fingers to force those elements back to air, but energy streams through me. The coursing riptides out of my chest and into my palm, setting the blaze to roaring, growing to twice the size.

"Ella." Declan jerks to his knees and grabs my hands. The occupants of the room whimper and gasp, and there's movement on the edge of my senses. He holds my wrists in a tight grip, using his available hand to wave at the burning destruction. The fire diminishes somewhat, then he grabs at the air in front of him, and the fire goes out.

I gape at where the fire had been and beyond where the horrified man and woman are huddled together. I look to Declan, still holding my wrists in his hand. His dark eyes narrow at me. His mouth is a hard line, his lips pressed together, firm enough to drain them to white.

I stare with wide eyes and a berating heart, the rune on my

shoulder burning and pulsing. He slides his hand under the opening of my shirt, pushing against my collarbone over the Vitale rune. I hiss through clenched teeth at the contact.

Energy pulsates in me, echoing my heartbeat. As quickly as he is pulling it out of me, it's brimming and threatening to overflow. I sway, dizzy with sweet intoxication.

His hand pulls back, an imprint of the spirit rune seared into his flesh. The blistered skin bubbles and fills in, healing within a minute. He drops his hand, flexing it before releasing me.

He turns, searching. "Marcus?" My brother is with us in an instant. "Get her out of here." I try to protest, but Declan holds his hand up. "Get her out of here," he repeats, "and keep an eye on her."

Marcus' golden gaze reaches out to me with weary consideration from under a furrowed brow. He offers me his arm. Being here is not high on my list of desires, but I do not want to be kicked out either. The room is full of shocked expressions and bent heads, everyone whispering to each other. As my eyes travel over the couple still quailing, I latch onto Marcus' offered escape.

We stride through the throne room, passing by the man and woman. They skitter back, and the man shields his wife from me. Their reaction burns the same as swallowing bile.

My brother directs me out of the room without a word, and once outside of those enormous double doors, he sighs. "Do you want to tell me what is going on?"

I shake my head.

"Ella, you spend your days in the city and leave Declan to deal with the court." We make a turn, and Marcus looks around as we do so.

"I'm helping people."

"You're hiding," my brother declares with a chuckle. "You haven't attended a single ball, party, or dinner since the ball thrown to celebrate your heroics for removing Viktor."

"Killing him," I grunt. "I'm not even so sure I did, but that's what everyone thinks. How am I a hero?"

"Viktor—" he starts.

"Dad," I snap. "He was our father."

"Yes, and neither of us referred to him as 'dad' unless we were being ironic or sarcastic. There's never been any kind of love in either of us for our father, so why the sudden outburst of affection?"

I swallow harder. "It isn't affection. And you're right," I say, facing my brother's golden gaze. Everything else about him is dark, his skin, his hair, and his expression. "Viktor was a fact of life, and I'm not sorry he's gone."

My brother smiles, a lazy movement tugging at the corners of his mouth. "I know you aren't, but something is hurting you." I sigh and roll my eyes. "No, Ella, I'm serious. You won't talk to either of the Bard brothers, so you're going to talk to me, or I'll set Legia on you."

"I'm fine."

He stops and looks at me. The skin between his eyebrows crinkle, and the lines around his mouth crease into deep ravines. We stand in silence as he studies me. I attempt to stare with defiance but give up, diverting my eyes to the window. My throat feels swollen and itchy. I try to swallow, but my stomach lurches at the taste in my mouth. The last shred of stubbornness in me is squirming pathetically in my gut.

"You aren't fine, Ella. There's nothing fine about starting fires or disintegrating artifacts by waving your hand."

"I've been doing that since I was nine."

"Losing your temper is what used to set you off, but something tells me that wasn't what happened a moment ago."

I bite down on my tongue. He is not wrong.

With a heavy exhale, he goes on without waiting for my answer. "So, it stands to reason that your control is being affected by more than anger."

"I have more energy in me than when I was nine," I tell him with a huff. "So, yeah, maybe it's harder for me to keep control over it all the time."

Marcus puts a hand over his eyes. The sleeves of his button-up shirt are rolled, exposing the white scars left in his ebony skin by Ravenna's torture, the only visible signs of the harrowing. There are others, embedded deep within him, but he hides those.

He drops his hand. "Okay, let's try this again. Ella, everyone is worried about you. You are more reclusive now than you ever were before, and your powers are out of control."

I bite my lip, look down, and left. "Really, Marc, I'm fine."

"Horse shit." His tone is harsh, the outburst steeped with frustration. "You're moody and sour all the time. At least I think you are because no one ever sees you. You are the queen, and you've burdened Declan with your responsibilities."

"He's—"

"Responsibilities that I know you want." He wags an accusatory finger under my nose. "You want to help and protect and do what is right, so do that. Not by sneaking around the city or far corners of Cimeria County—and don't ever let me catch word about you in the mines again—but by undoing the damage Viktor inflicted. Change the laws, make things right."

I stare at our feet and shuffle my own, running a hand through my hair. "I don't know if I can," I whisper. "I don't know how to fix what Viktor did to me, so how am I supposed to fix what he's done to this court?"

My brother wraps his arms around me and squeezes me tightly to him. "I understand."

"You do?"

"Yes, I do. You don't know what to do, so you're hiding and letting Dec figure it out."

I scrunch my face up in Marc's chest. "I can do more good outside of these walls. Dec knows what he's doing, and he's capable of making decisions. Viktor never bothered to teach me anything about the court or politics. I don't even know half of my duties."

"Why didn't you ask?"

He lets go of me, and I look around us, feeling exhausted. "It isn't just that. The whole court looks at me like some kind of savior from Viktor. But I'm telling you, he isn't dead. I don't know how I know, but I know it."

"Ella—"

"No," I manage through a constricted throat. "The court doesn't know the truth about me. They don't—"

"Stop," Marcus hisses, looking around. I bite my lip. "Haven, if someone hears..."

With another look around, he puts his hands on my shoulders. His eyes drop shut, and I feel a chilled tingle creep over my scalp just before freezing pressure rips through me. I exhale, giving in to it, allowing my brother to tear our elements apart and rebuild them where he wills. When I feel whole once more, I crack an eye. I recognize my brother's study and open both eyes to check if he made it here as well.

I grin at him. "You're getting better at dissipation."

He smirks. "Practicing with your suggestions has helped me a lot."

I nod at him as I step to the couch. He settles behind his desk and starts to shuffle papers around. The interruption has seemed to cease our conversation, so I lay back and contemplate.

I am still mulling things over and staring at the book-lined walls when Declan materializes in the room. I sit, and he comes to sit next to me. Our fingers lace together, and I rest my head on his shoulder.

He opens the link again, and his worry kicks me in the stomach. I wheeze, trying to catch my breath. "I'm okay."

"I couldn't put the fire out."

I frown, thinking he did.

He expels air, shaking his fingers from mine to stand. "It took me two tries and infinitely more effort than it took for you to start the damned thing. Your magic, intentional or not, is strong. Pretty soon, if your powers keep growing, if you keep going at this rate, I won't be able to change elements under your control."

"There's always Chase, or..." I pause. "No, really, there's just Chase. You're as strong as most mages get, and I know Wesley, Samuel, or Cannamore aren't stronger than you. Daphine might be—as a representative under the Gammet brothers leading the gild, she's as strong as mages can get."

Declan crosses his arms. "I'm not okay with you setting off explosions and destroying things without someone being able to put you in check."

My eyes drift to the chessboard.

*Dammit, now she's upset, and she's really going to blow something to Damnatus. Or turn it to ash. Fuck, she's going to kill me one of these days.*

"No," I say, staring him down. "You're right. I need to figure out how to control this." His arms drop, and he turns away. "Wait, Dec."

He faces me with hands on his hips and a glower. "Why did I deny the child?" His dark eyes pinch with irritation. "You don't listen, and you don't pay attention."

My mouth opens in shock as his words sing through me. He pinches the bridge of his nose. He is cranky. His frustration is boiling, but it is not only because of me. The pressure around my lungs lessens.

Declan lets out a bark of laughter, and my lips lift at the corners. From across the room, Marcus catches my eye with raised brows. I shake my head at him.

Dec drops down onto the couch. "How many children are there in the city without a home?"

I look from my brother to my fiancé, dazed. "I'm not sure. A lot."

"With all the lives ruined or claimed by Viktor and his policies, worst of all, he managed to start that lynch mob that burned down Polluck and decimated the south. There is a severe deficit of men and women, leaving a surplus of children. Those children are becoming a problem."

"You're trying to encourage couples to foster children from the city," I whisper, putting the pieces together with help from our link.

"Yes. They are starting to act more animal than elemental, running in packs and hurting others. They are destroying property and stealing food, and those in the city are coming to the crown, demanding a solution as well as monetary compensation for the crown's lack of order." He sighs and shifts to lean back against the cushions with our shoulders touching. "I've offered a stipend to anyone who takes in children to attempt to increase participation."

"It's not working, is it?" I ask with little hope.

He narrows his eyes. *"You are not stupid."* An audible sigh escapes him as he faces forward. He leans his head back and closes his eyes, trying to relax.

Regret stabs at me. I thought Declan to be heartless when he was doing the right thing. It might have seemed like he was being a monster, but he was making the hard choice with the thought of all the court instead of the single woman. My heart swells in my chest.

*"I want to help."*

*"You always want to help. I can barely tolerate how much you fucking care about everyone and everything, all the damn time. It gives me migraines."*

My thoughts flicker to another set of purple eyes.

"Focus, Ella." He draws the words out in a groan. "I'm out of ideas, and I could really use another mind, your mind." *Help. I need help. I need her. Her help. Her.*

I rest my head on his chest and curl into him. "I was focusing. I pulled Dean out of the city because he had nowhere to go, and I gave a stipend to that merchant who wanted his hand cut off for stealing apples."

"Where are you going with this?"

My eyes roll to the ceiling and then settle on Marcus. My brother is acting like he is paying no heed to us, but I would wager he is eavesdropping. I focus on the quill in his hand. With a yelp, he drops it and waves his hand. His yellow eyes train on me and narrow.

"He's asking for your benefit. He already knows what I'm thinking."

Getting up, Marcus comes closer and pulls around one of the armchairs. "I don't know who Dean is."

I wait, but Declan stays silent, just not in my head. *"I'm not going to say anything. Bringing Dean here was your choice. Not to mention, this idea is your crazy concept."*

"You don't think—"

*"I didn't say that."*

"You didn't say anything."

He snorts through his nose a sound of amusement, and I fight a grin. "Dean is a boy I brought from the city streets to the palace a couple revolutions ago."

"Okay, stop." My brother tips his head forward, his voice hardening. "You're thinking of dragging a horde of young children to the palace?"

I make a noncommittal motion with my hand, and both men inhale with sharp noises. I try to ignore it, and maybe I can pretend with Marcus, but Declan knows.

*"You cannot blame us. Every time you wave your hands, something turns to ash and smoke."*

"Not every time," I grind out through clenched teeth. I

verbalize the response for my brother's benefit. "And no, I don't think *all* the children will come to the palace, but it's an option. It's an option to provide food and clothes to help prevent theft. Those are two viable choices we can implement along with your encouragement for fostering and adopting."

Declan's mood is lifting, if only vaguely. He wraps an arm around my shoulders and drops a kiss on the top of my head. "It's a grand idea, but who is going to pay for it? There are going to be costs, and probably more than you realize. You could bankrupt the crown attempting to feed, clothe, and employ such a vast number."

My eyes lock with my brother's. He shakes his head. "You'll have no protests from me, but I doubt your sister will agree to open the Byron vault."

"This is Viktor's fault," I snap, my voice rising, "and I don't see why the Byron family shouldn't pay the price."

Marcus holds a hand up. "I said, I agree."

I slump into Declan's solidity. "I know, but I'll never convince Selene. She'll say no to spite me."

"You are the queen," Declan interjects, "and inherited not only the crown but the family estate when Viktor was pronounced dead. You don't need your sister's approval."

I lift my chin, rotating to lock eyes with Declan, my betrothed, my solid rock, my everything I need wrapped in a six-foot package of lean muscle.

His bronze hair is falling in his face, against his thin, noble nose. One side of his mouth twists and silver flecks glint in his dark eyes.

"So, yes?"

He drops his chin toward his chest and settles in, pulling me back against him. "Yes."

# CHAPTER 4

For the first time in a long time, I am in Viktor's old study, or at least the reconstructed room that was his study. I have hated this room my whole life, and regardless of it being destroyed and refurbished, this place holds too many memories. I avoided this hovel for as long as possible, but this project is more important than my petulant discomfort.

I have spent the last few days putting my devised plan into motion. There is a lot of legal paperwork, and I am frustrated. A noble family cannot pay for things that are the crown's responsibilities, even if they want to, without the proper paperwork and consent of the crown. Even if the noble is, in fact, the crown.

There is paperwork for establishing work and wages, papers to denote crown involvement and plan. There is paperwork for my paperwork, and twice the work as everything is funneled from the crown to Byron estate finances. It is an endless barrage of forms and submissions to various estates, dukes, and legal representatives within the court, and I want to punch something or cry at each new form. Possibly both.

*I have no idea what I am doing.*

Shuffling through papers, looking at too many numbers and

letters to compute, my brain refutes cooperation, and my temples throb. The rune along my shoulder is like an open, bleeding wound. The energy strumming through me is border-line painful and distracting.

"*Lover?*"

I focus on my surroundings. Papers are floating around, and even as I watch, several drift off the desk to hover in midair. Through the mess, I make out Declan standing in the doorway.

The confusion blossoming is not all his. While setting off explosions or destruction are not abnormal, manipulating elements at random in other ways is. My heart races. I need to calm down, or I know the last couple of days' arduous work is going to be ashes. I look through the whirling mess and lock onto his eyes, begging him to help me through our link.

He smirks and pushes away from the doorframe. One by one, he picks the pages out of the air to stack them on the desk.

"Thank you." I breathe out my relief and smile.

He holds his hand out. "Come on, court session is going to start soon."

I groan with displeasure, my head drops, and I throw my hands in the air. Every page on the desk disintegrates into ash. I let out a frustrated grunt, and my head drops further to hit the desk which implodes on contact.

The crack is deafening. Wood splinters burst outward from the epicenter of my accidental detonation. I curse and start to throw my hands up to shield myself, but Declan grabs my wrists.

"*That's only going to make things worse.*"

Helpless, I look at him. The Vitale rune is blistering, and my eyes are prickling with tears.

"*You have too much energy all the damn time.*" He lets go of my wrists to pull on the chain around my neck. I wait as he unclasps the necklace and pulls it away only to clasp the jewel around his own neck.

The reaction is instantaneous. I watch his chest swell and his pupils dilate. There is a faint echo of the jewel's rush through our link. The muscles that connect my shoulder to my neck twitch with an urge to take the sapphire back.

*"You don't need the damned thing."* He kneels and slides his hand under the left side of my blouse. *"But, you do need this."*

"Don't," I whisper.

"Shhh. It's okay, I can handle it. You need this."

I lean into the cool touch of his hand. The humming stream of energy through me into him is a much-needed release. I exhale, a sweet taste lingering on my tongue.

"I need to let this out. I haven't been to the city for a few days."

"I know."

"I don't just go to help the people."

"I know."

"Making the food, using magic..." He is still pulling energy out of me, and the drumming in my core responds faster and faster. My thoughts go fuzzy, and words are difficult. The pull of energy is an extreme high, something that makes my body hum and my tongue taste like honey.

"I know. I get cranky," Dec says on a low breath, "but I understand."

His hand slides off the rune and up the side of my neck, pulling my face to his. We kiss, and I soak in the feeling of him, the taste of his mouth. For a tiny point in time, everything is right.

It is okay.

He pulls back. I lean my head to the side, and he takes advantage of it. His teeth slide into the side of my neck, filling his own needs.

When he is done, I slump forward into him. He kisses my temple but helps me sit upright. "We need to go."

*"I don't want to go."*

His lips twitch into a frown. Pushing a hand through my hair, I force my legs to work and stand. "Look on the bright side, court can't start without both of us, so we can't be late." His eyes narrow, but he is amused; the light gray of his eyes gives him away. I smirk and dissipate us to the throne room.

We take our seats on cushions at the head of the room, and everyone around us follows suit. Declan takes point, and I am more than content to sit by until the proceedings of those calling on the crown begin. At that point, I take over, and he is happy to hand over the reins. We communicate through the link when I need help, but he lets me decide unhindered.

I struggle twice, and both times for the same reason. Couples are still coming to request children, and both times we counter, proposing adoption and offering monetary compensation. Declan interferes both times, which I am thankful for. After the second couple turns to leave, I turn to Declan.

His shoulders are dropped, his head tipped back to stare at me with soft features. Despite the strength rolling from him, the menacing dark runes along his exposed forearms, he is capable of tenderness. *"You're doing fine. You're brilliant aside from denying children, but that's your fucking bleeding heart."*

I roll my eyes at him. *"I'm not worried about how I'm doing."*

Inhaling, I mimic his character by pinching the bridge of my nose. I need to find some semblance of inner calm before dealing with the next caller. I exhale, allowing my shoulders to drop and tension to release from the base of my neck. My eyes meet his gray ones as another caller is announced.

Forcing a smile, I turn to who is next and stop breathing. Two identical figures in ratty jade cloaks float along the floor until they reach the middle of the room. They stop in unison. Bow in unison. Stand straight in unison.

My heart skips a beat as the Gammet brothers stand motionless and silent. I cut my eyes to Declan, questioning. He shakes his head in response. He does not like that they are here, and he does not want to deal with them.

The last time the brothers were in Byron, they were focused on Declan. He had been implanted with bearings that sealed his memories and more that gave him false memories. The experience had not been pleasant for him, suffering through bearings broken to release his memories, and the subsequent blood released from those bearings almost killed me.

Declan grumbles, his dark mutters catching in the back of his throat and apprehension in my gut, but I am excited. I push myself off the floor and clear my throat. "Brothers, how may we assist you?"

"We are here—"

"To offer assistance."

I cock my head. "Assistance for what?"

"You—"

"Morella."

I whip my face toward Declan, but before I can accuse him of anything, he shakes his head, then lumbers to his feet to stand next to me. *"I didn't call for them, but you do need their help."*

"You need our help—"

"More than you know."

Declan clears his throat to say, "We appreciate your offer, and Ella will gladly accept."

The brothers put their hands together in front of them, moving fluidly in time and unison. "We are pleased—"

"And now request—"

"Er, request what?" Butterflies assemble in my stomach. *What on Caleum could the brothers need from me?*

"We must request an—"

"Audience with you, Morella."

Declan's angst fills me. I sigh, but he is growling in the back of my mind. *"The last time they wanted you for something, it almost killed you."*

*"That was my own fault for getting used blood on me."*

*"They're supposed to be the most powerful mages in Caleum. Like you asked yourself, what could they possibly need from you?"*

His snarky comment draws a disgusted look from me. I turn back to the brothers. "Of course, I will be happy to grant an audience."

They bow together, and I feel the cold seep through me. I gasp, but my body is in a million pieces. Everything comes back together in a blur of color and a snap of cold. The brothers are before me, side by side. I see gray stone and pink watercolored stains beyond an open square. Pain splinters at the base of my skull and my eyes roll back into the darkness.

⟳

*I* am cold, laying on a hard surface. Propping up on my hands, I look around, and realize I am where I fell. At least, I think I am. There is a brother in front of me with his back turned, staring out of a window. I curl in on myself for warmth.

I have an overwhelming feeling of panic coursing through me. Judging by how my stomach is in knots, the feeling has been conjured for some time. I drop my forehead against my knees and focus on breathing.

"Dec," I whisper.

*"Lover, what in Damnatus is going on? Where are you? Are you okay? You've been gone for hours. I couldn't hear you. Couldn't sense you, feel—"*

*"I'm okay."*

His barrage of questions is hard to respond to without learning some answers. I lift my head to find the brother has turned to face me. "Where am I?" He remains silent. "Can you not talk without the other one?"

The brother moves, lifting his hands. The robes fall around

his elbows, exposing what should be forearms. The boney fingers exposed in the light look like the legs of a spider, and there is scaly gray skin stretched tight over the bones. Indentations linger where the skin has been sucked tight between bones where muscles ought to be.

He grabs the hood and pulls it back, dropping it down to his shoulders. I shudder when my brain comprehends what my eyes are betraying. There is no nose, just two gaping nasal cavities. No lips to hide the yellow teeth. There are cheekbones, jaw, and scalp covered in the same gray scaly hide and no trace of hair.

My eyes stop focusing on his features to meet his gaze, and I gasp. His eyes are vibrant violet, twitching as he watches me. In the back of my mind, I hear Declan calling my name, asking me to answer him, begging to know I am okay.

*"I'm fine."*

*"You're terrified."* I close my eyes, holding tight to the image of the brother. Declan is repulsed. *"What is that? Where are you?"*

*"It's a Gammet brother."* I open my eyes and try not to shudder. "Where am I?"

"Aron," it says. I look around the room, not sure what I am looking for or expecting. After a moment, it speaks again, this time louder, but repeating the word. "Aron!"

I stand, wiping my hands on my thighs. "I don't know what that means."

"It means—"

"My name."

I turn to the voice behind me. Thankfully the other brother is still covered. I focus on him, trying to forget the repugnant thing behind me. I swallow hard. "Where am I? Why did you bring me here? What did you do to me?"

"We disassembled your elements."

"We apologize for it."

"The magic of the control rune—"

"Was stretched for moving you so."

I look out the window, dazed. "What do you mean it was stretched? Like, you negated it?" Fear causes my heart to skip.

"Dissipating at such a distance requires great control."

"We dissipated you, which controlled you far more."

"Greater control than the magic of the rune considered acceptable."

"That is the reason for the pain and your unconsciousness."

I nod, still unsure. A cold shiver runs down my spine that the control rune could be overridden. *Viktor is not dead. He can come back. He could force me under his control.*

*"He is dead. Gone. You killed him."*

I focus out the window and try to stay calm. "Where is here? How far did you take me?"

"You are in our ancestral home."

"You are in the spirit glen."

*"You're in Kennelton?"* Declan's exasperated.

*"Yes, your homelands, so less than a day's journey."*

*"To my estate. The glen is on the other side of Kennelton, a two-fuck-ing-day journey by horse."*

I shrug and walk to the window. There is no glass pane, and I lean onto the stone lip to crane my neck outside. I am several floors off the ground overlooking a forest. The trees are small in stature, with skinny trunks of gray bark, but the canopies are lush pink leaves and white flowers. The ground is mostly dirt but littered with patches of vibrant rosy moss, and the gentle babbling wafts from a creek from somewhere nearby.

I turn back to the brother, watching me, who revealed his face. I shudder, stepping away from the window and him. "It's beautiful, but why am I here?"

"We requested an audience with you, and you agreed."

"We did not want to be disturbed or heard."

I groan and scrub my hands over my face, taking a moment to think, but also to convey what is going on to Declan. He is acrimonious that the brothers whisked me away to Kennelton without permission.

*"They could have killed you or seriously injured you. You were unconscious for hours as it is."*

"So why here?" I ask.

"This is—"

"Our home."

I nod, tempted to argue that their reply does nothing to explain being here. "Okay, so what did you want an audience for?"

"It is easier to show you," the brother behind me answers.

He walks forward, and I am relieved he has pulled his hood over his head again. They stand next to each other, and their faces are directed toward me. After a moment, their hooded faces turn toward each other.

"Can she handle that so soon?"

"She is strong."

"You are clouded."

There is a hissing noise that makes the hairs on my body stand. "She wears our father's Vitale rune."

Both faces swing to me. "We will pull your conscience in."

"Pull my conscience, where?"

*"What?"*

The brothers step forward in eerie unison. I step back, sharing Declan's trepidation at what this might do to me, to us. "What do you mean, pull my conscience in?"

Their hand closest to me reaches out, and I feel them land on each side of my face. There is a snap between my temples and a ripping sensation from my toes up my body and to the base of my skull. A bright flash of white causes me to blink.

My vision clears. Two young boys, identical with purple eyes and yellow hair, are before me, and I am reminded of Dean. They are sitting on the floor of the room, laughing and playing with the elements. The scene changes to two young men with the same violet eyes, but the hair has gotten darker with age. They stand before two gravestones near a stream somewhere in the red-leafed forest.

"Should we do it here?"

"There's no better place."

One of the men slices his palm open before passing a blade to the other. The second repeats the action, and they grip hands, wound to wound. A ribbon wrapped around their hands shrinks and bleeds into their flesh. They speak in low voices, harsh tones, and winded words, their faces contorted with exertion. The energy streams between them with a shimmer, bouncing back and forth, stitching them together with glittering elements.

The scenery does not change, but the men begin to age. Their hair is gray, then white, and then it falls out, and the skin shrinks against the bone. Their bodies wither away, their skin turns gray, then dry and cracked with scales that shimmer green in the light.

When their hands leave my face. I am back in the same empty room, gaping at the brothers. The world moves about me, circling. My muscles ache as if I spent hours punching a practice post, my organs covered in deep bruises freshly made, my body tender from abuse. The sound of my heartbeat is like a chisel against stone.

In the back of my mind, under my own agony, I can make out Declan's distinctive growl. *"Fuck whatever they did to us."*

"Your shade will want to rest."

"Your conscience was ripped from his."

*"Are you okay?"* I ask him, horrified.

*"That. Fucking. Hurt."*

I cringe. Dec is fuming and in pain. Anger and suffering bring out his bloodlust, and together they are dredging his cravings from the bottom of his soul. Shades are noted in history as unstable with a penchant for blood that demands to be answered by any means.

Panic clogs my airways and makes my voice shake. "Can you take me back now?"

The brothers look at each other in unison, then their faces swivel to me. "Your shade will have to wait."

"We have not concluded our request."

"Declan. His name is Declan," I tell them, rubbing my right temple with two trembling fingers.

"Apologies."

"Inconsequential."

My eyebrows rise in disbelief. The brother on my right turns to look at the brother closer to the window. There is a hiss, which I think comes from the brother who is turned away from me. The one still trained on me bows.

"Aron believes him to deserve respect."

"He is a king, her king."

"He is no king."

"Show some respect, Erac."

Another hiss rips the air, and the brothers stare at each other. I clear my throat. "Aron and Erac, those are your names?"

"Yes."

"Morella."

I wave a hand, and they stay still, no signs of flinching. "Ella is fine. What is your request? I need to get back."

"It seems we do not die as other elementals would, but our bodies are gone."

"Our bodies have withered away, and with them, so have our powers faded too."

I nod as if this is making sense to me. "How can I help? Do you want to take energy from me?"

The figures before me shake with the sound of smooth rocks tumbling together. I realize they are laughing and clench my fists. *Declan is losing his grip, and they dare to snicker?*

"We need your power, yes, but not to take from you. "

"We would like for you to use your power for us."

I clench my jaw and bite back a groan of despair. My head and body hurt, and Declan's thoughts are degrading further into an accretion of violence. Staying here is an imposition. I need to get to Declan.

"What do you want me to do?" My question is met with silence, so I scream, "Tell me what you want from me or take me back to Byron Palace now!"

"The bond you share with the shade is detrimental, and merely a beguilement the would-be-king maintains over you for his own benefit. It would do to sever the link."

My ears go back and grow warm as my jaw drops. The remark does nothing to soothe Declan's brewing wrath. His guttural growl rings through our link.

The brother on my right, the one I believe to be Aron, steps forward. He holds a hand out to stay his brother a pace behind him. "Erac is overly anxious. We hold Haven's choice for you in the highest regard and mean no harm. We hesitate out of fear of distressing you, but our request is simple."

I exhale long and slow, looking around the room. There is not much in the room for me to ignite. I relax. "Get to the point."

"There is no point in this requisition if your attentions are divided. The results would be insufficient."

"Okay, I've had enough," I snarl. "I don't know what that means, and I'm leaving now. If either of you tries to stop me, you'll regret it."

Aron waves his hand, and the other brother disappears. He sways. "Forgive us, Ella. Erac has always been cantankerous," he wheezes.

I peer with caution at his visible deterioration without the other. "Can you exist without him?"

His hood bobs. "We are linked, much the same as you and Declan. It is easier with him, but I can manage without." He pauses, and there is the sound of dead, brittle reeds in the wind clacking together. "I believe he was doing more harm than benefit."

I sigh. "What can I do for you?"

"We need new bodies."

I blink with my mouth wide open. "What?"

"You've made fruit a thousand times. You've made the flesh and the meat inside. We are asking for that."

There's a revolting slime coating my innards. "Those aren't the same thing."

There's the sound of rocks rubbing together again. "Indeed, they are. We will help you learn."

"To some extent. We will instruct you how." Erac has reappeared.

"If you acquiesce to make us new bodies—"

"We can help you to control your power."

The hooded faces turn toward each other. "We must take her back."

"She hasn't given an answer."

"She has not."

"Then, we wait."

Rage billows in my chest, and my throat feels tight. I try to reach Declan but get a hazy, vague response. "Fine, I'll do whatever you want if you can teach me to control..." I pause, waving my hands over my body, "this. But I am going back to Byron now, and I don't need you to take me back."

Both faces turn toward me. I blink and focus. Cold rips through me as I rush to Declan's side.

# CHAPTER 5

*T*he muscle twitches in my hand, the color a mixture of mud and berry jam. The pound of flesh clenching and releasing with a smooth transition. I watch it work, mesmerized. Sticky fluid begins to leak out, puddling around the muscle in my grip. The lump spasms and quits moving altogether. More blood flows forth, running across my palm, beading and rolling down my forearm. I stare at it and squeeze as if that is going to keep it from dying.

Blood spurts out, spraying my face. "Argh," I groan and drop the thing. I swipe at my face with my other hand, smearing the blood over my cheek and forehead. I curse and try to use my sleeve to clean the mess.

"That's enough."

"For now."

I look to the brothers nearby, watching me work. My gaze drops to the thing on the floor, sitting in a pool of its own fluids. I nudge it with the toe of my boot. I never thought I would be in the dungeons again. Being here brings on grisly flashbacks of atrocities and agony, but here I can work away from prying eyes.

I look from the bloody mass to the scores of body parts on a table next to me. My stomach churns and clenches. The nasty thing in me is queasy. Not even my demon likes playing with dead things. While the hissing voice wants to cut apart a body and peel back skin to expose flesh, it wants the victim alive.

*If the wretch had been squirming and kicking, it would have been more fun.* The thought is equal measures unbidden and disturbing.

The man had been dead, a modicum of relief present in that, and the brothers would not say from whence the body had come. They brought the corpse for me to study, to overcome my abysmal ability to picture muscles and tendons. I had seen them before, of course, and my demon is always keen to recant those experiences, but I never focused on them. I would bury my conscience, and with it, all intellect. The only thing left had been my thirst, far too engrossed in enjoying the inflictions to study how the elements work.

The brothers thought seeing muscles and tendons would help construction, so the dead man was procured. Once I got past the grotesque nature, I found my work intriguing, but coming back to my senses makes me itch all over. I swore I would never do this sort of thing with Viktor gone, but here I am, in his dungeons, dismembering a body and playing with the parts.

I shudder, bend over, and heave out the contents of my stomach. Not much empties from me, and I swipe away the spittle from the corners of my mouth. Facing the brothers, I try hard not to think. "I'm done for the day."

They bow to me in unison and are gone as I blink. I close my eyes, picturing my bathroom. The cool rip of energy slides through me as I dissipate. I peel my clothes off to shower, scrubbing for what feels like hours, as if I could wash away my sins.

With pink and pruned skin, I dress, dissipating to the dining hall to join others. My eyes scour the room, meeting my brother's gaze from a table at the end of the hall. The Bard brothers are with him. Even sitting down with his back to me, Seth's messy mop of brown hair sticks a head above everyone else.

I tug on his left ear in a gentle tease, then slide onto the bench next to him on his right. He rubs his ear on his shoulder and glares at me. "Where have you been?"

"Helping the brothers." Rather than meet his curious gaze, my eyes travel to where the head table used to be. It is easier to lie if I do not look at him. The table now serves to collect wine and plates for the servants to disperse without traipsing to the kitchen.

The removal of the head table was a joint decision between Declan and me, much the same as the decision to remove the thrones from the courtroom. We want to be amidst our courtiers and subjects, not above them. We are still working toward removing barriers and avoiding setting ourselves apart. Viktor enjoyed power, reveled in leering over others, but that is not something Declan or I want.

I swivel my eyes across the way. Declan has a plate of food while his brother and mine are nursing wine goblets. I look around, rubbing my hands on my thighs.

"I thought you went to dinner a while ago," I say, eyeing the plate. "Aren't you hungry?"

Declan shoots daggers at me from black eyes. He knows what I was doing in the dungeon. "I'm not one to judge, but playing with dead things is morbid."

I wince.

"'Playing with dead things,'" Marcus repeats. His eyebrows lift into his shaggy black hair. "What is he talking about?"

I glare at Declan. He settles back and crosses his arms over his chest. He might be wearing a button-up shirt and playing king, but the flickering of his eyes and his drawn mouth remind me he is dangerous. He may be a caged animal, but only because he chooses to be. My eyes slide from him to the waiting expressions of Seth and Marcus.

I sigh. "I wasn't playing with dead things. I was studying anatomy."

"Is that what Erac wants you to believe?" Declan's voice is low, threatening.

I sigh again. "It's easier to look at it that way."

Beside me, Marcus rests a hand over his eyes. "What is going on?"

"You don't want to know," Declan and I say together.

Marc drops his hand and stares at me with emblazoned yellow eyes. "As your brother, I wouldn't respect that answer. As the chief advisor to the queen, I cannot accept that answer. What have you gotten yourself into?"

I glance around to ensure no one is paying us heed. "The brothers asked me to make them new bodies, and in exchange, they will teach me to control my power."

"Make them bodies?" Seth's features display disgust. "What exactly does that mean?"

"They equated it to making fruit." I am met with three pairs of eyes, all boring into me with deafening disbelief. I shrug. "That's what my response was."

"Then why—"

"What does this have to do with something dead?"

I glare at Seth. Not thrilled he was interrupted, Marcus shoots pointed eyes at Seth, but he does little else. "The brothers brought me a body. I am to disassemble it so I can understand how the elements create the different tissues."

"Why in Haven's name would you ever—" Marcus snaps but quits talking. His eyes dart around us. He lowers his voice. "Haven above, Ella, if the court finds out."

"I'm working for the brothers," I say stubbornly.

My line of sight travels to Declan, but he still has me shut out. Ever since I agreed to peel back flesh, he has had me shut out. His black eyes meet mine. Faster than my eyes can follow, he stands. I watch him walk away, willing him to open our link or at least come back. He does neither.

"What you are doing is revolting enough to get under Dec's skin, and that isn't an easy feat." I turn back to Seth.

"It's not?" I stare at him.

"I know Dec wants us to believe he wasn't changed when he was away for all that time, but he's let things slip. The court might believe he has no recollection of his time away, but it is insulting that you and he think we don't know better." He wags a finger indicating himself and my brother. "So, you need to realize that if it's bad enough to make him sick, then you should reconsider."

I swallow hard. "You're right." The words hang in the air. "I hate to say this," I whisper, "but will you—"

"Keep this from Selene?" He scoffs. "Ell, I've always kept your secrets, and I will continue to do so. You don't have to ask every time. I appreciate you annulling the engagement between us, by the way."

I nod. "You're welcome. I don't suppose you've found a way to break the bond?"

Seth scowls. "Not yet."

"I could ask the brothers?"

"I think you should be cautious about asking them for favors," Marcus chimes in. "You're already doing despicable things for them, and you've burdened Declan with the court again."

I look above us to the massive wood support beams. "I don't care what I have to do if they can help Seth."

"If it is your soul or me, I'm not worth that."

Now I scoff. "My soul will never see Haven regardless of what I may do for the brothers." They both fall silent. "And I didn't drop everything on Declan again. I'm still working on preparations for handling the orphaned children in the city."

"There are about twenty other problems Declan is dealing with. You're dealing with one." Marcus holds up a single finger. "You've shouldered him with the burden of court."

Seth drains his goblet. "This is where we disagree. I think it is best Declan takes the reins. No offense, Ell."

I smile at him weakly. "I know. You're right."

"She is the queen, and she cares about the people."

Seth nods. "She's passionate, and she does care. She's also emotional and prone to explosions. Declan makes the hard choices for the betterment of all, and I don't think she's capable of doing that." He looks at me and flashes his teeth in a faux grin. "Sorry, Ell."

I shrug. "You're right."

"I have to go. I'm meeting Mekie." Seth stands.

Marcus and I watch Seth go in silence. "I'll stay with you while you eat if you want," my brother offers.

I shake my head. "I'm really not hungry."

"You need to eat something." I keep quiet. "Are you alright?"

Startled, I look over at him. "I..." I start, but words fail me. A ball forms in the back of my throat. "No. Not really. I promised the brothers I'd give them new bodies because I needed to get back to Dec, and I need to learn how to control all this power." I pause to draw in a shaky breath. "Dec needed me. The brothers ripped my conscience away from his, and it hurt him. He was angry and in pain, and I was worried." I pause again. "I made a hasty promise because of that, and I'm doing what I'm doing because of that promise, and it's pushing him away."

Marcus spins the wine goblet by its stem between two fingers and his thumb. He contemplates me but motions for a servant. He requests broth and bread.

When the meal is served, I pull it close and dip bread in the broth.

Marcus smiles at me, but he looks tired. "You're doing what

you can, and for what it's worth, I think you're doing well." I open my mouth to protest, but he holds his hand up to stop me. "I do my best to push you. I want to incite motivation and make you think. That does not mean I don't believe in you."

I reach out and touch his exposed left forearm. I run my fingers over the scars left by Ravenna. "You've always been there, Marc. You've always tried to be the father Viktor never was. We never discussed what I did. I'm sorry."

His hand covers mine, pinning my palm against the rippled flesh of his arm. "You don't need to be sorry."

My eyes jerk to meet his. "Are you sure? You didn't want to annul the marriage."

My brother laughs. "Venna is dead, along with Viktor and the duchess. Why should I bother annulling the marriage? Spend your time more wisely."

A shadow crosses his face despite the twist to his lips. "Do you know I still get ghost pains? My whole arm will light up like all these cuts are fresh. The healers say it is normal because of the psychological trauma that accompanied the physical damage." His eyes drop from mine to our hands. "These scars are visible, but they aren't the ones that matter."

I shift and lean against him with my head on his shoulder. "I know. I have those too."

"You more than anyone would understand. You carry that weight with you every day. Every time I catch sight of these scars..." he begins, holding his forearm aloft, "I am reminded of her, of what she did." He swallows, and I hear it clearly. "The only reason these scars matter is because of the mental ramifications." He rests his head on mine. "I cannot imagine the pain you feel when you look in the mirror."

"Yeah." I snort a chuckle through my nose. "Dear Dad really screwed me up."

Marcus pulls back, staring down at me with a grave expression. "He screwed us all. I think you got the worst of it, but I am not innocent. Spaulding and Selene, they got their fair share of doing Viktor's bidding too."

I open my mouth, then close it. "Precious, delicate Selene?" I tip my head back and laugh. "Haven above, that is hard to imagine."

Marcus sips his wine, hiding a grin behind the brim of the cup. "Yes, well, she might be more like you than she lets on."

Snorting through my nose. I cackle. "Right. Selene, my drop-dead gorgeous sister that knows more fashion styles than fighting combinations?"

My brother gives me a half-hearted smile and huffs. "She may have blood on her hands too, although she was never abused quite like you. Viktor was always hardest on you."

I scrub a hand down my face. Selene having metaphorical blood on her hands is a comfort. All my siblings were subjected to some of the same tortures. Marc may not have sulked in shadows and slit throats, but he had his fair share of demands from Viktor. My eyes scan the room, but it is mostly vacant.

Still looking around, I let out a sigh. "Marc?"

"Yes?"

I stare into his golden eyes and open my mouth only to close it. I chew on my lower lip. "If you can move on, and if Selene and Spaulding are just fine, then why am I so stuck?"

Marcus tilts his head and peers at me. "Little sister..." he pauses to rub a hand down over his face, "you've had the worst of it. By far. The blood. Total control. The errands. The abuse. *All of it.*" He stresses the last words and jabs a finger on the table.

"Yes, but I know you got the crap kicked out of you by him too. Hell," I say, pointing at the exposed scars along his left fore-arm, "Viktor used Venna, your own wife, against you."

He gives me a lopsided grin, but there is no humor to it. "You were always his favorite, and Haven only knows that is the worst thing to be to Viktor. But," he adds, rolling his shoulders, "there's no easy answer. You're going to have to find a way to live with what was done. By you. To you. It makes no difference. You just need to find a way to live with it."

I puff my cheeks and spit air out. "Great." I roll my eyes. "How about you tell me how?"

He drains his wine glass. "I can't. It doesn't work that way."

# CHAPTER 6

*S*itting cross-legged on the floor with eyes closed, I see the elements. I focus on them to pull this group into this form, and that set I push into a different state. I pull and push and press on so many elements that it is hard to keep track. The energy streaming out of me feels like I am constantly breathing out. At first, I barely notice the energy flowing, but as I continue to work, fatigue begins to gnaw on me.

I keep spinning the elements together, wishing for my sapphire, which is still hanging around Declan's neck. Now would be a good use of the amplifying abilities of the jewel. I inhale deep and slow, holding the air in before letting it trickle out of me. I concentrate on assembling the elements. Forcing them into a certain state isn't difficult, and binding them together into a single thing is not much harder, but layering multiple pieces to link and work together is tricky.

A body is made of so many different components. There is the bone, muscle, the obvious components, but also the blood vessels, cartilage, and sinew to account for as well. The bones I was able to create and then take a break. All the other tissues intersect in a beautiful coexistence of harmonious use and benefit that requires my steady diligence.

My outstretched arm is so heavy it feels like lead. My shoulder is burning, and so are my lungs. The energy pulsing through my chest and down my aching arm no longer feels pleasant. The flow feels as if glass shards have been running through my veins for hours. Everything in my torso throbs with raw pain.

*"Lover?"*

Declan's voice in my mind breaks my concentration. It has been a cycle since I have heard him inside my mind. I blink, the thing before me nearly complete. Exhaustion clouds my vision, but I am almost done. The fatigue is draining, but sheer will and want to finish helps me push energy through the air, converting elements.

Despite the interruption in my concentration, the flowing continues. The energy knows its task while I have become nothing more than a channel. My vision is slipping to gray around the edges, narrowing and fading into the distance.

I watch mesmerized, only half in disgust as muscles knit together. The tissue ripples, growing along the ligaments and bone the way moss grows along roots. After the muscles form, they swell in size, forming long lines and smooth pieces independent of each other yet still of the same part.

*"Stop. You're drained. You're draining me."*

I ignore him, letting my eyes haze over to see the different elements. As pieces breakdown into smaller orbs of red and yellow, each with its own texture, Declan dredges my conscience back to him.

*"Ella!"*

He wrenches my conscience out of the dungeon into him. He is panting, leaning against a wall. My eyes close, and I slump forward. With maximum effort, I interrupt the strum of energy. I let my outstretched hand drop. Exhaustion and pain fracture through my chest into my skull. I double over, hands on the stone floor in puddles of something I pretend not to be able to name, gasping between dry heaves.

Fighting to breathe, choking on air, I cough, my lungs burning. My chest is on fire, the muscles I need to draw in air refusing to work. Hands, strong, warm, and calloused, grab my shoulders and pull me back against something solid.

"What are you doing?"

*"Just breathe."* Leaning back against Dec's chest helps. The steady strum of his heart and the rise and fall of his chest are comforting. His thumbs roll up my spine between my shoulders. *"Breathe."*

"You should not be here."

"He is here to help."

"Help who?"

"Help her."

"He interrupted her."

"Only her work."

"That is everything!"

"No, it isn't."

Air is a sweet-tasting delicacy, chasing the burn from my lungs. I blink, my eyes refocusing on seeing the world in wholes rather than pieces. I let my eyes close again and lean into Declan. I throw myself through our link into him.

Touching him is like being thrown against a brick wall. His worry and anger slams through me. I gasp, my eyes snapping open. My vision is blurry with salted tears.

Declan's lips whisper against my ear, "Breathe."

I gulp down air, nodding against his shoulder. I listen to my heart stammer and relax against him. The feeling of his hands on my shoulders is soothing. I nod again and roll forward to sit, causing my abdominal muscles to burn in protest. My body trembles. I hold a hand up and watch it shake. I look to Declan, who stares back with black eyes.

*I'm tired,* I think, trying to bury my conscience in him. *"I'm sorry. I miss you. I want to stop fighting. I hate not feeling you, and I hate what I have been doing."* I say nothing, though, staring into Dec's murderous eyes.

His lips twitch, and his expression of rage softens. He reaches out with a steady hand to tuck hair behind my ear and cup my face. I drink in his gaze as he peers down at me. I hear the brothers in the background, but they sound so far away.

"Morella, you need to finish!" Erac demands.

"Can you not see her?"

"She is not focusing."

"She is barely upright."

I ignore them. *"I'm sorry."*

*"I know."*

I fall face-first into Declan's chest. He rumbles, containing a laugh as he squeezes me tight to him for a second. With his hands on my shoulders, he pushes me back to arm's length.

*"Are you alright?"* His words are carried on the tides of care and worry.

*"I'm tired."*

*"And you're in pain."* Dec sighs and shifts his focus to the brothers. "She is done for the day."

"You play pretend well, but you are neither king nor husband and cannot speak for her."

Declan's nostrils flare, and the acrimonious expression returns. His lip curls back, and he snarls. "I said she's done. She's almost drained. She was pulling energy from me."

"Give her the sapphire around your neck then."

I am too depleted for the gem. I remember the harrowing experience of touching the gem when drained once before. I cannot muster the energy to speak. I try to shake my head, but it is too heavy. It sort of rotates and flops on my neck in a dismal attempt.

"Erac, brother, you push her too hard."

There's a hiss. "He is holding her back too much."

"Erac, stop, please."

"She was nearly done, and now her work is atrophying before our eyes. What we've always wanted, needed—"

"Patience, brother, and allow me a turn."

"We'll not last much longer even with our link, despite our ancestry. We need her to finish her work without the boy meddling because he craves her attention."

"Erac!"

"Her work here is much more important than her being overwhelmed. I recommended breaking the bond. Do you see now?"

Brilliant light flashes, flickering through the air accompanied by a thunderous crack. I am still reeling, ears ringing, as one of the brothers falls sideways. His body hits the ground.

"This is why." Erac turns to help him.

"This...was..." Aron is wheezing. "You."

I stare, trembling, and helpless. My eyes dredge over the rotting corpse. My work, all that energy and effort are decaying at rapid speeds.

"He is dying."

My heart lurches, and my stomach drops. "No."

I try to stand, but my legs give way. Declan catches me. He cradles me in his arms and kisses my temple. "You're too drained. You cannot help. Even you have limits. You need to rest." Each statement is punctuated with a nuzzle or butterfly kiss to my skin.

"I need them. I need them to teach me."

There is a loud hiss. "Then finish your work! Finish what you've started. Save him."

With wide eyes and panic balled in the back of my throat, clogging my breath, I turn to Declan. "Give me my sapphire."

He takes my offered, shaking hand. "No."

"Dec, I need—"

"I know," he grunts, pulling me into his lap. *"You need them, which means I need them. So, I'll help."* He shifts me so my back is against his chest. *"I can adjust how much energy the sapphire feeds into you like a filter to keep it from overwhelming you."*

I exhale, long and slow. My eyes drift half shut as I hold my hand up. The muscles scream in protest, searing hotly. I do my best to ignore them. I see the elements, some hazy, some strong and vibrant. Not everything has been lost. I focus on what has atrophied the most, the muscles.

I feel the energy roll through me, dragging like little daggers through my outstretched arm. I feel the trickle of energy from Declan into me. It starts off as drips, but as I force the muscles to rebuild, as I begin to form flesh and skin, that drip turns into a stream.

My arm shakes, and the pain ripping through me is almost unbearable, but I refuse to surrender. Declan props my arm under his to ease my struggles. He is doing what he can to help, but I can tell it is starting to take a toll on him as well. I squeeze my eyes shut. Wetness dribbles from my lower lashes and down my cheeks. I try to conjure the last bit of strength and energy I have. I hurl it all at the body in one giant burst of energy and slump back against Declan.

The feed of energy from him slows but does not quit. For that, I am thankful. Through half-shut eyes, I glare at the thing on the floor.

The skin is waxy and yellow. The nose too small and angling to the left. The scalp is covered in patchy dust-colored hair and dips in the skull. There's nothing attractive about the face, but the body appears sound. I cringe.

Declan kisses my temple. "That face is better than green scales stretched tight over bone."

I hear Erac laugh, the sound of rocks rubbing together. "The appearance is unimportant. His blood will correct the features, assimilating the body to Aron's true form."

Breathing is difficult. I can do nothing but watch as Erac lifts his brother's body. He goes to one of Viktor's contraptions and hangs his brother upside down. He moves around, placing a bowl under his brother's head. In a daze, I stare, too drained to care.

There is a glint in Erac's hand. He steps to his brother and slits Aron's throat from ear to ear. I jerk as if I could do anything. The pain, the exhaustion, it all gives way in lieu of shock. Declan holds me against him.

"What have you done?" My voice sounds strange to my own ears. The words feel like prickly stones dragging along my esophagus.

Erac faces us and folds his hands back into his robes. "What I must. The blood is the lifeforce, and it must be removed from one body to be installed into another." He falls silent. Aron's blood draining into the basin creates an eerie pelting echo around the room. "I have no need of you now. This is blood magic only I can perform, and you are too wasted to be of use even if I could accept help."

He draws one hand out and waves it in the direction of Declan and me. A cold tingle spreads through me, and then I am alone in my bed. I hear Declan's faint growl, but I lose consciousness.

# CHAPTER 7

$\mathcal{M}$y conscious unfurls, sleep pulling away like the wings of a bat, abandoning me to harsh reality. The further it ebbs away, the quicker it goes until I am left exposed and shivering.

Bright light catches my eyes through tentatively shut lids. I groan in displeasure. I shift, stretch, and yawn before trying to hunker back down and reclaim the peace of delirium.

"Morella?" The little hairs at the nape of my neck stand. "Are you awake?"

I bolt straight up to see who is in my room. My gaze whirl around the space to see the rows of white beds lining the long corridor. Above me in the steeple roof are large windows filtering in the soul star's bright light.

"Why am I in the infirmary?" I ask. When my sight turns to who is next to me, I jerk hard enough to throw myself over the edge of the thin bed. Cold streaks run through me, and I am sitting in the middle of the bed, left to gape at the smirking man.

"I do understand this is quite a shock, but I daresay you shouldn't be too surprised."

I stare through wide eyes, forgetting to blink. His close-cropped golden hair accentuates the ears that are too small and stick out. His round face beams at me, the skin around his vibrant violet eyes crinkling. A strangled noise escapes from the back of my throat.

He laughs. "Ella! It's me, Aron!" Another strange noise whispers past my lips. Comprehension is sinking in. "To answer your question, you are in the infirmary because you've been asleep for a couple of days. I thought it best to have a shaman brought to tend to you. The expenditure of energy is a costly one, and you did so for hours on a grand scale. Declan is quite furious with us all, but I am ever grateful."

"Declan." His name conjures him at the foot of my bed. "Dec."

He comes around to the side of the bed, opposite Aron, and sits to face me. His conscience is digging around in mine, checking if I am alright. A small smile curves my lips as I close my eyes and throw myself back into him. I hear him sigh as he accepts I am fine. His hand cups my jaw, and the bed dips as he shifts, coming closer to press his forehead to mine.

*"Will you please stop doing this?"*

A giggle bubbles out of me. My lashes flutter. Slate gray orbs penetrate my soul. "I'm sorry."

The left corner of his mouth twitches in a half-smirk. "I know. You're always sorry." He pulls back and faces Aron. "Where is your brother? Aren't you two conjoined?"

"He is resting still. He may never recover." Those purple eyes trail from Declan to meet my gaze. "He will need a body."

"Absolutely not," Declan growls. He sits, squaring his shoulders. "Damnatus will freeze before I allow you to put her through that fucking nightmare again."

Aron smiles. "Your adoration for Morella is touching. I do believe Haven could not have picked a better suitor for her. She doesn't need your protection now, though. I will be helping her this time."

"No."

I sigh. "Dec."

"Not going to happen."

"Dec." I frown. "*I need them.*"

He looks at me with a blank face, but his nostrils twitch. His lip curls back to expose sharp canine teeth, his slate irises shifting darker. Blowing out a harsh breath, he shoves his hair from his face. "You need to eat something." The skin of his nose furrows. "And a shower."

~

*I* shower, donning a dress to please Declan, the color of storm clouds or his eyes when I have done something vexing.

"*So, the color my eyes have been for the last twelve cycles,*" he jests, gleaning my thoughts.

I grin in the mirror before dissipating to the dining hall. He meets me at the door, and his eyes travel my body. His head bobs around before he grips my hips. Hauling me against his solid frame, he kisses me, slow and deep, his tongue rolling against mine. My knees begin to give as I sag into him.

All too soon, he is pulling away, taking my hand, and dragging me under the eyes of the court. When we enter the dining hall, we are stopped by Lady Devereux.

"Declan." She beams at him. "Your Majesty." Her expression is plastered on, but the tone is flat as her caramel eyes rivet on me.

"Elizabeth," I greet her with a raised eyebrow, questioning her motives. She is a friend of Selene, never eager to approach me before.

She grins, her too big mouth exposing larger than normal

teeth. The structure of her face is overall masculine despite her dainty build. "It is good to see you in the dining hall again so soon. Helping the Gammet brothers regain their strength? How exciting."

I force a smile. "Yes, it was all very exciting. I am glad I could assist."

"It is good to see you assisting *someone*." She draws her last word out, putting emphasis on it. I narrow my eyes. "Oh, my dear," she chortles, "that did come out wrong, did it not? I think my mouth can run away with me sometimes, and how I was hoping to be friends."

I hitch my smile. "I'll not hold miscommunicated words against you. After all, there may come a time when I have difficulty phrasing my own words and may need to beg your understanding."

She flutters her lashes, looking at Declan. "How gracious your wife-to-be is."

"She is indeed much kinder than I," he responds. His thoughts travel into a dark recess of his mind recalling atrocities he committed and reveled in.

"Perhaps you might come by my suite tomorrow, so that we may have tea?"

My eyes stretch and blink rapidly at her. "Er, tomorrow I have to return to helping the Gammet brothers. Perhaps we can arrange for some other time?" I take a half step to the side, starting my retreat. "Won't you excuse me? I am famished."

"But of course, Majesty. You've been in the infirmary for a few days."

I nod, shuffling back and away to the other side of the room, Declan on my heels. I slump onto a bench in a dazed sort of stupor. I stare ahead, trying to comprehend what happened, my expression borderline blank. But there is a lot of shock and disbelief, also a bit of annoyance percolating there too.

Legia waltzes over and sits across from me, Wyatt and Chase

in tow. "What, in Haven's name, were you talking to Lady Deveraux about?"

"She says she wants to be friends and asked me to have tea with her."

Legia blinks her turquoise eyes with gusto. Her freckled face stays blank as she does so, and I cannot help giggling at her antics. She rolls her eyes and scrunches her nose. "Well, that explains the look on your face. She's just sniffing around looking for power now that you're queen." There's a collective shock from Wyatt and Chase. "What? It's true. She's never bothered with Ella before."

"I see," Wyatt hums. "Anyone who has not spent their entire life throwing themselves at Ella's feet shouldn't bother to befriend Ella now?"

My eyes grow, and I suck my lips between my teeth, diverting my gaze to the table. I watch Legia bristle at her brother's words from the peripheral of my vision and lean away.

"I've never thrown myself at Ella's feet, and I'm not going to accept those implications." She smacks the tabletop.

"Ella was hardly around before," Wyatt snaps. He hunches over, laying crossed arms on the table. "I'm merely pointing out that not everyone was as active as you in pursuing a friendship."

"She had her reasons," Declan growls.

"Which she's never made known."

Chase leans forward. "There are very few of us who know those reasons."

Wyatt shoots me a nasty look. "Why does everyone know something I don't?"

"Because she doesn't talk about it," Legia answers for me. "I've seen the scars. I've heard..." she pauses, "things. Ella's been through terrible things, and I wouldn't talk about them either."

Ever and always faithful Legia, standing against her brother for me like it is no big deal. There are a lot of times when I wonder why she has been my friend. My eyes meet hers for a second, and I smile before dropping my gaze.

"What scars?"

I stare back into Wyatt's honey-orange eyes and fidget under his stern gaze. I am not sure how to answer his question.

*"You are not obligated to."*

"What scars has my sister seen? If something happened, the court has a right to know."

I find the courage to glare back. "This has nothing to do with the court."

"Your business is the court's business." Wyatt sneers at me. "You don't have a choice about that."

Declan's bitter laugh ripples through my mind. *"The court certainly thinks they are entitled. You don't owe this information to the court, the same as I don't owe the court knowledge of my time and actions while living with Marx."*

I cut my eyes to him. He keeps his face clear of expression, squared to Wyatt with a straight back. He wears no signs of the angst and rage in his thoughts.

"Seriously, what has gotten into you?" Legia is leaning away from Wyatt, glaring.

"Nothing."

"Why are you so cranky? You've never said one bad word about Ella before."

"I'm not cranky," Wyatt snaps back. "I just don't think it's fair to judge Elizabeth for only now trying to get to know Ella."

Legia huffs, turning to me. "Whatever. I stand by what I said. Be careful, Ella. Elizabeth is a snake just as much as your sister."

Wyatt smacks his open hand on the surface space between him and his sister. "That is hardly fair! Selene has gone out of her way to belittle Ella. Elizabeth has done no such thing."

The siblings cock a bow at each other, glowering as if looks could prove their side and sway the other. "You can't prove that she hasn't. We've never paid much attention to her, but she's also friends with Skylar, and Skylar has attempted public humiliation and worse. There's a lot to be said about the company kept."

A twisted laugh bursts from Wyatt. His head tips back, the cruel sound booming from deep in his chest. "This coming from you? Ella wasn't gone a cycle before you were cozying up to Mr. Blackburn over there." He jerks his thumb at Chase. Legia jerks back as if her brother had slapped her. "The Blackburn family has never been a fan of the Princess, and you couldn't get engaged to him fast enough. You aren't friends with Skylar, but you're marrying into the family. How dare you degrade Elizabeth for her company? Are you so blind to your own?"

My eyes cut toward Chase, who slides further away from the Wyndams. He grimaces at me as he does so, and I frown back. Chase might not have started as a friend, but he has been good to Legia and has kept my secrets. He was tortured for information about the Vitale rune the day I tried to kill Viktor because he was my tutor.

*"It wasn't your fault, and he doesn't blame you."*

Chase's face is to the table, a grave expression dug into his flesh. There are deep creases between his brows and around his mouth, so deep they are stark black in his skin. I guess he feels my eyes on him and looks to meet them. I incline my head and try to smile. One corner of his mouth pulls back.

I take a deep breath. "Don't lump Chase in with the rest of his family."

"Haven above." Wyatt lets out a low whistle. "Now, you're defending a Blackburn?"

"Chase has earned it," I snap back. I squeeze my hands into fists in my lap under the table. "Ravenna tortured Marcus that day, and Skylar tried to do the same to Declan, but their father...?" I point to Chase. "His own father tortured him." Wyatt looks over at Chase, who looks back with a blank stare.

"His father tortured him because Viktor told him to, and all because he was my teacher."

I pause to draw in a breath, count to three, and exhale. I want to keep my temper in check. I want to keep my voice down. Most importantly, I want to keep the table and dining hall in good condition. "The potential for him to know where the rune was by being associated with me was all the encouragement needed for Viktor to give the order, and his father did it. That is his family. He isn't like them."

A deafening silence follows in the wake of my words. Legia moves to sit on the other side of Chase. She wraps herself under his arm and rests her head against his shoulder. Chase leans his head against the top of Legia's, his dark eyes on mine.

Declan worms his fingers between mine under the table. He swirls bright colors through our minds. *"Calm down. You're okay. We're okay."* He squeezes my hand.

Wyatt clears his throat. "I didn't know."

I stare straight back into his melancholy expression without much guilt. He looks miserable, but so does Chase. Chase volunteered to train me on his own time for my benefit. He has been good to Legia, and he was tortured because of me. I always liked Wyatt, but my loyalty is owed to Chase.

"He's courting Elizabeth," Declan says.

Legia bolts upright, glowering. "What?"

Wyatt slumps in on himself. "Yes, I've been spending time with Elizabeth." Legia curls back like a snake getting ready to strike. He holds his hands to shield himself, leaning away. "Wait, Legia, I didn't know any of that."

Legia splutters as Chase wraps an arm around her waist. "If I may..." he begins. His gaze flickers to me, I shrug, and he looks back to Wyatt. "There's a lot the court doesn't know, and I'm willing to bet Skylar wants to keep it that way. Her exact involvement was kept quiet, so Elizabeth may not know her character or allegiances."

I bite my lip, knowing full well Declan made that deal with Skylar. He ceased torturing her and promised immunity to know where I was. I was miffed about the arrangement, but he insisted it was necessary due to time constraints.

"Ella and I have each received a chance to prove we are something other than what our family would have you believe. If Wyatt thinks Elizabeth deserves a chance, maybe we should give her the benefit of doubt."

I look to Declan, who squeezes my hand. *"It's your choice, lover."*

I roll my eyes to the ceiling. Inside I am a wrecked ship tossed about in a sea of guilt and apprehension.

I meet Chase's, who raises his eyebrows at me. He used to dislike me, and even after he learned the truth about Viktor's abuse, he still did not care for me. His opinions of me did not rise until he started to train me, to spend time with me, and learn who I am.

Looking around the room, I wonder how many people here feel the same about me as he did back then. I hear Declan assuring me it does not matter, and I have a lot of support within the court. He tells me that often but I never believe him. If Wyatt trusts her, and Chase thinks she deserves a chance, then so be it. I need allies around court.

I direct myself to Wyatt. "Do you think you can talk Elizabeth into inviting Legia to tea as well?"

# CHAPTER 8

$\mathcal{I}$n the gardens with the Gammet brothers, working on meditation like I have been, every morning for the last cycle, I cannot clear my mind, failing miserably at gaining dominance over the Vitale rune. Dozens of little pops of energy keep slipping out of me. The pops are getting louder the more frustrated I get, and then I set fire to a nearby plant.

I let out a string of curses and throw my hands in the air. "This isn't working!" I yell.

"The rune is an alien force. You must meld with the rune to harness the power. Accept the rune as part of you, accept the power into your life force."

"Isn't there something else to try?"

"For the moment, no." Aron smiles and nods his head.

"Someone is here to see you." Erac lifts a shaking arm.

I questioned if he should be here, given his condition. They both insisted fresh air and meditation would be good and not strenuous. I look over my shoulder to see Marcus standing a pace behind me, arms crossed. His features are at rest on his face betraying no reason for his visit.

I turn back to Aron and sigh. "I guess I need a moment."

"Take what you need," Aron says.

"Do not take too long," Erac warns.

I stand to face Marcus. "Yes?"

His yellow eyes flicker toward Aron, and he holds an arm out. "Let's walk."

I take his arm and he pulls me away. I try not to fidget. I try to remind myself it is just Marcus.

"Ella, what is going on?" he asks. "And don't say nothing, because I know something is wrong. You refuse to speak about it with anyone, and I'm done trying to be patient. You haven't been to a session since you recovered from helping the brothers. In fact..." He stops and drops my arm. He meets my gaze and scowls. "You are pulling away even more. You spend all your time with the Gammet brothers."

I keep my eyes straight ahead and sigh. "I am doing what needs to be done. I need to control this." I point to the rune. "I can't handle this much power."

He scoffs. "What you are doing is selfish."

I wince. "Maybe. Probably." I scrunch my face and try to piece together my thoughts to form words.

He watches me with a scowl, arms crossed. He is closed off, black hair amuck about his head.

I run hands through my hair and collect it in one hand while I run the other over my face. "What I am doing lets you and Declan do some real good in this world. I'm training with the Gammets. I'll get myself under control. I won't hurt anyone. I won't set things on fire or start explosions around the court. I won't scare those that come calling on the crown."

His frown has only deepened the longer I rambled. His features change as he exhales, transforming to a melancholy expression. "Ella."

"The city, the court, it needs more than me and my best of intentions," I whisper. "So, I'll be here training, or I'll be in the city. I'll figure out my power. I'll help who I can. Maybe I should just take care of the salt mines. That should be my responsibility since I killed Gordon Pym."

Marcus shakes his head. "I take care of the mines." He stabs himself in the chest with his finger. "That's my responsibility as the eldest member of the Byron family." His voice is steadily rising. "You need to focus on the crown, on the court, and helping Declan. You've left him to tend to your responsibilities."

"They aren't mine!" I scream. I look around us and lower my voice to a hiss. "Nothing about that crown or court should be mine. I don't have an ounce of royal blood in me. I've done despicable things, and I'm as guilty of those crimes as Viktor. Those shouldn't be my responsibilities. I'm not—"

I manage to suck in air in a cracking gasp. "I shouldn't be queen, Marc. I shouldn't oversee the court or any part of this land. I shouldn't be allowed to be responsible for anyone's life, and I probably shouldn't be allowed anywhere near another living soul. I have one set of skills, one thing I am good for, and it isn't queen material. I just... I'm not responsible. I'm not honest. I'm not good. I'm just Viktor's stupid tool, and I don't know how to get past that."

Blackbirds fly high through the sky. I recall a time when I was a little girl chasing them around a courtyard. Gopi, the first life I ever took, he died that day. I shiver at the memory. I wipe my forehead and run my hands back through my hair to push the strands out of my face, finding the courage to look my brother in the eye.

"No one deserves to have to be near me," I tell him, "including you, so don't come back."

I close my eyes and hold my hand out. I send him back to his study, knowing full well he will be outraged. He claims being dissipated by another hurts.

Making my way back to the brothers, I do my best to seal away my emotions, to blink back the burn in my eyes, and stay my trembling hands. When I drop down to sit cross-legged in front of them, I hope there are no traces left.

They do not ask, and I do not say. I close my eyes and focus on breathing, feeling a numbness spreading through my gut. Meditation is absorbing, so I try to consume the raw pain into my blood and breathe.

I have had very little luck controlling the power within me, evident by the burned foliage and pile of rubble that used to be a stone bench. I grind my teeth, a nearby potted plant dissolving to ash. "This isn't working."

Aron opens his brilliant lilac eyes. "You must calm yourself. Still your mind. Control your emotions."

"You have been saying that for cycles, and it isn't working." I shake my head, sneering.

His shoulders drop. "Emotions can be constrained. They can be tempered. Controlling the elements starts with controlling yourself. You have enormous power and no mastery of manipulation. You are able to force elements into accepting direction from you out of sheer force." His eyes drop from mine to the burnt patch of stone between us. "Connecting with your life-force must be difficult for you, given your unique circumstances."

*My father's blood. Viktor's blood.* I roll my shoulders, shifting. "What does that have to do with anything?"

Aron's eyes snap to mine. They are wider, his eyebrows lifted. "Everything."

My head tilts, and I shoot daggers at him with narrowed eyes. "I don't get it."

His head tips back, and he laughs, eyes dancing. "Either my friend Chase is a very poor teacher, or you paid attention as little as he claims."

I purse my lips and look away. "This isn't Chase's fault."

Aron snickers. "I know. This isn't your fault, either." Those words sing through me, drawing my gaze back to him. His features are softer, radiating kindness. "Erac and I should have trained you. For that, we apologize. You needed more tutelage than you were given. Chase was not equipped with the proper knowledge."

I trace the grout between stones in front of me with a finger. I puff my cheeks then expel the air. "I don't think I can do this."

"You can, but I never said this would be easy. You are going to have to accept the foreign lifeforce, meld the power of the rune to your own source of life. Once you find inner peace, you can harness all the power."

"Inner peace," I sigh. "Great." I straighten my legs, pushing myself onto my feet. My lips twist to the side. "I'll work on that, but in the meantime, I'm going to get rid of some of this energy."

I go to Cato to expend my excessive energy, making fruits for the hungry and repairing busted wagon wheels. I even heal a broken bone and a few lesions. Learning to make a body has its advantages.

The soul star begins to set, hours gone, but the rune is still burning hot. I wander down an alley toward a group of children. I talk to them, offering them fruits, and one asks if I can make them a shelter. I offer that if they come to my estate, they can have more than just a roof over their heads. They decline, so I wave my hand and make a hovel out of the enclosed end of the alley for them.

I exit the alley considering I have not heard or felt Declan in my mind all day. Distracted, I get entangled with a few men. One of them recognizes me as the queen and spits at the ground by my feet. He insults me, calls me names, and blames me for the problems in this land. I do nothing to contradict him, pursing my lips.

I know I am partially to blame. I stare at the spit on the toe of my boot and wait for him to finish his rant. When I lift my eyes from the drool, a ring of spectators has gathered.

"The city is a dangerous place for one such as you," he sneers, cracking his knuckles and rolling his shoulders. "There are all kinds of folks who would love to see you strung up for the misery you've caused."

I fidget and nod. "I understand. I'm trying to help."

"Help? Help who? The elemental mutts that are running these streets? Do they know you're the reason they're here? The reason their families were driven from their homes, their fathers killed in the mines, the reason for needing help?"

I realize he is moving toward me. I step back. My heart rate accelerates, but I draw in a breath and wait, not daring to move. The last thing I want is to set someone on fire or set off an explosion that will cause mass panic. Either thing will cause someone to get hurt, and really, if they want to wail on me, what is the harm.

"Sir, I apologize for any inconveniences I've caused." I stay still as we stand toe to toe. He towers over me, glowering. "Is there anything I might do to right the misery I've caused you?"

"You can rot in the inferno." He leers with a malicious grin, balling a fist. He pulls back. He swings.

I do not bother with any maneuver. His hook cracks against my face. Jarring pain whips through my nasal passages, radiating through the whole side of my skull. My left ear rings as I stumble down to one knee. The flesh over my cheekbone pulsates hotly where he struck, and I put a hand to it and wiggle my jaw.

When I start to pick myself up, I glance toward my attacker, but someone stands between the man and me. He is taller than all the others, a mop of frizzy brown hair and enough muscles bulging to scare a dozen full-grown men.

"Walk away," he says in a deep growling voice. "Now. All of you."

With a silent sigh, I get to my feet. I crane around Seth to the man glaring at me. Our eyes meet, and then he turns and strides through the crowd. As he leaves, the crowd starts to depart, and I toe the ground.

Seth turns around, frowning and glaring all at the same time. "What the Damnatus?"

I hang my head, a hand pressed to my throbbing cheek. "Thanks."

"I shouldn't have needed to step in. You could have taken him." He narrows his eyes in his round face. "Easily."

I smile with pursed lips. "I appreciate the gesture."

"Why'd you let him hit you?"

I shrug. "It doesn't matter."

"Ell," Seth snaps, "I don't know what's going on with you, but I do know you let him hit you. Why?"

I shove my hands in my pockets and eye a few passing by as I rock on the balls of my feet. "Because he's right. It is my fault, and if it makes him feel better..." I say, trailing off and shrugging.

Seth gapes at me, then shakes his head. "Ell," he groans, "what in Damnatus is going on in your head?"

I swallow the lump in my throat and grin at him. "Nothing," I whisper.

He shoves fingers into his hair, gripping at the strands and his skull. His eyes slip from dark gray to a dark inky coal. "You're still a terrible liar. You let him hit you, and you're making me fucking crazy."

"I know." I do my best to grin and wink at him before I dissipate to my rooms.

I peel off my grungy clothes and shower. Slipping on a dress, I go in search of Declan. I find him in the dining hall, where he sits in the corner alone.

When I slide onto the bench next to him, he runs a hand over his mouth. Without looking at me, he sighs. "I know you've been trying to manage that rune, but you missed session, *again*. You were unconscious in the infirmary for days, and you haven't bothered to attend session since."

I shrug and hold a hand over the table. A plate appears, and I start piling food on it. "So? No one cares but you."

"It's been a whole cycle."

"You've got it covered."

"Ten days."

I roll my eyes. "Thanks, I didn't know what a cycle was."

He grabs my hand as I reach for my goblet. I frown. I lift my gaze to his.

"I am tired," he says. The words are shoved through clenched and bared front teeth. "I am doing everything. You've even dumped your orphan program for me to handle."

I jerk free. "You deal with those things better than I do, and anyway, you're the one who was so desperate for me to fix this power issue I have." My finger points to my collarbone.

His lips press together hard enough to disappear. His temper spikes. I roll my eyes, causing his irritation to double.

"Ella," he snaps, "you needed to deal with it. I've tolerated you making a vessel for—"

"'Tolerated?'" I reiterate the word, stressing the syllables. "'Tolerated?'"

His eyes flash darker, and the muscles in his jaw jump. "Lower your voice, Morella."

I smack the tabletop and narrow my eyes. "Do not call me that! How many times do I have to tell you?"

His lips hitch to the side. "How many times do I have to tell you to take care of your responsibilities?"

My jaw drops. "Excuse me?"

He shakes his head. "You need to help me."

"What would you have me do?"

"Stop spending so much time with Erac. I don't like the way he talks to you or the way he speaks about me. In general, I do not like the way he acts toward you—"

"There is nothing wrong with how he treats me." I laugh with a hollow ring.

"And how he treats me? Is there nothing wrong with that?" I bristle with indignation, but Declan goes on. "I am here because of you. Everything that I am doing to take care of the crown is for you, and I am tired." His tone is low and edged like broken glass. Something about him is warning me to tread cautiously. "I am done with holding your crown while you fawn over another man."

I swallow hard and twist fingers together under the table. "I am not fawning. I wasn't even with Erac today."

The skin on the bridge of Declan's nose crinkles as he snarls with black eyes. "I have been allotted none of your time nor attention for the last two cycles other than when *I*," he stresses, "wake you from a nightmare to calm you down. Perhaps Erac would be kind enough to manage your pathetic dreams so that I might get a decent night's rest."

I gape at Declan and he stands. "Your orphan program needs a signature but has the majority support of the court. See Marcus when you deign to have time."

Declan leaves. Most would not notice the straining muscles in his neck or the clenched fists at his side as he moves out of the dining hall, but they are glaring signs of his rage. I swallow bile and stare at the untouched food in front of me.

My tongue tastes of ash as I consider eating. I push the plate away, looking around. Seth catches my eye. He shakes his head, turning so he is facing away from me. I run a hand over my face and take a deep breath, expanding my ribcage.

For once, I am glad Declan has our link shut off. There are all these emotions cascading through me. I cannot even name them all, and I do not need his emotions adding to the turmoil. With my appetite ruined, I dissipate to my rooms to end this day.

# CHAPTER 9

Over the next few days, I steer clear of the brothers. Erac is still lingering between life and death, but I need time to recover. I work toward finishing the ordinances for the orphans in the city and start the paperwork to repeal Viktor's levied taxes in Cimeria. I was too busy to investigate a cave-in within the salt mines, but as that is a Byron family issue and the court is left uninvolved, I delegated it to Marcus. I made it on time to court the last two mornings and even took charge of session, mostly without Declan's help.

Now I am rushing to make it to tea on time. Legia shoots daggers at me with her eyes for being late. I sit down, having zero chance to say anything before Elizabeth insults Legia. Legia flares and I do my best to hide in my chair, eyes wide, as the two women hurl insults and insinuations at each other cloaked by smiles and pleasant voices.

I do my best to mediate between them, receiving a kick in the shin from Legia at one point. I set fire to the table in shock. Elizabeth squawks and flings her arms around. Legia laughs at her while I extinguish the flames.

We all stare at the table. Elizabeth is glaring at me, but I shrug. Legia stands, dropping a curtsy. "Thank you so much for your generosity, however sub-par and lukewarm the tea was." She pulls me to my feet. "Honestly, Ella, I think you did us all a favor."

Legia storms out, pulling me by the wrist as she mutters to herself. I follow along for a minute, nervous that if I say something, she will turn her wrath on me. Somewhere far overhead, the bells toll the time.

I grit my teeth. "Is it really already four?"

Legia stops, looking over her shoulder at me. Her head cocks. "I suppose." She drops my wrist. "I cannot believe it!"

"Can't believe what?"

"That Wyatt believes her. That he is courting her. Haven, staring at her face for thirty minutes made my eye twitch. Look at this." Legia jabs her extended finger toward her eye in a repeated motion. She groans, throwing her hands in the air. "Haven above, Elizabeth is as much a devious snake as Selene, and we all know the accepted opinion of your sister."

I raise a single brow at my long-time friend. "I don't know, I didn't think Elizabeth was that awful."

"You never think anyone is awful."

I jut a hip and place my hand on it. "I thought Viktor was awful."

"And you killed him." She wrinkles her nose. "Maybe it's a good thing you don't think anyone is awful."

Despite Elizabeth's best attempts at persuasion, Legia still thinks the worst of her. I cannot say Elizabeth is as bad as Selene, but I requested Legia's attendance at tea for that reason. If Legia does not trust her, that is all I need to know. Right now, I push it all from my mind.

I grimace and act like I am checking a watch. "I have to be going."

Her turquoise eyes sparkle. "Plans with your handsome, hunky husband-to-be?"

My face flames as a blush spreads. "Shut up. But yes. I have spent so much time with the brothers as of late." I pause, biting my lip. "I planned this whole dinner in my rooms for us. I told him I wanted to show him how much it means to me that he tolerates everything with me and is basically running the entire Byron Court."

She bobs her head, pushing me down the corridor away from her. "Well, thank Haven for that. Chase has mentioned Declan's dislike of Erac and the lack of your attention."

I arranged dinner, but Declan is not going to meet with me until five. With time to spare, I head for the library to clear my head.

I tiptoe down the library levels to the mage's section, hoping to avoid running into Seth. Not that Seth and I are at odds, but things are strained now that he is Duke of Kennelton, and I am Queen. Politics is a nasty business, derailing the best of people into pits of their soul, where disparaging and depraving triumph compassion and intellect. He may have been my best friend while Viktor, the sadist, was ruling my life, but things are shifting ever further from those days. We spar most mornings before the soul star climbs the sky, but these days I cling tighter to Legia, who weaves me through social graces and gossip circles.

A dark, jade-cloaked figure steps before me as I wander without purpose. I jerk and put a hand to my chest. "Cripes, Aron, you scared me."

"Apologies," he answers, "but it is Erac, not Aron."

I tilt my head and narrow my eyes at him. "You're supposed to be resting."

He nods and folds his hands in front of him. "I am, but I wanted to speak with you."

I fold my arms and eye him. "Where is Aron? Don't you still need him until you get a new body?"

"He is strong enough to support both of us for the moment

no matter near or far. I can feel his energy, the strength of his life-force returning him to full power." Erac's shoulders lift and drop.

I nod. "What do you need?"

"A body," he answers.

I frown and look at the ground. "You just said, and Aron said he was going to help this time."

There is that strange noise of rocks rubbing together. "You asked me what I needed. That is what I need. I do not intend for you to create a body for me at this moment."

I look at him from under furrowed brows. "Then, what?"

"I simply have a desire to speak with you, Ella. I have no ulterior motives or agenda to speak of."

I stare at him and force a smile. "Okay, well, I'm just wandering the library for quiet right now, and then I have a dinner with Declan."

His hooded head nods. "There is much you deal with."

I roll my eyes and scoff. "No, Declan deals with a lot. I run away and hide." I wave my hands to indicate my current surroundings.

"The would-be-king seems to enjoy doing those things."

"He doesn't." I laugh.

"He handles them well."

I shrug. "That's true. He does, but just because you're good at something doesn't mean you enjoy it." My thoughts sink into the demon in me, and it's grinning. We enjoyed those things, as much as I hated them. I shudder and look at Erac.

"Is the boy upset with you that you do not help him with those things?"

I glower. "Declan is a man, and yes, he has to take care of a lot of things. I don't always help him like I should." I cross my arms over my body to hug myself. Saying those words out loud sends a pang of cold through me. He and Marcus have said those words a hundred times, but somehow, saying the words myself seems to make them resonate in me. I curse. "I'm sorry, Erac, but I should be doing other things."

His head inclines. "Ella, you do enough. You have the right to do as you wish. I daresay the bond between you and Declan doesn't allude to a clear understanding of things."

I hesitate, biting my lip. Seth said not to, but I wince and sigh. "Erac, about bondings..."

"Yes?"

"How much do you know about them?"

His head tilts to the side. "What would you like to know? I am well versed in many things old and forgotten." His tone is light and teasing. "I have had quite a bit of time to read and learn."

"Ha," I half-heartedly let lose a laugh. "I bet." I bite my lip again, knowing Seth told me not to ask for any favors.

"Why do you hesitate?"

I wince. "I was told not to ask."

He laughs, that unnerving noise wafting through the library's still air. "Who would dare to tell you no?"

I grin. I cannot help it. "One of the very few that can." Heat spreads across my cheeks. "It's my friend, Seth."

"Ah, the would-be king's brother." The hood bobs. "Why does he tell you no?"

I make a waving gesture with my hand, then brace myself. When there is no explosion or fire, I exhale in relief.

"He's, er, he..." I shuffle my feet, staring down at them. "It's a long story." I expel air. "But, anyway, Seth is bonded to my sister, and, well, he doesn't want to be."

"A bond is an unnatural thing." Erac draws a breath like reeds rattling in the wind, and his figure shudders. "The creation of shades was an abomination against Haven. A shades' ability to bind another to them, to rip the soul of themselves and their claimed—"

79

"Beg pardon, what did you say? Rip the soul?" I blink, my head cocking to the side. "Did I hear that right?"

Erac inclines his head. "A bond is nothing more than perverted blood magic." The hood bobs from one side to the other. "The bond between a shade and its claimed is a bit more complicated than simple blood magic, but the principals are the same. Break the magic, and the bond dissolves."

"What did you mean, rip the soul?"

He waves a hand toward a set of nearby chairs. "Please. I will explain."

I take a step, then bite my lip and look around. There is no sign of the time available, but I imagine I still have some. Declan may forgive me for being late for the sake of his brother.

"Alright." I step forward and sink into the chair next to him. "But only for a minute. I have somewhere I need to be."

"Of course." Erac inclines his head. "But to answer you, when a shade claims or binds another to them, both souls are ripped in half. The shade transfers half of their soul into the claimed's body, taking half of the claimed's soul into their own."

My mouth hangs open. "Half of my soul is in Declan?"

"And half of his soul is within you."

I flop back into the chair and stare forward. After a few heartbeats, I rest my elbows on my knees to lean forward. "That explains why it hurts so much, I guess." I rub the space between my eyes. "So, how do you break the bond?"

Erac lifts a hand.

I jerk with unease and show him my palms. "I don't want to dissolve my bond to Declan."

He scratches his other arm and then rests the hand back in place. "I cannot break your bond with the would-be-king-boy. A bond must be removed from the source, from the shade. The magic is in his blood, not yours."

"Oh, okay. So...well, that's good. That means Selene isn't going to get a say in what happens with her bond to Seth."

"A claimed never gets a choice. They do not have a choice in being claimed. They do not get to manipulate the bond the way the shade does."

I shove hair out of my face and work through the strands detangling them. "You're referring to how Declan—" my fingers catch on a knot yanking several strands, "—can shut me out or use the bond to know what I'm doing or thinking even when I can't."

"Precisely. He is manipulating you, controlling you."

The demon in me curls and hisses. My eyes drop to the control rune on my forearm. The flourishes and dots are beautiful, but I run my fingertip over the scar nestled between lines. I love the scar. Hurt like hell and took forever until I could squeeze my hand into a fist without the muscles in my arm throbbing, but I love it. In a way, the scar brought Declan back to me.

I let my finger drop away and lift my arm for Erac's benefit. "I have this to keep from being controlled."

"Oh, sweet innocent little mage." Mirth is evident in his words. "The rune freed you from Viktor's control, severed his blood in your veins from his own. It does prevent you from being controlled, within reason. Aron and I were able to dissipate you a quarter of the way across Caleum without your consent."

He chuckles. "That rune broke Viktor's blood magic, however unintentional. Disgusting," Erac scoffs, "the way he used magic, really. A disgrace to all mages that such powerful magic could be weaved by one of the warrior clan."

I chew on my lip. The humor is gone from Erac's tone, something darker lacing through his words. I bob my head, staring at the floor, continuing to work to remove knots.

"There's no chance..." I stop, then try again. "If Viktor's not dead...?"

Erac waves a hand. "Even if he removed the rune, his absolute reign over you has ended. Once blood magic is broken, it cannot be repaired."

I frown. "Declan was able to bond with me a second time."

The Gammet brother lets out a hiss. "That you would choose to be controlled is beyond me, but no, that is not repairing the magic, that is repeating the magic. Viktor would need to remove the rune and instill his blood within you once more. A sufficient amount too."

"But he *can*," I stress, "regain the ability to order me around?"

"In theory." The words are dismissive. "I am curious why would you choose to be bound?"

I coil into the chair, opening and closing my mouth. I look away from him, my brow furrowing in contemplation. "It helps."

"Helps what? Him? He keeps tabs on you. He orders you around. You, something so rare and beautiful, and he wishes to strap you down, laden you with burdens below your abilities."

My lips twist to the side. "I don't know about that. I mean, yes, Declan is always asking me to do things, but those are things I should be doing." I prop my head on my hand and gaze at Erac. There seem to be no judgments from him. I smile.

"You are a young queen. You have yet to learn the ability to rule your chessboard with strength."

"What?" The mention of chess makes the hairs on my arms stand.

"The queen is the most powerful and precious of pieces. She guards her king, she fights for the others, and has the ability to determine the outcome." I cannot see under his hood, but I can feel his gaze burning through me. "You are a true queen. Do not allow him to rob your power from you or to control you. A king is only a puppet, a shadow, a mirage of power."

I strum fingers against my cheek. "Viktor referred to me as his queen, much in the same manner."

"Then Viktor managed to get one thing right."

I scoff and look around the library at the shelves and books. We share the silence for a while. There is no awkwardness, no need to fill the world around us with chatter. It occurs to me that we have strayed far from the purpose of our conversation.

"How do you break a bond?"

"Do you recall the way you broke the bearings?"

"Yes."

"Much in the same manner. Concentrate on the shade maintaining a bond and focus energy into its blood. Always remember, intent with blood magic is as important as the energy provided and the spell being weaved. Two mages can weave blood magic with very different results."

I nod. "I know casting blood magic requires intentions, but dissolving the magic?"

He laughs. "There is much for you to learn." He stands and stretches. "Would you care to learn?"

Excitement sparkles in my chest. "Yes, please."

# CHAPTER 10

*I* approach the practice field in the morning to find Declan jabbing at a wood post. I drop to the ground, grinning as I stretch. Erac is full of wonderful knowledge, and I am thrilled to be gleaning every bit. We talked for hours, well into the night, about the thorough workings of blood magic. I had returned to my room exhausted and even slept through the night without a single nightmare.

Limber and ready, I step to the post next to Declan. "Morning."

"You're in a chipper mood," he grunts, swinging at the post. It splinters at the contact of his fist.

I frown. "I would say you're not."

"Is that so?" He steps and swings, never looking in my direction. The next strike shatters the post.

"I would say so," I mutter.

He looks at me with black eyes. I make a futile attempt to reach him through our link, but I am shut out again. Maybe still. I have lost track of being allowed in his mind. I cock a hip out and cross my arms. "Dec, what—"

"Did you have a good time with Erac last night?"

I scowl. "Yes, we spent a lot of time talking. He was explaining to me about blood magic and—"

"Wasn't there something else you were supposed to be doing?" His voice is dangerous.

I look to the sky, and then my stomach drops. *Dinner*. I curse and drop my arms. "Dec, I—"

"Don't," he snaps. "Just..." He pauses and bares his teeth. "Get away from me right now, Ella."

I shake my head and move closer. "Dec."

He takes a step away, putting hands up. "I said, don't."

"I'm sorry."

"How many times have I heard that?" He laughs, a twisted and hollow sound. "In fact, I think dinner last night was to be an apology, or was it to show me what I really mean to you?"

Hearing my own words repeated back under the circumstances makes me blanch. The air feels warm around me, and I cover my face with my hands.

I inhale, then drop my hands and meet his putrid gaze. "That is what I said."

"There were nicer ways to show me how little I mean to you." He crosses his arms and leans against another post. "You have a choice, you know. I will not force myself on you."

I open and close my mouth, fighting to breathe at the thought of losing him. "Dec," I manage.

He scoffs. "I wonder if you don't want to lose me or don't want to lose what I do for you." His features are taut, pale with rage. He shakes his head. "I am not the king or your husband. Erac keeps reminding you of that, so it could be easy for you to replace me. Erac seems happy to take over."

Anger sparks me to life. "You're out of your mind."

"No." The word is harsh, but his voice low. It is worse than the yelling. "I've told you so many times that I am here for you, so if you don't want—"

"I don't!"

"—me."

"No, Dec, no that—"

"Then, make up your mind and make a choice." His growl is full of warning.

"You," I whisper.

"You say that, but everything you do tells me otherwise. I am here for you, doing this thing I despise, doing—"

I throw my hands up. "Argh! I am so sick of hearing that. Stop guilting me."

"Guilting you? Is that what you feel?"

I do feel guilty, but that is not something I want to admit right now.

He chuckles. "You don't have to say it. I hear you loud and clear."

I grind my teeth and clench my fists. *"Bastard. Blocking me out and still listening to me. You've had me shut out for cycles. You've been pushing me, controlling me ever since I became queen."*

He straightens and snarls like a rapid animal, biting at the air. He stands, quivering with rage.

I deflate, giving in. "I know you're upset, and you have every right to be mad that I missed dinner."

"A dinner you planned to show your intentions, or was it to show me your choice?" He shrugs, backing to rest against the post.

I sigh, shoving both hands over my hair. "Yes, and—"

"And I think I understand your choice."

"Dec."

He looks me dead in the eye, and the words die on the back of my tongue. His eyes are coal-black and ringed in red. The skin around his eyes and mouth are white, the perfect picture of a gorgeous monster.

I lift my hands in a defensive motion and take a step away. He smirks, one corner of his mouth tugging up.

"No," I manage to get out past the clog of fear in my throat.

"You see," he whispers, "you say that, and you keep saying that, but lover, everything else you are doing contradicts that." His face tips up toward the soul star. His hair falls back from his face. Furious or not, he is gorgeous.

He shrugs again. "I won't fight you, and I will not force you to accept me. You have a choice, but I expect you to make a choice soon, or I will make it for you."

The air is knocked from me like he kicked me in the gut. I liked him yelling at me better than the harsh whisper caked with despair. I blink back tears, and he is gone. I look around with blurry vision at the rest of the practice field. This sick feeling in me is burning, and I need to let it out.

I am stepping and swinging. Motion catches my eye. Seth. Our eyes lock, and he turns his back to me, choosing a post at the far end of the courtyard.

Another wave of emotions washes through me. I try to grit my teeth. I blink and focus on technique. I bash my hand into the pole so hard I pretend the pain is the reason for my tears.

My thoughts blossom into anxiety. My chest contracts, my heart feeling the squeeze of iron lungs. I falter in throwing a punch. My ankle rolls, and I flail as I hit the ground.

"Are you crying, Your Majesty? Because I am not going to empathize. You've got Dec so twisted and torn up with this infatuation you have..." Seth trails off and shakes his head. "I'll tolerate you loving my brother, but for Haven's sake, Ell, if you want something else..." He stops talking again, looking harrowed.

I gasp on all fours. His words seep through my panic. My head whips toward him, standing nearby. "You mean if I don't love Dec, you expect me to love you?"

"You've really become an arrogant bitch, haven't you?" He spins on his heel, leaving me in the dirt.

The world is reeling. My head and heart feel shredded. Disparage courses through me, and I do my best to force the burn in my eyes to retreat.

*I deserved that.*

I sit back on my heels. Seth has returned, offering me his hand. "What in Damnatus are you doing, Ell?"

"Nothing," I snap. "Just leave me alone." I smack at his hand and reclaim my feet without assistance.

I punch and wail and kick anything and everything. I move hard and fast until my lungs are burning. I am panting, but I register it all as a passenger. I focus on what Declan said, what Seth has said, what they all have said about me and to me.

*I need to do this. I need to do that. I should be, should be, should be.* I growl in the back of my throat, throwing a punch that explodes the post. *All these should bes.*

"Ella."

I ignore my name, punching a new post. It shatters. I splay my fingers, hand out, freezing the elements mid-explosion. Closing my fist pulls the fragments together. I get in another couple of swings against the post before it disintegrates.

*"Lover."*

The demon laughs. My own lips twist into a sneer. I spin around, throwing energy at him. Declan flies back through the air, nearly out of the courtyard.

"And stay out," I yell, turning to find a new post.

But he is there, wrapping an arm around my waist, his other arm wrapping around my shoulders, pulling my back to his chest. His hand slides under the collar of my shirt to press against the rune. I slam my elbow into his side and dissipate several feet away from him.

I look at him and glare. "I said, get out."

"You're going to hurt yourself or someone else," he growls back with black eyes.

"Only if they come in here." I laugh. "Now get out."

I turn away from him and realize not a solid standing pole is left in the field. My temper spikes. Energy pours out of me. The posts reassemble as if I never destroyed them.

I grin, swinging at the closest post, but Declan's hand closes over my fist. "What has gotten into you? Do you have any idea what the court is going to think of this?"

I try to wrench my fist free, but he locks on tight enough for it to hurt. Nearby posts shatter. One cackles to life with flames. "I don't care what the court thinks."

I pull my fist back while I extend my other hand, pushing energy at him. He must have been ready for it because he does not go but a foot. However, the combined push and pull free my fist.

He shows his long, pointed teeth. "You need to stop. You're done."

"You act like it, but you aren't really king." I smirk. "So, as queen, I am giving you an order. Get out of this field." He does not so much as even twitch. "Now," I say, turning back to a pole.

He scoffs. "You can hardly claim to be queen." I punch another post, and it explodes. "In fact, if it wasn't for your engagement to me, you and your family would have been stripped of the crown after the truth about Viktor came to light."

I drop my hands to my hips, staring at a post. It shatters from my glare, but Declan's words have given me a thought. I turn to eye him, and he crosses his arms, glaring back. His face slides into horror as my thought sinks into both of us.

"Don't you dare."

I laugh, doubling over, gasping for air, laughing hard enough to bring tears to my eyes and make my gut hurt. There is no reason I should be queen, and he just gave me what I need. I can absolve the engagement and then step down, knowing that the court would accept it.

The bond screams between us, vibrantly alive and pulsing,

but it is more than anger. There is a bitter pit of despair yawning within him. A pernicious churning of despondence mingling with noxious seething of putrid bile leaving sulfur in the air.

I stand and grin at him. "Yeah, that'll be the first thing I bring up in session tomorrow."

He is snarling at me again, and I hear him howling in my mind. *"You won't. You can't. We're bound to each other."*

My grin grows wider, and so do his eyes. "Erac told me how to break a bond." I say the words aloud for my own satisfaction. The terror tightening my chest does not belong to me. The only time Declan lets me feel him is when he wants to dictate my actions. It does not stop me; it only bolsters my resolve. "It's easy, in fact."

"Don't." The word is a single breath released from deep in his chest, bathed in revulsion.

I hold my hand out toward him. When I blink, he is before me, grabbing my wrist, twisting my arm behind my back. I squirm, breaking free with the help of the elements, and then go on the defensive. He is furious. I can feel it. I can feel him. I push back, swinging as hard as I can, adding energy to each hook and jab, thrilled to know he feels the impact.

We throw punches and block attacks until Seth cuts between us. He gets a blow from both of us for his efforts. Swearing and ducking behind his arms as protection, he turns his back to me, pushing Declan away.

"That's enough," he roars, turning to glare at me. "Both of you. Done. Now."

I meet Seth's heather-gray eyes with all that rage burning in me, and his expression softens.

He sighs, stepping toward me. "Ell," he whispers, "what the fuck?"

I stare at his eyes. They never shine anymore. They are the color of stones, a lackluster matte. My eyes prickle. The idea that his never shine because of me rankles. I open my mouth, about to tell him everything.

*"I don't know what I'm doing. I don't know how to do this. I miss my friend. I miss Declan. I can't do this. I can't be queen."*

As I am conjuring words into my addled brain, Erac appears.

*"Oh, great, this asshole,"* Declan thinks. He pinches the bridge of his nose. "What are you doing here?"

Erac crosses his arms, turning to me. I can only stare with wide eyes, stunned. "The bond removal will take a bit out of you, but after an abbreviated time, it will be beneficial for you."

A gurgle escapes my constricted throat.

"The bond you share with your would-be-king has become a parasitic poison. This escapade has made that much clear."

There is a harsh laugh, and my eyes jerk to Seth. "You are insane. I think that bond is the only reason they haven't killed each other."

My eyes slide toward Declan. He thinks Seth has a point. My temper flares at his thought, and a nearby post crackles to life with fire. We all look at it.

Erac extends a hand to douse the flames. His hooded face is directed at Seth. "Insane? No. The would-be-king came to me, requesting to know how to break a bond. Ella has requested the knowledge of how to remove a bond, as well. You, also, have expressed a desire to remove a bond. To Ella, not to me, but perhaps, you all understand the ability for a shade to bind its mate to them is a design flaw. Allow me to help you." The shadowed face rotates to Declan. "All of you."

One of Erac's hands lift, his palm directed to Seth. Boney fingers splay out, palm level with Seth's face. He closes his hand into a fist. Seth howls, dropping to his knees and then hitting the ground with a thump. My mind races, trying to catch up.

"Seth?" I scramble to him.

He pushes himself to all fours, head snapping up. "What?" His voice is hoarse, laced with pain.

"Did that…?" I hesitate. "Are you alright?"

"Yes, it worked." His fingers dig into the ground, tearing the earth. His eyes are ringed in red, magnified by the bubbling, glossy surface.

"Of course, it did." Erac's confident words irk me.

My head whips to Erac. "You're the one who's insane!"

Seth tries to reclaim his feet but stumbles and uses a post to keep his footing. I reach out toward him, but he bares his teeth at me.

I withdraw, crossing my arms. "Are you alright?"

"That fucking hurt." He takes a step away from the post in Erac's direction. His legs crumple beneath him. He drops to the ground on his knees, then doubles over on all fours and growls.

I get my hands on him, trying to pull him up. "Seth?"

He wrenches free of my grip, rolling to his back. "I'm fine."

I roll my eyes. "Fine."

Declan crosses his arms. "What the Damnatus do you think you are doing, Erac?" His voice is quiet, his presence swelling. The black eyes glitter in the light of the soul star.

"I am fixing your problem, would-be-king."

I wince. Seth gets to his feet with a grunt, taking a step toward Erac. Declan steps forward, clasping him by the shoulder. He looks at me. "Ella?"

"What?"

His nostrils flare. He looks ready to slaughter, but the bond is closed again. "Ella."

"What?" I repeat. "I'm not doing anything. He is." I point at Erac.

Declan turns his face away, not responding to me. His focus centers on Erac. "What are you fixing for me?"

"You can be free."

"I am free."

Erac laughs. "You detest your life and what you must go through for a woman who no longer needs you. You've come to me to learn how to break a bond, so we both know this is true. Allow me to break the bond, and you can leave."

"Did you really ask to break the bond?" My words carry through the silent air. My eyes straining to convey fury at Declan, wide and unblinking. In my chest, my heart is shriveling, pulling in on itself. Breathing is difficult.

"You requested the knowledge as well," he answers in a low growl.

"For Seth!" I scream as loud as I can. "Did you ask to break our bond?"

His face never so much as twitches, but I can tell the difference these days. His eyes flicker ever so like he is looking at the corner of my eye instead of meeting my gaze.

I shake my head, covering my ears to block out his shouts. Seth's words overlay Declan's. Each intake of air sends shards of my breaking heart through my lungs. The bond rips open to slam his conscience to mine. Declan is in my veins, but the taste of honey on my tongue makes me sick.

For the first time, he feels wrong. His presence in my mind is blistering cold. His thoughts coursing through my mind like shards of iron.

I open my eyes. They roll until they find violet eyes. "Do it."

Declan grabs my shoulder. "Ella, no!"

"Of course."

There is a snap at the base of my skull. My vision hazes and blurs, splitting in two. I blink the pain away, lying on my back. My legs are bent at odd angles under me. I roll over and get on all fours, fighting to breathe. A low, guttural growl wafts next to me, and I look over into Declan's black eyes.

My chest aches as I realize what I have just done. I close my eyes and dissipate, but not to my room. I open my eyes to look around the dungeon. It is the only place I deserve to be, the only place I have ever been worth my ounce of salt.

My heart crackles in my chest, an ache gnawing at me. I

double over and hurl, hitting all fours, heaving until I am crying. My chest burns, my stomach refuses to release. I cough and gag, unable to breathe.

I roll to my back next to vomit, tears rolling down my face. I stare at the ceiling, and the world spins into oblivion around me. Cold seeps from the icy stone floor stained with blood into my veins, freezing my limbs in place as I sink into darkness.

# CHAPTER 11

*I* wake and roll over right into my puke. The puddle of fluid is cold, slimy, and congealed. I almost throw up again. My head throbs in time to my heartbeat, and I hate myself. I dissipate to my bathroom, scrub myself raw, and when I exit the bathroom, Legia is on my couch.

"Thank Haven." She lurches to her feet.

"What are you—"

"You've been missing for days. Selene hasn't woken up yet. The Bards are furious. Where have you been? What in Damnautus is going on?"

I move past Legia to get dressed in head to toe black. I sit on the edge of my bed and stare at the ground. Legia stands in my doorway, blue eyes ablaze. Her jaw is cocked, arms crossed.

"You have a lot of explaining to do." She moves to sit next to me on the bed. "You had the bond broken. I don't understand. You love Declan. I know you do."

"He is miserable."

"Because of you, because you do not pay attention to him. You haven't paid attention to any of us in a bit, but, well, never mind Chase or me, we can— Well, no..." She stops and scowls.

"What the Damnatus, Ella? When was the last ball you came to? Or the last time we had tea? Other than that horrible experience with Elizabeth. When was the last time we went to the city, or even the gardens? Do you know what the color of the season is? Do you know that snakes are ruling? Elizabeth, Skylar, even Selene, are setting the trends."

She rubs her eyes and looks around. "I've always known when something is not right with you, and right now, things are as far from right as possible. I mean, Seth and Marcus aren't even on your side."

I bob my head, then look out the window. "I..." Tears burn my eyes. I curse and drop my head, clutching it in my hands. "My head hurts. My head and my heart." I blink, shedding tears. "I didn't want any of this."

Legia hugs me. "Well, at least you know you still love him. He loves you too, I can see it. We can all see it in everything that goes on. You love him, and he loves you. You can fix this." She pulls back to look me in the eye. "You can fix this, and you will fix this, or so help you, Haven, I will shoot a thousand arrows into you."

There is a chuckle, and I look to Chase, leaning against the doorway between the sitting room and bedroom. He jerks his head. "That is a magnificent view you have."

I frown. "I know. I can't tell you how many hours I've sat there staring at it. It never gets old."

He nods again. "I can only imagine," he answers, staring over his shoulder. I cross my arms and watch him stand there, staring out the window. He turns to me and shakes his head. "You caused quite a stir. Legia's been having fits."

"Of course, I have been having fits." She throws her hands in the air. "Ella loves this court and those in it." She wags a finger at me. "And I know you love Declan above everything. Something is very wrong with you that no one knows about. You don't talk to anyone, hardly ever. We have to fish you from the

96

library or your rooms or beg for you to even eat dinner. You don't come to session most mornings, but when you do, everyone talks about it because you do such a fine job."

I drop my face in my hands and groan.

"What are you doing, Ella?" I look at Chase, lost in a tidal wave. "Like, what are you really doing?"

I laugh at him through the tears. I breathe. I blink and swipe at the tears pushing out. "Haven above, but I don't actually know. You know, I've been killing since I was eight?" Legia winces, but Chase continues to stare at me deadpan. The expression is reminiscent of Declan's face, frozen in polite interest. I exhale and go on. "I've been hiding and dodging things for so long, I don't know if I know how to do anything else. I'm just a monster, and the only thing I've ever been good at is killing. I have no business being queen."

I let myself drop to the ground, sitting with my knees bent and my back against the bedframe. I swallow the lump in my throat, and my gaze rolls to the ceiling.

"Well, piss on that," Legia says in a matter-of-fact tone. "You've told me what Viktor did. 'You've told me about the blood." She waves a hand. "I don't care what he forced you to do. I don't care who he forced you to be. I damn well know that you have a temper, but who doesn't?"

She leans over, bringing her face close to mine to wrinkle her nose. "The things Viktor forced you into being isn't who you have to be now. Pull yourself off the floor, put on your best dress, and go find Declan."

"I—" My voice cracks, and I grit my teeth. I am failing at keeping this in, so I ram the heels of my palms into my eyes hard enough to draw stars. I force a few deep breaths. I try to collect myself, blinking out more tears. "I love him. I love him more than anything, but Declan doesn't deserve what I'm doing, and he doesn't deserve to be tied to me. He doesn't deserve someone so broken or worthless."

Chase chuckles. "I've thought you were useless. I've thought you were pathetic, childish, and I rued the day I saw you were in my class. I used to be afraid of the day you'd be queen. I thought this court would be doomed the moment you took over, even as much as I disliked Viktor, I thought you'd be the greater of two evils."

Legia hisses at him like a wild cat. "And look how wrong you were. Haven, I cannot believe I am in love with a man who thought Ella is evil."

I scoff, shaking my head. I swipe at the tears on my face and sniffle. "No, I wonder if he isn't right."

"I'm not." My eyes jerk to his, and he smiles. "I got dragged into this that day in Marcus' study, and I still wanted to hate you. I didn't want to feel pity. I didn't want to start asking questions about why you were always missing, where you were, or *why*." He pauses, his lips twisting into a sneer. "I didn't want to have empathy for the girl who never paid attention in my class."

I laugh, staring at the ceiling, "Sorry about that."

He rubs the back of his neck, gazing down at his shoes. "You've got enormous power in you, Ella, and I am grateful to Haven that you have an equally enormous heart in you." He glances with a sly side smile, and I realize why all the women make a fuss about him. "If you were anything like Viktor, all of Caleum would be destroyed by now."

"I feel like Viktor," I tell him. "I hate myself."

"That's bad." Chase chuckles. "I didn't even hate you after I realized I was being tortured because of you."

"You really should. I hate myself for that."

"I get what Legia sees in you," he says. "Why Declan loves you, and Seth." Chase scoffs, shaking his head. "I never understood until now."

I do not understand why any of them might love me. There may be nothing worthwhile about me. I have done terrible, awful things, and it is the only thing I have been good at in my whole life.

I raise my brows at him. "What do you mean?"

"I mean, you royally, no pun intended, screwed up by breaking the bond."

I roll my eyes. "Technically, Erac broke it."

Legia makes a noise of disgust. "That's even worse. You know Erac has feelings for you. You know that Declan is jealous of the time you spend together. He worries you consider Erac better than him because he has the same kind of power you do. You know they cannot stand to be in the same room as each other. Erac belittles and taunts Declan at every turn. They despise each other, and they are both pining after you. You essentially let Declan's enemy break the bond. *What were you thinking?*" She is on her feet, screaming at me.

I blink, confused and dazed. My eyes focus on her splotchy red face. "Erac has feelings for me?"

Her eyes bulge. "Haven, Ella! Are you so naïve? Do you really not notice these things?"

I roll my eyes in response.

"Keep rolling your eyes. Maybe you'll find a brain back there," she says.

Chase comes into the room. I watch him take her in his arms with blurry vision. He presses a kiss to her temple. "Dear, I really don't think she pays attention to those things." He turns his face down toward me. "No matter how bad what you did was, you did it for the right reasons. You detonated, but…" He sighs, shaking his head. "You did it for love."

Chase lets go of Legia and holds a hand toward me to help me off the floor. Once on my feet, I brush non-existent dirt from my pants. I cannot bear to look them in the eye right now.

"Erac has feelings for me?"

"Erac goes out of his way to be vicious to Declan, and you

never stand up for Declan either, you idiot," Legia mutters. My eyebrows raise at her subdued volume.

Chase clears his throat. "Erac has been challenging Declan since the moment he came here. Declan is furious about it, and the time you give Erac, the way you don't discourage him..." Chase trails off again, crossing his arms over his chest.

I close my eyes and swallow the emotional knot at the back of my tongue. "I need time," I manage. "I need time to sort this thing out with the Gammet brothers to get control over my powers, and then I can send them away." I breathe out and look around my room. "I need to learn to control myself, and then I'll send Erac away."

"You need to send Erac away," Legia squeals. "You need to find Declan. You need to apologize. Haven, you two are the worst at communicating, and you have a mental link between you. How is that even possible? Anyway, you need to go find him right now." She shoos me toward the door.

There is no point in arguing. Although I have no intention of finding Declan, I slink toward my door as the two of them call after me that they will be around if I need help.

I wonder if they will be. Part of me wonders if they are here because this is detrimental to their stature at court.

# CHAPTER 12

The following morning, I am alone at session. I struggle with the duties, and Marcus must step in to help my floundering a few times. Each time his scowl deepens. I try my best and do what I can to ignore Marcus and move things along without his help. Frustration gnaws in my gut, and several times I scare subjects from the room with mild explosions.

After court, the room empties. I continue to sit on my cushion, gaping in front of me. I sit and stare for so long that when a hand lands on my shoulder, I jerk. The cushions for Declan and I disintegrate. My brother smiles down at me.

"You did alright this morning. You know that, don't you?" His smile stretches but remains tight.

I shrug. "Have you seen Declan?"

His forced smile dissipates faster than I can in the blink of an eye. He drops to sit on the floor in front of me with legs crossed.

Those yellow eyes fixate on me, and I wonder why he is here. "Have you seen Declan or not?" I ask again, raising my voice.

I peer at him, confused. He is watching me, not responding to my inquiry. I study his face, the dark lines. His skin is ashy, his hair wild. Exhaustion weights his features.

He shakes his head, sitting with his arms draping over his knees. "Yes. I have."

I nod.

My throat is thick and swollen, clogged by something that begins to restrict my breathing. Even thinking about trying to fix this mess makes me want to run to the base of the salt mines and never come back. Owning my little cottage and herding sheep, shearing them for wool—I have never done that, but I could figure it out. I could become no one, responsible for nothing. I swallow, trying to remain calm, trying to remember to just breathe.

"I have concluded that you should take some time away from this place. As your, *I assume*, most trusted advisor since you don't talk to me, I feel that you need to fix whatever is wrong with you."

*"Whatever is wrong with you." "Something's wrong with you." "What is wrong with you?"*

Tears threaten to come. I blink to keep them at bay. Still, my eyes burn. He must notice because he sighs. "Ella, I'm trying to help you get right."

*Everyone knows there is something wrong with you. You aren't normal. You're always setting off explosions or disintegrating things. You're never doing what they want you to do. You never do anything right. The only time they come to you is because they think there is something that needs to be fixed, something they can fix.*

The demon laughs in the back of my mind. *They can't fix you.*

I swallow hard. Forcing a smile, I answer Marcus in a warbling voice. "No." I clear my throat to shake the emotion from it. "No, I get that. I get that something is wrong with me." I look down at my hands and begin cleaning dirt from beneath my nails. "I'll go to the estate."

"Very well," he says, standing. "I will handle the necessary obligations in your stead."

"Of course." I smile at his knees. "When you see Declan, will you please tell him I wish to speak with him?"

"Of course."

$\sim$

*a* day later, my things arrive at the Byron estate, and I set about unpacking. Not even halfway through the first trunk, someone knocks on my door. I turn to Maybelle, eyeing the trunks.

"Majesty," she grunts. "How long should we expect to be graced with your presence?"

I smile at her with closed lips. "Maybelle, how are you? It's just Ella, please, and I am here until I can fix whatever is wrong with me.

Maybelle scowls, or maybe that's just her face. She's always frowning, her lower lip sticking out further than the upper. "Ain't nothing that's wrong with you. You're just a spry young queen trying to find your way."

She leaves, and I go back to pulling things out of trunks and putting them in places. When I am done, I look around myself, feeling alone. The ring on my left hand is heavy, weighing my limb down with great weight.

Holding my breath, I twist the silver band and large yellow sapphire off my finger. I wait, not daring to breathe, inspecting it, and then step to the nightstand and drop it. The gem glints in the light of the soul star, and without drawing air, I dissipate to the estate gardens.

There are memories here, all kinds. The good kind. Marcus and me. The kind I would gladly forget when Declan was presumed dead. The pathways are an old familiar feeling. A stoic calm slithers through my veins as I wind my way along the stone trails I walk around, stopping in places to laugh at the ghosts of my childhood.

I stay until dusk, recalling more pleasant times and expending energy tending to the plants. A little brush here and there causes flowers to bloom and trees to grow in inches. I just finish growing a fully matured dragons' fruit tree when the Gammet brothers appear before me.

With a gasp, I take a step back, eyeing them with suspicion.

Erac sags against Aron, who looks pale and pants a bit. "Ella, we heard you were gone from the palace only a few moments ago."

Aron eases Erac to the ground and stays bent over, hands on his knees. I frown, crouching next to Erac. "Is he alright?"

"He could use a body," Aron wheezes.

I nod. "I'll do it. Whenever you're ready."

"I'll need to rest first." He flops to the ground, chest heaving. "But then, yes, please. He is very weak, and although we are tied, I doubt he will last much longer without his own strength returning."

Erac topples onto his back. The hood slips back, exposing that gruesome face. I curl my lip at him, but his chest is moving, so I am not going to panic over him dying.

I shift my focus back to Aron. "How'd you know where I was?"

"Logically, it was the only place we could think you'd go, the same as we would go to our home if we were forced out of Dis."

"Makes sense," I sigh then move to stand, but Aron grabs my wrist.

"You broke the bond?"

"Yes."

Aron looks dazed. "Why? I thought Haven's choice for you was rather immaculate."

I force a grin. "I don't know if I believe in that crap about it being Haven's choice. My friend..." I stop, frowning. "Well, he used to be a friend. Seth, he bonded to Selene, and they hate each other."

Aron shakes his head. "Who are we to question Haven? Dad used to say all the time, Haven is the oldest, and therefore, the wisest. I can tell you, being as old as I am, I know a few things that might make your head spin."

I raise my brows. "Yeah? Would one of those things be this rune? How to control this power?"

"It is," he sighs. "I know we promised to help, but it's hard to do so when we are hanging on death's door."

Aron pulls one side of his lips up in a chagrined smile. "I'm curious, why did you break the bond?"

I turn my head, looking away. "Declan deserves better than me."

The sound of rocks rubbing together draws my eye back. I realize the noise is coming from Erac. "There is none better than you."

"I deserve to be cast into the inferno for the rest of my life. I've been nothing but a monster since I was old enough to be a pawn on my father's chessboard."

"Hmm," Aron hums, looking disinterested. "You've spilled blood? So has Declan. We know who he is. We watched him collect our father's runes, saw the things he did to find them, to get them. How dare you think yourself lesser to such atrocities."

Rubbing the skin between my eyebrows with eyes closed, I groan. "I keep forgetting the legend of Virgil, the spirit runes in Caleum... This is all your family history and not a children's story."

Aron snickers. "We certainly weren't happy when our legacy became a silly bedtime story."

I shake my head. "What were we talking about?"

"Declan doing despicable things to collect our father's runes?"

"Oh, right. I know he did, but he's moving on, being something more, something better, and I'm... I'm just... I don't know. Nothing?"

A hiss rips the air, so loud and violent from Erac that it startles me. "You are beautiful and rare. You have the blood of a spirit. You are capable of anything."

"Wait. What? I have the blood of what? I have my father's blood." My eyes twitch back and forth between them.

"Viktor tainted you." Aron sighs. "Yes, we came to realize that."

I gape at them. "Tainted? Male blood more than taints. Using male blood gives the father absolute control over the child. He forced me to do things, commanded me, and I just hopped to it without being able to say no."

Aron winces, plucking at grass. "We're not referring to the consequences of injecting male blood. We are referring to the fact that you were born of elemental and spirit, with no need to be injected, and yet Viktor saw fit to instill his blood into you."

"What?" My heart is pounding loud enough to be deafening. I gaze at Aron's violet eyes, and he gazes back.

His eyes crinkle with a grin. "Mom said it was Wyoma and Sordello who conceived you."

"Mom?" I yelp. "The mage in the legend? Her?"

"Mom," Aron repeats. "Yes, you'd know her as the mage, also the woman who the spirit Virgil fell in love with. Her name is Amadia, if you care to know."

My heart sinks. "I do. I'm sorry. We don't have to talk about this."

Aron shrugs a bit. "You have the right to know. You wear our father's rune. You have made us one body and have agreed to make another. Our family story is now yours as well."

I chew my lower lip. "So, your mother, Amadia, isn't she dead?"

"In some ways," he says, the words wistful. "After Dad, she waited and waited, but she didn't die. They said she would, and soon, but Haven had other plans. She was broken, and when they came to her, she accepted the offer and cut her heart out."

106

My head is spinning. "Who? What offer? Cut her heart out?" I look at Aron. He blinks at me, tilting his head to the side. "*What?*" I yell.

Erac is back to laughing. "You're very ignorant. It is cute."

I clench my jaw. My eyes narrow at Erac on the ground with an urge to kick him. "Explain."

Aron grins. He sits on the ground with his legs stretched out before him, resting back on his hands. "A long time ago, before Erac and I were even born, I believe it was during Tyle's reign, a group of elves disappeared in the south. That's what is denoted in history, but what really happened was that the land was falling off, large chunks at a time."

"Yes, yes, Tyle, the bastard emperor who killed his uncle for the throne, created shades by experimenting with his blood and various other atrocities. His rule was horrible, and the land was dying. Get to the point."

"The elves trekked deep into the caves of the south, where they began blood rituals and cut out their hearts, planting them within the deepest core of Caleum to give it life. Those hearts, and the hearts of those who have since followed, are what now keep Caleum alive, not those silly rituals you do during the solstice and slumber."

"So, they cut out their hearts, and someone buried them? Okay, so, your mom cut her heart out, and someone buried it in that cave too?"

"They bury their own heart," Erac says.

"That is not possible." I laugh. "There's no way that is possible."

"It is, if you're powerful enough," Aron continues. "In fact, you could, but only if you'd like to be a dragon."

"Dragon? Those elves that buried their hearts are the dragons?" My words are weaklings, trickling out of moving lips.

Aron nods, appearing amused. "Yes. They become living, breathing entities of Caleum."

"Giant, scaly, winged, fire breathing entities," I manage, "after cutting out their heart and burying it."

"Yes." Erac lifts himself into a sitting position, pulling his hood over his face. "You really are quite cute with how daft you are."

I gape at him. "I am going to kick you." The words blurt from my addled brain without the hindrance of recognition. I sit then lie in the grass to stare at the sky of light purples and blues with the fading soul star light.

My heart rate slows, the blood stops drumming in my ears, and my breathing evens out. The numb ache in me is consistent, but I know it well. It is the same anguish I lived with the last time I was here. This misery is never going to leave my chest. My heart is Declan's, and I ripped it out and left it with him far away from here.

I decide to focus on trying to solve this new riddle. "Your mother is a dragon, and she said I'm half-spirit and half-elemental? Wyoma, or something?"

"Wyoma is your mother. Sordello is your father," Aron says. "According to Mom, Wyoma was a warrior. She has a sad tale like all the others."

"That's how they get you," Erac cuts in. "The brokenhearted are the ones who willingly cut out their heart."

I stare at the sky. "Are they going to come find me?" I prop myself on my elbows. "That's how it works?"

Erac and Aron shake their heads. "You aren't just an elemental. You cannot give life to Caleum as you are of a higher dimension."

"So, Sordello? My father is a spirit? But how?"

"Dragons can ascend as they've ascended beyond mere elementals."

"Why haven't you two ascended? And ascended to where?"

"Medius," they say together.

"Oh. I should have realized…" I trail off, shaking my head. This all sounds ridiculous.

"We cannot," Erac says.

"Not yet," Aron answers.

"You have the rune we need."

"Father's rune is required to ascend."

I raise my brows, wondering if they realize they have fallen into their old ways of speaking. I try to look at my collarbone. "You need this rune? Are you going to take it off me?"

"Taking it off, or—"

"Removing the rune—"

"Will kill you."

"You'll use it for us."

I frown. "You asked me to make you bodies in exchange for you teaching me how to control all this power the rune has given me."

"We did."

"You'll learn."

"The spirits of Medius will—"

"Know what we do not."

My temper flares, singeing the ground around my hands. "You don't know how to control this rune and power?"

Aron looks at me with a melancholy gaze. "We know much—"

"But not that."

I sigh. *Great*, I think. *More doing things for the Gammets. Just what Dec said would happen.* The thought makes me cringe, and the numbness to spike burns like flagrant alcohol on a wound.

I exhale and lower myself back down. "You lied to me."

"Er…" Aron starts. "Not intentionally."

Irritated, I contemplate telling them to pound rocks for salt in the mines. I watch the light change the sky. There is no coming back from what I did, so there is no use in pretending like I have anything else to do with my life right now.

 ith Aron's help, making Erac a body took no more than an hour. Not even a day later, the Gammet brothers were requesting to be delivered to Medius, but I have delayed, hoping Declan would come.

I have stalled for a cycle, wringing my hands and waiting. I put my ring on. I take my ring off. No matter what I do, Declan is still not here. Either Marcus failed to tell him I wanted to see him, or he does not care to see me. I believe the truth to be the latter, as I am incapable of believing Marcus would hide my request from Declan.

I cannot ignore the obvious statement Declan has made in not coming to find me. Part of me knows I deserve this. Another part of me wants to scream and yell and thrash until I have burned down my family's estate.

I want to cry and destroy something. I almost want to kill someone. I want Declan.

My eyes lock on the yellow sapphire on my left hand. The intricate, ornate ring he made for me. The amount of time and care that went into crafting the piece had given me hope at the beginning of our engagement when I thought there was none.

Declan has had ample time to find me. He knows where I am. He knows I am waiting on him. I grit my teeth, wrenching the engagement ring off my finger for the hundredth time to toss it in a jewelry box on my nightstand, slamming the lid.

I go to find the brothers in the gardens. "Explain this again? How do we get to Medius?"

"Are you ready?" Aron asks. "We can wait longer."

"No." I blink a few times and face Erac. "Tell me again."

Erac sighs. "You have to dissipate to Medius."

He shares the same features as his brother, but his face is slimmer, more handsome, and less boyish. His eyes are a bit darker, indigo to Aron's violet. Other than the face, there is no difference between the sandy hair and average build.

My eyes cut sideways toward Aron. He smiles sympathetically. "You are concerned by dimension travel?"

"You have no reason to be," Erac assures me, his words brisk.

"I have never dissipated somewhere that I could not envision. I was taught that in order to dissipate, you have to focus, to see yourself in that place."

Aron nods along with me, but Erac answers. "For a weaker being, yes, those steps are necessary. You are not weak."

"What Erac is trying to say," Aron interjects, shooting a disgruntled look at his brother, "is that the immense power you have will compensate for the focus. As I told you, you have power enough to lack finesse and still make the elements comply."

I narrow my eyes at him. "I have tried to have finesse."

"We should have trained her."

"We were not strong enough."

"We should have come to her sooner."

"She could not have helped us, brother."

A pop of power strikes in front of us, and the brothers refocus on me. "You two keep falling into your speaking thing."

I move a pointed finger between them. "Where you speak in turn and broken thoughts."

They grin in unison. "Old habits—"

"Die hard."

I grin at them. I cannot help it. The brothers understand me, my power. They are not afraid of me. My little explosions or loss of control does not scare them.

"Tell me," I say. "Dimensions, how do they work?"

Erac and Aron exchange glances. Aron has the ghost of humor on his features, where Erac dons an expression of contempt.

Aron pats his brother on the back. "Yes, I know, we should have taught her, but we are teaching her now."

Erac curls a lip and ignores his brother. "The dimensions are like rings, each one larger the lower you go, time moving quicker in those places. Haven is at the top, then the angels in Aspire, and then Medius." Erac layers his hands, shuffling one beneath the other as he speaks. "After Medius is Caleum, then Terra with humans, Damnatus and its demons, and finally the Inferno. Any elemental of Caleum with great enough power can travel amongst any dimension."

"What?" I ask for the thousandth time since they arrived.

Aron pushes Erac's hands down and smiles with kindness. "Caleum was not made of Haven—you know this—and so because this land is not made of Haven we are excluded from his order. That is why women cannot bear children, and why we can travel to any dimension."

My eyes narrow as my lips twist to the side. "So, Inferno, the lowest dimension full of damned souls and iron gates guarded by kangers... I could go there?"

"Theoretically," Erac snorts. "Why you would ever want to is beyond me."

I sigh and rub sweating palms on my thighs. "So, close my eyes, think of Medius?"

"And us, please."

"Don't forget us."

I laugh at the absurdity. They are the only reason I am going to Medius. "And you are certain that once there, they can help me get this rune off or, at least, do something to help me control it?"

They exchange glances. "We believe this to be so."

"We have not been to Medius."

I grit my teeth. They promised me help in exchange for what they wanted, and now I am doing something else for them, in exchange for the same help they promised, which may or may not even be obtainable.

I try to exhale, to focus on pushing the air out of my lungs, collapsing my ribs around the organs. Thinking of the action helps keep my mind off other, less desirables, like being conned by the brothers.

At last, I let my eyes close, and the look of frustration melt away. I do not have many options. I need to be able to control this power, or at least be rid of it.

"Alright," I say, drawing the word out. "Medius."

Pictures and prints of a castle floating amongst clouds fill my mind. I picture a castle, turrets soaring, and stone walls sprawling. I exhale slowly, picturing the Gammet brothers and me standing in a room of the castle. I imagine stone walls with tapestries hung on them. I add a bookshelf, a small table with a chess set, and two high back chairs framing it.

*Medius*, I think, over and over as I build the picture in my mind. *Medius. I want to go to Medius.*

Another image flickers through my mind. Slate gray eyes and yellow eyes glaring at me in those high back chairs with a half game of chess played between the two men. *Declan.*

My heart aches. My temper flares. *Medius.*

Energy pours out of me with a deafening crack. My body feels constricted, like a ton of iron crushing me. I cannot breathe. Energy flows from me, being drawn in a violent rush. I hit my knees, coughing and gagging. I splutter, drawing ragged gulps of air that burn my chest.

Tears are shedding from underneath my closed lids. Everything hurts. So much energy was ripped from me. The world spins in a blurring whirlwind. My stomach churns, threatening to toss out the acid.

I collapse to the stone flooring, knees first, then fall to my side, shivering from the bitter cold. Through kaleidoscope fracturing tears, I make out brilliant gold and red on the wall. I roll to my back, and the sweat soaking through my shirt starts to chill me as I'm pressed against the cold stone flooring.

I struggle to pull in air and force muscles to release a breath. Through graying vision, the image of two chairs swim into focus. I blink, sending wet rolling down my cheeks.

An animated suit of armor clanks and clings. The noise reverberates around the room. Each step echoes around me as my sight narrows to nothing more than blackened metal. A silver gauntlet, worn dull around the knuckles with gold details, looms toward me as my sight tunnels to nothing more than blackness.

~

Opening my eyes, I find myself in a room with red and gold tapestries decorating the walls. The floors are made of the same massive slate blocks sealed with black mortar, and two red velvet chairs flank a small, dark wood table with a chess set. I look around, my mind reeling, and perch in the middle of a massive four-poster bed.

The room is familiar and foreign at the same time as I eye the bookshelf at the end of the bed. In a daze, I stare at the spines of rich brown and gilded reds. I bite my lip, looking around.

Sighing, I curl into a ball, arms wrapping around my legs, forehead to my knees, and knock my head against my joints. *Think, dumbass, think, like you probably should have before you did whatever you did.*

Everything comes rushing back to me. The narrow pinhole of light expands to show me a large being in heavy plate armor with a creamy fabric hood drawn over a head, no face, just a shadow beneath. The beam widens, encompassing the Gammet brothers standing, violet eyes looking about the room as other armored beings enter through the doorway.

I had jumped from Caleum to Medius, bringing the Gammet brothers with me. My head jerks as I look around me. The room seems so familiar because I pictured it. It's an eerie familiar resemblance to Marcus' private study.

I force myself off the bed, moving toward the door. I stop in front of it. Dark wood, like the small details in the rest of the room.

I stare at it. Nothing happens. I scream at myself in my head as loud as I can manage.

I reach out with a shaking hand to grasp the gold knob. It rattles as my hand closes around it, shaking with violent force. Steeling myself, I open the door. On the other side is a corridor, and I am face to face with that metal suit of armor, something that would tower over even Seth.

The thought gives me a pang in my gut like my soul is wincing. Chewing on my lower lip, I focus on the being. The pauldrons are rounded, contorting over the shoulders, layering over a shimmering gold mesh that wraps around the upper arm. Couters guard the elbows, and gauntlets protect the hands, while massive, thick vambraces encircle the forearms.

An off-white fabric flows from beneath the armor of the torso to cover the head, draped, so the face is obscured in shadows. The hooded face lifts. It says nothing. I stare, not sure what to say or do.

It straightens, pushing away from its position of rest against the wall. "Ella?"

I blink. "Yes?"

"I am to accompany you to the hall of nutrients when you have returned to consciousness."

I blink again, then reach to vigorously rub my eyes. I am hoping when I open them again, the being will be gone, and I will find I am in Marcus' library. Declan will chastise me for missing court.

*Declan.* My heart skips.

The rich voice speaks again. "Are you conscious?"

I drop my hand. "Yes?"

"Very well." The face turns to the floor and then returns to me. I assume it is a nod, so I mimic the movement, and the being turns, marching down the stone hallway. I follow it along through several turns.

I eye the metalwork covering its body as I trail in its wake. The lavish niello and filigree inlaid in the tarnished blackened armor are as delicate as they are intricate.

We stop in front of two gold doors, twice the size of the Byron throne room. He pushes them both open, one hand on either door leaving a space wide enough for six elementals to walk through shoulder to shoulder, probably in about three rows high.

I gape. The doors are sized for giants, and he pushes them aside as if they were nothing. I scurry through the doors as they begin to swing shut. Inside are dozens of other beings, all the same; full metal and gilded armor with creamy cloth hoods pulled up to obscure faces from sight.

I stand inside the doors, my eyes stretched wide and unblinking, so they become dry and hard to focus. The being I had followed here has disappeared from my senses, lost in the sea of glinting and clinking metal. As I stand there, another approaches. It looms closer, and I edge away until my back is against the door. The cold solid form pressing back against my sweating skin is euphoric.

"Ella, you are awake," the voice booms like a shock wave in the dim noise, full of joy.

"Um..." My eyes hedge left then right, my heart palpitating.

"I was worried the energy drawn from you to make the distance between Caleum and Medius was so great that you might not recover, but you have." The metal hands fall on my shoulders, the edges of the armored fingers sharp through the thin fabric of my shirt. "How do you feel?"

There is an answer somewhere in my brain, but I cannot find it. My tongue is held hostage between the teeth in my lower jaw, and piecing together words has taken a seat while my dumb-founded mind is fathoming this situation. "Uharghumph."

The unintelligible noise squeezed out of my chest in confusion draws a booming laugh echoing out of the walking and talking suit of armor in front of me. "Please, relax."

Tension fades from between my shoulder blades. My breathing comes easier as I pull in long, even breathes. The scowl on my face melts away, transforming to a peaceful expression.

"Let us sit." The heavy hands move from my shoulders. The suit of armor turns, sitting in one of the available chairs. He points to the open chair next to him.

I move to the chair, afraid of what may happen to me if I refuse. The way he commanded me to relax with instantaneous compliance on my part is unnerving. Still, beyond the thought of something wrong, I feel nothing but ease within me.

I sit in the chair, the table's surface at eye level. Another laugh sounds and the chair raises so I can sit with elbows resting on it. "Um...?"

"My name is Sordello."

*My father?* My insides quiver and lurch, my heart lifting into my throat, making me choke on air.

"I am sure you have questions, but allow me to offer some information before you begin your barrage."

He pauses. Somehow I imagine he is attempting humor. The only thing I can think is to hum another um in response until my organs rearrange to correct positioning.

I receive a chuckle. "You are out of sorts."

He sets a cup in front of me. While the marbled white material fits in his one hand, I struggle to use both hands to tip it toward me, inspecting the contents of blue liquid.

His massive metal gauntlet waves in a half-circle in front of him, indicating the room. "This is the convergence room. This is where you will come for nutrients, gatherings, and is also used as a common room for socializing." He points to the cup in my hands. "The liquid is everything you will need to maintain life. There are nutrients and energy within it. We call it nourishment."

I eye the blue liquid before attempting to consume any of it. I touch my mouth to the brim, tipping the cup enough to have the liquid reach me. Pulling back, I lick my lips. The liquid has a pleasant taste, light, thin, crisp. I take a sip. It tastes like apples and honey. My stomach gurgles as I begin to chug the stuff.

Breathing is necessary, so I stop gulping the liquid to pull air into my burning lungs. I narrow my eyes at him. "You said your name is Sordello?"

The hood inclines. "I believe that Erac and Aron mentioned my name to you once before."

"They said you are my father."

The hooded face drops down like he is hanging his head. "Yes." The word is soft, not the deep booming voice he has spoken with thus far.

"You are not happy about that." I do not ask. The tone and change in demeanor are telling enough.

His pauldrons droop. The metal clinks as it settles with his hunched form. "It is a complicated matter. Spirits are undying.

We are old, so very old. Nearly as old as Haven. We were made before the aspires, and so are older than even Haven's favored creations."

"Mmm," I hum and take another drink. "What's that matter?"

"As a collective, we do not love. We do not have individual relationships but one collective relationship. My dalliance with Wyoma is an oddity, one that induced strife within our community."

I prop my chin on a hand. His hooded face remains positioned downward as he goes on. "The relationship, the emotions and affections that Wyoma and I shared were erosive to our joint commune. I am what you would consider to be a king, the second of my kind, given divine right to rule after the first chose to remain in Caleum." The hood lifts, as does his tone. "Virgil. The original one, the first, our leader, he too shared an odd relationship that caused disrupt amongst our collective. He chose to break free, to live and love in your world, but I could not leave this world, and my passions and attraction to Wyoma created something like a war amongst us. So I ceased contact with her."

I look about the room. "So, I'm a product of a relationship none of them are happy about?" I jerk a thumb toward the other end of the table. "And I am sitting in a room full of spirits that could just step on me and end my life?"

"They would do no such thing." Sordello appears offended, his voice taut. "We are not that kind of beings."

I pinch the bridge of my nose and then rub a hand over my face. "Alright, so I don't have to worry about them coming after me in the middle of the night?"

His form bristles to attention, metal clinking and glinting. "Certainly not." The response is abrupt and gruff. "We are proud beings and strive for a higher understanding."

I nod.

His shoulders slump, and the deep voice smooths with defeat. "I had hoped this first meeting would go better. I worry I may not be making the impression I want." He lifts a cup of his own, tilting it under the shadow of the hood. "Ella," he says, his voice softer, "I have watched you, your whole life. I have not been a father to you, but there are obvious reasons and limitations that have prevented me from intervening."

My mind reels. I put my hand over my eyes and breathe out. My eyes burn, and my throat is clogged by an impasse. Swallowing, I drop my hand and look around, blinking. "Um... I, um..." My brain is numb again. "I just—"

"You are still recovering."

I drop my face into my hands, snorting a laugh through my nose. "Recovering? Haven, like I am not in some other dimension talking to a suit of armor that is my father—my actual real, gave me life father, because the first one was so great, and I needed another one of those—drinking blue water from a cup ten times too big for me." A strangled sob trickles out of me as I half-way laugh. "What in Damnatus?"

He curls in on himself for a moment, then stands. "This is much for your mind to accept. You are far from what you have known your whole life. Come," he offers me an open hand. "I will return you to your room."

# CHAPTER 14

*I* stare at him in disbelief. "My room?"

He shrugs. "When you brought the sons of Virgil and yourself to this dimension, you created the room in which you arrived. As a collective, we agreed that the room will stay as part of the palace in honor of how it was made. It is only fitting that you should stay in that room."

"I created a room? In your palace?" My mind is spinning. No, the room is spinning around me. Maybe I am moving. I reach out and grip the lip of the table. "I changed your palace to dissipate to a room that didn't exist until I dissipated to it?"

"Yes. Your natural abilities, melding with our power rune, have given you great force. The energy consumed in the feat was dangerous, though. I expressed that I had my doubts about whether or not you would recover."

I have expended great forces of energy before, most notably was when I allegedly killed Viktor. I was in the infirmary unconscious for a cycle after that.

Swallowing my fears, the room still spinning, I ask weakly, "How long was I out?"

"Nearly two days."

*Well, that is not so bad.*

"I should clarify to you that is nearly two days in Medius time, which I believe equates to nearly twenty days in Caleum."

My heart stalls. "What?"

"I have realized you refer to the grouping of days as a cycle. I have counted those days. I believe it to be ten."

"Um..."

"Those ten days in your dimension is roughly the same as one day here in Medius."

*Twenty days? Someone must have noticed I was missing. Oh, Damnatus, you fool!* I scream at myself. The room begins to rotate faster. I press my forehead to the tabletop, inhaling to a count of three, holding for a count of three, and exhaling to a count of three.

*One, two, three. One, two, three.* I count time in my head. I picture myself dancing around a post, swinging my fists in time with the counts. It is a pleasant distraction from what Sordello is telling me.

I raise a hand, but my forehead stays planted against the surface of the table. "Um, I think I need to lay down. I, um, I need... I need something." My voice cracks. "Air. I need air."

Cold spreads through me, and then fresh air dances across my skin in a gentle breeze. The tip of my tongue glides against my lips, searching for it. I open my eyes to find myself lying on my back, staring at a dusty-blue sky with silver clouds.

A suit of armor stands next to me. I look around a stone balcony surrounded by an ornamental parapet and lift myself. Next to me is a large round opening, nothing but blue and silver visible beneath. Horrified, I skitter backward on my hands, my feet propelling me away from the death hole.

"Calm down," his deep voice commands.

Relief washes through me. My anxiety fades away as my heart rate evens out. The way I respond to his words with absolute obedience makes my skin too tight, compressing me as I overheat under the restriction. The demon in me is baring its teeth, wanting to rip the armor away to find flesh beneath, to peel the flesh for the way it commands me.

"Stop," I sob. "Stop controlling me." I drop my face into my hands, sobbing. I curl into a ball, and the calm his words brought disappears in the presence of that bloodlust in me.

His hand lands on my shoulder. "I did not mean to distress you further, nor to control you. I am unaccustomed to being around one susceptible to my powers of persuasion."

I lean against the stone wall behind me. It might be a railing, something the height of Sordello in his crouched position. I suck in air, slurping in through nose and mouth as my eyes search the dim blue sky above. To my right, the enormous structure of a castle made of gray stonework looms into the sky, sprawling into the vast expanse of clouds.

I long for my window seat, the view of Cato and Salt Canyon. Sighing, I find the courage to stand, shrugging his metal hand from me. My legs are shaking, working through fatigue. Still, I force myself to take shaking steps toward the opening.

"Okay," I breathe to myself, "okay. You're in Medius. You have a father who may not be a monster."

Sordello's laugh causes me to glance over my shoulder at him. "There are those who may think less highly of me, but I dare to proclaim myself better than Viktor."

I use the back of my hand to wipe my leaking nose, looking to the opening once more. "How would you know? Have you met Viktor?"

Sordello moves toward the hole in the balcony floor. "This is the septal." He gestures toward the center point. "It acts both as partition and connection between Medius and Caleum." He shifts from pointing to extending an open hand to me. "If you please, step forward, and I will show you."

I do not take his hand but move to stand with my toes on the edge. I stare down through the hole but see nothing but darkening sky and gray clouds. I blink, looking around. The dusty, light blue has faded all the way around the castle, the clouds dimming with the fading light.

"It is night." His words draw my eyes to him. "You were looking at the sky. I noticed the change in light from the last time you looked about."

I look back to the hole. "It's called a septal?"

"*The* septal. There is only one." He stands behind me, his presence making my skin crawl. It would be so easy for him to push me through the hole. "Now, look, and think of Caleum, of anyone you wish to look in on."

My eyes fixate through the hole, my mind and heart focused on Declan. The clouds swirl and sparkle like a glitter-filled fog. Shapes begin to materialize, taking on color and definition, details emerging as the blue smog clears to reveal images of Declan and Marcus. They are sitting in his study, and I watch them like an unseen shadow on the ceiling.

The chessboard between them has only a few pieces on it, all knocked over and askew on the board. The rest of the pieces are strewn about their feet. A half-full glass decanter of amber liquid sits in the middle of the board.

They are not speaking, each wearing a threadbare expression of exhaustion. Declan's eyes are dark, Marcus' brows furrowed. Both men are scowling, dark lines evident on their faces.

Chase walks in, looking as haggard as the other men, dark circles under his eyes and a grave, set expression mirrors back. He stops in front of them, hands on his hips. No one says anything, and after a moment, he reaches for the decanter. A tumbler appears in his hand from thin air, and he fills it.

He throws back the liquid, then refills his glass. He sets the decanter down, the noise loud as thunder in the silence of the room. "Legia is still having fits."

One of Declan's shoulders twitches, rising and dropping against the back of the chair. Marcus does not even act as if he heard. The room returns to deathly silence.

124

"Has anyone heard from Seth?"

No response.

Chase sighs, moving toward the desk. He rests his butt against the surface and leans back, his legs crossing in front of him, one hand acting as support. He takes a drink, watching the men across from him. "Then I suppose we have all given up hope?"

Marcus flinches to life, downing the amber in his glass. He shudders. His tumbler skitters across the smooth surface of the board to clink against the decanter. "The Byron estate is nothing more than a crater, and whatever wasn't destroyed in the blast was burned beyond recognition." He jerks, moving with stiff joints to refill his glass.

Declan bares his teeth, one hand clenching tight into a fist, so his skin turns white, and the knuckles protrude. The hairs on my spine tickle.

*I destroyed my family's estate when I dissipated to Medius? No wonder Marcus looks to be in pain. The expenditure will be taxing on our family's fortune, not to mention the work required for rebuilding. Declan must be furious with my absence. Maybelle, the others, Haven, what have I done?*

Declan takes a drink. Marcus settles against the chairback, tumbler in hand to stare past Chase. He and Declan may be moving, but there is something dead about them.

Chase takes another drink then sets his tumbler down, pushing away from the desk. He paces back and forth, hands running over his close-cropped hair. He drops his hands and faces the other men.

"Look, the estate, it looks bad, but—"

Declan hurls his tumbler straight at Chase. Chase throws a hand up, and the tumbler shatters against an invisible barrier. Glass shards and alcohol scatter. I stare in shock. Chase swipes a hand over his cheek, smearing blood.

Declan shoves himself to his feet, kicking the chair. It skitters back and tips over. "It's been two cycles. If she wasn't dead, she'd have come home by now. The court ruled her deceased this morning." His voice is elevating, and he raises his clenched fist into the air, shaking it at Chase. "I declared her dead!"

His words rip the air from my lungs. I blink, staggering. I nearly swallow my tongue on a shriek as I pitch forward toward the septal. The image of the men is gone, replaced by nothing but clouds.

Two hands grab my shoulders, pulling me back away from the edge. My heart is beating furiously against my breastbone. It slams against the cage as if finding freedom would lessen the pain. The world is tilting this way and that, beginning to sway. Everything starts to swim through unshed tears in my eyes.

"Forgive me," Sordello's deep voice cuts through the haze. "But sleep, now, and rest."

My eyes slip closed. The last thing I am conscious of is being swept into his arms. Not even the sharp edges of his armor digging into my flesh through my clothes can keep me awake.

# CHAPTER 15

*I* awaken to two chairs and a table with a chess set. My heart wrenches as I think about Declan screaming that he had declared me dead. Each one of them had appeared taxed. I had assumed they were upset by my lack of responsibility.

Chase said Legia was having fits. Declan had attacked Chase. I roll over, replaying the scene a hundred times.

I stalk to the bookshelf. The spines are all barren, so I select one at random. Sliding it from between the others and into my hand, I crack the cover. The page is blank. I flip through various pages, then skim the edges of each in rapid-fire. All blank.

I drop the book to the ground, pulling the next one from the shelf. I pull the next and the next, dropping each in a heap on the floor. Blank, every single page in every single book. With a sigh, I drop the last book at my feet.

"Great, not like I need a distraction right now," I tell the pile of rubbish. My frustration fizzles, and the books disintegrate. I slap a hand over my eyes. "Even better. This whole stupid thing is because I can't control this damned rune, and I still can't."

There is a knock. I drop my hand and stop speaking to myself. My eyes train on the door, but it remains closed.

"Yes," I call to whoever is on the other side.

The door opens, and a suit of armor walks in. "Hello. How are you doing, Ella?"

"Sordello?" The hooded visage bobs. "You really need a name tag or something."

There is a deep rumble, his shoulders shaking. "I believe I may be able to help with that. I have come to bring you to our healers."

I raise a single brow, my hands on my hips. "And that's going to help me with being able to discern one suit of armor from another?"

"By receiving all of our runes, you will become one with us. As part of our collective, you will begin to realize the difference in our energies."

My eyes stretch open. "You're going to put more of these things on me?" I jab at my shoulder. "I can barely keep things from blowing up or disintegrating as it is." I indicate the pile of dust that was fifty books with a thrust of my hands.

"The rune on your forearm, the blood of your mother—"

"What?" My eyes bulge. "My mother?"

"That is for another time. The rune on your shoulder is pure power. If not for the rune on your forearm, you likely would not have survived the Vitale rune taking to you. We were sure to apply Vitale last when outfitting Virgil's sons with their runes."

I run a hand through my hair. "So..." I bite my lip. "So getting the other runes, it'll help me control all this power?"

"More importantly, it will help you discern one suit of armor from the other."

His teasing draws a half-hearted chuckle from me. I am almost smiling. "Alright, then lead the way."

We traipse through the castle, weaving down corridors. Sordello stops in front of a polished wooden door. There are runes carved along the border, a cloaked figure carved into the center. He rests a hand on the door, his obscured visage in my direction.

"The collective has agreed you should receive the runes, but I have spoken with the healers regarding other remedial actions."

I lift a single brow. "Such as?"

"You have dozens of scars, physical reminders, permanent marks left by that monster. I requested our healers to inspect them. Their erasure could be therapeutic for you."

My other brow lifts to match the first. "Oh!" My heart skips in elation. "Can they?"

His hood inclines. "They believe so but will need to inspect you."

My head bobs. "Sure. Fine."

Sordello pushes the door open and ushers me inside with the wave of a hand. "Then, enter and know this is a sacred place."

I smirk but make no comment as I slip inside. The door closes, leaving me swaddled in shadows. I blink, my eyes trying to focus. There is a spark, followed by a snap. Light radiates from where the walls and floor meet, a dim glow circling around the room.

Three figures approach me. The shape of form is discernable beneath light-colored cloaks, but they wear hoods obscuring their faces from sight the same as the armored spirits. I crack my knuckles as they approach and then lace my fingers together, turning my hands outward to stretch them.

"Hello, Ella, daughter of Sordello, wearer of Virgil's life-force." All three dip into a bow from the waist in unison. They are smaller than those in armor, more akin to me.

"Hello."

The middle cloaked figure indicates a platform in the center of the room. "Please, remove your clothing and sit."

I look at them, and then the round, elevated tabletop. With a defeated exhale, I kick my boots off and strip my clothes away. Naked, I pad across the floor in silence and lift myself on the slab.

The three of them gather around me. They rotate behind me, and I curl my knees to my chest, grateful for the low lighting.

Warmth brushes against my back as they study the scars. "They can be removed."

"To be subjected to such agony. Such a poor creature."

My emotions are mixed at the pain in her voice and being referred to as a creature. In the back of my mind, my demon sneers. *What else are we?*

"The removal of these marks would be salubrious." Warmth brushes over my back.

I let my eyes close. "Please take them."

"And the others? There are many, not just these."

I open my eyes and nod. My gaze drops to my right forearm and the scar between the lines of my control rune. The white line in my skin was left behind after Declan had pinned my arm to a wall with my own small dagger. Not that the experience was grand, but it led to him coming back to court, coming home to be with me.

"Not this one." I show them my forearm over my shoulder. "I want to keep this one."

"Scars are physical representations of pain. Why would you want to keep such a token?"

"I just do." I drop my arm. Trying to explain to them about Declan and that the mark was from him is too difficult. "But if you can fix my knee back to new, that would be nice."

One of the robed figures steps in front of me. "Show me."

I stick my leg out. There is an audible gasp, and the sleeves on the robe of the healer before me lifts. Two translucent hands assembled from veins of light reach out. The contact of fingers against my leg is a pleasant warmth.

The fingers trace over the long scar on my thigh. "Such horror." Her voice is aghast. "The violence of elementals has always surprised me, but this..." She pulls back, the glowing hands extinguishing beneath the robe. "I believe we can try."

I nod. "Thanks."

"We have a potion that will induce sleep, but we can also speak to put you out of consciousness. Sordello mentioned your dislike of being controlled. If you prefer the potion, I shall fetch it."

I cock my head at the healer. "Why is it that I have blood magic that prevents being controlled, but you all can just command me about?"

She chuckles. "The blood magic of your mother was intended to remove the bond between yourself and the origins of the blood in your veins."

"And the intent of blood magic is more important than the magic itself." I sigh.

Her arms move in front of her in an open gesture. "If you prefer the potion—"

"It's fine," I sigh. "You can just knock me out with your words. I don't mind."

The hood inclines. "Very well. Sleep, Ella."

～

*I* wake in the four-poster bed facing the chairs and chess set once again. I sigh, rolling onto my back. I lift my left arm above my face, using it to shove hair back from my face. Black runes running along my skin catch my eye. It is hard to determine where one ends and the other begins.

Shocked, I sit, holding it before me to examine the intricate swirls and flourishes. There seems to be no end. Each black line connecting and flowing between the other. I scour my arm, unsure of which lines are the control rune. My heart slows as I catch sight of a single white line between the black. Relief washes through me as I draw my finger down the scar.

I scramble off the bed, craning and spinning, trying to get a good view of my back. With the snap of my fingers, I create a mirror on the wall. Standing so I face away, I look over my shoulder. I forget to breathe, my eyes growing wide. There is nothing there. I reach around, trying to touch every part of my skin, to feel nothing under my fingers but soft, smooth flesh.

I do not know how long I stand and stare, but I begin to pet every inch of me that I can reach, fingers searching for any fibrous connective tissue. Scars once pink, white, raised, and ghastly are all gone. I begin to move, looking over the rest of my body. Bending my knee, I put pressure, testing the weight it can hold before it gives out, pleased to find applying weight and bending is pain-free.

I return to staring at my back, and then, ever so slowly, I turn to face the mirror. I stare at myself, searching my body for the little imperfections that have plagued me for so long all over again. They are gone. Every. Single. Blemish. Gone.

My eyes find themselves in the mirror, and I stare. Bright violet returns my gaze. My nose is straight in my face. Even my hair, the red-tinged purple strands more lush as they hang around me down to my waist.

My throat feels tight, and my eyes well with tears even as I watch myself beginning to cry in the mirror. There is no deep wailing that follows. Instead, I smile at myself. A flicker of pleasant emotion washes over me, and I laugh at myself, as the drops start to slide down my cheeks.

Inhaling deeply, I grin, blinking the tears away. I stand, frozen in the moment, ebullient until there is a knock on my door.

Sordello calls my name. I clear my throat, wiping away any lingering tears. I look at my naked body and glance around the room. There is no closet or evidence of clothes, so I picture a robe for myself like the healers wore. I imagine feather-soft fabric against my skin and close my eyes, exhaling.

There is another knock. Now covered, I rush to open the door. Sordello seems pleased, although nothing about his appearance tells me so. It is just a sensation that wafts through my chest.

"Sordello."

"I see you are conforming to our collective." He indicates the robe.

I grin. "I needed something to wear. It was the first thought I had."

If he had a face to show, I would bet he is smiling. "It is suiting. Have you had your sustenance for the day?"

I shake my head. "No."

"I would be honored if you would join me. I wish to speak with you."

"Oh." Some of the happiness welling within me disperses. "Yeah, that's..." I puff my cheeks full of air and blow out hard. "That's fine."

"I did not mean to upset you. I maintain no hidden intentions. I wish to be acquainted with my daughter."

My eyebrows shoot up. The only time Viktor ever spoke to me was when he wanted something, or it benefited him in some way. My lips twist as I shove fingers through my long hair of burgundy strands and work them into a braid to hang over my shoulder.

"I am not Viktor and wish nothing more than to allow you to determine such through my actions." He steps back, allowing me to exit the room.

I step into the corridor and follow him to the convergence room where we sit, drinking our fluid, and conversing. He asks so many questions, it makes my head spin, but I answer everything.

My cup is empty, and we have talked so long I find the courage to say, "You haven't asked about...." I wince. "Well... about Viktor's errands."

Sordello's hand rises, staying my words. "I have no need to speak of such things. The scars have been removed. The memories will never leave, but I hope they will fade. What that monster did to you is unspeakable."

I nod, swallowing a lump at the back of my tongue.

"Ella, as your father, your true father, I feel as though I have failed you. I could not protect you, and the result of that has left scars too deep for the healers to reach." He sounds broken. His shoulders slump forward, his shadowed face staring downward. "My deepest regret is that you have been subjected to Viktor and his control. I watched in horror and hatred as he beat you and forced you to perform acts of violence. I was radiant with happiness as you glowed with love for Declan, then watched with a broken heart and mourned alongside you when Declan was believed to be deceased. I have watched you your whole life but failed to be there for you or protect you."

I force myself to swallow the welling burst of emotion. Absent-minded, I try to take a drink from my empty cup. The thought of being watched is uncomfortable. The thought of having someone who cares, despite my screw-ups, accidental explosions, and lack of responsibility, heals a crack in my heart.

Sordello reaches out, his metal-clad hand covering mine on the table. "I wish to be in your life. I wish to act as a father might now. However, I realize that you are beyond needing a father as you have matured into a young woman. If you can forgive me, if you could look past my failures and find a place for me, I will not fail you again."

I fiddle with the empty cup. There is a whirring in the back of my mind as my brain works double-time to unravel what he has said. I look toward his shadowed face. "Was there anything you could do?"

His head shifts back. "No. If there were something I might have done, I would have. But, a spirit in Medius cannot reach Caleum without being called forth." He sighs. "Had my falling out with Wyoma not ceased the visits of the dragons to Medius, I would have been able to request her assistance."

"Then, there was nothing you could do." I shrug. "Viktor..." I sigh and investigate the bottom of my cup. I roll my eyes. "Viktor did what you are blaming yourself for." I look toward Sordello's shadowed face once more. "So, no, I won't forgive you for something you didn't do. I blame Viktor."

"And yourself."

My mouth flaps.

Sordello chuckles. "Did you think I would not know?" He sweeps a hand around the room. "We feel each other. We feel each other's emotions. You will learn how, but for now, be aware of it."

I frown. "Great. Just what I need, more thoughts and emotions in my head that aren't mine."

"I do not have experience with a bond, but I daresay this will be similar." He leans on the table with crossed arms. "My daughter, Ella." He chuckles. "I believe you hate being called Morella."

I wince at the mention of my proper name. "Yes."

He bobs his hooded head. "You asked me if there was anything I could do. Allow me to ask if there was anything *you* could do." He pauses, and I stare at him with pursed lips. "Was there anything you could do?"

I lean back, crossing my arms and legs while scowling at him. "I was his puppet."

"You were controlled by his blood."

"And then I wasn't."

"And you did something."

I narrow my eyes and cock my jaw to the side. "I should have been able to do something. I knew Viktor was scheming. I helped him. Me." I wrench my hand from beneath my father's and use it to jab myself in the chest with a finger. "I did those things for him."

If he had a face, I would expect it to be an expression of dejection. "That man—nay, *thing*, for I detest calling him a man —controlled you. You were the blade in his hand. Is a dagger responsible for how it is wielded?"

"I enjoyed it." The words are a breath from my lips. I don't know if they are even audible. My secret. The thing I could never admit.

"I imagine a dagger would enjoy being used, having its blade sharpened to cut. That is its nature." There is no judgment in his words, no condescension. He rumbles, "Who am I to judge you?" He shakes his head. "Nay, my daughter, you are what you are. A young queen, learning to lead, to find a new use, one that may not come so easy to your nature. The feat would be no easy task. I do not envy you."

I fiddle with the cup in front of me. "I have felt like I am drowning, struggling to stay afloat. I don't know what I am doing. I don't know how I am supposed to act." Tears sting my eyes. "I want—I mean, I really want to be what I am supposed to be, but it's not as simple as learning to be a queen."

"We have removed the physical scars, but the deeper ones concern me. After years of abuse and no control, I understand you may not be what everyone expects of you. You are learning to be free. I imagine you have yearned for these days, but I fear they are overwhelming you."

I force the ball in my throat down and bob my head. "You have no idea."

He shrugs. "No, I do not. How can I? Being controlled and then set free? You've been taught a lot of things, but independence is not one of them."

I feel like the piece of me that has been missing is found, and all I want to do is share this with Declan. My heart aches. Sordello places a hand over his chest where a heart ought to be.

"Careful what you wish for, I guess."

"Do you wish to see him again? I can show you to the septal."

I nod. "Yes, but tomorrow, okay? Right now, I don't know if I can handle it."

# CHAPTER 16

*W*hen I wake, I dress, creating garments to wear beneath the robe. Instead of a cream color this time, I opt for black, taking comfort in the caliginous. I brave the corridors to find my way to the convergence room, using the elements to open a door far enough to slip inside. Once there, the Gammet brothers wave me over to join them.

"Ella." Aron beams at me. "I was wondering when we might see you."

I smile with closed lips and give them a little wave. "How are you?"

"Never better. This place is amazing. Have you met Malik and Orso yet?" He motions toward the two spirits next to him.

"A pleasure," I tell them, inclining my head.

The spirit next to Aron indicates me with his gauntlet. "So, you're Sordello's daughter?" I incline my head, and he goes on. "You wore the Vitale rune before the others. That is impressive."

The spirit second from Aron bows his head. I get the feeling that this one is Malik. "Virgil was our best warrior. You should wear his rune with pride."

"Oh." I glance toward the rune over my collarbone. "I didn't realize the runes were spirit specific."

"It is an odd arrangement. The rune likely does not know the difference." Orso waves his hand.

I nod and glance toward Erac. The feeling of his eyes on me must have drawn mine to his because he is staring at me. I give him a small smile. "So, how do I get sustenance?"

A cup settles on the table in front of me. "You can get it yourself from the fountain next time."

Sordello settles next to me. "Malik. Orso. Aron. Erac."

They incline their heads at their respective names, and I look to where my father points. At the far end of the room is a grand set of windows exposing golden clouds strung in a pink sky. Beneath the windows is a pale, cream-colored stone fountain of three tiers.

How I managed to not notice that until now is beyond my comprehension. I glance at the container in front of me, the same marbled white material as before. It differs from the vessels being used by the others. In fact, it matches Sordello's cup, but they are the only matching pair.

"You make your own cup and disperse of the elements when you are finished," Erac says.

I jerk, startled that he has answered my thoughts.

He grins at me, laughing. "You have the remaining runes and are part of the collective now. We can all sense what you are thinking or feeling."

Rolling my shoulders, I focus on my beverage, unsure how I feel about this. I lift the cup, taking a drink to hide my face. I roll my eyes at myself, knowing damn good and well that hiding my face never stopped Declan from knowing my thoughts.

"The collective cannot be far from what the bond was like for you."

I wince as Aron mentions the bond, glad I am hiding my face regardless of them feeling the pang in my chest at his words.

"Hardly," Erac scoffs. "The bond between her and Declan was a poison. The collective is peaceful. Have you begun to feel it yet, Ella?"

Setting the cup down, I meet his indigo gaze. "No. Not yet."

"I started to feel it the instant I was fitted with the last rune." He frowns. "Have you even tried?"

Sordello holds an open hand to Erac. "Please, leave her be. She will come to the collective in full in her own time. When she is at peace within herself. It will be difficult for her to connect until she finds that solace."

Malik picks up the words. "She has quite a bit of negativity within her. Feelings of worthlessness and insecurities are clouding her soul from ours."

"Self-hatred," Orso says, lifting his cup of red marble. "Loathing, hurt, fear."

"Orso, please," Sordello says. "There has been quite a bit my daughter has faced. We removed the scars we could; there are deeper pains she will need to heal before the collective is open to her."

I stare around at them. "I am sitting right here." I point toward the table. "There's no need to discuss me like I am not present."

Malik shrugs. "Even if you were not present, we would still feel you. You are a thorn in our side."

"It will take time." Sordello's deep voice is taut. "She needs to heal."

Orso inclines his head. "Malik is not being malicious. It is a fact."

Sordello makes no response that I can tell. There may be a response within the collective, but I am not an assimilated piece. We all fall silent, drinking.

Malik stands and turns to leave. Orso looks after him and then to Sordello. He shrugs, and Orso nods. I grit my teeth. This collective thing seems to be the bond all over again. Then again, this may be worse than the bond. I cannot imagine how I am going to manage having a hundred voices in my head.

*One entity sharing my headspace was*—my thoughts falter—*bad enough... The best thing in this whole world. It was beautiful and strange and everything, not needing to speak, to let the complex array of emotions speak for themselves without complicated words adding noise and confusion to even the simplest thoughts... To feel his love, never having to wonder if it was real...*

The thought sends a pang of regret and pain, singing through the beating mass in my chest. I force myself to take a drink and ignore it. "Sordello, you said you were going to show me around?"

"I will. Would you care to see the way to the septal first?"

I shrug. "First, last, doesn't matter. I need to know my way around."

He laughs. "You will want to know your way to the library."

My heart skips with excitement. "There's a library?"

Aron winces at my shrill decibel. "Of course, there is a library. You haven't been? It is enormous, even bigger than our library in Dis."

My jaw drops. "But that's the largest library in all of Caleum."

Erac laughs. "Yes, and this one is bigger. I'll show you to it right now. Aron and I are going to go."

Sordello is intrigued. I narrow one of my eyes at him in an irritated twitch, but he makes no remark.

"Thanks, but I think I'll let Sordello show me around. This is his home after all."

Aron smiles. "Of course, Ella. He is your father. You should get to know him better."

"There is plenty of time for that." Erac looks disappointed, his voice betraying a petulant pout.

"Brother, there will be time for us later."

Erac gives him a look of disbelief, but Aron stands and grabs his brother by the arm, dragging him away amidst protests that he wants to stay. Aron gives a wave as the great door swings open, and he shoves Erac through it. I smile behind my cup. They look like children in a giant's hall, and Erac is not having any of Aron's suggestions willingly.

Sordello is watching me. "Erac cares for you."

I take a drink. "I've heard that before."

"From your friends?"

I frown. "Yes."

His head tilts. "You do not think they are your friends?"

*I don't know if they are.* I can sense he is curious. Not wanting to discuss my potential friends, I change the topic. I shove fingers through my hair. "So, I think I can feel you. Not the others, though."

"You are my daughter. The link between us is established through blood. It is bound to be stronger."

I nod, then drain my sustenance. "So, the septal?"

He finishes his own drink and stands. "I will show you around the castle and the library first, then deliver you to the septal to give you time there on your own."

～

*B*y the time we get to the septal, the clouds appear to be dark storm clouds, the sky black behind them. I look around and rub my eyes, fighting back a yawn.

"I did not realize how vast this castle is." Sordello looks toward the expanse of stone. "I apologize for keeping you from the septal. I believe I may have underestimated my home and the history to share."

I shrug. "It is not a big deal. There is always tomorrow, right?"

He crosses his arms. "Lying is offensive, although I suspect there was a touch of truth. Do you not want to see your friends?"

I bite my lip, glancing at the hole. Looking away, I shove fingers through my hair, then shuffle my feet as I begin to pop my knuckles. "I do, and I don't. They... I mean, to them, I am dead." The word slips off the tip of my tongue without thought. Hearing it aloud makes me stop.

"Go on."

I sigh. "They were always too busy for me unless it was to tell me to stop screwing things up for them. Legia and Chase only came to find me when I put their position at court in jeopardy by fighting with Declan. For the last few cycles, Declan was only ever mad at me for one thing or another. Seth stopped being my friend. And Marcus..." I shake my head. "Marc has always been more father to me than Viktor, but lately he seemed cold, distant."

"I never saw those things in such a way. For example, I saw Legia and Chase drop everything to be there when you needed them the most, despite their plans that morning."

My stomach drops away. "What?"

"Those close to you have often been there for you when you needed them most."

I hug myself against the cool breeze. "Yeah, I guess."

"They care for you, despite your self-doubting and the distrust you place against them. Believe me, they care, even if you do not see it."

My arms squeeze around me. I try to reach further, to cocoon myself in my own embrace. My eyes fall to the ground as I mumble back, "I don't get it. They never thought I did anything right." I snort through my nose. "Dec—Declan." I turn my head further away and stare out over the expanse of the balcony. "He was always mad at me."

Sordello's heavy gauntlets rest on my shoulders, jagged

metal digging through my robes. "Listen to me. No one who cares about you is going to settle for you wallowing and whining. They will push you, try you, and hope to make you better."

I swallow hard, almost downing my tongue.

"Shame. You feel shame." He sighs. I listen to his armor clink, and his hands leave me. "Why?"

My face whips to him in shock. I stare, blinking at him. "What?"

He crosses his arms, hooded head held high. "Why do you feel shame?"

I open and close my mouth. "I don't know."

His hood shakes from side to side. "You are lying."

My face flushes with heat. "I'm not."

"You are." His response is lightning quick.

I grit my teeth. "I'm not lying; I don't know." He makes no response, but there is a feeling in my chest... Dissentient? "I'm not."

"Then you are lying to yourself."

I stare. I splutter. His shoulders roll as his torso leans away from me. I drop my arms and glare at him. "What's that supposed to mean? That I'm just pretending I don't know what you're asking? Like I don't know there is something wrong with me?" I am not sure when I started yelling, but my chest feels about to burst, and my lungs are burning. I pant, hugging myself once more. "I *know* there's something wrong with me." The defeated whisper is barely audible to my own ears.

He drops his arms and steps closer. "What is wrong with you?"

I glare at him through welling tears. "What do you think?" I feed venom into the question. "I'm barely able to keep from blowing everything up and scaring other elementals. I'm a queen who doesn't know her own duties, who can't be, who shouldn't be." I cannot catch my breath, and I run the heels of my palms under my eyes to clear away moisture. "Everything I do is wrong."

"'Wrong.'" His head cocks to the side. "You have used that word twice now." He twists, looking back at the castle. "Here, I am a leader. To you, a king, and yet I have made many mistakes." He turns back. "Do you think that makes me wrong?"

My lip curls. My nose even scrunches. "No, but—"

"But? But what? Have you made mistakes? Yes, but so have the others." He waves a dismissive hand. "Mistakes teach powerful lessons. The bigger a mistake, the more knowledge there is to be found, but only if one is willing to learn. A mistake, a failure..." he huffs and pauses, "A wrong. These things must be evaluated and learned from."

I return to holding myself and staring out into the dusty-blue sky full of silver clouds.

"Ella, my daughter." Hearing the way he says it, the tenderness that was never there when Viktor made the claim, my blackened heart turns rosy in my chest. "All your life, you have been abused. You have been forced to atrocities and that monster." The word is ripped from him with a harsh ring. "Viktor did little more than harm to you. I doubt you are capable of making choices, never having learned how to."

I stare, lost and untethered.

"You do have much to learn, but the only thing you can do wrong is to not even try. You will make mistakes. Learn from your failures. Move on." His hands land on my shoulders again. "Let go. Let go of the shame and fear. Let go of the idea that you are ever going to be perfect. Stop expecting so much from yourself. Look to accomplish one thing at a time. Look for the small victories. Let go of the fear of failure. You can only learn by trying."

My head bobs, and I force myself to inhale. "I'm tired."

His hands drop away, and I move around him. Without looking through the septal, I walk back into the castle. I pass by the library but head to my room. I push the door shut with a click and lean back against it, staring at the chess set with blurry vision and a racing heart.

# CHAPTER 17

*I*n the morning, I go through the forming routine. Wake, roll over, remember I am in Medius, and everyone I love and care for believes I am dead. I stretch against the cool sheets. When my feet hit the cold slate flooring, I force myself to take one step and then another, dressing in the black clothes and robe before heading for the convergence room and my cup of nutrients.

*Why couldn't there be food? I miss food.*

With a huff, I remain standing next to the fountain to avoid the brothers before heading straight to the septal. I sit cross-legged on the edge, tucking my legs tight against each other to be as close as possible to the septal's ocular. My heart rate stays even, but the pressure of the rhythmic thunks pushing blood through my veins rises until I think my heart might break a few ribs.

*Declan.*

Shimmering gold clouds swirl, and I see him sitting against a thick tree trunk, legs sprawling out in front of him. Next to him is— My stomach churns.

*Nope. That's— No. Please fucking no. What in Damnatus is he doing with her?*

Selene is sitting next to him, taking a drink of wine from a bottle. To her side is cheese and bread laid out on a burlap sack.

Bile lurches in my throat. The gas burns my nasal passages. The view of Salt Canyon from the orchards is all too familiar. They sit, side-by-side where Declan used to take me when he wanted us to be away from the prying eyes of the court as his stallion, Shadow, picks at grass nearby.

I fight to breathe, to maintain the image in the septal. I employ deep, calming breaths the way Aron taught me to meditate. I want to break down and cry, but maybe there is more to this than I realize. Forcing my jaw to relax, I wiggle it back and forth.

*Just breathe and see where this is going. Do not jump to conclusions.*

My sister picks at a piece of bread in her lap, licking her pretty pink lips. Despite having ridden on horseback and sitting in the dirt beneath the tree, she wears a short blue dress. A pair of heels lay in the grass near her feet, her beautiful golden curls twisted in an updo. A few wisps hang free in a flawless fashion I could never achieve.

She turns toward him, her expression soft. "Thank you for this. It's nice."

Declan's head inclines.

"I know that our engagement is strictly business at this point, now that I am to be crowned queen, but..." She hesitates, offering a dazzling smile. "I am hoping that this might become more."

He raises a single brow at her, fixing her with his blank stare. Maybe there is horror on his face. I want there to be horror, disgust, something negative. She stares back and then makes a funny face. His lips turn up at the corners, and she tips her head back and laughs.

"Okay, so I know that this might take some time, but I want

you to know that I am willing to try. I learned a lot from..." Selene looks away and then back. "From Seth."

Declan's eyebrows lift as much as they ever do when there is surprise littered in his features. I wonder if Selene can tell.

She tosses the bread aside to twist to her knees, kneeling to face him. "I know that sounds odd, and I certainly didn't learn what you're thinking."

The right side of his lips twists up as he adjusts his grip around a bottle of wine. "What am I thinking?" There is a cruel humor in his words. I know what he is thinking.

"Everyone knows that she and Seth had a relationship before your engagement, and now you're getting Seth's ex-fiance, but I swear to you, he and I never touched each other."

Declan takes a drink. "You two were bonded."

"Haven, that was..." She looks around and then rubs her hands on her thighs. "He was beaten bloody, and I was trying to determine if he was even alive when he bit me. But the point is, I know that my jealousy of her had a lot to do with Seth. I let certain feelings of mine get in the way of keeping an open mind to—my future husband."

Declan takes another drink, this one longer. "I see."

She shifts toward him a bit. "My previous engagement was a business transaction as well. My father and your father had exchanged something, and I was to be payment to your family by marrying Seth."

She tilts her head, looking toward the roots of the trees. After a moment, she blinks, coming back to life. "I was furious about being treated in such a way, and..." She grins, her cheeks tinging pink. "To be honest, I was jealous she had gotten you, and I got Seth instead."

Without responding, Declan takes another drink. He is draining the bottle, but Selene bats her eyelashes. Liquid leaks from the corner of his mouth, but it is not wine. Instead of a dark coloring, the liquid is clear. The bottle stays bottom-up, pouring contents I suspect are much stronger than wine down his throat. I watch his throat bob and work to keep up with the stream of fluid.

She grins wider and then looks down at her knees. "Ahem... Well, so, that's out there now." Her features wobble, like it is taking a massive effort to maintain the hopeful grin. "I have always had a bit of a crush on you."

Declan stops drinking, tossing the bottle to his feet, where it rolls away in the grass. He contemplates her. The breeze shifts his hair against his nose, and I flush with heat.

Watching all of this is making me sick. My fists are clenched so tight my knuckles are white. My jaw is aching from tension, but I cannot pull away. Selene is throwing herself at him, and I am waiting for him to push her away.

She gets up, moving to straddle him on her knees. She slides her hands up his neck into his hair. Her small mouth presses against his. Declan makes no immediate response, and I feel as if I have been kicked in the chest.

Declan's hands come up in a stiff movement to grab her hips. His mouth drags along her neck, and she mewls in response. Horrified, I watch. Not able to breathe as they struggle to remove barely enough clothing. She straddles him, impaled, moving up and down. Her head is tipped back, her hair tumbling over her shoulders and down her back. Her eyes are closed, lips parted.

I wrench myself away, throwing my body toward the railing, scrambling, crawling on all fours, clawing at the stone. My fingers find the balustrade, clutching spindles for something solid. My stomach churns; the taste of acidic vomit burns. Tears cloud my vision but do not fall.

Sweating and shaking fingers lose their grip, and I fall to all fours. Revulsion and sorrow overcome me. My chest aches, my lungs begging for air even as my abs sear from abuse. Still, my body keeps trying to throw out the images now ingrained in my mind.

Crawling on all fours, mewing, and sobbing like I suffered one of Viktor's beatings, I drag myself away. Through the open threshold and inside the castle, I manage to get control enough to run through the corridors lost until I find my room at the end of a dead-end hall. I slam the door shut behind me, tears streaming down my face.

My demon is hissing, clawing at the nothingness in me. I want to hurt something, but the only thing I catch sight of is the damned chessboard. I grab it, yanking it off the table and sending pieces everywhere. I turn, throwing it to the floor. The marble cracks against the stone with the sound of lightning.

I get on my knees, grabbing it and slamming the corner into the stone over and over until the noise echoing around me drowns out my wailing.

Two hands reach out to stay mine. They are shaking blurs before me, stained with hues of deep reds and thin pinks.

Erac is crouched in front of me, his face full of concern. One of his hands lets go of mine to wipe away a tear rolling down my face. He does not say anything but pulls my hands from the broken marble. He stands with my wrists in his grip and pulls me to my feet.

He wraps me in his arms, pressing me into his tight embrace as I sob. I cry into dry heaves before he pulls away from me. My arms are hanging at my sides, my body convulsing. Snot and tears are dripping down my face, and I stare at him with swollen, blurry eyes.

"I want to go home," I manage.

"We are home." His voice is a gentle chide.

"No," I sniffle, swiping at my nose. "I want to go home, home. To Caleum, to Cato, Bryon. I need to go home now."

The frown on his face deepens. "Ella." He drops his hands

from me, sighing deeply. "This is home. You wear all our runes. We are spirits."

"So?" I take a deep breath, closing my eyes. I tip my head back, drawing in air through my nose until my lungs are full. "Unless we are called by those below, we are stuck here?"

"I am afraid so." The tone of his voice is soft, compassionate. He does not look afraid. He looks relieved, his features at peace.

The room is too warm. My sight is tipping and spinning. "No."

"It's alright, Ella."

"*How is it alright!*" I scream. I clench my fists, wanting to draw blood from his body. I want to reach through the septal and break my sister's delicate neck. Little explosions of power pop around the room.

"Haven, calm down!" His roar barely reaches through the hurricane of pain in my mind.

"*Get out! Get out, just get out!*"

Erac holds up his hands and backs toward the door. "Alright, Ella, alright. Just calm down. We can talk tomorrow."

When he is gone, I pick up one of those stupid high back chairs, breaking it into pieces against the stone floor. When I am done, I reach for the second one, but it cracks before I ever lay a finger on it. I fall to my knees, hands grabbing at my hair, screaming as loud as I can for as long as I can until my lungs are on fire.

Exhausted, in hell, I crawl to the bed. I crawl onto it like an animal ravaged by fearsome wounds. Facedown, I scream into the mattress until my lungs are empty and then roll onto my back. Tears roll from the corners of my eyes down my temples into my hair. The realization that I have lost Declan once and for all settles over me like a shroud of iron, carrying me into an eternity of despair.

# CHAPTER 18

$\mathcal{I}$ do not leave the bed. Contemplating the idea to move, to sit, or touch the floor never crosses my mind. Declan screaming at Chase, throwing a tumbler, and yelling that he declared me dead plays in my mind. The image transitions to Selene straddling him. I dry heave a bit over the edge of the bed, and the loop replays.

Erac comes by, as promised. He fixes the chairs and chess set, he makes right all the damage in the room. If only he could fix all the destruction I have wrought.

When he finishes, he perches on the edge of the bed, frowning at me. "Do you want to play?" He jerks his head to the side at the chess set.

My eyes fixate on him, unseeing beyond vague shapes and muted colors. The sound of his voice is muffled as he talks to me. His words are soft and low, murmuring nonsense. I never speak. Trivial words are a waste of time.

At some point, he leaves. The loop plays over. Tears slide down my face. I roll over to the middle of the bed and sleep.

*I* wake numb, unable to move. I do not have the strength to even lift my limbs, and bending them would be a great feat, like bending an iron rod with my bare hands. As I lay there, I start to count back how long I have been here.

*Seven days. Today is the eighth.*

I roll to my back.

*That's seventy days in Caleum, almost half a revolution. By the end of today, it will have been eighty days. A complete half-revolution.*

I think back.

*How long did it take before I felt okay? Had I ever moved on after Declan was declared dead?*

I move. I shower. I try to envision washing my old life away. The soap suds rolling off my body are all the memories of my old life. After the shower, I piece together tight black pants and shirt and a pair of boots. They embrace me like a hug around my broken pieces.

Rather than drinking in the convergence hall, pretending to be merry or in the mood to socialize, I take my cup and return to the septal. My thoughts go to Declan, but I shake my head to loosen those thoughts.

Instead, I check in on Seth and then Marcus. I pull away from the septal to stretch, moving through positions, meditating to do my best at clearing my mind. I shuffle through old memories, the good and the bad.

I try to pay attention, try to evaluate, as Sordello mentioned. After reliving each memory, I picture shoving it in a box and slamming the lid. My head is pounding in time with my heart, and I decide to take a break.

I return to the septal with great joy as I watch Legia marry Chase. They are glowing, radiating felicity. I grin and clap, cheering along with the others present to share their bliss. I catch sight of Declan and Selene next to each other. My stomach rolls over, but I switch my focus to the others.

After the wedding, I pull away from the septal. I create a post near the far end of the balcony to swing and practice form. When I am sweating enough that my clothes stick, I retire on physical activity.

I am leaning against the balustrade, watching the sky fade from pink to purple as night descends, when Sordello joins me. The air is warm, a cool breeze making my auburn strands dance before me. "Everything about this place is peaceful."

He chuckles. "You seem to be finding an ease within you."

I tilt my head back and relax. "I think I am starting to feel the collective."

"It will take time. There is still a weight in you, though." He pauses. "Viktor."

His name sends chills crawling across my skin, and my face wrinkles. "What about him?"

"You still carry a belief he is alive."

I lean over the railing, watching the sky flow by in a gentle waft. "Yes."

"Why?"

I glance at Sordello with disbelief, then stand and sigh. "He —I..." I sigh again and shake my head, gripping the railing. "Were you watching then?"

"I was."

"Did you see him disintegrate?"

"There was much deteriorating and imploding. There was a brilliant flash of light. When I could see again, there was only you in the rubble."

"Damn," I mutter and grit my teeth. I grip the stone in my hands until my knuckles go white. "Earlier that day, I pulled Ravenna apart and thought of Damnatus." I shake my head. "I have no idea if she went there or what, but the last thought in my head when I was trying to kill Viktor was that Damnatus was too good for him. I'm scared. I'm scared I might have focused too much on that, on Damnatus, that I didn't destroy him."

Saying the words aloud, letting that thought solidify in my mind, moves a massive weight from me. I release my grip and stand straight.

"I was hoping you could tell me that I accomplished my goal, that he was dead and gone, disintegrated with everything else, and that's why there was no body."

His body shifts. "Use the septal."

I look at him, then over my shoulder at the septal. "What?"

"We can use the septal to see into all other realms." He moves to the opening. "If Viktor is alive, we can see him wherever he is."

I curl my lip, pushing away from the banister. Standing next to my father, I toe the edge of the septal. "Alright." I take a deep breath and drop my gaze.

I focus on Viktor. The clouds swirl, and poisonous green eyes materialize. I yelp, my knees buckling. Sordello grabs me to keep me from toppling through the image.

Anxiety shreds my veins and highjacks my heart. "No."

"He is in Damnatus."

"No."

"The septal doesn't lie."

"No, no, that can't—he can't." Words are failing on the back of my tongue. Fear strangles me. "No."

Sordello pulls me from the chasm and helps me to the ground. He kneels next to me, keeping a hand on my shoulder. I fight to breathe, resting elbows on my knees.

"Ella?"

I glance to Erac and Aron, staring with concern. My eyes flicker to the two spirits nearby. Malik. Orso. I recognize them. I nod, forcing myself to swallow.

Sordello stands. "Viktor is alive."

"He wears Virgil's runes."

"A threat to our collective."

I gape at them. "Can't we do something?"

Malik shakes his hooded visage. "He is in Damnatus, a lower dimension we cannot reach unless called upon."

"If he breaches Medius, we will end him to remove the threat to our way of life," Orso assures me. "It's okay." He kneels beside me, resting a hand on my arm. "He will be unwelcome here."

I nod and run a hand over my face. Medius is safe from Viktor. Viktor is in Damnatus away from Caleum. Both pieces of information are good news.

"Indeed, it is," Erac bristles. "He will never be allowed here." He offers me a hand. I accept it and allow him to pull me to my feet. "You are safe here." I stare into his violet eyes. He pulls me into an embrace, holding me against him. "You're safe. He can't reach you here."

I rest into him. He is warm and solid. I press my ear to his chest, listening to the mass beating inside. The rhythmic pulse is comforting.

I take a deep breath and push away from him. I swipe at my face and clear my throat. "Thank you, Erac. You're a good friend."

His eyes flash, his features flinching. He scowls at me, crossing his arms. I roll my shoulders and move away from them all, wanting space, needing air.

I hunch over the balustrade and stare at the nothingness below. My heart rate is returning to normal. My hands tremble as I reach out and place them flat on the surface. I press the sweating, hot palms against the cool, smooth stone and close my eyes. I breathe deeply through my nose and exhale out of my mouth. All I can do is accept that Vikor is alive and pray he finds his way here to Medius, where I can kill him.

I turn around to find them watching me. I meet their gazes

and nod. They all incline their heads in turn and then dissipate. Sordello remains, approaching me.

I hold my hands up, and he stops several paces from me. "I just want to be alone."

There is discontentment in my gut, but he dissipates, granting me solace.

# CHAPTER 19

*I* glance at the septal. I want nothing more than to glue myself to the edge and watch them all. I want to feel like I am still a part of their lives, and I wonder if this is how Sordello felt, watching me all this time. A couple of days have slipped by; my anxiety is dulling, less prevalent in my mind.

An image of Declan appears in the swirling clouds, conjured from sheer desire. I know I should walk away or concentrate hard enough to force the septal to show me something else, but to me, only ten days have passed, not a hundred. My heart is stubborn, refusing to let go. Inhaling deep, I sit, promising myself to only watch a moment.

He rolls out of his bed, and I am giddy to find he is alone. He dresses in grunge clothing, dissipating to the practice field. I watch him move, graceful and powerful. His movements and body mesmerize me until he returns to his rooms for a shower.

With a burning face, I keep my eyes rolling around the sky and the balcony, only sneaking peeks at him. I bit my lower lip, grinning every time I sneak a look at him. This is probably a gross violation of his privacy, and part of me feels bad. The other part of me is thoroughly enjoying this.

He does not dissipate to the courtroom but walks slow and deliberate through the hallways, staring blankly ahead of him. At the great doors for the courtroom, he pauses, smiling with tight features at the servants who open the door for him. He moves into the empty room where cushions are laid out in a circle already. He stops in the middle of the room, looking around him.

One hand is on his hip, the other falls over his eyes. His shoulders square, his spine straightens as he stands there. Letting out an audible exhale, he drops his other hand to his hip.

"Damn you, Ella," he curses and then tips his head as if meeting my gaze. His noble features are strained, and he clenches both fists at his side, speaking in a quiet, strained voice. "Damn you to the fucking Inferno for all of eternity."

I shrink back from the edge at his hoarse growl. After a moment, he moves forward to drop to the floor. He drops his face into his hand, his long golden brown hair falling forward. He remains alone and stationary until Selene enters the room next. She sits next to him and puts a hand on his shoulder. He looks up at her.

"Hi," she says, smiling.

He nods. "Hello."

"Are you alright?" Her brows draw together, and she frowns.

He nods again. "Tired."

She nods. "You don't need to be here." She reaches out to brush the hair resting against his nose. "You can go relax, or beat a post, or whatever you want. I will make the proper excuses and handle everything this morning on my own."

He looks away. I watch his throat bob.

Selene leans into him, her arm looping beneath his. "You deserve a break." He looks to her again and frowns. "You're surprised, aren't you? I can never tell." She bats her lashes at him. "*She* never did that, did she? She never understood. But how could she? She never knew anything about politics or the courts. She didn't understand the trials of the crown or the weight of it all. She never even paid attention to sessions."

"No, she didn't," he breathes, staring at the middle of the empty floor.

"She was selfish and ignorant." Selene stops leaning into him and sits tall. She fusses with her skirt, then fluffs her curls. "The court is better off now."

My heart breaks as his head bobs. The images in the septal fade away as I scoot on my butt away from the septal to the balustrade. I lean against it, staring at the opening.

My heart is hammering, and sewage is running through my veins, my stomach boils with acid. The taste lingers on my tongue, stinging my nasal passages, and rots my insides.

I bend my knees and put my head between them, focusing on breathing to keep from regurgitating for the umpteenth time since my arrival here. I swallow the bile. It burns less than the truth. They are right. The court is better off without me.

I looked my brother in the eye and confessed the court needed more than me and my best of intentions, so this information is not new. Selene belittling me is neither new nor something I put weight to but seeing Declan nod hurts. I close my eyes and swat my self-pity aside.

Instead of throwing a tantrum, I decide to do something about it. I stand, brushing sweating palms against my pants, and head for the library.

I meander through the main floor, idly looking about, not sure what I am looking for. The demon in me still wants to peel the skin one layer at a time from Selene's face. It would be painful, and she would live, albeit scared. My demon curls in a ball, purring in satisfaction of the thought.

Selene understands the court and the burden of the crown's

responsibilities. She spent her whole life craving the position. I am certain she learned everything possible, just hoping to be queen one day. I realize Selene is doing for Declan what he had been begging me to do all along. He had just wanted me to do enough to show that I might give a damn.

I stop in the middle of a row of shelving, wiping away tears. A spirit approaches me, so I smile. "Hello."

"Good day, Sordello's daughter. I am Diana, keeper of these records."

"It is nice to meet you, Diana."

Her hooded face inclines. I think she has a pleasant feeling. "Are you enjoying Medius?"

I do my best to smile instead of cry. *This is home now.* "Medius is lovely." I glance around. "Where do all of these books come from?"

She laughs. "Where do any books come from?" She looks to the nearby shelf, metal-clad fingers running down the spines. "We have spent eternity collecting knowledge. We have written extensively about your world as well as our own."

"There are books about Caleum?" My hopes perk.

"Yes. Jesa and Theron have spent countless days watching through the septal to record much. Jesa recently finished a book about the current fashion in your world and the way women wield it like weapons."

I blink, then tip my head back and laugh. Chloe was forever trying to get me to learn things such as that, maybe now I can.

"Yes." The word is bathed in a chortle. "When you have eternity, you look for anything to interest you."

I grin. "I suppose." My smile fades. *I have eternity. Here. Now.*

"Is there something I can help you find?" Her pleasant voice draws my attention back to her.

I wrinkle my nose, channeling Legia. "If I were, let's say, looking to learn how to be a queen, what do you think I should read?"

She is pleased. "I think there may be a book or two. Come, I will show you."

# CHAPTER 20

*N*ineteen days. One hundred and ninety days. Over an entire *revolution. No, just nineteen days. I'm not living in Caleum anymore,* I tell myself as I get dressed for the day.

Erac collects me from my rooms and escorts me to retrieve our daily nutrients. He shares some of the new magic he has learned, and I do my best to be polite. I smile, attempting to entertain a conversation before excusing myself.

I retrieve one of the hundred books from my room that Diana had given me. I dissipate to the septal and think about the Byron courtroom. I watch with diverted attention, reading, and waiting until the court is in session.

I set the book aside to watch the Byron court maneuver through the politics and the commoners. I pretend to be oblivious to the small touches and intimate glances Selene gives Declan throughout the morning, focusing on my objective to learn. As far as they are concerned, I am dead. It is as it should be. I can never go home, and Selene seems to be caring for him. As much as I hate her and my demon is ready to pounce, Declan deserves to be cared for.

When session is excused, I turn away. I flip through the book on political ideology. The pages are yellow, the spine stiff. I can only imagine, given the sub-context and examples provided, how long ago this was written.

Every day, I do the same thing. I watch session, and I read my books. I have even started to pry into the Clemm Court and Elven Court sessions for additional experience. Sordello stops by. As we interact, I start to feel more of him, finding it less and less necessary for him to speak aloud.

I lift a hand, scrunching my face, and studying the sky. "Excuse me, but a session should be starting."

"I will wait, and we can continue our discussion after if you would like?"

I smile at him. "Yes, please. Learning different things helps to keep me distracted."

I look to the septal, calling the image of the courtroom. Normal proceedings start, and then as two commoners argue before Declan and Selene over a debt to be paid, the air starts to shimmer. The room shakes, and a tear in the air forms, red light seeping through as it grows wider.

A foot attached to a leg juts into sight. Then comes the torso, and a man materializes through the rift. My mouth goes dry as Viktor's poisonous eyes gleam mean around the court-room. He smooths the starched white dress shirt down the length of his chest and slides his hands into the pockets of his dark slacks.

Behind him comes a hulking being, covered in thick rope muscles and black horns protruding from the eyeless head. It shuffles behind Viktor, yellow teeth scintillating with saliva. Drool drips from the long-curved fangs in a lipless mouth.

Viktor glances over his shoulder at the demon. It lets out a deep noise between a groan and growl, and one side of Viktor's mouth hitches up.

He faces Declan and Selene. "Declan, my boy, how are you?"

Declan's eyes narrow. "Turn around and walk right back through that portal."

"Ah, pleasantries are beyond you." Viktor rubs a hand over his bare scalp, and his lips press in a fleeting frown. "To the point, then, yes? You will relinquish Byron Court to me, once more, its rightful ruler. After a short adjustment period, Byron Court will declare war against the others. There will be a fight, but I assure you, we will win. I will rule over all of Caleum, and you all," he makes a small wave of his hand, "will be spared the atrocities of war as my most dear subjects."

Declan stands, crossing his arms. "You are not welcome here. You have been stripped of all rank, declared dead. Stay that way."

Viktor slides his hands into his pockets. "I was hoping you would see reason." He turns toward the demon, jerking his head toward Declan. The creature releases a snarling breath, a long-forked tongue licking the air and spraying spittle before tipping back its head and roaring. It brandishes a massive double-headed ax and lurches forward.

Declan's eyes widen a bit as the thing charges. He dives out of the way, rolling and coming to his feet with a sword in his hands. There is screaming as everyone rushes to escape the room. Seth appears next to Declan. Declan hands him his sword, producing another one. They exchange glances and then split to flank the demon.

My heart is thundering against my ribs, beating in horror. Declan goes toe to toe, parring the swings of the demon's ax. Marcus stands off to the side, hands waving to control the elements. The Bards are striking against the demon as Selene sits, mouth agape, staring at the thing. It swings the great ax toward her, and Seth darts forward to intervene on her behalf.

He rolls her out of the way as the ax slams into the stone floor, where she had been only moments before. He scrambles, looking furious. "Run, you fucking idiot," he roars, kicking at her.

Declan intercepts the demon's attack directed toward Seth's turned back. There is a skirmish, and Declan manages to take the head off the thing.

My hand is over my hammering heart. I am leaning so far forward that I fear I may fall through the septal. Everything in me and around me is trembling as I watch Declan double over, panting from the effort of the fight.

There is a snap, and I look toward Viktor. Others pour forth from the shimmering air. More and more demons are streaming into the courtroom carrying weapons of great size.

"No. No–no–no–no–no," I say over and over.

Sordello's hand lands on my shoulder. "Go, my daughter." A blade is offered to me. "Go and call us forth."

I turn, mouth hanging open and unblinking. "What?"

He points to the septal. "Go there, now, and call the rest of us forth. A life offering is necessary, but that doesn't have to mean death."

I watch Declan and Seth going on the defensive. There are others there now too. Legia has a bow, and Chase is with Marcus. They are waving their hands, but Chase starts to yell their magic is useless. Others with swords are appearing, group-ings of three and four needed to attack a single demon. Only the Bard brothers manage a single demon as a pair.

"Ella, my daughter, go, now, through the septal."

"But," I blink, looking from the scene to him. "But how? I can't. I can't leave. I—we have to be called."

"You are of Caleum, not of Medius. You are not bound here as we are."

"What?" I breathe, mind reeling. "I can go home?"

He offers the dagger to me once more. "Yes, you can come and go as you please."

I take hold of the hilt, looking under the hood toward the

shadowed face. There is only blackness, but I sense an approval. I nod, my eyes training back to the battle below. I suck in a breath and stand. With a final nod of encouragement from my dad, I step through the septal.

Air rushes around me as I concentrate on the Bryon courtroom. Freezing air rushes past me, whistling in my ears and whipping strands of my hair across my cheeks, leaving my skin stinging. The cold ripping through my body is an augment of dissipating. This is ice shards running through every inch of me, blistering pain tearing through my elements.

I crash into something solid, rolling and skittering across stone. Groaning, I push myself to my knees, looking around. The blade Sordello gave me is a few feet away. I get a shaky leg beneath me to stand in a crater within the middle of the Byron courtroom.

Fumbling and tripping on weak legs, I step to grab my dagger. I pant in silence. Glancing around, I notice every eye is turned on me. My eyes stop surveying as they lock on Viktor. His eyes are wider than I have ever seen before.

"Morella," he says in a trembling voice. "My wonderful daughter."

My lip curls back. "I am *not* your daughter."

"Come now," he opens his arms wide. "How can you speak such words? Have I not raised you? Have I not given you life? Molded you?" He slides his hands into his front pockets and rocks on his feet. "I had been informed of your death."

"Clearly, I'm not dead."

"Well, this is a pleasant surprise, and you know how I detest surprises." He extends a hand with a curve to his mouth. "Come, you belong with me."

I sneer at him. "You're right. We should rot in the inferno together."

"Ella?" I hear the defeated tone of my name and look to

Declan standing at the edge of the crater. He stares down at me, pale, his sword hanging in his grasp.

"Hey, Dec." I jerk my head at him. "Sorry about," I shrug, "you know, everything?" I turn back to Viktor. "Take your demons and leave, Viktor."

"I will not. I will have Caleum on its knees before me."

I shake my head. "No. I won't let you," I tell him through clenched teeth.

His head jerks back. "Ever the stubborn child." He shakes his head at me. "I have legions of demons at my side. What could you possibly do to stop me?" There is a triumphant ring to his words. He already thinks he has won.

I sigh, turning the point of the dagger against the base of my ribs. "You will never rule the Byron court or any part of Caleum ever again. I will stop you, and when I kill you, I'll make sure you're really dead this time." The cold ring of my words causes him to rock back on his heels.

I tip my head back, looking to where I know my dad is watching. "Dad," I breathe and close my eyes, lips twisted in a grimace. This is going to be one of those experiences I hate. "Spirits help us."

I shove the blade up and inward. It hurts beyond compare to all the times I have screamed until I could not breathe. Nothing before has ever burned the way blood filling my lungs does. I cough, spitting up wet and tangy fluid.

"Ella!" Declan roars.

I hit my knees, falling forward to all fours, gasping, regurgitating pink spit and sticky, stringy red mucus. I wish I could force my body to stop trying. Each pulse of my heart sends waves of pain spasming through my chest, my lungs fighting to work despite the steel lodged in them.

"No! What have you done?" It is Marcus who is pulling me to my back, his ashen face swimming above me. "What did you do? Why?" He lifts me into an embrace.

A laugh bubbles out of me at his horror, but it is agony. My vision goes out of focus, dimming further and further. I am hoping each spluttering breath will be my last.

"Get my daughter."

# CHAPTER 21

$\mathcal{I}$ come to, groggily groaning and pulling rough canvas from my face. I shove the cover from my legs and twist to all fours, panting. My lungs are furious with me.

There are bodies laid out in a neat row on either side of me, dull canvas sheets covering them. I rest back on my heels, wiping my face and collecting myself. Voices, clear and gruff, come from outside of the tent. The smell in the air is atrocious. Nearby a fire crackles and pops with chipper life.

The flap on the tent pulls back, and two men with a makeshift stretcher enter. I watch them, and one freezes, dropping the stretcher, blanching at me with wide eyes. He is younger than his partner, a squat golem with a big, bushy gray beard. The golem peers at me with a frown, but the young fae turns, running from the tent squealing.

"The dead are rising! The dead are rising!" His shouts fade.

My eyes cut to the other man as I stand. "Hello."

He leans back, studying me with distrust. "Eh?"

"Yeah." I draw out the word and shove fingers through my hair. It is greasy, and I pull my hand back, wiping it on my shirt.

His eyes drop lower, and I look down at the bloodstained

hole at the base of my ribcage. Looking back to him, I purse my lips. They twist together, and I cross my arms over the evidence of my wound.

"This looks weird, but..." The words hang in the air.

He straightens. "Only the dead were brought here for disposal."

I nod. "I'm sure I seemed dead." I drop my arms. "Are the other spirits here?"

His head drops and lifts a few times very slowly. "Aye, they are."

I grin. "I'm like them."

"Don't look like them."

I glance at myself. "Er, well, sort of like them." I sigh. "Can you tell me where I am?"

"Northwest corner of Byron Palace."

I nod. "Perfect."

As I pass by him on the way out of the tent, he shuffles to keep his distance. I ignore it. The young fae had run out screaming about the dead rising for a reason.

Outside the tent, I recognize the courtyard as the same one I killed Gopi in. There would have been poetic justice in my body being burned here. I move glacially, impaired by exertion. I stop several times, leaning against walls to pant and catch my breath.

During one such stop, a group of servants passes by. One of them stops, his purple eyes lighting at the sight of me. "Ella?"

Glancing up, I eye Dean while still bent over with hands on my knees for support. "Hey."

"Haven, I thought they said you were dead. Uh, again."

A strange gasp escapes me, something between a chuckle and panting. "I'm sure." I manage to get upright but stay against the wall for support. "I need to find a spirit. Sordello?"

Dean waves at the others. "I'm going to get her to the court-room." They move on, and Dean gets his arm around me. "Come on, Yer Majesty."

With Dean's help, I get to the courtroom. There are servants posted at the door. Their eyes go wide at the sight of us. They exchange glances, and then one steps forward.

"I'm sorry, Your Majesty, er, I mean, Ella, but..." She bites her lip, looking strained toward the other. "We aren't supposed to—"

I wave a hand at her, doubling over, trying to breathe. "Yeah, yeah, I'm sure I'm not welcome in there."

Through the door, I hear Sordello's booming voice. "I have asked you a dozen times, where is my daughter?"

"Morella is outside with the other dead commoners to be burned." Selene's voice is full of sweet syrup.

"She is not dead," my dad insists, his voice grave. "Fetch her before she is burned."

"She shoved a blade through her lungs. She had no pulse." Declan. "Three days ago." The words twist my gut.

I hear a hollow laugh. "You know nothing, young king." There is a pause, and then, "Until Sordello's daughter is brought forth, you'll receive no further assistance. She is one of ours, and we protect our own."

The voice could be Malik or Orso, neither am I familiar enough with to label under the circumstances. There is a murmuring on the other side of the doors I cannot decipher.

"Sordello, Sir," Marcus says, "we are ever appreciative—"

"I like you, boy, you've done right by my daughter, but don't push your luck with me. It is ill-advised."

"I didn't do it for you." I am shocked upright at Marcus' tone. He has never sounded so violent. "Perhaps you might give us all clarity on your claims of 'daughter?'" The word is spat out with a vulgar twist.

Having heard enough from this side of the doorway, I push the servant aside. "Don't worry, I'll tell them you tried to stop me." I offer her an empathetic grin while patting her on the shoulder, then force the door open with the use of the elements.

The room stops, every head snapping toward me as I shuffle through the door. But controlling the elements proves too much, leaving me to slide to the floor in a breathless heap on the other side.

"Ella," Sordello yelps. He strides to me, pulling me back to my feet. An open hand runs from my head and down my frame about a foot in front of me. "You are not entirely healed. How are you moving?"

"Entirely is the keyword, and I don't know. One foot in front of the other?" I am panting but give a small chuckle. "I've been told I'm stubborn."

Something hurtles at me with an ear-splitting screech. The orange blur collides into me, breaking me from Sordello's grip. I stagger backward, all the air knocked from me. My ears ring.

Legia pulls back, beaming at me. "You're not dead?"

Her shout is louder than the squeal. I move my head away from her mouth as far as possible. "Haven. Gia. No. Seriously. Can't breathe."

She lets go of me. The room moves around me as I take rapid, short pants. Sordello's hands land on my shoulders from behind me, and I reach up and rest mine over his. "Thanks."

"Sit. Your lungs are still damaged. You will heal faster without exerting yourself." He moves me toward a chair. Legia stays next to me, helping me into a chair.

"Excuse me?" I look toward Selene, pale-faced and standing on her feet. Her features flinch when mine meet hers. "This is a meeting of the war council. This is a collection of nobility and guild leaders. What do you think you are doing by bringing her in here?"

"She is my daughter," Sordello answers. "As I am the leader of the spirits that makes her nobility by your standards. Furthermore, she is embroiled in this mess, responsible for bringing us to your aid, and will prove to be useful in this coming war."

"But 'she's–she's— We pronounced her dead. She's been stripped of any rank or title."

There is a bark of laughter from across the room. My eyes meet Seth. "Repeating yourself isn't going to change the answer, you stupid git." He crosses his arms and nods at me. "Good to see you're alive."

I rest my head back and breathe. Marcus approaches, kneeling in front of me. "Ella?"

I peer down into his forlorn expression. "Marc?"

He hangs his head, shaking it, so his frizzy dark hair wiggles on his head. "What in Damnatus?" he yells, lifting his head to fixate his eyes on me. "Where in Haven's name have you been?"

I try to push myself further into the chair. "Um…"

"And why the hell does he," Marcus begins jabbing a finger toward something behind me, "keep telling us you are his daughter?"

One side of my mouth pulls back in a grin, the other side uncooperative with fatigue. "Because he is my father, my *real* father. It's a lot to explain, but Sordello and a dragon named Wyoma gave birth to me. Wyoma dropped me in the city, where, she assumed, I would be taken in by someone. Someone found me, claimed I used magic to warm myself up, and brought me to Viktor. So, naturally, Dear Dad—"

Sordello clears his throat. His hand lands on my shoulder. "I will never force you to refer to me in such a way, but I will not listen to you use that term for *him*."

I scoff. "Right, Dad, it's a joke with us." I manage to shrug one shoulder. "*Viktor* decided I would be useful, so he injected me with his blood."

"That's impossible. That's–that's," Selene stammers. "You aren't the rightful heir."

"Where she came from makes no difference in being an acceptable heir," Declan says.

I look at him for the first time. He is still sitting on the floor, his arms resting over his knees. There is nothing about his face at this distance that tells me what he is thinking or how he is feeling.

I pull my eyes from him to my brother and back to Selene. Her glassy eyes and her trembling lower lip make me giddy. I grin, thinking about how much I would enjoy strangling her. Selene reaches out, sitting down and latching her hands around Declan's arm. He does not shrug her off, and I feel like that blade is being shoved through my lungs again.

Before I can do something regrettable, I crane to look at Sordello. "Where is Viktor?"

"All we know for sure is that he is south. There are reports of him being in the southernmost parts of Salt Canyon."

"But sending demons everywhere," Marcus chimes in. "You cannot be contemplating going after him so soon."

"So soon?" Legia yelps. "Soon? She should not be considering it at all." She grabs my wrist. "Tell me you aren't even thinking about going after him."

"She may be the only person able to get to him." Declan's words are low, his voice tight.

"You cannot be serious!" Seth exclaims. "This is Ella we're talking about. She's got the power to control the elements, sure, but those demons weren't responding to the manipulation of elements. She's inept for what we really need, and besides—" he winces, "—her powers are totally out of control."

"No," Sordello says. "Her powers are not an issue. She is no longer unstable. Wearing all of our runes, she has assimilated that power."

"Unstable powers aside, this is Ella's life we are talking about," Seth retorts. "She cannot be expected to face Viktor."

"She cannot be trusted to face Viktor, you mean," Selene snaps. She lets go of Declan, getting back to her feet. Her pretty face whips around the room as she points an accusatory finger at me. "Morella very well might side with him. She and Viktor have always been close."

"That's an outright lie," Marcus counters. "She's hated Viktor nearly her whole life and justly so."

"Why? Because she blames him for all the murders she has committed?"

The room implodes. Declan lurches to his feet, grabbing hold of her by the arm and snarling at her. Marcus dashes across the room to intercept Seth on his way toward her. Legia is arguing with those around us in my defense, and even the deep voices of the spirits blend into the din.

I watch the noise and chaos, Chase wagging a finger at a group, Marcus and Seth scrapping, Declan shaking Selene, the skin on his nose wrinkled with fury as he yells—that bit makes me grin. With a sigh, I get to my feet, holding a hand up to snap.

As my fingers rub together, a small explosion detonates in front of me. Everything goes quiet. All eyes return to me.

"I am going to find him," I say, looking at Seth and Marcus. "I am going to kill him. And this time, I am going to remove his head and burn the body to be sure he is dead."

"You are going to hang as a murderer," Selene snarls.

"Viktor poured his blood into her," Sordello says, his voice ringing around the room with authority. "She had no choice in those atrocities. I'll not allow her to be strung up for your misconceived notions regardless of whether or not it will last." He looks at me during the last part.

Selene laughs in a hysterical meltdown, hands running down the sides of her face, and the pitch of her words as shrill as steel dragging against stone. "That is the defense you've prepared? That is worse than a murderer. That is a direct breach of the laws of the land, not just of Byron."

I glare at her with a hatred I have not known before, even for Viktor. Viktor did things for his own gains, but Viktor was honest about those gains and his motives. He stood there and told me he had Declan killed because he felt my relationship with Declan weakened me. Selene has no spine. She is selfish and a coward, hell-bent on having me killed because of her jealousy.

Selene takes a step back under my gaze. I wonder if she can sense my hatred and rage. Her gaze drops from my eyes toward the floor. I exhale, allowing my lungs to empty. "Killing me will not last, and it will not make you any less jealous of me." I raise my voice. "Killing me is not going to do any good for anyone in Caleum."

Selene's face turns pink. "I am not jealous of you," she snarls, stepping forward. "What would I have to be jealous of you for?"

My eyes shift from her to Declan, who stands over her shoulder and then back to meet her gaze. "Killing Viktor is the only death that is going to matter." I must stop to breathe. "Now, someone is going to tell me where Viktor was according to the last report."

"You can barely stand," Declan snaps. "You are out of your mind if you think anyone is going to let you near Viktor right now."

I meet his eyes, but Selene starts screaming. "We are not going to let you near Viktor ever. You will rot in a cell until he is dead, and then you'll die too."

Seth laughs. "There was hardly a cell in Caleum that would hold her before, and there is nothing anywhere in Caleum that can hold a spirit." He moves toward me. "Dec's right. You're barely upright. You look like you need food and rest. Come on, I'll get you to the dining hall."

"Seth," Selene hisses. "You will not."

He is already putting his arm around me, bending to scoop me into his arms and against his chest. I look up into his face.

His head is up, though, focused straight ahead. "Go fuck yourself."

His words ring loud and clear through the room, and there are more than a few muted and strangled coughs abound. He turns with me in his arms and walks out of the room.

I am grinning. "Bet you loved that."

His chest rumbles. "Every syllable."

I laugh, gasping at the end as my chest wracks with pain. He shakes his head, glancing down at me with dark gray eyes. "Where the hell have you been, Ell? Do you know we all thought you were dead?"

I rest my head against his shoulder and close my eyes. "Yeah, I knew. I was in Medius. I didn't know I could come home. Someone—Erac—told me that I was a spirit, and we couldn't leave without being called on." I look up at his scowl. "He lied to me."

Seth grunts and adjusts me in his arms. "Go figure. Let me guess, he wanted to keep you up there with him?"

I shake my head. "I don't know. I only found out it was a lie a second before I came back and haven't seen him since to ask. Anyway, there's this place, the septal, and it is, I mean, Medius really is a giant floating castle. Just clouds, pink and gold clouds all around when it is light. They turn to blue and silver when it is dark. There's no soul star or sun or anything, just light—"

"Get to the point, Ell."

I snicker. "There's this place, the septal, where you can look into another dimension. That's how I knew. I heard Declan say he declared me dead."

"We mourned. I mourned. Haven, Ell, I really thought…" He stops walking, looking down into my face. "It was rough. Every single one of us took it hard. Chase blamed himself for not being able to teach you better. Legia thought she should have talked to you more. Hell, Marcus shut down for days. And Declan…" Seth shakes his head.

He starts to move again. "I don't think anyone was right for cycles." He kicks his foot out in front of him, and I realize he is kicking open the dining hall door. It opens with a bang, slamming against the wall. Seth just walks in and sets me on one of the long benches. "Wait here. I'll go get food."

I look around the empty room as I wait, focusing on breathing with half functioning organs. The door opens, and a stampede of familiar faces comes straight at me. I drop my head to the table as the bench moves beneath me, others sitting around me. I lift my head, staring across the table into Declan's black eyes.

Legia is pulling me against her from behind, smothering me in another hug. "Haven, I am so glad you aren't dead. Did you know we thought you were dead? Wait, was that said yet? We so thought you were dead. Your family estate was destroyed, and we all thought you lost control."

I scoff. "Yeah, I know."

She lets go of me, and I notice Chase is with her. He claps me on the shoulder with a shake. "It is good to see you. Do try to stay alive for more than five minutes this time, won't you?"

"Ha." I smirk. "I think I can manage that this time."

"Ella, where the hell have you been?"

I smirk, turning toward Marcus, but he glares, his cheeks sunk in, his eyes dark and tinged with sickness. "Do you realize we thought you were dead? This isn't funny."

"No, what's funny is Seth said those exact same words and in that same order."

He mutters a string of curses under his breath. "What do I care what Seth said or how? Answer me."

I nod, my eyes flickering toward Declan. Wyatt is next to him now with Samuel and Cannamore on his other side. I blink, startled, not sure when they arrived. I turn back to my brother. "I was in Medius."

There is a brief flicker of surprise in his eyes, but Seth

returns with steaming broth and bread. My mouth waters, saliva forming as pinpricks under my tongue. I rip the bread to pieces, smelling it. I dunk it into the searing hot soup and tip my head back to drop it into my hungry mouth.

Sordello laughs. "You have missed food."

I grin, but the grin disappears as Declan growls. "Nearly twenty cycles. You've been presumed dead for well over two hundred days. That's eight days over a full revolution."

I give him an irritated glance. "Thanks. I wasn't aware of the number of days in a revolution." My eyes flutter and roll as I turn back to my meal. "What do you want to know?"

"What in Haven's name happened? One moment you're here, the next you're gone. The Bryon estate was in wreckage when I went to find you," he says, his voice tight. The tense muscles in his face twitch, and there is a flicker of something beneath his drawn expression.

There is no time for me to answer him, but my eyes never leave his as the questions bombard me from all directions. *"When I came to find you."* He came after all?

"You fell out of the sky in an explosion of fire at the exact time Viktor returns. There's more than a coincidence there."

"You burned down our home and left us to think you were dead. How could you do that to me? To us?"

"You promised me you were going to fix things. I have half a mind to keep my threat and fill you with arrows."

"Are you really a spirit?" Dean glances around, then looks at the table with embarrassment.

I turn and point to Dean with a smirk. "You, sir, are as well." Everyone turns to stare at him, but I snicker as Dean's lower jaw drops. "You're gonna need some help figuring that out. Maybe get with Dad," I jerk my thumb at Sordello. "He can get you with Mattio."

"Great. That is fucking great," Declan snaps. "You have been dead for two hundred days, and that's the first thing you're going to say to anyone?"

I blink at Declan. "That was really important to Dean. He needed to know." I fan my hands out flat on the table. "Believe me."

Dean gives me a sly smile. "You have no idea."

My head tips back as I laugh. "Oh, trust me, I know." I meet Declan's black eyes and do my best to quit grinning. "Alright," I hunker down over the bowl. "What did you want to know?"

Rapid fire questions come my way, and I do my best to answer. Sordello stands behind me, helping to explain the things I can not. There are so many questions, and I find myself laughing at some of the very same thoughts I had myself.

Dean volunteers to get me more soup and takes off with the empty bowl. Legia eyes me with a cocked jaw. She huffs and rolls her eyes, scrunching her nose at me. "I still want to shoot you."

I turn toward her and open my arms. "Go for it. I'll heal. I deserve it. I know."

She stands, and Chase follows, lacing his fingers with hers. They start to leave, but she turns back and glares at me. "You, Your Highness, are going to keep your feet planted to this world, and you are done dying. Got it?"

I wink at her. "Promise."

Chase and Legia exit the dining hall hand in hand, and I watch them go with the ghost of a smile on my lips. Then kick myself mentally that I had not offered them congratulations on their marriage.

Most of the others leave, making polite excuses for why they are going. I acknowledge them, making small talk, and send them on their way with a grin. Soon it is just me with my brother and the Bards. Selene had slipped in at some point as others were leaving. She sits, pressed against Declan without speaking. She glares at me every time I speak, and soon enough, I am rolling my eyes at her.

"You need rest," Sordello says. "You still are not completely healed."

I nod, yawning. "Yes, alright, but before I go, I have one question of my own." Marcus inclines his head, and I take that as consent to answer. "Did Aron and Erac come with the other spirits?"

Seth curls his lip. "You really care if—"

I hold a hand up. "I want to know if they are present in Caleum."

"They are not welcome here," Declan says quietly.

My face jerks toward him. "But are they?"

"Yes, they are in Caleum. They are south, with the bulk of the army and spirits."

Selene tenses and grips Declan's arm harder. "She doesn't need to know where the army is. She doesn't need to know what is going on."

I rub my temples. "Please refrain from speaking; you're voice gives me a headache."

She leans forward, glossy-eyed, and opens her mouth. Seth cuts her off. "I'll second that motion." He chuckles, then turns to me. "Looking for Erac?" His tone has shifted to a nasty connotation.

I give him a look of exhaustion. "More accurately, I am going to want to steer clear of him. He lied to me, telling me that I couldn't leave Medius."

He is taken aback, but Selene retorts instead. "You should have just stayed there."

"Oh, do shut up," Seth groans. "She brought the spirits here."

I put a hand against my chest and wince as I stand. Sordello offers me aid, and I accept, leaning on his arm.

My eyes meet Declan's, and Selene leans between us. "Go away."

My eyes drop to the table, and I take a deep breath, sighing in defeat. "Anywhere away from you will be a pleasure." I look to Seth then Marcus. "Night."

Sordello sweeps us away during their vague responses and helps me along to my suite. He ushers me inside. "I have a terrible weight in me. This fight, this vow to kill Viktor, it will not end well for any involved with this madness."

I furrow my brows. "Is the madness simply the plan to kill him?"

"The madness feels as if it is this course which we are all set upon, fixed to the rails of fate, destined for pain." His head shakes a bit. "It seems no matter which course of action we take, this war will not be easy for any. I want you to prepare for the heartbreak and agony that will come. When it comes, you must remain steadfast. Allowing your emotions to control you as you have before will only bring worsening conditions."

"I will do my best."

He leaves then, with the sense of dread closing in around me as darkness is closing in around the palace. I stare out the window, and tears collect in my eyes. I want to return to the dining hall; to go find Declan. I want to talk to him, but I know I need to stay away from him. I have done enough damage. He does not deserve for me to drag him into an emotional mess with me when there is the war to consider.

I head for the bed, rolling into the middle still in my boots and bloodstained, ruined clothes. I stare at the ceiling and blink. Thick tears roll out, and I shove the memories away. I close my eyes and do my best to get some rest.

# CHAPTER 22

Sordello shakes me awake. "Come with me."

Rolling off the bed, I hit the floor as I change my clothes with the elements into something less bloody. He dissipates us, and when I reassemble, I stand before him in the practice field.

Through a yawn, I scratch my head and ask, "Why here?"

"You need to learn to fight," he says, handing me a wooden sword.

I look at it with a single cocked brow. "I know how to use a blade."

He starts an attack, and I go on the defense. He disarms me in seconds. "You know how to kill with stealth and how to fisticuffs. You are not a trained warrior with a sword."

My face grows warm as I fetch my sword. "Okay." Facing him, I draw the word out. "I have magic, though."

"Try it." He launches into an attack before I have time to set up.

I lose my sword, hitting the dirt on my butt. I throw a shock wave of energy toward him. He steps through it, a single pause before his sword rests against my neck. "Demons are as impervious to the manipulation of your elements as spirits are. Trying to use the elements of Caleum will be ineffective."

I prop myself on my elbows, still laying in the dirt. Gazing up at him, I twist my lips and consider. "So, every skill I have is worthless?"

"Not worthless, just not the skill you will need. Demons swing weapons two or three times the size of elementals. You have neither strength nor size on your side."

Gritting my teeth, I shove his sword away and roll to my feet. "Fine."

"Those other skills will help. The rest I will teach you. Once you have learned, I will get you to the frontlines. I know that is where you will want to be."

I nod vigorously. "I want to find Viktor."

"You will. *After*," he stresses, "you learn. I will not have you out there unless I feel comfortable that you will be safe."

"I mean, I'm a spirit."

"And if the demons rip your Vitale rune off your body, you will die." My jaw drops. He chuckles. "You were unaware that they can do such?" His hand lands on my shoulder. "A spirit can die if the rune is removed or if they destroy your body. You have much to learn. Every morning, when the soul star rises, meet me here. I will train you, and when you are ready, you will join us in this fight."

I nod my agreement, and he begins to review proper grip with both hands. It differs from holding a dagger or any of the smaller blades I am comfortable with. He must keep stopping to correct my grip, but he teaches me basic swings.

He insists I use no magic and learn each step and swing with both hands. Then he leaves me there to continue working through swings. I practice with slow swings, paying attention to form, then adding speed as I feel comfortable.

After a while, I grab the discarded sword left by Sordello and return to my rooms. I pilfer bread and cheese for a light break-fast and then find my way out of the palace walls.

The gardens are filled with tents, and I weave through them, realizing the setup is to help the wounded and house recovering warriors. I worm through the makeshift shelters. Everywhere I look bandaged warriors and healers are skittering around. There are hushed tones and grim silence.

I catch sight of Gemma, wrapping white around the arm of a dryad made up of pure muscle. I stop and wait until she has finished. The man has the darkest skin I have ever seen, offset by bright orange eyes. She hands him a sword, struggling with two hands to lift it for him. He grasps it with the hand of his injured arm, testing the weight and flexing the muscles.

He nods at her and then sets the sword aside, speaking in a voice tinged with a slurring accent. "Good."

Gemma turns from him to me. She frowns. "I see Selene didn't hang you." Her tone is cold.

My brows furrow. "Not yet, but it will come."

"Good."

Shocked, I jerk. It is full well what I deserve, but hearing my friend wish for my death is unexpected.

Gemma stares back with fury blazing in her cinnamon-ringed verdant eyes. The colors match the strands of her hair, braided and wrapped like a crown around her head. "You're surprised? You've taken life away from another."

I grimace. "I have, but it wasn't my choice."

She shakes her head. "All these revolutions, Legia and I stood by your side thinking everyone else had it wrong, thinking the court's opinion of you was unfair because we knew who you were, but we didn't know, did we? Who are you?" She twists those words with a cruel sneer. "I don't know who you are because my friend Ella wanted to help others, was kind and generous. She wouldn't have ever been capable of killing another."

I stand, rooted to the spot with an open mouth. I blink, but my mind is numbed from shock to dumb.

"Excuse me, Your Highness." Gemma laughs. "Actually, you aren't even that, are you? Selene is right. You aren't even rightfully a princess, not to mention wrong for the throne. Haven help us, you'd be like the monster, Emperor Tyle." She shakes her head. "I have work to do, injured to tend to. Go away."

Gemma turns, but I grab her forearm. "Wait, Gemma, I'm…" I look over her shoulder to the man waiting on her. "I'm sorry. There are things I should have said, wish I could say, but I couldn't. I really couldn't."

Gemma wrenches herself free. "I do not have time, nor want of time, for this."

She marches away from the tent. I look toward the dryad. "Should I call her back for you?"

He shakes his head. "No need. She has done what she can." His voice is a soft baritone. "She said she thought you incapable of killing." He jerks his head in the direction Gemma stormed off. "Have you been fighting on the frontlines?"

Shaking my head, I shuffle my feet and avoid his steady gaze. "No, she is talking about…" I stop and exhale. "Have you been on the frontlines?"

His head inclines. "Yes."

"Where?"

"We pushed them," he grunts, shrugging into a shirt, "back from the canyon and further into Cimeria." He sits back on the cot with a heavy breath. "You haven't even seen the frontlines."

"Not yet."

"A small thing like you?" He shakes his head. "The women are being held back now." His eyes become misty. "The small, like you, the demons rip them in half."

My lip curls back slightly. "They'll have to try really hard."

Those eyes appear sunken as they fixate on me. "Star was one of the best."

"Star?" My voice is a whisper. "They killed Star? The warrior guild leader, Star?"

His eyes fall to the ground. "She was next to me."

I glance toward the wall in the direction of Cimeria. My blood boils. I breathe through my nose, biting back emotions. War is going to take too long. Training with Sordello to even get to the fight is going to waste precious time, cost lives that should not be lost.

I turn back to him. "Where in Cimeria?" My voice is a harsh hiss.

His brow crinkles. "You knew her?" I shrug. He shakes his head. "You seem to be a lady. What can you do?"

"Where?" I grind through clenched teeth.

"Two days west of Palik before I was brought here for healing." He works to shrug a jacket on. He winces this time.

"What's wrong with your shoulder?"

He stares at me. "Nothing, 'Ma'am."

I narrow my eyes. "You can't fight like that."

He laughs. "Nothing's going to stop me from getting back there, not this," he holds up the injury Gemma treated, "nor a sore shoulder."

I step closer. "Which shoulder?"

He glares at me. "There's nothing wrong with my shoulder. If I say nothing is wrong, then nothing is wrong, and they take you back."

"Tell me which one it is, and I'll fix it."

His face shies away. He is watching me with distrust. "The right."

I reach out, touching fingertips to it. I let my eyelids drop to half-mast, focusing on the elements. Things are wrong, out of place. The fuzzy red muscles are jagged, not cleanly bound together. My eyes close, and I push energy into his shoulder to rebuild the muscles. His shoulder jerks from under my touch, and I look at him.

He stands, rotating and flexing. "Not bad. Are you a healer?"

"No."

"Name's Gamal," he offers me his hand.

I accept his hand but do not offer my name.

He holds tight to my hand and lifts brows over a wide nose and orange eyes. "No name?" He chuckles. "Well, no name, thank you."

I drop his hand and smile. "No name. I'll take it."

We release our grip, and he secures his sword, shoving it into a sheath. "The orders are to push them back as far as south as possible. They want to flank them, rounding them together, pushing them into a group. I've heard talk that the spirits are going to shove them back through a dimensional tear." He buckles the sheath on a leather belt around his hips. "Don't know much else."

I nod. "That's enough for me to work with." I glance at Gemma, who is headed back this way. With a sigh, I jerk my head toward her. "She doesn't look pleased that I'm still here."

Gamal glances up at her. "If I were you, I would be running in the opposite direction."

I laugh, moving away. I meander through other tents, doing what I can to help others the way I helped Gamal. I do not ask too many questions. I listen, trying to glean information without notice.

When dusk comes, I make my way to the dining hall. I sit at the end of a bench near the back wall where part of the table is deserted. A servant, a young fae girl, comes to bring me food. I wave the food away.

"Take it to someone else who needs it. I just want a plate and goblet."

The confused girl brings me what I ask for, and I create my own dinner of wine and fruit. I sit alone until my sister slithers over, an entourage of girls with her. Her eyes narrow, her heart-shaped face tinging with fury.

"You are not welcome here."

"Slither back to your hole, snake."

I glance over my shoulder at Legia staring her down. I look back to Selene. She scoffs, tossing her blonde curls over her shoulder. "Be careful, Legia. Those defending Ella are being ostracized and cut out."

"Not to mention deemed expendable and shipped to the frontlines," Elizabeth giggles.

Legia's form visibly hardens. Her stance swells, her shoulders roll back. "Declan would never stand for such a thing."

"Poor thing," Skylar snickers. "Who do you think has arranged for the others to be moved to the frontline?"

Selene grins at me. "Daphine confessed to me that she was on my side, but her father?" She shrugs. "Declan was so certain that the Medici would support you that he sent her anyway."

My jaw drops. Nausea overcomes me, sweat beading where my neck and hair meet. Two guild leaders, two of the strongest women in Caleum are dead. "Daphine's dead?"

"You are a liar, and we all know it." Legia is on the balls of her feet, ready to pounce.

Selene tips her head back, laughing. "Am I now?" She looks around at the girls surrounding her. "I am Queen of Byron, and you? The daughter of a duke, right? You have no title, nor does your husband. Who do you think Declan is confiding in?"

My sister and her ladies stroll away snickering. Legia drops her hands from her hips and takes a seat next to me, straddling the bench to face me. Her attire of tight jeans and laced up boots caked with mud is odd. Her orange hair is still braided, which helps soften the outfit.

"That snake is lying and delusional." Legia grabs the goblet in front of me, raising it to her lips. Choking, she spits the wine back out. "Haven, has your sister tried to poison you?"

My stomach knots. "I wouldn't put it past her." Legia stares down into the goblet, inspecting. I take her silence as opportunity. "Daphine's dead?"

Legia's gaze lifts to mine. "A horde broke through the ranks." She sets the goblet down ever so slowly. The look in her eyes is distant as she stares at it. "Daphine, I, a mix of hunters and mages for ranged attacks, we were surrounded." Her eyes shift to a darker blue. "They're resistant." Her eyes meet mine. "The demons, they're resistant to magic. Daphine got the worst of it. She held them off long enough for the rest of us to escape."

Legia grabs the goblet staring down into it. "What is this?"

"Wine."

"It's terrible."

"I made it." Legia gapes. "I'm much better with fruit." I push the plate toward her. My appetite has dissolved.

Legia picks up a piece and looks at it. She shrugs, takes a bite, and groans. "That's delicious. I haven't had fruit in ages. Not surprising, though, is it? Not with the south a total war zone. Viktor and his demons have destroyed or blocked almost every trading post there was." She grabs another piece and snaps to a servant, handing the goblet over. "Get rid of that and bring us new."

"Please," I say for her.

Legia waves her hand at the stunned woman. "Go on." She wrinkles her nose. "You've been gone so long, I think everyone's forgotten your necessity of common courtesy to the servants."

She sighs. "Speaking of being gone for so long, what do you know about what is going on? Selene has taken your place. She went and blabbed about you being a murderer just so that you couldn't take the crown back. Oh, I hate her!" She slaps the tabletop. "And Declan. She sunk her fangs in him from day one by arranging their engagement. And do not believe her for one second. Declan is not shipping your supporters to the frontline. Daphine was there for the same reason I was. We wanted to be. Declan has actually ordered all women to be removed from the frontlines because they were being slaughtered without resistance."

"Um…" I hedge the word in to get her to stop talking long enough for me to get a response in. "Doesn't it bother you that I'm a murderer? She's right. I should be hanged or burned."

"Pull your head out of your perfectly shaped backside, Your Highness." Legia rolls her eyes and takes a bite of fruit. "Damn, this is really good." Her eyes roll back into her head as she savors and chews. When her eyes pop open, they are hard. "You've been coerced and beaten by Viktor your whole life. It was a shock when I first learned." She waves a hand about. "It doesn't change anything."

"Gemma thinks it does."

"She didn't know?"

Grimacing, I shake my head. "No one knew except Seth and Marcus. Declan learned with our engagement and bond, then Chase found out. Then you."

"Well, and then because of that bond to Seth, your wretched sister knew. Haven, what a mess. What are we going to do to fix it?"

"We?"

"I did not spend my entire life devoted to you to be left standing empty-handed while I watch my friend hang for crimes she is not responsible for." She takes a drink and shakes her head. "No. You and I are going to fix this. We're going to get you Declan back, and then we are going to rule Byron."

I stare at her. "What? I became your friend, knowing you'd be queen one day. Don't think I don't know you became my friend, hoping I'd show you how to fit in at court." She glares, taking a drink of fresh wine delivered by the servant. "But neither of those reasons are why we are still friends. Gemma is a bloody idiot. I saw the scars long before I knew. I knew things weren't right, and I knew that every time you'd come back after an absence, there were new scars, more bruises. I didn't know more because I didn't want to know." She stares at me, her expression softens, and she dips her head to clean dirt from under a single nail. "I'm sorry."

Leaning forward, I throw my arms around her. "Thank you." She hugs me back. "Thank you for everything, for it all. For showing me how to act in court and for helping me through all of those balls." My throat becomes thick with emotion. "Thank you for sticking by my side, and for being my friend."

Legia squeals in my ear, and for once, I do not mind. She tightens her grip then pulls back, laughing and wrinkling her nose. "I love you like a sister, Ella. You *have*," she says, applying a heavy emphasis to the last word and a roll of her eyes, "to know that."

I drag the heels of my palms along the underside of my eyes, looking upward as I do so. When I blink and look down again, Chase is sitting across the table from us. His eyes lock on the plate of fruit. His hand snakes out, snatching up a piece of dragons' food.

"Where'd you get this?" he exclaims, juice slipping down the corner of his mouth. "Haven, that is good." He pulls the plate to him. "Legia, you perfect doll, who'd you charm this time?"

"I didn't."

"I made it."

Chase stops, inspecting the half-eaten piece in his clutches. "It's damn good," he says, inhaling what is left on the plate.

I concentrate, palm directed at the empty plate. More fruit appears. Chase and Legia quickly tear into what is there, gushing over how delicious it is. My mind is far away from here. I want to talk to Declan and find out what is real and what is not.

I drop my face into my hands, then shove my fingers back through the strands. I grip the hair around the base of my skull and inhale until my lungs are full before letting my hands drop away. I want to talk to Declan for so many other reasons, but I wonder if he feels the same.

"What's going on with you." Legia has a piece of star fruit halfway to her mouth. Her eyes narrow. "You aren't thinking about staying locked up in here, are you?"

"Declan," I reply, fluffing my long burgundy hair over my shoulder. I have always enjoyed the way the cool, silky strands feel against my skin.

Her lips press together, and she sets the fruit down. "Have you talked to him yet?"

I shake my head. "Not yet. I don't know what to say."

She snorts through her nose and pops the fruit into her mouth. "Start with an apology, something better than that piss poor thing you said in the throne room, and then tell him you love him."

My jaw drops.

"What?" she gives me a curious look. "I saw the way you looked at him in the courtroom, all doe-eyed and blushing. Even if I didn't, I don't need to see how you look at him to know you're still in love. It broke you when we all thought he was dead, and it was like he never left after he was reinstated." She waves a hand. "Just tell him the truth."

# CHAPTER 23

The following morning, I meet Sordello in the practice field, but he informs me I have been summoned to face Declan and Selene as king and queen. I curl my lip at him.

"I will be there with you. They will not dare test me knowing how reliant they are upon us."

We dissipate to the throne room. Around me are the whispers and murmurs I have hated all my life. Somehow, they are different this morning, though. They no longer bother me. I stand tall, not caring to pay attention to them.

"You wanted to see me?" I train my eyes on Selene.

Declan is next to her, resting back on the cushion with his legs out straight. My eyes flicker to him, and I wrench them back to my sister. I do not want to look at Declan if Legia is honest about my obvious affections.

Selene stands, brushing wrinkles from her skirt. My eyes drop to the fitted, dark clothes and boots I wear. I roll my shoulders, thinking I should have worn something more appropriate.

"Yes, Morella, I requested your presence as the court has established what is to be done with you. Should you ever care to follow proper etiquette, you should arrive at the door and wait to be announced when the court is ready for you."

I roll my eyes and cross my arms. "Sorry. I don't actually know anything about proper etiquette." I bat my lashes and use a syrupy sweet voice. "Maybe you can teach me sometime?"

I draw a few strangled noises from around the room for my efforts. I drop the façade and raise my eyebrows. "I am here. There's no use in wasting precious time in dalliances not required." I cock a hip, resting weight solely on my left foot, the right in front of me.

She clears her throat and straightens her spine. Clasping her hands in front of her, she smiles around the room at the others. I keep my focus on her. "Jokes. Quaint for one of your station, tiresome nonsense for someone in mine. I have things that require attention." She indicates me with a wave of her hand. "You are an annoyance. You are confined within this palace. You are to be locked away within these walls as a prisoner."

Declan stands. The movement draws my eyes, and I try my best to stare at his boots. "We agreed to request you stay within palace walls, but you are free to roam the gardens."

I lift my eyes, shifting back to Selene. Her eyes are narrowed slits. She turns her face to his. Her lips move, whispered hissing reaching my ears, but I do not know what she says. My eyes are pulled to Declan as he crosses his arms. I shift my gaze back to my sister and away from his hard, lean body. I do not need to go all gooey-eyed and incur Selene's temper.

She faces me, forcing a grin. "If, at any point, it is determined that you have left the palace, you will be executed as the treacherous trash that you are. Do you understand me?" she begins nodding her head. "You are a prisoner within these walls, a prisoner for your crimes. You are in direct breach of the laws of Byron and Caleum. Your existence is unnatural and should not be. You have taken life. You are a liar, a thief, a treacherous little crumb that needs to be swept up by the servants after I have roasted your body and removed your poison from this world."

I raise a single brow, keeping my lips pressed together. I do not bother responding. I am not wasting my breath to tell her that my existence was not my choice, that I had no control over anything she is deeming to hold me accountable for. I was the dagger in Viktor's hand, and when I was more than his little tool, I attempted to kill him for all that he had done and used me to do.

I roll my shoulders and wait, keeping my lips pursed tight. Fighting, resisting is only going to inflame this situation and will not aid me. There is a rolling pride in my gut I know is from Sordello. I clear my throat and drop my chin at Selene.

Her smile becomes genuine, pleasure smeared across her delicate features. "You have been stripped of all rank, any titles you may once have had. You were declared dead, and the court will not reinstate you. You have no claim to the crown or the Byron name. You have no family, no possessions other than what is on your being, and no link to me or my position in any manner. Anything that was once yours is no longer yours."

My eyes snap to Declan, so I quickly look down to inspect my nails. I use a thumbnail to clean dirt from a couple of nails on the opposite hand. I shift my weight from one foot to the other and cross my arms. I blink at her, waiting, sure she is going to continue this degrading tirade.

Silence fills the hall as I wait. My eyes shift around the room, and I look over my shoulder at Sordello. I look back at Selene. "Have you finished your decree?"

"You are not to involve yourself in matters of the crown, in matters of politics, or in matters of war. Everything you touch, *you stain*," she stresses. "It turns to ash. It disintegrates."

Her smug tone matches the gleam in her eyes as she steps

forward to meet me. "You are a poison in this court. So, stay out of its affairs, stay away from those of importance within this court, and keep your treachery from destroying anything else." Standing toe to toe, she lowers her voice so no one else will hear. "This includes Declan Bard."

My eyes move over her shoulder to Declan. I nod, returning her gaze. "Mmm," I hum, for all to hear. "Sure. Anything else, *Sister*?" I emphasize the word, smiling at the end.

"I am not your sister," she hisses.

I smirk. "No, of course not. That would make things too complicated for you, wouldn't it?"

Her head jerks back. "There is nothing about you that affects me." She points a finger at her chest. "You," she says, pointing that same finger at me, "are not capable of affecting me."

I smirk, knowing full well she is lying. A throat clears, and Declan's voice rings around the room. "Ella, please. It will be best if you stay out of important matters until the court reaches a decision. Your future is not finalized, but the less you are involved in situations, the less precarious the court will feel at this time."

"Oh, her future is pretty certain." Selene turns to face him. "She is a murderer. She was declared dead by you."

At her words, I scan his face for some evidence of his feelings. The mention of him declaring me dead does not sway his features. He stares at her without expression.

"They claim her a spirit? Then she will return to Medius with the rest of them, or she will be killed here in Caleum." She turns back to me with a snarl. "You are nothing here. You have no home, no family, and no money. You will never be welcomed back at this court or any other. You are nothing at all."

Sordello steps next to me. "Careful with how you treat my daughter." The boom of his voice is quiet, but it ceases Selene's tirade. "I have established she is as good as royalty to you, and she has the entire collective as her family. I have tolerated your disrespect thus far, but no more. You will treat her with integrity."

The volume of his words is soft, but the tone is sharp-edged. I know he is angry. I turn to look at the shadows beneath his hood. "It's okay."

He rests a hand on my shoulder. "I was not there before."

"Really." I laugh. "'It's alright. This is the least of things, an absolute joke compared to what you did miss." I flourish my hand at Selene. "She doesn't bother me."

"Excuse me?" Selene snaps.

Declan has moved forward to stand next to her, his hand resting on her shoulder. The pose mirroring Sordello. The implication is clear. Sordello is supporting me, but Declan is supporting Selene. Something cold slithers through my stomach. I do my best to ignore it and breathe.

Declan inclines his head, his words as quiet as my father's. "This court will accept her stature as nobility. We will see her as your daughter and treat her with the same respect we give to you and all of your kind."

I glance at him and flash a small smile. There is no reaction in his expression, no change in the dark color of his eyes. I incline my head to him. "Thank you."

"I will request that you stay here in the palace and within the grounds."

I nod, swallowing the ball on the back of my tongue at his cool, detached voice. With him this close, touching her right in front of me, my chest aches. Cold seeps through my veins and lungs. I want to step forward and bury my face into his chest, inhale the scent of him, and feel his strong arms around me.

Instead, I dig my thumbnail into the tip of my pointer. I force a smile and make my best attempt at a curtsy. I am not going to make any promises or even agree, but I will allow them to think as they wish.

I turn away, Sordello's hand dropping from my shoulder. My eyes lock on the door. I need to be away from here. Declan touching her, siding with her, it is going to get the best of me.

Selene calls out to me. "Where do you think you are going?"

Every ounce of me wants to ignore her. She has made her point, and Declan has made his choice. I have no reason to be here or to say anything else.

Still, I pivot on my heels to meet her gaze. She has stepped toward me several paces. "You were not dismissed."

I cross my arms. "My apologies."

"Your Highness."

"Yes?" Color burns her cheeks at the scattered laughs about the room. I do my best to swallow my smile.

"How dare you?"

I sigh, dropping my arms to my side. "I am not fighting you. Please, don't do this."

"You will address me by—"

"Shut up."

Her words cease. I watch her mouth move without sound. I stare, watching her try to conjure words to no avail.

My eyes travel over the exposed black runes twisting around my forearm. I brush a finger against the lines, knowing one of the runes is Pith, responsible for being able to control lower beings.

I drop my finger away and tilt my head. Her mouth has stopped moving, her eyes glassy. I straighten my shoulders. "You may have a title, Selene, and you may be queen. You may have taken my place, taken my life, and you may cast me out, claim I am nothing. But do not for one second believe that you have power over me."

I step toe to toe with her. I meet her eyes. This close, I can see the unshed tears welling up, ready to spill over her lashes. The yellow of her eyes is ringed with gold, and once more, I remember how much more beautiful she is than I.

"I will never bow to you, *Sister*." I sneer at the term. "I will bend a knee. I will show loyalty and accept the rule of others, but it will never be you." I take a step back, my eyes never leaving hers. "Choose your words and actions carefully. A title is not power."

I turn my back on her and stride out of the room.

# CHAPTER 24

$\mathcal{I}$ spend my day in the gardens. I do what I can to assist others, fixing tools and mending broken bodies. I keep my head down and my mouth shut, listening to gossip and whispers, anything that might lend knowledge to where Viktor is.

When the light starts to fade from the sky, I head for the dining hall. I sit at the end of a table, making my own food. Chase and Legia join me, making requests for fruits. Seth and Marcus arrive, and the four of them talk, even drawing a laugh or two from me.

I keep distracted by Legia's constant chatter and making fruit until Declan arrives. He sits on the other side, with Marcus and Seth, the furthest from me, but when he sits, my eyes connect with his. I lick my lips, his eyes flickering at the movement.

Legia elbows me in the ribs. "Ow," I complain exaggeratedly, rubbing my side.

She wrinkles her nose. "We are out of fruit."

I focus on the plate and more appears. "Happy?"

She looks at her goblet. "Nearly." Her head lifts, shoulders back, neck craning from side to side. "This war is killing service."

I roll my eyes. "Would you like wine?"

"Not from you." She hugs the goblet to her chest, covering the top with her other hand. "That was awful, and you are never, ever to make wine again."

"It wasn't that bad." I reach for the goblet.

She shakes her head with wide eyes. "It was terrible. I thought Selene snuck poison into it while we weren't watching."

My eyes flicker toward Declan to find his are still on me. He leans forward, resting crossed arms on the tabletop. His eyebrows lift and press together. I bite my lip, but words fizzle in my throat as Selene sits next to him. My eyes roll away from him, and I sigh.

"Well, there went that." I mutter the words under my breath as I stand.

"What was that, urchin," she snaps back, wrapping her arms around his closest bicep.

Seth leans forward, looking across Declan. "No one actually wants you here."

Marcus runs a hand over his face then plucks a grape. "I second the motion." He lobs the grape at Selene. It bounces off her forehead, and she jerks. Color rises in her cheeks.

I try not to grin, knowing it will only encourage them. Declan could have easily caught the grape if he wanted to. Knowing he let it hit her warms my heart.

"It's fine. I'm tired." I start to back away, but Legia grabs my wrist in an iron grip.

"First of all, you leaving does not negate that I will carry this motion. Second, before you go...?" She looks to the plate.

A giggle escapes me. "Alright."

I close my eyes, picturing an enormous amount of fruit, red and blue berries, dragons' food, and star fruit. The stream of energy pulsates through my chest, giving me a lingering sweet taste on my tongue. When I open my eyes, the whole end of the table is covered in a heap of fruit.

I wink at her. "That ought to hold you until tomorrow."

She lets go of my wrist. "Now, if you will only get rid of the snake in the garden."

"Darling." Chase kisses her temple, a smile to his voice.

Legia wrinkles her nose, and I take the opportunity to slip away. I head for my rooms and lock myself inside. Leaning against the door, I concentrate on feeling the collective. I breathe out, dissipating to most of the energy.

Opening my eyes, I find myself in the middle of tents. I peer around at the collected canvas constructs going as far as my eye can see. A group of men approaches, all muscular, carrying swords strapped to their bodies. They are talking, laughing as they move in a group, and I skip between two tents. I wait as they pass by. They have not noticed me, or if they did, they do not care.

A sigh of relief washes out of me, and I start to move between tents. I avoid the sound of voices and other beings as I try to find my way out of the maze to the outer edge. The position of the moon above tells me I am moving east through the camp, toward what I hope is the active war zone.

Standing between two tents on the edge of the camp, I stare out across the desolate landscape. I peek around to see if anyone else is about before starting to move out. There are gouges in the ground, evidence of massive claw strokes. I weave past a couple of craters and then stop. Hands on hips, my eyes rove over the barren, flat wasteland.

I need more information before plowing headlong in the wrong direction; information I am not to be given by those who have it. I kneel to the ground, placing my hand in the dirt where something was dragged through. Cimeria was full of marshes and wetlands, but the earth here is dried and destroyed now.

Pushing up, I grit my teeth and turn back to the camp. There must be a setup; somewhere, someone is mapping out the enemy and information. I just need to find it.

I start to work through the tents, staying out of sight. The further in I get, the harder moving becomes, the process turning tedious. The sky is tinging with light before I find the largest tent in the center of the camp, my hours of roaming finally yielding fruit. I slink around the edges, looking through gaps in the canvas walls.

Inside I hear muffled voices. I sense Sordello and Malik are the spirits inside then catch a clear view of Seth standing by the wall, leaning against a support pole. He picks at his nails with a dagger.

"There's no use in that. There's no use in headlong fights. We are massacred every time."

"Keep your army back. Allow us to make the charge." Malik.

"Young King," Sordello speaks with a heavy weight to his voice, "my daughter can be of great use."

"No." The growl from Declan is full of venom.

I shift my view through the crack in the canvas paneling. Declan reclines on a rickety wooden chair. His legs are stretched out on another chair. He is dressed in a dark, fitted shirt and jeans with boots, much more casual than he was dressed for dinner.

His high cheekbones are colored with fury, his nostrils flaring. "Ella stays at Byron."

My mouth goes dry. I wonder if he would execute me for leaving the palace, what he would do if he knew I was here right now. Part of me wants to rush in there and demand my chance to fight. But I must be smarter, not let my temper best me and ruin this chance.

I slide along the outside of the tent, peeking between cracks. I stop listening to their debate, craning to peek through the cracks of adjoining tents. I have yet to find a map, but with the soul star rising, I need to meet Sordello at the practice field.

I dissipate to the field. I drop to the ground, planting nose to knees. I bite my lip at the intense pull in my hamstrings but force myself to stay in the position. Easing into the stretch works much better, but for now, I need to maintain pretenses that I have been here for a while.

"I believe you were ordered to remain on these premises under pain of death." Sordello's warning carries low on the breeze. I wonder if I heard it or just know his thoughts.

"Can you prove I didn't?" I lift my chin, keeping my torso folded forward to release my tight muscles.

"If I were compelled to speak truthfully in the matter, yes." He stands, sword tip dug into the ground with both hands resting on the hilts.

I pull one leg in at an angle and drop my head to my outstretched leg. "I was careful. No one saw me."

"The entire collective is able to feel you. None of us are going to reveal your presence, but you should be cautious."

I stand to face him, and his arms cross. "I can't just sit here and do nothing. You can't expect me to stay here and let others fight for me." I dig my toe into the dirt. "I mean, I heard you. You asked to let me fight."

"Yes, but I received the answer I expected. You are not ready, but I am trying to garner support for when you are." He holds a sword out. "As for what I expect from you? I expect you to be smart. I expect you to be careful. I expect that you will do as you perceive to be right. That is all that I expect of you."

I look at my feet and nod with burning eyes and a lump in my throat. Viktor never would have responded that way. He would have given me a direct order. He would have told me how to act. I exhale, lifting my gaze to Sordello's shadowed face with an urge to hug him.

"Alright, let's do this." I take a stance, gripping the hilt of my wooden sword in clammy palms.

The hood inclines, and he attacks. We skirmish, and I do my best to fend off the attacks while parring with my own. He disarms me, then knocks me to the ground.

I groan and roll over, dirt and my shirt sticking to my sweating skin. I push myself to my knees and lift my eyes straight to Declan's face.

He stands a few feet away, leaning against a post with dark eyes. I swallow hard, hoping he has not been there long. Getting my butt kicked by Sordello is humiliating enough without an audience. I regain my feet, putting my back to Declan.

Sordello holds a hand up to me. "Wait, Ella." His face shifts over my shoulder. "Is there something requiring attention?"

"Yes."

Sordello nods. "Then we are done for this day." I feel a glowing happiness in my chest. "You are doing fine. Keep practicing. Keep helping the wounded here." His arm waves in the direction of the gardens. "You're doing important things."

I make a face of disbelief and roll my eyes. I chuck the wooden sword off to the side. It clatters against the stone, and I wipe the grime off my hands and onto my pants. Without answering, I dissipate to my room, heading for a shower then to the gardens.

When the sky begins to dim, I walk to the dining hall. I sit and make enough fruit for dozens to eat, but only Marcus joins me. I look from the pile of fruit as he drops to the bench. He plucks up an orange and begins to peel the rind.

"Just you and me tonight."

I bob my head. "I'm noticing that." I glance around. "Is something... Did something happen?" I keep my voice low.

"If something has happened, I have not heard of it, nor am I at liberty to say." He arches his back in a stretch. "Every few days, Chase and Declan bring themselves and others back from the frontlines for a decent bed and food, so they will not be gone long."

I wince. "Excellent. For now, it's the Byron family locked in a stalemate." I eye Selene a few tables over with Skylar and Elizabeth. "Has there been any news of Viktor?"

Marcus frowns at me. "I am not at liberty to say."

I furrow my brows and glare at him. "Seriously?"

He pops a piece of orange into his mouth and chuckles. "Yes." He peels more of the rind away to expose the yellow flesh beneath. "Selene is out for blood."

I scoff.

He shakes his head. "We are doing our best, wrangling with her, but she is determined to watch you burn, and alive if possible."

I grimace. "That would hurt."

"She is quite piqued with you."

I roll my shoulders, looking around. I pretend to find interest with the wood beams high above us. "I've noticed." I bring myself to look at him. "Then again, she's always been this way."

He presses a finger to his lips, chewing. "No, not quite like this. This is worse." He sighs and rubs a hand down his face. "Something changed."

I shrug. Picking up a piece of dragons' food, I run my thumb over the green hide. "Declan."

"How dare you speak the king's name, filth." I lift my eyes to see Selene sitting down at the table. Elizabeth sits on her one side and Skylar on the other. My sister tosses her perfect curls over her shoulder and reaches for the fruit. She holds an apple aloft and inspects it. "Who did you kill for this?"

Marcus smacks the table. "Dammit, don't. If either of you would like to recall, we are family."

She wipes the apple on the front of her blouse, then takes a bite. She moans, eyes closing as she chews. "Divine." Her eyes open. "And certainly not for the likes of you to enjoy." She makes a shooing motion at me with her hand. "Be gone and be careful who you speak of."

"She has every right to say Declan's name."

Selene releases a titter and beams across the way at me. "You claim she has the right, and yet, Declan has not been to see her, to speak with her." She clicks her tongue against her teeth. "Declan has moved on. He wants nothing to do with murdering garbage. She lost the right to speak his name."

I drag my nail along the surface of the dragons' food, watching it split under the pressure. My veins hiss with joy at the idea of splitting her skin in the same way. Clear juice flows out of the wound, and the taste of blood lingers in my nose and on my tongue.

I set it on the table and turn my torso to Marcus. "I heard women were removed from the frontlines, so if Chase and Seth are on the frontlines, where is Legia?"

"Legia has been shipped to the frontlines to die as one of your precious, little supporters."

Marcus' face whips to her. "Legia is there of her own free will."

Elizabeth shakes her head. She rolls an orange between palms. "Wyatt tells another story."

Marcus runs a hand over his face. "Why?" His gaze fixated on Selene. "Why are you three insisting on causing her pain?"

Selene's crystal blue eyes stretch. "I simply do not care for murderers."

My eyes cut to Marcus. There is no logical argument he can make on my behalf. Still, his eyes narrow. "You were at the mercy of Viktor. You, yourself, have committed acts on his behalf."

Her lips turn white, pressed together. The color lifts to her cheeks. Marcus scoffs, head jerking back.

"And you." One of his crooked fingers indicates Skylar. "You supported Viktor. You went after Declan without a qualm."

I place a hand on Marc's shoulder. His golden gaze falls on me. The hard fury there draws a wince, but I hold steady. I shake my head.

His brows draw together, and I give my best court smile. His brows lift, lines creasing his forehead. I roll my eyes to the girls on the other side of the table.

"S'not worth it," I manage through a forced yawn.

"You deserve a fair trial." He shakes his head. "Actually, you don't deserve to have to suffer even that. And," he glowers at our sister, "you damn well know that's the truth. You know what Viktor did to us, to all of us. None of us should be held accountable for the actions forced upon us."

Selene laughs. "Oh, dear brother, do watch your words. Those speaking in favor of Ella are dying fast these days."

I stand. "Enjoy the fruit." I step over the bench. "I'd hate for the energy I spent making it to be wasted."

Elizabeth chokes on her orange. Selene turns a lovely shade of green. I squeeze Marcus' shoulder and dissipate to my rooms.

# CHAPTER 25

*I* double and triple-check that my door is locked before dissipating south. This time, I start at the main tent, picking up where I left off.

Somewhere there must be charts, maps of where Viktor's armies are, where the Byron army is, where Viktor might be suspected of being. I need to find them, and then I will have a direction to start.

I find a small tent in the ring around the central source tent. It is not part of the ring but instead positioned inside the ring and outside of the central tent. I slide to a crack in the burlap paneling, moving around the tent, looking inside for an occupant.

Deciding it is empty, I slide inside. I eye the map tacked out flat on the rickety table. Little figurines are sprawling across the surface, and I stand there, trying to make heads or tails of the thing.

A miniature tent is tacked to the map. I circle it with my finger, moving my finger south to a grouping of red figurines. I pick one up, inspecting the miniature demon, surprised by the weight of it.

I set it down with the others. The tiny demons are scattered through the south, most in clusters. There are single demons here and there to the west, one even further north near Cato.

To the west, a taller, black figurine catches my eye. My lips twist to the side in amusement. A king chess piece. Viktor. Declan's twisted sense of humor must have created this map.

"Ella?"

I jerk, my heart leaping into my throat. I rest a hand over my heart and breathe. Sending a silent thanks to Haven, I smile at him. "Samuel."

He appears baffled. "What are you doing?"

I wave at the map. "Looking at this."

"Aren't you restricted to the palace? In Byron?" He pauses, his head swiveling around. He glances back at me with a twisted face and draws in air, so his chest swells. "Seth!"

Samuel's shout rings in my ears. I stare with open mouth and wide eyes. "What the—"

"Samuel?" Seth's voice calls out. "Sam, what's wrong?" Seth is coming closer by the sound of it.

I dissipate to another part of the camp. My elements collide harshly at the abrupt and poor dissipation. I grimace, my body splintering in pain. I bend over, then drop to a knee.

My muscles spasm with the pain of dissipating too fast. I grit my teeth and force my body to move. I glare with blurry vision at a nearby tent, hands on hips as I catch my breath. Gemma. Samuel. Those I thought of as friends are against me, and it rankles worse than dissipating too fast.

I look west. Tents as far as I can see sprawl into the distance, but westward is where I need to go. I step out of sight, sliding between tents as others approach. Haven help me if someone else sees me. Selene will enjoy ripping body parts off until I am dead.

I can change my appearance, altering my elemental composition, but that is not enough. I puff my cheeks and release a silent sigh. I need help. I need someone who can track, someone who can help me follow westward.

I curse under my breath and think of Legia. Coolness trickles through me. I scrunch my eyes shut and wince, giving in to the separation of my elements, in no hurry to go through discomfort again so soon.

As I piece together, a sharp inhale of breath makes me cringe. "Sorry! I didn't mean to."

I brace myself and crack one eye open. Legia is staring, bright blue eyes stretched wide enough for me to see their entire orbs. I open the other eye and relax as I realize I am in a small tent with just her. She has a shirt gripped to her naked body.

"You scared the ever-living piss out of me." She is snarling at me, but for her, the volume is low. She turns her back to me, rummaging through clothes on the low cot. "What are you doing here?"

I avert my eyes, trying not to let her words affect me. Still, my eyes burn. "Um…"

"If Selene finds out…" Legia huffs. She grunts. "Haven, if Selene finds out this and that you'll be dead, and dead for real. Chase says spirits can die if 'their bodies are destroyed enough. Selene finding out…" Legia chortles. "I wish she would. Let her dare try. 'There's no way, no freaking way."

I look back to my long time friend sitting on the edge of the cot, working fingers through her hair. I nod. "I know Selene wants me dead," I whisper. "I know it's possible too. If she catches me. And I know she's waiting and watching like a hawk for me to screw up, but I can't just…" I exhale, long and slow.

Legia's eyes sparkle at me. "Sit on your ass and do nothing? Wait for someone else to clean up this mess?" Deft fingers are braiding her hair. "If you were okay with it, I'd question your merit to be queen." She ties the braid off and runs her hands over her scalp and the braid. "What's the plan?"

A timid smile creeps across my lips. "You're okay with this?"

She rolls her eyes at me and tosses the braid to hang down her back. "Okay with it? Selene is belittling you, degrading you, and spreading lies about you. Haven, the things I hear about you around this camp." She shivers. Her features draw in on themselves as her gaze drops to the ground. "She's evil. Pure flipping freaking evil."

Legia inhales, crossing her legs, leaning forward to clasp her hands over her knees. "She's after Declan, you know."

I smirk. "I know."

Legia shakes her head. "I listened to her telling Elizabeth about how he loves her and would do anything for her as she was touting that gaudy ring she stuck on her own finger." Legia scoffs. "As if. If anything, he hates his betrothal to her. She bought that ring herself, according to Chase and Seth. Declan won't talk about it, or her." Legia makes a face of disgust.

"He's been dark ever since his reinstatement, but it's worse now, so much worse." She trails off and begins to twiddle her thumbs, fingers laced over her knee.

I cross my arms and shift my weight. "I don't know if he hates his betrothal." I wince.

Legia laughs, head tipped back, humor spilling from her chest in droves. Watching her is contagious, a smile tugging one side of my lips back. Her face turns red, and she swipes tears from the corners of her eyes as she focuses on me.

"Haven," she chortles and wrinkles her nose. "I needed a laugh like that. There's been so little to laugh about lately." She looks up, blinking rapidly then beams at me. "There wasn't a sober moment in his life since he declared you dead, and there wasn't a kind word he's ever said about that snake. He's been suffering and hiding at the bottom of a bottle. And you still haven't talked to him."

She narrows her eyes at me. I frown, glancing at my feet as I shuffle in the dirt. I open my mouth to tell her what I saw, but

Chase materializes in front of me. His back is to me as he drops to his knees.

"Hello, my beautiful, gorgeous," he clasps her hands in his, lifting one to his face, then the other followed by exaggerated lip-smacking sounds, "absolutely stunning ginger snap."

She giggles, a blush spreading across her freckled face. "Chase!"

He makes a playful growling sound as he tackles her back to the cot, kissing her face. She shrieks with laughter, trying to cover her face from his amorous attack.

"I am going to lick every inch of you."

I gag on a laugh, and he bolts upright, head whipping around to me. "Ella!" His yelp is loud, drawing a cringe from me and a whack to his arm from Legia. He looks embarrassed and rubs at the spot on his bicep. "Sorry."

I shrug. "Ginger snap?"

He gives a daft expression. "I love ginger snaps."

"That's gross." I grin. "But you two are cute."

He sits up, legs over the edge of the cot. Legia curls around his back, chin resting on his shoulder. "When you face off against demons every day and are just happy that the one you love is still alive, then you can judge us."

I bite my lower lip and make a divot in the ground with the toe of my boot. "I am, every time I see Declan."

"I know." She kisses Chase on the cheek. "It's been a long day; I'm cranky."

I bob my head and cross my arms. "I get that." I let out a sigh. "I wish I could help."

"You are. You're going after Viktor."

"What?" Chase cocks a brow at me.

"That's the plan."

He groans, leaning over, head in his hands. "Selene is going to go ballistic. Declan is barely keeping her from ripping your throat out with her bare hands."

I snort through my nose. "She doesn't have it in her."

Chase lets out a hollow laugh. "She does. She's been salivating over the idea of watching you burn, and Declan's having a constant conniption about it."

Chase scrubs his hands over his buzz-cut hair. "Ah," he sits up, resting back into Legia. "Fuck it. Viktor needs to go, and you're the only one who stands a chance at getting the job done." My former tutor snickers. "Don't tell Declan I said that. He's made up his mind that he's the only one capable."

I roll my eyes, knowing damn good and well Declan would think that. I know he's curtailed in his role as king, and I know what he is capable of. "He probably is. Probably, the best chance we have would be him and me going after Viktor together."

"Oh," Legia moans, "that's brilliant. He wouldn't tell Selene either."

"Darling." There is a warning to the term of endearment.

"What?" She snaps back with a glower, craning to meet his eyes.

"Declan is never going to agree to that."

"Well, fine." She huffs and turns her cerulean gaze upon me. "Ella can do it on her own."

I grimace. "No, that's why I'm here. I need help." Their eyes both stretch wider at my words. "I can't track."

Legia perks, eyes dancing. "But I can."

Chase shakes his head again. "No. It's bad enough Ella runs the risk of someone realizing she is missing." He sighs. "If both of you are missing together? It's too obvious." His eyes gaze at me from beneath heavy lids. "It's too much of a risk, and if Selene finds out Legia is aiding and abetting...?"

I wince. "That's not going to end well. She's consumed with trying to destroy anyone who will support me and—"

"She'll take any opportunity to eliminate Legia from court," Chase finishes for me. He tips his head back, staring at the canvas top. "My wife..." he stops and beams at her. "Haven, I love calling you that."

Legia giggles and taps the end of his nose. "And I love when you call me that."

He faces me. "She's brilliant, she's an enigma, and Selene can't attack her the way she's going after some. Selene's got too much support, so any chance she'd have to destroy Legia would be capitalized on. We need to be smarter than she is. We need to formulate a plan of attack and protect our dwindling pieces."

Legia wrinkles her nose. "You're talking like this is a game of chess."

"It is." His head rests against her shoulder, eyes slipping shut. She kisses his temple, wrapping an arm around his chest. "The usual suspects cannot be involved. Declan, Seth, me, you, we can't get involved. Selene is watching, waiting for any teeny-tiny window of opportunity." He sighs. "We need unassuming pawns that she isn't going to notice."

I bob my head along and then shift my weight from one foot to the other. "Makes sense." I breathe out low and slow. "Gemma and Samuel are out too."

"I wouldn't trust Gemma to even ask her for help, and she's no good to us in any case. We need trackers, fighters, not someone to fix a boo-boo." Legia's eyes roll. "What's wrong with Samuel?"

"He caught me looking at what I assume is Declan's map and yelled for Seth."

Chase winces. "That's bad."

"That's Selene." I shrug. "She's got everyone convinced I'm —I mean, she's not wrong, I am a murderer—but they all think... You know."

Legia nods. "We absolutely do, we absolutely agree, and we abso-fucking-lutely are still on your side."

Chase gives her a weak smile, only half of his mouth

conforming. "Selene is systematically destroying your name and reputation, going after anyone who claims to be your friend or is brave enough to speak against her on your behalf. It's interesting, really, to see how many are coming to your defense, and those are only the ones brave enough to speak out. You've got a hell of a lot more supporters than I ever realized." He stretches his legs out in front of him. "Selene even put a good bit of time in today trying to convince Canamore and me that you are a danger to Caleum. Not that it worked," he grins wide and winks at me.

"It's easier for her to get rid of Ella if she alienates her. What about asking the spirits for help? They aren't going to hand Ella over."

"Too obvious. Selene is out for blood, and she is much more conniving and intelligent than we have ever given her credit for." He gives me a wry smile. "She's really sunk her teeth into Declan and the crown."

I lean back on my heels as the memory of her straddling him smacks me in the face. "I'm aware."

"Haven, but I cannot even imagine why in the world she might ever believe he would want her."

My stomach clenches and churns. "Because." They stare at me. I convince myself I can do this, I can say those words aloud. "Because he—"

Legia claps her hands in excitement. "Oh, oh! I know. I know the perfect man for the job. Well, men, really." She wrinkles her nose. "They're warriors, but they're perfect, they are. They can track, and they can work together to take down a demon, so they will be able to keep you safe."

"I can handle a demon." I sound more defensive than intended.

Her eyes narrow at me. "Have you faced one yet? They're resistant to magic, and I don't think you can punch them. These two are the only pair that can kill a demon other than the Bards." Legia rolls her eyes. "And really like the Bards, they don't even need to team up, but all the others work in teams of four or five."

I lift my eyebrows. "They sound impressive."

Chase sighs. "Now, to find out if they are willing to help us."

# CHAPTER 26

$\mathcal{I}$ meet Sordello at the crack of dawn and train until the soul star rises. The heat is beginning to beat down, sweat making tendrils of hair stick to my neck and face.

I lean against a post and toss the sword to my feet. He pulls back, still at the ready. "I'm done for the day."

His shoulders roll forward, and the wood sword drops to his side. I run hands over my arms, swollen and pink skin disappearing as I feed healing magic through my flesh.

Sordello's sword disappears. "You were at the encampment again." My head bobbles as I keep my eyes to the ground. "I know I cannot stop you, my daughter. There is nothing that can stop you if your mind is made, but please, *please*," he stresses, and one of his heavily armored hands lands on my shoulder with the sound of chinking metal, "I do not want to experience the pain of losing you. I heard you were spotted."

I roll my eyes and peer at his hidden visage. "There's no proof I was there. I'm being careful. I promise."

He leaves me with a sense of insecurity looming in my chest. I kick at the sword, feeling I have been struggling with the weapon for far too long. Sordello's fear mingles with my frustrations, and I decide to beat against a post for a while.

Several days on end has left me exhausted as I trudge to my rooms. I shower and lay down on my bed. My eyes drift close, my limbs heavy.

The memory of Declan telling me I am beautiful, down on one knee before me, plays out in my mind. I feel excited, thrilled, happiness as I accept. My head bounces on my neck emphatically as tears of happiness spring to my eyes. Declan stands, sliding the ring over my knuckle and seating it on my ring finger before he spins us in circles.

My head is tipped back, and I am laughing and crying all at once. He sets me down, one arm wrapped around me, pressing against my lower back to keep me against him. His other hand reaches for me, resting along my jaw. His shimmering silver eyes look deep into mine.

"Haven, Ella," he breathes. For a moment, I think he is going to kiss me, but his hand shifts. His fingers dig into the side of my neck as his hand closes around the base of my jaw. "Do you really think I can forgive you? For everything you've done?"

He sneers down at me as confusion blossoms in my mind. I struggle to breathe past his hand clamped down on my throat. "Dec?"

He starts to squeeze his hand tighter, and I grab at his wrist. "Please, Dec... I can't... I can't breathe."

Blood is building pressure behind my eyes, and they feel ready to burst. My lungs are starting to burn. I try to pull in air, try to breathe, but I cannot. He has my airway crushed beneath both hands now. I pull uselessly at his wrists. My neck hurts. There is so much pressure between my ears, and behind my eyes, it is excruciating.

I bolt up, a hand to my throat, gasping for air, eyes bouncing wildly around the room. There is no one and nothing but me. I breathe in rapid succession and try to calm myself.

I drop my face into my hands and sob. My whole body is wracked and shudders violently, feeling the pinprick of tears beneath my lids. I do my best to hold back, to keep the sorrow in.

"Ella." My name draws my eyes to Erac, coming closer. His face is pinched with concern. "Are you alright, sweetheart?"

I drag the heels of my palms under leaking eyes and look to the ceiling. I purse my lips, bobbing my head. "Fine."

"You are not fine." His voice is sharp-edged. He sits next to me on the bed. He brushes loose strands of my hair away from my face and over my shoulder. "You are hurting. Your heart." His fingers trail over my collarbone and rest just above my breast. "It is broken."

I turn my face to meet his gaze. This close, I can make out silver and black flecks in his plum eyes. A dark ring of violet circles the iris. They blink at me, opening wide, staring into my soul.

His fingers are warm through the thin fabric of my shirt. I shiver, looking away, swallowing my heartbreak. "Yes."

He inclines his head. His fingers dance over my shoulder, then down my back as he nudges forward, closer. "Your would-be-king has torn you asunder. Cast you out. Abandoned you. Left you broken."

His words are softer than his caress as his hand strokes my back. I pull my knees to my chest and hug them close. "He didn't cast me out or abandon me."

Erac pulls me against him. I do not fight, falling against him. He kisses the top of my head and cuddles me. "He keeps you locked away, cooped in this palace as a prisoner. He gives you no thought or any of his time."

I sigh. "Selene has me locked away as a prisoner, and that's only because otherwise, she's worried I'll take the crown away from her."

He rubs a hand between my shoulder blades, then shifts

behind to massage my shoulders. "The crown should be of no consequence to you."

*He is right. I have no business being queen,* the demon hisses in the back of my mind. It's pleased with our history.

"Your thoughts are negative." His features draw inward in a pinched scowl. "I only meant you should take your rightful place in Medius next to Sordello." He meets my eyes, grinning. "And me."

My brows push together. "What?"

"As peacekeeper, leader, mediator." His hand flourishes. "Call them what you want, but they are at the forefront of the collective. Sordello. Malik. Orso." A forlorn shadow steals his expression. "Virgil. He was a leader too." His voice drops to a whisper.

Erac rests his cheek on my head. I feel his muscles moving as he speaks. "He was not a leader, but *the* leader. When he decided to stay in Caleum, Sordello took his place. The collective thought it best to have more than a single leader after the debacle."

Erac stops, scoffing a chuckle. "The spirits think of Sordello's relationship with Wyoma as a debacle, but..." He pulls back to stare down into my eyes. There is something there. A spark, an ignition I do not want to name. "But, I think you are the best thing to happen to this world, to any world."

His face is looming closer. Those violet eyes shift from mine, dropping lower. His head tilts.

My heart is racing, pounding, trying to break my breastbone. The tip of my tongue darts along my lower lip. His eyes shift to mine, then flicker closed.

*He is going to kiss me. Erac. Erac is going to kiss me.*

I can smell him. He smells of campfires and cool air with a warm breeze. It is a vast difference from Declan's scent of musk and metal. I sit, pulling my body away from Erac's grasp.

"What are you doing?" My voice is shrill. I am not sure who

I am talking to. I shove him away. Maybe I shove myself away from him. "This is wrong."

"Wrong?" Anger flares to life in his eyes. The purple blazes. "I am the son of Virgil. You are the daughter of Sordello."

I throw my body forward off the bed. My skin feels too tight. "That means nothing."

"Nothing?" he snarls. "We are prince and princess of Medius. Your place here in Caleum is no more. You are an outcast. They call you murderer and abomination." His shaking finger is pointed out toward the city. "They scorn you, hate you, curse your name and spit upon the ground. You are not wanted, not even welcomed. And your precious, minuscule, would-be-king has all but forgotten you. He has found a new bride, a new way to claim the power of the crown."

I step back away from Erac. My arms curling into and over my chest. He stands, stepping toward me as I find my back against the wall.

He appears wild, looming over me. "He treats you like garbage, discarded when no longer useful to slake his lust for power."

"No, that's not—"

"Did you really think he came back for you?" His eyes dart down and back up my body. "He knows nothing of what makes you special. You're just a pretty face to him." He flicks a piece of hair over my shoulder. "He saw you as a steppingstone, stomping you down and dispersing your secrets as weapons against you to keep you where he could control you."

"No."

"How do you think she knew?" Erac's hoarse sneer sends shivers down my spine. "He told her, knowing he could no longer control you."

I am shaking my head. "No. No, you're wrong. Seth. She knew because of Seth, because of the bond."

"Then tell me," Erac demands as he leans in, hands around my waist, body firmly weighing mine into the wall. His lips graze my ear, warm breath drawing the hairs to stand. "If Selene wanted the crown so badly, why did she wait until now?"

Air is difficult to pull in. My heart is lurching and skipping. My mouth is dry, flapping open. Words are failing my numbed mind. All I can conjure is, "No."

He snarls, smacking an open palm against the wall next to my head. "Yes. Yes, a thousand times. I told you, he was controlling you, using you, raping your innocence for his own gains."

My ears are burning as much as my eyes. I lean in toward Erac. "Declan would never."

Erac laughs from deep in his gut. "Oh, but sweetheart, he did, he has." His eyes narrow. One of his fingers draws over my cheek. "But it is of no consequence. No, none at all. You should be my wife in Medius. This is no place for you, and these elementals that have discarded you are not your friends. They do not deserve your loyalties."

I grind my teeth and inhale to scream at him as loud as I can manage. "I am so sick of being told whom I should marry." I shove him away from me with both hands on his chest. "Sick of being treated like a pawn, like a piece to move across shiny squares." I shove him again. "Sick of being told what to do." I step into the next push, and he stumbles back a pace. "I'm done. Do you hear me? Done!"

We stare at each other as I pant. I swallow to soothe my aching throat and catch my breath. I lean back against the wall and glare at him.

"The only person who is going to decide who I should marry is me," I tell him, pressing a finger against my chest. "And you are *never* going to spew garbage about Declan again. He's twice the man you think he is and three times better than you."

Erac inhales sharply with a hiss. "Ella, I have only ever—"

I kick away from the wall and point to the door. "Get out."

He bares his teeth at me but dissipates, leaving me alone. I stand there, trembling, trying to wrap my head around the words and emotions streaming through me in a violent torrent. I ball my fists, squeezing as tight as possible.

# CHAPTER 27

*L*egia and I sneak through camp in cloaks I created of canvas. Our faces are altered, erring on the side of caution as we move through the camp. Legia dances between the tents with grace and a light step. I work to keep up with her, knowing the camouflaging cloak will make it hard to pin her down if I lose sight of her.

She sidesteps, grabs me, pulling me inside a shelter. I gasp at the suddenness. "Damnatus, your grip is like iron."

"You try gripping a bow for hours on end and see how manly your hands get."

I snicker. "I didn't say manly."

"Shut up." She drops her hood, and I realize there are two men watching us.

Two dryad warriors. I raise a brow at them. Dryads typically took to being healers and scholars, occasionally joining the mage guild and becoming shamans.

I eye the one closest to me. Bald, wide, flat nose and orange eyes. I drop my hood around my shoulders, letting loose the control I maintain on the elements to return our features to normal.

"Gamal?"

"No name?" His rich voice carries surprise.

The other man is tall and thin with darker skin than even Gamal or Marcus. In fact, his skin is akin to black, his bright amber eyes widen. He lets out a low whistle. "Queen Morella."

Both straighten their backs and square off with Legia. Gamal's eyes narrow. "They call her killer, a disgrace..." He spits at the ground. "And say she's loyal to Viktor."

Legia's eyes narrow, and her face pulls tight. "That's piss lies from Selene to keep Ella from the crown."

"And Declan," I mutter under my breath. The men eye me with distrust. I hold my hands in a defensive pose. "I am not loyal to Viktor."

"Says you." The other man grips the hilt of his sword. "Not much good in your word."

Legia plants hands on her hips. "Says me. Are you going to question me?"

Gamal shakes his head. He shifts his body toward me. "You were asking for information, looking to know plans, asking if we knew where Viktor was. How do I know you aren't here gathering information for him and his dogs?"

I give him a quizzical sneer. "How's the shoulder?"

He glares. "Give me one good reason I shouldn't hand you over?"

I scoff. "Because I'd have to let you?"

His chin drops to his chest, and he glares at me with disbelief from the tops of his eyes.

I sigh and offer open hands to him. "Because I want to find Viktor."

"To help him," the other man snarls.

"To kill him!" I snap back in a hushed shout. Gamal's head jerks. His face displays open shock. "I am going to find him and kill him."

Gamal and the other man exchange glances. Chatter wafts

through the air, muffled by the tent as the silence grows. Gamal returns his gaze to me. He eyes me, full of distrust. His gaze moves over to Legia. "Can she do it?"

"Do what? Kill Viktor? Absolutely."

"She was said to have tried before," the dark man says. "What's different this time?"

I bite my lip, looking to Legia. She lifts her eyebrows and stares back. I shake my head. "Me. I'm different." I cross my arms and shift my weight. "I thought just unleashing power would be enough. I was wrong. I lacked conviction, and I promise you, that is not a mistake I will make again."

My words are a sharp hiss, hanging in the dead air. Legia steps next to me, putting an arm around me. I give her a timid smile with lips pressed together.

The darker man lets go of his sword and steps forward. "Lumor." He offers me his hand.

I take it, heat radiating into me, the callouses rougher than mine. "Ella."

His large eyes are set narrow in his face. Black stubble clings to his lower jaw and the top of his head. Those dazzling eyes meet mine, dark chocolate melted on a hot day. "You helped my brother." His eyes cut to Gamal. "For that, I will help you." He squeezes my hand then lets go. "What do you need?"

"I need to find Viktor. He's heading west according to the map, but I could use help with tracking him."

"You need a tracker." Gamal looks at Legia and inclines his head. "She's been recommended for guild leader, an expert on the subject."

My head swivels to Legia. "Guild leader? What? When did this happen?"

She fights a grin. "Yes. Just this morning. I'm excited, but I'm not. I'm not sure if I want the position. I know how much Chase struggles with family duties and being a leader. I'm going to be duchess, that's much more than Chase handles, and I don't know if I'll ever see him if..." She flips her braid over her shoulder, her face hardening. "Not the time."

I lean my shoulder against hers. "It's always the time."

"After Viktor's dead, but until then, my life choices are bottom of the list." She faces Gamal. "I cannot help her. Someone else needs to. Someone Selene is not going to be paying attention to. Besides," Legia continues, crossing her arms, "you and Lumor are excellent trackers as well as capable of taking down demons."

Gamal and Lumor exchange glances. Neither appears happy. "Look," I interject into their silent conversation. "I am asking for your help. You can say no without repercussions. This is your choice. I am going after Viktor." I drag his name out. "He is a master at manipulation and getting people to do what he wants with total deniability. He has a penchant for violence. He's got a disregard for life that is astounding. There is no telling what we will find, and there is no telling what happens to you if we get caught, with my sister out to ruin me and anyone who will support me."

Gamal runs a hand over his bare scalp, staring at the ground. He lifts his gaze to Lumor. "We've heard things." His voice is the sound of breath. "Things I'd not share with a lady."

I snort through my nose and cross my arms. "Have you heard the things I've done?"

He cocks his head. "You're called a murderer."

I give a scoff of humor. "That's like saying Victor is a bad guy. Hardly does it justice."

Legia gives me a petrified look of horror. "Ell."

"What?" I give her a skeptical glare. "You think what Viktor forced me to do was civil? You think it was just taking lives?" I drop my arms, my voice lifting. "You think Viktor was kind? He wanted his victims to suffer. He'd watch me, step by step, instructing me on what he'd want me to do, and there was nothing I could do to stop it or stop him."

She takes a step forward and throws her arms around me. She squeezes me to her, my arms pinned at my sides. I am shaking with fury, but she helps. I sigh and relax. Somehow it is easier to talk about what I did to others. Whispers of murderer and villain are better than pity.

She pulls back. "I know, and I know it wasn't just others. You were hurt too." She turns to the men. "If you want to know what he's capable of, ask to see her back."

I grit my teeth, eyes cutting to the men. "I can't show them my back."

"Why not," she pulls back. "It's... I mean, it is gruesome, but it is just a back."

I shake my head, focusing on Gamal and Lumor. "When I was in Medius, the spirits took all my scars." I smile. "Except this one." I run my finger over the remaining mar. My heart does a little flip in my chest.

"What?" Legia gasps, pulling and tugging on me, getting me to turn around, yanking my shirt aside. I let her, staring at the men and shaking my head. Her fingers brush against my skin. "Haven, they're gone. They're all gone." She pops back beside me. "Ella, that's incredible. How did they? Magic?" She waves her hand. "Of course, it was magic."

"They thought, Dad—Sordello thought, it might help me heal."

"Okay, but why would you ever keep one?"

I frown. "It's from Declan."

"The king?" Lumor tilts his head. "He's left a scar on ya?"

I bob my head. "Yes. Don't ask, it's a long story. Are you willing to help me?"

The men exchange glances, squaring up. Their faces twitch, their eyes shifting. Gamal crosses his arms, and Lumor shakes his head. A mental conversation neither I nor Legia are understanding.

Lumor grins. Gamal sighs. He drops his arms and faces me. "We will help you."

I grit my teeth, then release my jaw. Rancor in my gut makes me nauseous. "Great."

"When do we start?"

I focus on Lumor, ignoring the churning in my stomach. "Now."

# CHAPTER 28

*I* dissipate us in short distances following a trail of destruction. Lumor and Gamal ask about the scar. They ask about a lot, like why I am a murderer. I give answers to everything. Somethings I skimp on details, but these two are risking their lives to help me. I owe them at least to set their minds at ease.

Lumor paws at the ground, lifting and sniffing dirt, pointing out broken plants and gouges in the earth. Dozens of little signs I would have overlooked. Without them, I would have aimlessly wandered in search of Viktor, and I make a note to do something nice for Legia when this is all over.

As the sky lightens, I give up, taking a mental image of our surroundings before returning the dryad brothers to the encampment and dissipating to Byron Palace.

I train with Sordello and then make myself useful in the palace gardens. Gemma glares at me when we cross paths. I do my best to ignore her scathing mutters and cold stares. Helping wounded and assisting the Byron forces in any way that I can is more important than my pride.

The days repeat, resetting after every session with my

father. I try to get sleep the first few days, and each time Declan comes to me in my dreams. It starts out beautifully, my heart soaring only to be ripped out, suffocated at his hands. The misery I feel each time I wake is outweighing the benefit of the mere hours or minutes I achieve, so I abandon sleep as a useless torment.

Those times are the only moments I share with Declan, which only adds to my misery. He still has not come to me or so much as sent me a message. I do my best to remind myself he is busy with crown duties as well as a war, that I am not as important. I could try to contact him, but if he is content, I do not want to hurt him.

Every night I follow Viktor's path of destruction. Every morning as the sky begins to light, the soul star starting to ascend, I train with Sordello. Over and over, the days slip by until it is a never-ending loop. Repeating over and over. Viktor's trail of death, villages and towns destroyed in his wake. It is the only thing that truly changes.

Towns and small villages are burned, pillaged, bodies everywhere. I find a young boy with intestines dangling out of his body. Another burned village. This time a woman and a man, holding the body of a child. They lay in peace as if asleep if I ignore that waxen skin and deep claw wounds stained burgundy.

This night, we find a town with bodies strung from ropes across the rooftops, headless, like small electric lights decorating the town. Near the edge is a dead demon. I tiptoe around the remnants of a camp. The ropes creak as bodies sway in the wind. I find no solid evidence Viktor was here, but the way the townsfolk are strung up makes me believe he was. They paid dearly for slaying the demon.

Lumor and Gamal are around somewhere, out of sight, and searching for evidence elsewhere. I keep my eyes on the rubble and debris to avoid seeing the cadavers as I move between empty buildings. In the center of town, there is a pile of severed heads next to a massive battle-ax.

I stand staring down at the dismembered remains. *Viktor was here. This was him. It must be.*

The edge of my vision blurs with movement, and I whirl, hand out, fingers splayed. Energy pools in my palm, swirling in a bright shimmer. Lumor twirls the massive battle-ax in his hands, bobbing his head as he tests the weight.

For as big as they are, the men move without sound with an eerie ability. I lower my hand and let out a breath of release. The energy dissipates, the skin of my palm burning with warmth from the gathering. I narrow my eyes at him.

He chuckles. Gamal steps next to him from nowhere and whacks him in the arm. "She could have killed you. You saw how the demon disintegrated to ash."

Lumor winks at me with a jovial grin. "She is harmless."

"Demons are resistant to magic, even from the spirits. She's the only one that can affect 'em, an' you're out here startling her." Gamal shakes his head. "Fool."

I pull my face into a scowl. "He's right. You should be more careful." I turn my back and root through litter with the toe of my boot.

I fight a yawn and ram fingers into my eyes, rubbing away the exhaustion. I blink away the spots. For the last, however many days, we have followed this trail of destruction in vain.

We have been at this for a while, and for each encampment we encounter, my frustrations build. There was a demon once and a battle-ax now. It is the most we have ever encountered.

There are splinters, scraps of fabric, and ashes scattered about. I look around, the weight of sleepless days and lack of progress weighing down on me. Time gone with nothing more than useless training and fruitless nights.

A small doll materializes in my view beneath charred wood fragments. It must have been white at one point but is now discolored by ash, a blotchy red stain on one side, and splatter across the apron. Viktor's signature.

I kick at the mess and scream. My voice echoes around the shambles of a once village square. My hands are trembling, and I clench them, watching my knuckles turn white. I blast energy out of me in an explosion that implodes the village, turning the rubble to ash, leaving nothing but the tumultuous ground around me.

A hand lands on my shoulder, and I jerk. From behind, Gamal is watching me with silent intensity. I breathe in through my nose and out of my mouth in slow repetition, then shrug his hand off.

Lumor steps next to me, the battle-ax slung over his shoulder. "We keep looking." His voice is deep and blurred with his accent, but I have become accustomed to it. "We keep trying."

I stare around at the chaos. My vision goes hazy. "There is nothing here but destruction." My voice is hoarse and shaking. "Viktor was here; I know his handy work like the back of my hand." I blink and look to the sky. The tinge of the soul star is blazing to the west, pink edging the horizon.

"Morning." Gamal's voice is easy.

"We have time."

He shakes his head. "Lumor and I need to rest, to eat. We will be on the battlefields this day."

I lock my jaw and turn to the watch the sky illuminate. Tracking Viktor has sown no results, and I am still confined to the grounds of Byron Palace. Sordello insists on training me, but I am unable to help or fight. I shake my head.

"This is as good a place as any to stop," Gamal insists.

"I know." The confession is barely above a breath. But I don't want to stop. I don't want to go meet Sordello to train or waste another day while Viktor is free to create this kind of hell.

"We'll come back. We'll pick up here. We will keep tracking him. We will find him."

I nod and close my eyes, dissipating us back to the Byron camp. I stare at the canvas walls and glance over my shoulder to ensure Gamal and Lumor are safely returned.

Lumor winks at me as he drops the battle-ax to rest against the end of his cot then throws himself down. Gamal grabs my shoulder and forces me to meet his gaze.

He frowns. "Lumor and I need rest."

I bob my head.

"We are not spirits; we cannot continue."

I clear my throat. "I understand."

Lumor is already snoring on his cot. Gamal's hand falls limply from me as he turns to his own. He drops, the taut fabric and wood structure groaning under his weight.

He rubs his face and bare scalp. "Viktor is heading east. From all you have said, from all that we have seen, he is not a stupid man." The dryad lifts his head, staring at me. "The bulk of his forces lies here." He makes a sweeping gesture. "For all we do each day, we are not making improvements. For all I see each night...?" He stops, shadows drawing dark creases in his scowl. His eyes gleam hard.

I shift my weight from one foot to the other. "He has a penchant for causing pain."

Gamal twitches at my words. "He is barely a man. No man would create such morose things."

A small smile plays with my lips, tugging on them despite the mood. He sighs, dropping his hands between his legs. His shoulders roll forward. "I know not of the world as you do. I was a simple man before all of this. You may know what I do not."

His brows draw together as his eyes fixate on the ground. "Viktor is heading east and has left his swarm of demons here. Likely, he is searching for somewhere to make a stand, somewhere like a stronghold." His eyes lift. "He is looking for a home."

I stiffen and suck in a breath. "How do you know that?"

"Barely a man is still a man. He has lost his palace, his throne. He will be looking to remake what was, to return to power. In two days' time, we will be ready to continue. Study maps. Find where he is going. I cannot stomach another desolated town."

# CHAPTER 29

*J* sit at the dinner table, flanked by Seth and Marcus. Their voices are floating on the edge of my consciousness, loud and ever-present. My head feels thick, swollen, my eyes keep rolling into the back of my head. I lean against Seth, who makes no complaint.

I should be studying maps, searching for where Viktor is going. Not even the call of the library is enough to roust me, though.

*How many days has it been? When was the last time I got any sleep?* I yawn and shake myself to full consciousness.

I blink, my eyes are sticky and dry. Declan looms before my groggy mind. I snap upright, much more awake. I stare. Declan stares back. I blink again. He is still staring. My brain is screaming at my mouth to say something.

"Hi."

"Hello."

*Now what? What else do I say?* A million thoughts zip through my mind. Apologies and professions of love are the most prominent. I say none of them.

He watches me, and I look around, wondering where Selene

is. He is never far from her. She never allows him near me without her presence.

I yawn, rolling my shoulders and rubbing my eyes with the fingers and thumb of one hand. Clearing my throat, I sit, arching my back to stretch out the sore muscles. My eyes roll between Seth and Marcus to focus on Declan once more. None of them are saying anything.

He raises his eyebrows. I groan and let my head drop to the surface of the table. Marcus nudges me.

"You need sleep."

I snort, not bothering to look up or make any intelligent reply. There is nothing I want less than to attempt to sleep. Marcus nudges me again.

"Come on, get up."

I groan at him again. I am content to get this half-sleep between him and Seth. Seth joins in the nudging.

"He's right, Ell, you've been nodding off for the last hour."

"Um... I, um..." I am mumbling at the table, cut off by a yawn.

"Need sleep," Marcus says.

"Can't I just sleep here?"

"Ell." Seth rests an arm over my shoulders. "What's going on with you?"

I groan in response. "Right now? I'm tired."

"Then go to bed."

"I don't want to go to bed. I want to sleep right here. Sitting next to you, where I'm comfortable."

Seth squeezes my shoulders. "Alright, Ell, but we have to get back to camp soon."

With a sigh, I wrench myself up. I stand and catch Declan's eyes, watching me. I am stunned for a moment. A hundred other things I want to say to him cascade through my mind. I open my mouth and close it. I open it. I close it. With a sigh and slumping shoulders, I attempt to step away from the table, forgetting the bench behind my knees.

Not even Seth is fast enough to catch me. I land on my elbow, my other arm caught in my friend's steel grasp. I curse, half hanging in his grip with the back of my head on the stone floor.

Seth lowers me to the floor with care. "Are you alright?"

I look at him, then to Declan halfway over the table, his face choleric, his eyes wide. "Great. I'm just gonna stay here a moment."

Declan stands upright and pinches the bridge of his nose. "Damnatus," he grumbles. "Go to bed and get some fucking sleep before you kill yourself."

"It won't stick," I manage through a yawn. "Might make Selene happy, though."

Low growls emit as two armored hands haul me to my feet.

"Dad? What are you doing here?"

"Even spirits need sleep," he grunts. "And you've not had any for a couple of days."

My face warms a bit as I grin. "It's been a bit more than that."

"A couple days in Medius." His voice carries a waft of disapproval.

"Isn't that, like, nearly two cycles?"

I look toward Marcus and shrug. My eyes catch with Declan's. He scowls at me. I wince. "Um, it's..." I yawn, reaching up to cover my gaping mouth. I curse and rub my elbow.

"You fractured it." I frown at Sordello's words and then my elbow. "And you're too drained to fix it." There is a sigh. "To answer you honestly, daughter, I am here to speak with your king. A spirit was dismembered, and the pieces have not been located."

I am wide awake now. "What?" I look at the white and lax faces of the others. "I didn't feel—"

"You're too drained to feel it."

He sounds annoyed, and I throw my hands up. I regret the action, my elbow spiking with pain.

He shakes his hooded head. "Bed. Rest. Recovery."

"Not until you tell me what in Damnatus is going on," I mutter.

"With the pieces of Jyan missing, it is safe to assume that Viktor has a set of spirit runes at his disposal."

I jerk, staring with wide eyes. "What?"

Sordello holds a hand up. "You have no power to go after him."

"You're also condemned to this palace under pain of death," Seth reminds me. "Dec and I will find him, Ell."

I glare at him. "You can't! *I* have to."

Sordello's armored hands turn me to face him. "You have to rest. You're pushing too hard. You're going to kill yourself."

"Not like it'll stick," I mutter sourly.

There is a loud crack, a bright flash. I jerk and gape at him. His shoulders slump, and he breathes out heavily. "Did you think we had nothing in common?"

I snicker. "Fine. Sleep, and then—"

"Then nothing." Declan's order comes soft and low, but with a warning. "You are going to stay here. The Byron palace is safe for now."

I narrow my eyes at Sordello, knowing damn good and well that I am not going to sit and wait. He sighs. "For now, you are too drained to heal yourself. Regardless of your desires to help, you do not have the energy to do anything." He pushes me toward the doors of the dining hall. "Walk, Ella, or you'll damage yourself."

I grumble but put one foot in front of the other. When I

reach my door, I must fight and fumble to unlock the damn thing. Inside, I lock the latch and collapse face forward onto the bed. My eyes slide shut, and I am enveloped in soft darkness.

An arm wraps around my waist, pulling me to my side. His front presses against my back, and I wiggle, trying to move further into him.

"Mmm."

His fingers trail over my arm and then the curve of my hip. Even with eyes closed, my lids flutter in pleasure. I am grinning in partial sleep.

"Dec."

"It's me," he whispers back, his lips tickling against my ear and then my neck.

"I thought you were with Sordello. The missing runes."

"Shhh," he whispers in my ear, the warmth of his breath tickling my skin.

I am melting at his presence and touch. His lips brush down my neck and along the top of my shoulder. I feel his teeth rake against the side of my neck softly, sending shivers of arousal through me. My skin pimples, and my spine tingles.

"Dec."

"Mmm?"

His hand closes around my neck at the base of my jaw. His lips press against my cheek. "Do you really expect me to forget what you've done?" The whisper sends another tingle down my spine, but this one in fear. "How could I ever forgive you?"

His other hand closes around the base of my neck. I reach up, trying to pry his hands away. He laughs softly in my ear, kissing my cheek as I squirm against him.

I start pleading, tears burning my eyes, pressure building in my head. There is too much pressure. There is not enough air. I manage his name only once. "Dec."

I cough, gagging myself awake. Tears are leaking from

beneath my closed eyelids. I sob into my hands, rolling to bury my face in the pillow and scream as loud as I can. I begin to hyperventilate, wailing with deep wracks of my body until I am all cried out.

# CHAPTER 30

*I* try to sleep, but nightmare after nightmare plagues me. I toss and turn for what feels like endless hours. One thought burns in my mind. I cannot dislodge it. I cannot forget it.

*Viktor has a set of spirit runes.*

Giving up, I dress in all black and dissipate to the small offshoot tent where the map is. I am greeted by Samuel's eyes, wide and growing wider as he stares at me.

"Ella!" His cry of dismay is loud, and I shoot daggers at him with my eyes. I press a finger to my lips, looking around with meaning. He grimaces back at me. "Give me one good reason I don't yell for help."

"I'm just here for this," I tap my finger on the map. I glance over the clumps of figurines scattered throughout Cimeria County, then train my sights on the king chess piece. I trace my finger from the piece in the line that I believe the path of destruction leads. I keep moving my finger until it comes across the Asperheim palace.

I stop, tapping the image of a castle wrapped with a dragon. I sigh. Gamal is right, Viktor is looking for something, that much is evident in the path he's traveled. Nothing in Cimeria is fortified or large enough to house an army or firm enough to withstand assaults. Asperheim will give him a palace, a stronghold, a fortified place where he can expand from.

"What are you doing here?" Samuel's voice has at least dropped to a whisper. "You aren't supposed to leave Byron, even if the Bards turn a blind eye to it."

"Viktor." I glance at him, pointing at the map. "I have to find him."

Samuel's eyes shift a tad darker. "Looking to join him?"

The heat and venom in his voice make me take a step back. He had been my friend in training. They all had been my friends. "Not to join him, to *kill* him."

Samuel's face changes from rage to confusion. "The army is working on it. Declan, Seth, the spirits, they are working on finding him."

I roll my eyes. "They are trying to fight off his demons and keep Cimeria safe. I can read a map." I cross my arms. "Viktor is the root. Dig him out, and the rest dies."

Samuel frowns, his eyes twitching from the map to me. "You're to be in Byron, locked up for crimes like murder and breaking blood rituals."

I curl my lip at him. "I didn't have any choice in what Viktor did to me. I didn't have any choice in what Viktor made me do." The heat of rage fills my voice.

My former friend takes a step back from me. There is a flicker of fear across his face. "Wait, Ella, I didn't mean—"

"You did," I snap. "You meant it. Everyone means it. So does Gemma when she tells me she can't wait for Selene to burn me." I point a finger at him. "You have no idea what happened to me, what I have lived through, what I have done, and what was done to me and by me."

He is gaping at me with fear. The demon slithers through my veins. *Maybe they should fear you. Maybe they should all fear you.*

I drop my hands to my side with clenched fists. "Forget it. Believe what you want, it doesn't matter to me, nothing matters anymore except killing Viktor. After that, then, well..." I shrug and relax. "Selene, you, everyone can have what they want. I'll be done."

Samuel frowns at me, a mixture of pity and depression comingling on his face. "Ella—"

I shred myself apart, not caring to hear what he has to say. My thoughts are of the time I spent in Dragonsland at the Asperheim palace. I recall the room, the breeze through paneless windows and gauzy curtains, the sand dunes, and a stone garden view. I piece myself back together there.

The room is dark, lit only by the moonlight through the expansive window. The mattress has been ripped, and stuffing flung everywhere. It lays askew on the four-poster frame. There are large gashes and burns on the walls, the other furniture smashed and broken around the floor.

Glancing around, I move to the window. The gardens with stone and gravel paths hedged with cactus and dry shrubbery are filled with frolicking demons, gathering in clumps. There are torches and fires. Loud grunts and roars echo through the night air.

"Found you," I whisper on a breath of air.

My eyes close as I search within myself. I might be too damaged to be part of the collective, but I have his blood in my veins. I feel the strumming of power coming from nearby. If Viktor has a set of runes, that would be him.

I move through the palace the way a shadow flickers in light, dodging demon and elemental patrols alike. I maneuver, using elements to hide and dissipate larger distances to avoid notice all the way to the grand hall. I dissipate inside to the rafters above the room. I crawl along them, clinging toward the outer edge.

Beneath me, the room appears empty. I scale the length of

the beam to reach the middle of the ceiling to perch above three figures sitting in the corner of the room. There are demons, shoulder to shoulder, standing around in frozen attention. My heart ratchets as I recognize the woman sitting next to Viktor. The duchess, Declan and Seth's mother, although she was pronounced dead and no longer has a title.

She reaches to tuck her short-cropped brown hair behind her ear as she speaks, eyes fixated on the woman sitting across the way.

The third head is facing away from me, with black hair that reflects no light. Her head turns so that I catch her profile as she laughs, the musical sound wafting to my ears. I clench my jaw, realizing Lenore, Queen of Roget, is meeting with Viktor.

I stay where I am, torn between listening to the muffled voices carried by the acoustics of the room or moving closer. Here, I can only hear various words, but not enough to discern what they are speaking of. I worry if I move closer, Lenore will hear me. Being a shade, her hearing is heightened, and I know from the bond with Declan just how much a shade can hear.

Instead, I study the facial expressions of the duchess and Viktor. After a while, the duchess and Lenore rise to stroll through the room. They walk beneath me. I hold my breath as they pass, crossing my fingers that Lenore will stay oblivious.

The heavy doors close with a soft bang, and only Viktor and I remain in the room surrounded by demons. I sit, watching him. He appears at ease, resting his elbows on the table to steeple his fingers together. I crawl toward him along the rafters.

"Please, do come down from there, Morella."

My skin crawls at the sound of his voice. I pause, frozen in fear to gape down at him. His head tips back to focus on me.

"Sit." He waves a hand toward the other side of the table. "Create a chessboard for us to play a game like we used to."

Taking a deep breath, I dissipate to the bench across the

table from him. I sit, staring into his burning green eyes. "I'm not doing this."

He sighs. "Morella."

"What?" I create a blade in my hand, snarling at him. I pull back, ready to strike. A clawed hand wraps around my recoiled arm. Behind me, a demon holds my wrist from striking forward.

"I am the only one protecting you, Morella. Without me, these things would tear you to pieces." He waves a hand, and the demon wrenches the blade from me, stepping back to watch over my shoulder. A smile pulls his lips tight. "Very well, I could use the practice." He stares at the tabletop, and a chessboard appears. He smiles. "I have been steadily learning."

I stare back with a skeptical and disgusted face. "Really? You should try learning to be a decent man."

"You should learn to be afraid of me." There is an edge to his voice I have never heard before. "You scorn me, spit on me." He rests his elbows on the table, leaning over the board, eyes burning. "I have nothing but love for you, my daughter, but my patience is running thin."

I snort a forced laugh through my nose. I have never been so terrified of him as I am at this very moment. "Love for me?" I shove the board to the other side of the table, into his chest. "I'm not playing this game, and I will never be afraid of you again."

"You should," he whispers, sliding the board to the middle of the table. "You should be afraid, consider me a threat, and act with thought, with caution. You never could learn that lesson." He spins the board so that the white pieces are on my side. "White moves first."

With a huff and eye roll, I shove a pawn forward two squares. "So, when I kill you, the demons will just run around Caleum?"

He taps a finger on top of the king piece, gazing at the board. "Focus, Morella. Do you even know why you moved that piece?"

I narrow my eyes at him. My pawn, two from the end, sits two checkered squares out. There was no point to the move other than to comply enough to keep him talking. I need to know what is going to happen after I kill him. "Yes."

He shakes his head. "You gave it no thought." He moves a pawn of his own. "I want you to pay attention."

I sigh, moving another pawn. "And I want you to return to Damnatus." I smile at him. "Or better yet, just curl up and die."

He chuckles a bit. "You wish your own father dead?"

"You aren't my father."

He considers the board, rubbing a hand over his bare scalp. "I have heard the claims that you are the daughter of a spirit." He moves his bishop forward. "Let me assure you…" He meets my eyes. "You are my daughter."

"I'm not." My hands clench, my heart beats harder.

"You have my blood in your veins."

"That doesn't make you a father. That makes you a monster."

He frowns. "It is your move." I roll my eyes and move a knight. Viktor's eyes flash. "You are not paying attention."

I stare at the board. Two pawns and a knight moved from their starting positions. I glance around the room at the demons standing guard. My eyes rivet on Viktor. I shrug, crossing my arms and leaning away from him.

"Perhaps incentive is required." He grins, his eyes lighting up.

I do my best not to react. He lifts his right hand and snaps his fingers. A gagged but struggling Gemma is dragged into the room by two demons. They drop her on the floor. She struggles with her hands bound together in front of her to get to her feet.

I gape at her. Her red and green hair is strewn about her face. She has been crying; her eyes and nose are red, puffy, her cheeks stained by tears. My heart is in my throat as I gaze horrified at Viktor.

He indicates her with a hand. "Someone you believed to be a friend who has decided you deserve to die."

My eyes cut toward her, two demons gripping her between them. She tries to shake them loose. I can hear her screaming at me through the fabric gag. Beneath the table, I grip my fists, feeling a blade materialize in my right hand.

"Before you attempt anything rash, I will explain. If you attempt to kill me, she will die immediately." He holds his hand up, motioning the demons forward. They drag Gemma forward, her feet trailing behind her. He shifts to face her. "You will stop fighting." He nods at the demons, and they remove her gag and binds. A dagger is offered to her. "Take the blade you are offered." Gemma grabs the hilt with shaking limbs.

"You have the Vitale rune."

He looks at me. "Yes. The last rune necessary to properly assimilate me as a spirit, granting control over those weaker than myself."

He looks back at Gemma. "You will watch. For every piece Morella loses, you will plunge the blade into yourself. For every piece Morella takes, you will take a step toward the door."

"You're sick," I hiss, lurching to my feet. I slam my own blade tip down, embedding it in the table. "You cannot."

"I told you once we are what we are, and there is no point in feeling shame for it." He indicates the door closest, where she had been brought through. "If you reach the door, you will be granted freedom, allowed to leave this palace unharmed. If Morella wins, you will go free. If I win, you will die."

"What?" I feel myself shaking. I look to Gemma's wide eyes. There is white visible all the way around her irises. I grit my teeth, looking to Viktor. "What the hell do you want from me?"

"I wish to spend time with you, Morella." He rubs a hand over his scalp. "I was hoping to avoid this situation, but you forced my hand."

I remain on my feet, hands planted on the table on either

side of the board. My eyes are twitching as I look between Gemma and Viktor. Nausea leaves the taste of bile on the back of my tongue. Fear is causing my skin to prickle and chill.

I fixate on Gemma, envisioning us in my window seat back in Byron. Before I can assimilate the image, Viktor snaps his fingers. Each demon standing around the room draws a blade and slits its own throat.

The bodies drop with heavy thuds as the weapons clang to the polished floors. My eyes cut to Viktor, who stands, arms spread, head back. *"Enoi lotate,"* he yells.

The demons begin to turn to ashes. A whirlwind swirls around the room, a cloudy barrier forms. Viktor drops his arms and faces me. "I have a very astute teacher."

I grip my hands and glance at the lone demon, still standing behind me. "What did you do?"

"There will be no further magic. You will not dissipate to safety." He points at the game. "This is your only choice. This is the point of no return Morella. This is what your choices have wrought." He takes a seat and gestures to me. "Sit."

# CHAPTER 31

*I* stare at the pieces, knowing even my best attempts at chess fail, and I have not put thought into a single movement. Weakly, I move my hands, feeling beneath me to find the bench and sit.

"The moment I received the rune, I knew you would come. You've always been weak, caring for others. I knew you would act, try to get to me before I had the chance to use the power of these runes." His shoulders flex and then roll. "You are still failing to act with thought instead of emotion."

My body is trembling. I look from him to Gemma, who stands in place as a limp rag doll. The blade is shaking in her hand by her side. "Ella," she whimpers. "Help me."

My anger begins raising the temperature of my blood. My ears grow warm at her plea. The thing in me is rising to the surface, grinning with desire. I grit my teeth, trying to kick it back into place, but it is thrilled to see how this game plays out. It wants to watch her bleed.

*She deserves this.*

I turn away from her to stare at the board. I am screaming at myself to think. Fervently I wish for the bond with Declan. He plays chess with Marcus so often I doubt he would fail to save Gemma's life.

My mind is spinning fast, thoughts streaming like a cascade of water over a cliff. Though, none of the thoughts help me, adding to my despair. I drop my face into my hands, breathing deep through my nose.

*Focus!*

I shove my hands over my face, back through my hair. I only have to survive long enough to get Gemma to the door, then I can deal with Viktor. I square my shoulders to consider the board with a clear mind.

I shove another pawn forward. He moves a pawn in response. I move a bishop.

"My father did some of the same things to me when I was growing up."

"Yeah, I know."

"I hated him for it." He looks at me, his eyes soft as freshly sprung grass. "Did you know that?"

I roll my eyes. "Didn't stop you from being just like him."

He strokes his chin in contemplation. "For a while, I hated him, but what my father did made me strong, made me what I am today."

Scoffing, I cross my arms, curling in on myself. "Your move."

"I need you to understand that everything I have done, what I am doing, it is all in love for you, my daughter."

Tears are blurring my vision as I glare at him. "You're a monster, and you've made me one too." I point to the board. "Move."

"Very well." There is nearly a sigh to his words.

He takes one of my pawns. My heart skitters in its cage. I watch in slow motion as he plucks the piece from the board, using it to nudge his bishop into its place. My eyes lock on Gemma.

"For something so trivial, perhaps the arm is enough." There is a pause, where Gemma stares at me with horror. "Please stab the blade through your arm, Gemma."

She lifts the blade. It wavers in her hand. Her other arm lifts out straight, away from her body. Her cry as the blade sinks through her forearm rings out around the room. I stare, partially in shock, but mostly in intrigue, my demon slithering through my veins with happiness.

"Pull it back out, my dear. You'll need it again."

His tone is light, casual. It churns my stomach. He has no more care for Gemma than ordering more wine from a servant. Gemma's eyes are glassy, her lower lip trembling. Without hesitation, she rips the blade from her arm at Viktor's instruction.

She screams. I wince, both at the cry of pain and the realization that it is my fault. My demon is stretching languidly. Yawning with boredom.

*She deserves to know what it is like to be under Viktor's thumb. She deserves this punishment.* The smell of blood in the air is intoxicating, and I lick my lips.

I look at the board. I must be more careful. I start to move pieces with a bit more consideration.

I knock one of his pawns off the board. "Take a step, Gemma."

She spreads her legs as far as she can manage, needing no help from the incitement rune to move toward freedom.

Viktor takes one of my knights.

"Ella!"

I glare at her. "What?" I snap the word at her without empathy. The demon is taking control, the sight and smell of blood and pain clawing at my weak resistance. "I'm playing to win, to save your life, I can't keep every piece."

He sets it to the side. "Stab yourself in the leg this time."

Muffled sobs escape her. Mechanically she lifts the blade, plunging it into the mid-thigh of her right leg. She doubles over, crumpling to the floor.

"Stand up." Gemma lurches to her feet like a puppet on strings. "Pull the blade out."

She whimpers but does as commanded. She doubles over, dropping the blade and sobbing. She presses her hand over the wound, drawing it back to stare down at her palm coated in blood. Her eyes lift toward mine.

My brows are drawn together, my face pulled into a scowl. I look back at the board. Pieces are everywhere. I line each piece in my head, checking which piece is even moveable without being taken. I look for pieces in danger. I look for his king.

"Morella." I glance from the board to his face. "I have tried to do my very best. I have strived for perfection, to be the father you needed."

I scoff, returning my gaze to the pieces and checkered squares.

He continues in an even voice. "My father required the best from me, never believing that I was good enough. Nothing I ever did growing up was deserving of even the smallest sign of affection."

"He was a monster, that created a monster, and now," I pause to look toward Gemma, then his poison eyes, "you've created another monster. Congratulations." I return to surveying my prospects.

There is a hint of anger in his voice. "I am proving to my father once and for all that I am so much more than he ever believed me to be."

I cross my arms on the table. "A monster and a failure?"

"Make your move." His voice is edged with something dangerous.

My ears go back, and I focus on the board. I move. He moves. I move. He moves.

"Check."

My heart stutters. I swallow, eyes glancing toward Gemma.

"Do something," she whines. "Please, Ella, I'm sorry. Do something!"

I look at the board. I can take the rook threatening my king, so I do. Gemma takes a step forward.

Viktor removes a pawn from the board. "In the arm again, Gemma. Now."

My heartrate ratchets faster. The point of the dagger is visible on the other side of her arm. I remember the pain of Declan spearing my arm through with my own little dagger, pinning it to the wall. I try to focus on the game, but my demon is curling with pleasure, satisfied to be part of the reason she bleeds.

Viktor and I trade-off, piece for piece. Gemma has a dozen holes in her, but she is two steps from the door. I look from her to the door, then back to Viktor and the board. He has his chin propped on a bent elbow. He strums his fingers at me.

"There are exactly three moves you can make, Morella. None of them are going to change the outcome of our little game."

Gemma cranes her head. I stare at the board with absolute dread. I can take one more piece, putting Gemma one more step closer to freedom, but it leaves my king exposed. I can protect my king but lose the chance of Gemma's step. I can move a piece aimlessly.

No matter what I do, my move will be negated on Viktor's turn. Either I drag this game two more moves or allow him to end it now. Desperate for any sign of hope, I look at Gemma.

"I'm sorry." My voice is hoarse, a whisper ripped through the clog of misery in my throat.

"Sorry?" she squeaks. "Sorry? What does that mean?" I grimace, looking at the board. "What does that mean, Ella?" she screams at me with a shrill tone.

I bite my lip, digging dirt from under one of my nails. I cannot bring myself to look at her, to tell her the truth. I stare at the board, helpless, then raise blurry eyes to Viktor.

"Please."

He stops strumming and raises his eyebrows at me. "You are pleading for her life?"

"Yes."

He scoffs. "Do you not understand yet?" He opens his arms wide. "All of this is for you. All of this is to make you stronger, stronger than anyone, even me."

I blink, looking to Gemma. I should have known that taking so many of his pieces was too easy. She is close enough to the door that she might reach out and touch it with her fingertips. I look around the room at the swirling demon ash, trying to figure out if there is a chance for me to grab her and leave.

"You have more power than any other living being, and you are pleading for the life of one who claimed to be your friend then turned her back on you when you needed it the most." He smiles. "I honestly thought it would have been the orange-haired girl who broke." He rubs his scalp.

Coming here had been reckless, playing right into his hand. I wonder if not coming would have doomed Gemma anyway. I swallow, beginning to pop my knuckles.

"Ah, well, it does not matter." He pauses, considering me. Something about his face softens. "When I rule all of Caleum, I will have finally proven myself to my father. When I die, I will leave you the greatest legacy anyone will ever have known in this dimension. You will have Caleum and Medius at your feet as the one true queen of both dimensions." He extends a hand toward me over the chessboard. "Join me. Stand at my side as my daughter. Help me take control of Caleum. I will allow your betrayer to walk away."

I stare at his hand. My blood is pumping too loud in my ears, strumming out the sound of my own breathing. I stare at his hand, unblinking.

Gemma in exchange for Caleum. I look at her, pleading with my eyes that she understand the price is too high.

"You bitch! You aren't going to do it, are you? You aren't going to save my life." She is wailing and throws the dagger toward me.

I duck out of the way. The blade skitters on the floor behind me. My hand is shaking, my vision hazy and foggy with tears.

Gemma remains where she is, screaming at me. Tears streaming down her face, her flesh blotchy with rosy splotches. Some of the words make it through my anxiety-induced haze.

*"Murderer." "Monster." "Selene was right."*

Viktor turns to look at her. "You will be silent, or I will instruct you to cut out your own tongue." He turns back to me, pulling on the collar of his white dress shirt to straighten it. "It is your move, Morella."

I know he is not talking about the game. I have not given a response to the offer, despite Gemma's reaction. I shake my head, reaching out to flick my king piece. It topples, clattering against the marble squares in the deathly silence of the room. It rolls, tumbling into his queen, and lays still.

I lift my eyes to his. His brows draw together. A flash of anger sparks in his green eyes, making them shine the way lightning flickers across a night sky. He stands, shoving the chessboard sideways. Pieces go flying, the board skitters across the table's surface and falls to the floor with a loud crack.

He remains there, standing hunched over, eyes locked on mine with hands flat on the table's surface. He is breathing a bit harder than I might expect. The exertion of chucking the board was hardly significant.

He pulls my dagger from the tabletop and turns. "You will not move, Gemma." He strides toward her, the blade gripped in his hand.

I stand, trying to catapult over the table. Large hands with long, clawed fingers wrap around my wrists. They drag my hands behind my back. I squirm, trying to focus on the blade. I envision the blade in my window seat.

Nothing happens. Viktor stands behind Gemma. The blade lifts to her throat, Viktor's eyes lock on mine. "Your choices have consequences. You may despise me for this now, but someday you will understand."

I try to break free that I might stop him, but claws grip the back of my head. I feel my scalp burning, wetness dampening my hair.

I grit my teeth as the claws grip tighter, slamming my head against the table. Pain explodes in my temple. The world spins. Dazed, I stare, watching Viktor draw the blade across her throat.

My ears are ringing, pain clouding my thoughts. My head slams against the table again. My vision goes gray. I blink away the haze of water over my eyes, the world returning to color. I cannot hear anything but a high pitch ring in my ears. I squirm, kicking out.

My head bounces again. I kick as hard as I can against the most solid part of the demon I can find in an attempt to dislodge it. It jerks backward, hair ripping from my bleeding scalp. Pain makes the world an unfocused blur of colors before my eyes. The grip adjusts, the demon holding tighter.

Gemma's body lays at his feet. He inspects the blade and drops it next to her. He steps forward, straightening his blood-splattered shirt. "When you are ready, Morella—"

"I hate you," I scream, still struggling. "I don't care what you want; the answer is no!"

Viktor sighs. He inclines his head, and mine is bounced again. This time, the world grays and turns to black.

# CHAPTER 32

*I* roll over, groaning. My head is pounding. I drop my head into my hands, then run them through my hair. I hiss and wince, pulling back. Blood coats my palms. I force myself to move, to look around. The grand hall is empty. I am alone.

Viktor has too much sense to remain where I can find him right now, and I do not have time to track him down. Sordello will be furious. If I am not there for our scheduled session, things will escalate. On the other side of the table, Gemma's body lays white and still. I scurry over, pulling her limp form to its back. Her eyes are shadowed and opened. I sob, slapping my bloody hand over my mouth.

Closing my eyes sends tears rolling down my face. I grimace, picturing her body in my window seat. It disappears, and I stand with shaking legs. Looking around with tear-soaked eyes, I try to think of what to do next. With effort, I dissipate to the map room, startling Samuel.

"Ella," he growls, "what in Haven's name happened to you?"

Without responding, I move to the table, repositioning the

king piece over the Asperheim palace. I pull back, blood coating the king piece.

He points at the map. "Did you just move?"

I glance around and whisper, "He's there."

"What am I going to say when the king asks why it was moved?" His lip curls. "Or why it's covered in blood?"

I shrug. "Don't say anything at all."

Samuel's eyes are wide, his features slack with shock but soften, his brows drawing together. "Ella, you're bleeding."

With a pathetic chuckle, I dissipate to the practice field. Using my shirt and the elements, I do my best to remove the blood. I am sure the side of my face looks bad, but there is nothing I can do other than focus my energy inward to heal the wounds. I start to stretch, meditating as I move through positions, focusing on healing my physical wounds. By the time Sordello arrives the soul star has risen.

"You're late." My voice is hoarse. I blink, my eyes dry and swollen from too much crying.

"There was a discussion about why something was out of place."

I grimace. "I found him."

"I know." He kneels next to me. "Are you alright?"

I shake my head. "No, I'm not." I use my hands to push myself to my feet. "Are we going to do this or not?"

"Not." The word renders the air frosted.

I look at Declan. "What are you doing here?"

He leans against a post staring at me. "The damnedest thing happened to my map."

I do my very best not to react, but I am certain the flare of his nostrils tells me I failed. Still, I clear my throat to ask, "Oh? What is that?"

"Your blood was on that king." His eyes are black.

I swallow, running fingers over my left temple. Pressing on it still throbs, but I am hoping Declan cannot discern signs of my head being slammed against a table. He is watching me with intensity and anger.

"Why were you bleeding?" He pushes away from the post to stand on the balls of his feet.

I hold my hands up. "Do you see blood on me anywhere?"

He pinches the bridge of his nose, and when he drops his hand, he snarls. "You're covered in it." He points at me, and my eyes drop to my shirt.

"Oh. I forgot about that." I cross my arms over my body. "Whatever, I'm fine."

"You're not fine," he roars, chords of muscles straining in his neck as he steps toward me, cloaked in rage. "You're covered in blood. You appeared in the encampment where Samuel saw you, beat half to death."

I shuffle my feet and stare down at them. "I found—"

"Stop. Talking." He clutches at his head. "I don't want to hear a damned thing. Do you have any idea...? Any fucking idea what it is going to take to keep this from Selene?"

I scoff. *I should be dead, like Gemma.* "Then don't. Let her know."

His black eyes bulge. "What?"

I shrug, holding a hand out to stay Sordello. "What, what? Let her hear. I found Viktor. He's at Asperheim. Kill him. I couldn't, so you do it."

"You went after Viktor?" He swings at the nearest post. It shatters. "What in Damnatus were you thinking?"

I laugh. "I was thinking I could do it, but I was wrong, wasn't I? So, go." I wave a hand. "Go kill him and let Selene kill me." My eyes well up. "Just let this be over."

He stands there, staring at me, breathing raggedly. He twists on his feet, staring at the sky, then he puts his hands on his hips, looking right at me. He growls, dropping his hands, striding to me.

He grabs my face, tipping it up to him. "Ella."

I stare into his black eyes. "Declan."

He makes a noise in the back of his throat, an eerie mixture of groan and growl. "Do not touch my map. Stay here—" he points toward the ground, "—where you promised me you would stay for your own safety."

I want to laugh or maybe cry. *My safety? Gemma is dead.* I have no will to fight in me. My best attempt to stop Viktor was met with loss and death. The demon is curled up, licking its wounds. I step back to the wall and slide down it. "I never promised you anything, but fine, I'm done."

He stares down his nose at me, a breeze wafting his hair against the bridge. We are frozen in time, in that moment. I want to say so many things, but all that comes out of me are salty drops of water over my lower lashes.

Kneeling in front of me, he reaches out, fingers tightening on my face. His eyes search my eyes. "I can't." He stands and turns his back on me. He screams expletives and then points at me, directing himself to Sordello. "Make sure she stays here."

Declan disappears, and Sordello comes closer. "I believe you vexed your king."

I glance up at my father and then look around. I let out a breath I had not realized I was holding. Resting my head back against the wall, I breathe normally. "Yeah, I made him mad."

"Have you spoken with him?"

I crack one eye and watch Sordello crouch before me. I stare at the shadowed face under the hood, seeing nothing. I wave a hand. "Just that."

"Forgive me, but, if you wish to reclaim your relationship with him, I believe you will need to speak with him, more than..." He mimics my flourishment.

"There is nothing to say." I close my eyes, focusing on slowing my breathing and heart rate.

"Do you no longer love him?"

The words dredge a sudden tightness in my chest, and something lodged in the back of my throat. "No."

"You're lying."

I look at Sordello with blurry eyes and frown. "Fine. Yes, but it doesn't matter." I blink. "He deserves better. He *has*," I stress, "better."

"My daughter—" he begins, but I lurch to my feet.

"I saw how she treated him, how she showed she cared. I didn't do that. I had my chance, and I screwed it. I screwed it up so bad." My voice cracks.

I drive the heels of my palms into my eye sockets. I take a deep breath and exhale. I lower my hands and gape at Sordello's hidden face.

"I have little knowledge or experience with love, and therefore cannot help you. However, I do feel that if you care so deeply, you should speak with him about it."

I shake my head. "He's better off."

"Very well," my father sighs. "Do you wish to speak about your meeting with Viktor?"

I shake my head. "No."

"You are lucky he did not kill you."

"Lucky?" I grit my teeth and clench my hands. "Gemma," I breathe, "Gemma's... She's... Haven." I try to get control of myself. "It's all my fault."

He pulls me to my feet. "You once told me that I was blaming myself for things Viktor did." I blink into his hidden face. "Viktor is to blame, Ella, not you."

I nod and limp back to my room. Gemma lies in the window seat, her body crumpled, dripping blood. I wince and sink into a ball on the floor next to it. Grief punches me in the chest, knocking the air from my lungs. I sob and give in to the despair until I can no longer cry.

Finding what little strength I can, I say a prayer. I think of Haven, of glowing warmth and happiness. Holding tight to the thought, I take Gemma's hand in mine. Energy crawls through me, so slow like the control I have over the elements is dampened with mourning. The feeling of her hand slips from mine, and I open my eyes.

Blood remains, but her body is gone. I stare until my eyes focus outside my window. I can barely see over the city, just glimpsing the tops of the ashen walls of the canyon. I consider dissipating there, running away from everything. Hiding in the mines, I could pretend like I am dead, living out whatever time or life I may have and try to forget about everything.

I cannot bring myself to look at my own reflection. I shower and glance dejectedly at the camp in the garden outside of my window. There is no desire in me to leave the palace. There is no desire in me to go help the other healers. Byron lost one of their healers because of me.

I realize I need something, something other than fighting or drawing blood. An insane idea grips me, and I sink into the window seat. Staring across the expanse of tents, I figure there are others like me who are torn up and broken. Maybe everyone needs a little bit of laughter.

# CHAPTER 33

*I* practice making wine over the course of the next few days. I wander about the healing tents, finding willing subjects to test the wine on until I can make something drinkable.

I head to the city wall, where there are fewer tents. Sitting on the edge of the fountain where I spied on Declan and Skylar, I create two dozen casks of wine. I create a small stage and return to meandering through the healers' tents, looking for musicians, finding a few to who will play for the simple joy of performing.

I have managed to avoid Marcus and everyone else thus far. Several times in my toils, I hear others mention Gemma or ask if anyone has seen her. And every time guilt smacks me in the face, pulling my grief to the surface. I cannot bring myself to even be around others. I have no idea how I am going to manage to explain what happened to her.

Seven days slip by. I meet with Sordello each morning to continue my training. Each morning he indicates that the others are interested in seeing me, encouraging me to go to my friends. He complains they plague him to know where I am.

I sleep in rare clips of time. The nightmares of Declan

continue. Every time I close my eyes, the torment returns. They all begin as beautiful memories, the diversity sparking broken hope that this time will be different, but the end is always the same. I wake from the image of his eyes glowing red. He had been bellowing in my face that I am a monster, that I am responsible for Gemma's death. He keeps asking me if I thought he could forgive me as he crushes my throat.

Running my hands over my neck, too broken to even cry, I realize the soul star is rising. Dejected and exhausted, I dress slowly. I walk to the practice field instead of dissipating, feeling wrong and sick inside. I do my best to shake the sleep from my limbs as I wait on Sordello but end leaning against a wall with my head tipped back and eyes slipped shut.

"Morella."

I jerk to stand upright as a hand closes around my throat. I flail, panicking as Declan's face looms before me.

"What in Haven's name do you think you're doing?"

I gasp, "Dec?"

"You're never going to get better. You've never going to be able to fix this mess." He puts more weight on my throat, cutting off the airway. "Why don't you just find a way to rot in the inferno? I'm never going to forgive you."

I cannot breathe, and I pitch forward. The phantom Declan disappears as I fall to my knees in the dirt and then to all fours gagging and coughing. I am relieved to breathe and look around. I am still there when Sordello and Declan both appear.

Sordello kneels in front of me. "Ella?"

I sit back on my heels, pushing hair from my face. "Yeah."

Avoiding looking at Declan, I stare at the space of ground in front of his feet. I do not want to look up and see him staring down his nose at me like a piece of garbage. "Look, I'm..." Stopping, I sigh and try to get my emotions under control. "I'm not..." I inhale through my nose. "Not this morning, okay?"

"Of course," Sordello says, extending a hand to help me to my feet. I push it away, sitting back on my heels.

"Are you alright?"

Startled, I meet Declan's gray eyes. He sounds concerned, but his voice is soft. I try to force a smile at him. "Not really."

He crosses his arms and scowls. "Then stay in this palace and get some bloody sleep."

I want to laugh but release a strangled scoff. "Why are you here?"

"It doesn't matter now." He gets down on one knee in front of me.

The memory of his proposal slams through me. Throwing a hand over my face to cover my sob, I dissipate back to my room. Sleep is far from the only problem I have, but it is the most pressing. I can feel the days on end weighing down on me.

Lying down, I try to recover, at least dig my mind into meditation far enough to get rest, to recuperate energy. I toss and turn, waking up various times in different positions, gasping for air.

As I awaken for the umpteenth time, panting and clawing at my throat, I realize the soul star is setting. I stare at the painted sky, watching the light fade before getting up to shower. I scald myself with water to wash away the tears and grogginess. I slip out my door and stroll through the servant's passages in the walls to make my way outside without notice.

I find those who volunteered to be my musicians, working with them to create instruments to their desires. We weave through tents and shrubbery toward the fountain at the palace wall where the stage and casks of wine await. The five men take their instruments and begin to pluck strings and speak about songs. I serve them wine and force smiles their way. At least they seem to be genuinely enjoying themselves.

The sky is growing dark, the area flooding with shadows, so I release little balls of energy into the air. The energy is a soft light, and I create a hundred of them, tossing them into the air, making them float and spin, creating a delicate light source for this gathering.

The music draws a handful of other elementals. A crowd forms, and the men on stage begin to strum out melodies. A few younger children stand off to the side with wide eyes. I encourage them to chase the shimmering balls of energy around the fountain. I help them catch a few of the orbs, letting the children play with them.

There are smiles and laughter abound. More and more have come to join the ball. I laugh at myself for calling it a ball, but then a boy asks me to dance. Grinning, I apologize to him for stepping on his feet in advance. We dance, and when the song ends, another man steps forward to take my hand and spin me in circles. So, it goes through several songs until I am dizzy and warm in the face.

"Ella?"

I glance toward my name. Legia, bright blue eyes larger than gold coins, is standing with Chase. Her mouth is hanging open. In response, I wrinkle my nose at her before the man whisking me around turns me away from her. Soon enough, Chase is dancing Legia around, and I cannot stop my grin. Legia beams up at him, and it makes my mirth dissolve to ash in my mouth.

I stop dancing and get knocked into. "Oh, so sorry." I force a grin at the man, still holding onto me. "I'm sorry. Will you excuse me? I think I need to stop."

I give him a curtsey and slip away from the couples dancing. At the edge of the crowd, halfway hidden in a shrub to watch the merrymaking without notice, I gaze upon what I have wrought. There is not a single face scowling. The sound of laughter hangs in the air, like my energy balls. It is the first time in a long time since I have seen such happiness in the faces of my friends and subjects.

I wrap arms around myself as I wince. *They are not my subjects anymore.* I force a deep breath into my lungs, holding it and trying not to cry.

"Ell?" I glance over at Seth, who is beaming at me in a way I have not seen since before I was engaged to Declan. "Was this you?"

I nod, gripping myself tighter.

"You made a ball?" He laughs. "Haven, I've seen it all now."

I try to smile. "I needed…" I wince. "I needed something."

He holds out a hand to me. "Dance with me then." I raise a single brow. He looks to the sky and chuckles. "Come on, I'm just as horrible as you."

He grabs my hand and drags me into the fray. We square up, and we both step forward, knocking into each other. He laughs. "I'll lead."

I roll my eyes. "Since when?"

I follow and step on his toes. We laugh together at each misstep, blaming each other at each falter. It is so flawed it is flawless, and I love it. The way he is beaming at me, the way he dredges laughter from me despite the despair gnawing at my heart, Seth is managing to give me the something I needed.

He spins me, loses his grip, and I trip over my own feet. I knock into something solid, whipping around to make apologies.

"Tis alright, Your Highness!" They wave me back toward Seth.

I make a faux grimace at him as I step back to take his hand. I catch sight of Declan twirling Selene. Pain rips at my heart, nearly pulling it from my chest. I grunt, gripping Seth's hand and wrenching us around so that I can no longer view them.

"What the hell, Ell?" His brows are furrowed, and then his eyes flicker behind me. He looks back at me. "He doesn't—"

I shake my head. "Don't."

Seth sighs, dropping my hand and stepping back a pace. "You need to—"

"Please," I beg him. "Don't. Please? Okay? Just..." I swipe at the wisps of hair around my face. "Just don't say anything about it." I look up at him pleadingly, and he frowns back.

"Ell."

"Leave it alone." My voice is harder.

He shakes his head. "What is going on with you? We all know you've been trying to go after Viktor."

My eyes are full of tears in a split second. I sob, my face contorting with grief.

"Haven, Ell," he breathes, gripping me against him. "Come on."

He leads me away from the dancing and the stage. We step to the other side of a shrub. He pulls me in close, and I fall against his chest, sobbing and blubbering those words I thought I would never know how to say.

# CHAPTER 34

*S*queezing me tight, Seth grunts. A string of low curses erupts from him, and he presses his lips to my temple. "You're damn lucky to be alive."

I shake my head. "Viktor was never going to kill me."

"Everyone knows he wants you. I'm more surprised he left you there."

I pull back, swiping at my face. "I think he wants me to choose him."

Seth shakes his head. "We all know that is never going to happen." He sighs. "And we all know you've been leaving this palace. Declan was screaming about chaining you up after you left blood all over the king on his map and Samuel's description of you showing up looking like someone beat you half to death."

I grimace. "I should have known Samuel would tell him."

Seth cranes back to meet my eyes with a skeptical expression. "Are you going to tell Declan no?" I curl my lip back. "Yeah, me neither. He is terrifying when he isn't stoic."

I smirk, rubbing my nose against the middle of Seth's chest.

"You need to relax and trust that Declan and I are doing everything we can. You need to trust us." He cups my face in both his hands. "You used to, Ell. Trust us. You haven't so much as spoken three words to Declan since you've come back. You look like absolute fucking hell too." He pulls us to a stone bench nearby. "Maybe this isn't what you needed. Maybe you need sleep."

I let out a hollow laugh, resting back on my hands and staring up at the sky. "Haven." I sigh. I hold my hand out over the space between us on the bench. A goblet appears, with wine. He plucks it up, taking a drink.

Legia and Chase come around the corner. She gushes, letting go of Chase to skip to the bench. She sits next to me, knocking her hip against mine to make me provide her room. "I can't believe you did this!"

I roll my shoulders. "I didn't do—"

"Stop! I don't believe you! None of them do either." She waves a hand toward the festivities. "They all said 'the girl with purple eyes' or, Haven, some of them said 'the queen.'" She laughs. "Selene heard that and turned red, don't you know?" Legia tips her head back and laughs again. "Of everyone I can name, I never would have thought you'd throw a ball."

I grin. "I needed a distraction."

Legia wrinkles her nose, eyes dancing. "Something other than trying to find Viktor?"

Chase hangs his head and sits on the ground near Legia's feet. His legs cross in front of him, and he yanks Legia down into his lap. He presses his lips against her temple. "Darling, you are loud, and those words will condemn her to death."

I scoff. I deserve whatever Selene may do to me.

The others fall into silence, and Declan comes into sharp relief around the corner next. Nausea sweeps through me, and I sigh, sitting upright.

"Don't Ell."

I glare at him, and Legia turns to wave. "Oh, now it is a party, isn't it?" She wrinkles her nose and claps her hands together. She lifts her goblet toward me. "I am out of wine, though, Your Majesty."

I hold out a hand, but Declan's hand rests over the goblet. "I did not know you'd request wine from me," he says dryly.

I drop my hand to look up at the sky. There are hundreds of thousands of twinkling white lights about us pinned against an inky background. I plaster a polite smile on my face as Legia and Declan banter back and forth.

Seth sighs, stands, and stretches. "I think I'll go see what is available in the kitchens."

I shake my head. Snapping my fingers, a pile of dragons' food appears where he had been perched. "You could just ask," I tease.

I pick up a piece and toss it toward Legia. Chase's hand snakes out, catching it. Legia wrinkles her nose. "Nice try."

Chase holds an open palm up, and after a moment, a knife appears. "You know, I think the student has surpassed the teacher."

I smirk. "I really don't think that's a fair comparison. I'm a spirit, apparently." I hold my left arm out, showing off the black lines swirling in delicate beauty across my pale skin.

Seth takes a piece of dragons' fruit and tosses it to Declan, who catches it with one hand. He looks at it, and his eyes travel over the others slicing and munching on the food. "Can we all agree to take the night off and forget about this fucking war?"

"Absolutely," Chase says with a mouthful.

Legia pokes him in the chest. "Manners."

He tries to kiss her with a mouthful of fruit, juices running over his cheeks and chin. She squeals, and I cringe, throwing hands over my ears. "Haven, Legia."

"Haven might indeed hear her," Declan says, picking up the last couple pieces of fruit to sit next to me.

My stomach drops away. The skin on my left arm tingles, feeling him in such close proximity. I remind myself to breathe.

The thought draws a strangled laugh from me, considering the man next to me makes sure I cannot breathe in my dreams.

Declan begins to juggle the fruit. "What is so funny?"

I look to Seth as he shoves a whole piece of fruit in his mouth. Our eye contact causes him to freeze, fruit halfway bitten off in his mouth, juice dripping down his chin. He winks and returns to eating.

Clearing my throat, I answer Declan. "Oh, you know, that Haven might actually hear Legia."

Declan lifts an eyebrow in a skeptical glance. "You are still an awful liar. It's nice to know some things never change."

I duck my head away from him and fluff the hair on the side of my head to obscure my face from his sight. My eyes meet Legia's, and I stretch them wide at her. Her brows raise, and I cut my eyes in Declan's direction. She wrinkles her nose.

"What are you two plotting?" Chase asks. "I hope it's more fruit."

A piece is lobbed toward him, and Declan has ceased juggling. I raise a brow at him. "Since when do you know how to juggle?"

The shoulder closest to me lifts and falls. "Since when do you plan and host balls?"

I roll my eyes. "This hardly constitutes a ball."

Legia laughs. "I second that. If this were a ball, I'd be wearing something much more elegant."

"Darling, what you are wearing is fine. You look beautiful," Chase says.

I never take my eyes off Declan's, but one side of his lips twist into a smirk at the sound of a slap. I roll my eyes as Legia retorts to her husband. I raise a hand, picturing Legia in a bright blue ball gown. My fingers snap.

"Ella?" I glance toward her. Her cheeks are tinged pink, and she runs her hands over the bodice of her gown. "Haven, if I knew you were so fashionable, I would never have bothered commissioning all those dresses. I'd just have had you snap your fingers and been the best dressed at every ball."

Seth starts to laugh. I glare at him, doubled over. A hand slaps his knee as he laughs and laughs. "What is so funny about that?"

"You? Fashionable?" He dissolves into hysterics.

I narrow my eyes. With a quick mental image, I snap my fingers again. Seth now dons a black sheath dress. He shuts up, his eyes growing wide. Legia rolls on the ground, shrieking with laughter. Chase has his lips sucked between his teeth, trying to maintain his amusement.

Seth gives me an evil look. "Fix it."

"I think you look good," Declan says, his tone dead serious.

I smirk, covering my mouth with a hand. "Yup." I choke on a giggle. "Black is very figure flattering."

He glares at me. "Ell, now." He points at his chest. "Change me back."

I shrug, resting back on the bench. My head tips back. I exhale slowly, energy trickle from my core to return Seth to his jeans, boots, and long-sleeved shirt.

"Aw, you're no fun."

I grin as Chase responds. "Darling, do try to be quiet. For now, Selene has not managed to find us, but if she hears you, she is going to slither over. She never leaves Dec alone for more than the few minutes he can manage to slip off."

Legia makes a noise of frustration. "She'll ruin this for sure."

"Yes," Declan sighs, "and I am telling you if she comes 'round that corner, I am running as fast as I can in that direction."

His thumb jerks in the opposite direction. A smile tugs on one corner of my mouth. "Not a happy betrothal?" He narrows his eyes at me. I smirk fuller. "Could have fooled me."

His hand brushes the hair off my shoulder. "What's that supposed to mean?"

I snort through my nose. "You know how I said I could watch from Medius?"

He pulls back, fear filling his eyes. "Yes." The word is tight. "That's why you..." Declan stops talking. He stands, rubbing a hand over his mouth. He turns back to face me. "That's why you aren't speaking to me."

"What's going on over there?"

I study his face. The crescendo of breaking and wailing or gnashing of teeth is a distant memory, but my chest still constricts when I think about it. "I saw you and her," I say, floundering my hands in front of me.

"Excuse me? Others present. What is going on?"

Declan growls, emitting a string of foul and crude words. "That was copious amounts of alcohol, and she was a convenient toy."

Legia gasps. "Oh, Dec, tell me this isn't what—"

Her words cease. Chase has a hand clamped down on her mouth. "You really didn't fornicate with her," he begins, his voice is hoarse. "Because if you did, you deserve whatever Ella does to you."

Seth shudders. "Not even I was that desperate."

"Shut up," Declan grunts. "All of you."

"No, nope, not going to happen. You nailed Selene. We are going to make sure you never forget it too. Oh, you stupid, stupid man." Legia wiggles from Chase and sits next to me on the bench, encircling me with her arms. "Why didn't you say something? No wonder you've been so upset."

I shrug. "Thought you knew."

"What?" Legia pulls back, giving me the most exaggerated expression of shock. "No. No, I did not know that. I would have tried to smack the stupid out of him." She shivers and then hugs herself to me once more. "Ew, so gross."

I giggle as Declan's shoulders slump. He pinches the bridge of his nose. When his hand drops, he shakes his head. "You were declared dead for more than a revolution. I declared you dead." His words are terse and clipped short. "I was..." his jaw clenches, "not in my right mind."

Seth chuckles. "Clearly, if you boned Selene."

Declan looks to the sky exasperated, throwing his hands up. "And after Ella dropped like a ton of iron into the Bryon courtroom, I told Selene to screw herself, I was done."

A laugh rips out of me in a shrill bark. "What?"

He glares at me. "What, what?"

"I think you declared me dead after that." I lean my head to the side. "Again."

"Yeah?" He puts hands on hips. "And? Sordello was busy telling us all that you were a spirit and not dead. Seeing as you'd come back to life once—" he bites his words off. "I was going to..."

I hold my breath. "To what?"

The breeze wafts his hair in front of his face, the strands settling on his nose as he stares into my eyes. Now more than ever, I want to run to him. Legia rests her chin on my shoulder. Declan's eyes flicker from mine to her, then toward the others before returning to me.

"Ella." He stops and puts his hands on his hips. "Lover."

My heart skips a beat, and then another. *Could he really still...?* My lips pull to one side, my whole being shaking. Even my voice wobbles in the air as I ask, "Who are you talking to, exactly? Me or...?"

"Don't." He pinches the bridge of his nose. "Do not fucking say it."

Seth laughs, "Oh, no, please say it, Ell, please, pretty, pretty please with a bright red cherry on top," he begs with glee.

Declan snaps his teeth. "Shut. Up. Now. All of you. I screwed—"

"Selene," Seth snickers.

"—up. Yes, but you were dead. Gone. I declared you dead. I

was in a special kind of hell, and I thought I was never going to see you again." He draws in a shaky breath. "Fuck!" he yells and takes a swing at the shrubbery.

I glance at Legia, who is quietly resting her head on my shoulder. She wrinkles her nose and shudders. "So, so gross."

My head tips back, and I laugh. "Haven," I say to the sky, then focus on Declan. "Come here." I pat the bench next to me. "I'm not mad anymore."

He peers at me with skepticism. "No fucking way."

I give him a smile. "I was. I was angry and, and I mean, I'm pretty sure I threw up. I was a lot of things, but it's okay now."

He moves stiffly and drops next to me. His jaw is tense. I reach out and brush one finger over the bulging muscle. He twitches away from my touch. I sigh.

"I've missed you." His voice is a hoarse croak as he reaches up, pressing my hand against the side of his face.

"I've been right here." I shrug, and Legia's head rocks against me. "I figured you were—that you and her were..." My eyes slip closed, and I take a deep breath. "That you replaced me."

He groans, pulling my hand from his face. He keeps it in his possession, worming his fingers through mine. "Fuck no. Fuck a thousand times, fuck no." A twisted laugh worms from his chest. "I hate that bitch."

I wince. "You say I wasn't talking to you, but you never..." I trail off. "Well, you didn't exactly say much to me either. You wouldn't let me leave the palace."

He cocks a brow, and one side of his mouth tugs up. "You really think I wanted to stay away from you?" He shakes his head and sighs, dropping his head back. "I didn't want to pour fuel on the fire. She's going to go ballistic when she hears about this as it is. She wants to rip your head off, and I'm trying to keep it attached."

I shrug. "She can try, but Sordello and the others, they're

never going to let it happen. I'm never going to let her," I say and stop, my face drawing in on itself.

"And?" Declan's voice drops to a gravel filled snarl. "You were confined here to prevent what I assume happened before you moved my king piece."

I grimace. "Whatever you are assuming, make it twice as bad."

He curls his upper lip back, exposing wicked teeth. "Don't tell me that."

I sigh and shake my head. "I thought I could kill him, but I can't." Legia picks her head up and smacks me in the back of the head. I glare at her. "Ow."

"Oh, sorry, I thought you were the other queen."

I rub the back of my head. "What's that supposed to mean?"

Declan snorts. "Have you forgotten who you are?" He wraps his arm around my neck and pulls me against him, his lips brushing against my forehead. He pulls back with a wicked grin and brushes the hair from my face. "I haven't. You can do anything."

"I'll second," Chase says.

"Carry," Seth chimes in.

I sag against Declan. "I really don't know. I tried."

"What happened?" Declan asks, his voice thick and low. "Something happened, something different."

I snort and nuzzle against his shoulder. "Yeah. He has magic, and not just control the elements, normal mage magic, but a full set of spirit runes. He claims he has a teacher. He cast some kind of blood magic that kept me from controlling the elements."

"Shit," Seth curses. "Who in Damnatus would be teaching him?"

I frown even as Declan pulls me closer, his arm flexing as if he could protect me. "We'll figure it out," he says. "Us, this group, we'll figure it out and fix it."

"Carried," Legia says and moves away. "You two need to talk this through. Like really talk. Figure this out." She wags a finger. "This is killing me, and more importantly, I need to get away from someone who screwed Selene because..." She shivers. "Because that's just... 'That's gross and wrong, and I just can't even imagine or think about it. And I cannot believe you are letting him touch you."

Declan vibrates with rage, but his arm tightens around me as if he is afraid I will pull away. "We are never discussing this again."

"Don't count on it, lover boy." Seth puckers his lips and makes wet, slurping noises.

Legia shoves Seth forward and grabs Chase, dragging him backward. Chase salutes us with a grin. "Gotta go, but we'll keep Selene busy."

They disappear around the corner, and I lift my eyes to Declan. He makes a disgusted face. "I really fucked up."

I jab my finger into his chest, but there is no give of the muscles beneath my touch. "You screwed Selene. Repeatedly."

He grabs my wrist, twisting my arm. I yelp, but he has me in his lap and releases the painful grip. "Morella Rowena Annabelle Byron..." He nuzzles my ear. "I know what I did, but if you say those words to me again, you are going to be in trouble."

I giggle. "You're not going to hurt me."

He smirks. "No, but you are still going to scream."

My lips twist. "Sort of like—"

"You are like a dog with a bone," he growls.

"Of all the women possible, why did it have to be her?"

He pulls back to stare at me with gray eyes and drooping shoulders. "It never crossed my mind who she was. It wasn't you. That was the only thing that mattered to me. I didn't think it would ever be you again, and she was there." He shrugs.

I grimace. "Okay, but, *her*?"

He cups my jaw, pressing his lips to my forehead. "I am telling you that's all it was. A distraction, a use when I was drunk. I'm not making excuses, I'm not trying to ask for forgiveness. I know it's bad."

I press my forehead to his. "So bad." I make a gagging noise. "So, so bad."

He chuckles. "I hate myself for it. I cannot imagine how you must feel about me now."

Getting up, I straddle his hips, knees pressing into the rough cement bench on either side of his legs. He's built thin and lean, and I clasp my fingers around him by the corners of his square jaw. "I don't hate you."

"Ella," he groans, his eyes rolling into the back of his head as they slip closed. "Lover."

"I'm sorry about before, letting Erac break our bond."

"Me too. I've missed the feeling of you." His nose finds my neck. "I miss feeling all of you."

I hum, dragging my nails over his scalp in a gentle scratch. Pain streaks through me. I gasp, twitching, and jerking forward. I scream as the feeling of a knife impaling my heart hits me. I claw at his arms around me, ripping myself away from him. I hit all fours on the ground, panting for breath. Another stab rips a growl of pain from my chest.

My name is being called. A hand grabs me, and I jerk. I hear Declan's voice next to me, begging to know that I am alright.

I gape at him, eyes watering. His hand grips my shoulder. The other hand lifts my jaw, tipping my head back to make eye contact.

"Tell me you are alright," he is whispering. "Please, breathe and let me know you're okay."

I nod as much as I can. His hand is holding my face to his, making the movement difficult. "Diana."

He grimaces, using both hands to pull me to my feet. "Diana? Who the fuck is Diana?"

"A spirit. I can feel it—her, it's the collective. She's hurt."

"There must be a fight. Can you tell me where they are?"

I close my eyes, focusing on her. I grip the front of his shirt in both hands. "Yes."

"Where?"

I shred us apart and piece us together at the source of my pain. There are demons everywhere, rushing around us. Several shoot by, but others take notice, beginning to circle us. I cling to Declan as he starts yelling at me.

A sword appears in his hand, and he shoves me to the ground, swinging at a demon hurtling toward us. I look around, clawing at the dirt to crawl a few paces away from him. The demon's head plops in front of me.

"Ella, where in Damnatus are you going?" Metal on metal clashes and rings out.

Claws sink into my side, and I scream. I shove my hand toward the thing pulling me closer. Energy blasts out of me. The claws retract, and the demon skitters back a few feet. It catches itself on all fours and lunges toward me once more, yellow eyes blazing.

The demon head has leaked onto the ground. The blood and fluids have created a sickening yellow puddle, and I stick my hand into it. My flesh bubbles and sizzles, but I throw every bit of energy I have into the ground. I want to destroy those elements burning my hand. The demon rushing for me barks, dropping to the ground, clawing at its internals. It is making noises of agony and pain.

Others start to drop to the ground. The air is filled with howls of pain. I push harder, digging deeper, feeding as much energy through the ground to seek and destroy the elements making up the demon's blood.

Squeezing my eyes shut, I do my best to ignore the blistering rolling through my arm. I cannot discern if the enormous stream of energy or the contact with the demon blood is causing the sense of shards of metal dragging through my skin. Either way, I try to push past it, to force the energy faster.

"Ella, stop." Two hands grab me, pulling my hand out of the blood. "Haven, Ella, look at me. Come on, stop, let go, it's over." A hand on my face tilts it toward the blurry form of someone.

I blink, wheezing, and pain blossoms through my side. I hiss and wince, looking down to see four holes punched into my side. My blood is soaking the shirt, showing visible glints of the primal fluid against the black fabric.

"You're hurt." His voice is thick. His eyes are black and furious. "Sordello!" he yells, looking around. "Malik? Orso? Damnatus, one of you fucking answer me!"

"Friend." My eyes flicker to the spirit kneeling next to us.

"Lyr," I say. I try to sit up but roll out of Delcan's grasp. I groan and curse.

"The hell are you doing," he growls in response, dragging me back into his arms and cradling me against him. "Lyr is it? Fix her."

A metal armored hand lands against my side. "She destroyed a legion of demons with magic," the spirit says. "She barely has enough energy to breathe."

"I thought they were impervious to magic?"

Breathing hurts. Every inhale sends hot throbbing through my torso and warmth trickling down my side.

"They should be, but Ella is different. She is of Caleum and Medius, she is far more powerful than any of us."

Declan grunts. "Do something. She's bleeding. Dying."

"She'll be okay. It will just take longer."

"I don't fucking care. Do something to make her okay now."

There is a heavy exhale. "The jewel around your neck, give it to her."

Something is forced into my undamaged hand, and a wave of energy crashes through me. It makes it harder to breathe.

Declan rocks me. "Come on, heal yourself. You can. I know you can. You can do fucking anything, so do this."

I try to answer. There is a gurgle coming from the back of my throat. He keeps rocking me in his arms, his head pressed against mine so I cannot see his face.

"Don't you dare, don't you dare die on me," he grunts. He squeezes me against him tighter. "Not again," he whispers. "Please, not again."

"Dec." My eyes roll into the back of my head as pain wracks my body.

"Lover, if you die on me, I will chase you through the Inferno if I—"

# CHAPTER 35

*I* open my eyes. Declan is lying next to me with eyes closed and his chest rising and falling in even slumber. He looks peaceful, bathed in bright, white light filtering through my bedroom windows. I reach out, drawing a finger down his nose.

His eyes snap open, shimmering gray orbs twitching as they watch me. He smirks. "Lover." An arm drapes over my hips, drawing me against him.

"Dec," I breathe, nuzzling into him.

He rolls us over, so I am pinned beneath him. His teeth nip at my neck. My eyes roll into the back of my head, and my breath catches in the back of my throat. The feeling of his mouth against me is incredible, and I moan.

He chuckles as one of his large hands wraps around the base of my jaw and throat, tilting my mouth up. I scream.

He wrenches his hand away, lifting his torso from mine, eyes wide. "What the hell was that?"

I reach out, grabbing his biceps. "Oh." He is solid beneath my grip. "It's you."

He gives me an incredulous glare. "Of course, it's me. Who else would it be?" There is an edge to his voice.

"Not you?"

"You scared the hell out of me," he grunts, settling his weight down between my legs and on top of me. "Again."

"Sorry," I glance around us. "What do you mean, again?"

He stares at me stone-faced. He shakes his head, and the bare bones of a smile touch his lips. "Take your pick. Breaking the bond. Dying." He nods. "Dying. Seeing that chess piece coated in your blood and hearing Samuel tell me that you showed up with half your face covered in blood. Dissipating us to the middle of a battlefield." He clenches his jaw and shoves his next words through bared teeth. "On the wrong damn side."

I wince. "I didn't know. I just went to the source of pain. Diana." My heart ratchets up. "Diana was—"

"Diana is fine," he says, cutting me off. His jaw and face relax. "You, on the other hand, *died again*." He emphasizes the last two words and glares at me. "Haven, I cannot handle you dying this much."

A giggle escapes me. "Is it really dying if I don't stay dead?"

He narrows his eyes. "Yes. And then there is whatever that was." He jerks his head at me.

I cannot bring myself to look at him. He chuckles a bit, pressing both my hands above my head together in one hand, using his second hand to lift my face. "What was that?"

"Um... It was, uh..." I try to look away, but he grips my chin in his hand. "Um, well, you uh, you show up and then... They're like, memories, but not. They start off really good, though."

"They?" he asks with a terse voice. "Nightmares," he scoffs and shakes his head, dipping his face lower to nuzzle the corner of my jaw. "I should have known. That's why you wanted to sleep in the dining hall, why you haven't been sleeping at all."

I wince. "I mean, I tried at first."

He holds my gaze. "So, these dreams start good, and then what?"

"And then, um, well..." I make a face and fidget. "And then you, uh... Well, you—"

"Take a deep breath and tell me."

I close my eyes. "It's always just you and me, and they start off nice, sometimes reliving memories, and then, well, you..." I exhale. "You say all kinds of things, mostly that you'll never forgive me, and then, well, you mostly strangle me."

My eyes remain shut. The feeling of the thumb of his free hand rubbing over my cheekbone feels nice. Tension releases from me.

"Look at me." My eyes snap open to stare into slate gray eyes. "I forgive you." My eyes burn, and I blink but try not to look away. "I forgave you the moment I found your family estate destroyed. It hadn't been worth..." He stops, his jaw muscles tense and bulge, and then release. "I thought I had lost what little time I had with you over... It doesn't matter. I forgive you. Do you hear me? I forgive you."

"I hear you."

He bends his head down and presses his lips to mine. I sigh into him, my lips parting, my fingers curling, and his hand baring down onto my wrists. His tongue licks against mine. I rip my face to the side, leaving him gaping at me with daft confusion.

"Lover?"

"No." Crystal orbs cling to my lashes and burn like pinpricks. "No. Selene."

He bares his teeth at me. "Do not say those words." I am startled by his abruptly developed and displayed rage. "I made bad choices. I can't go back and undo what I did. All I can say is I honestly believed you were dead, and as soon as I knew you were alive, I remedied the situation."

"Remedied?" I shake my head, attempting to pull my wrists free. "No, Dec, that isn't what I mean at all."

A growl emits from low in his chest as he bears down on me, forcing me into the plush mattress. He crushes his mouth against mine, his tongue licking along mine. The kiss is demanding and hard, his weight suffocating me, but it is exquisite. After a moment, he pulls back, breathing raggedly.

"She's better for you," I pant. "She—"

He is kissing me again, ceasing my words. He pulls back, his teeth biting and pulling my lower lip. His hands grip my face, forcing me to look at him. "I cannot stand Selene. She is a vain and jealous creature. If she were not so stupid, she might be more akin to Viktor in her endeavors." He gives me that lopsided grin I adore. "I really hate her."

I glance at the ceiling over his head. "She tried to show that she cares." I look back with tears in my eyes. "I never did that, never."

He smirks, then presses his mouth to mine. His mouth is softer, his hands roaming over my body. I cling to him as he assaults my mouth with his, enjoying every second.

"I know you care. You always care. About everyone." His voice is low and deep, full of emotion. "You could have what Viktor wants. You can do what he is attempting to, and all you want to do is help. I find it insufferable, the way your heart bleeds for others. It is maddening and unfathomable, and I adore you for it." Two fingers lift my chin, and he lands little butterfly kisses on the tip of my nose. He presses his lips to my forehead. "I want you to stand by my side and stop hiding. You don't have to hide anymore."

He tips my head back further, and his mouth comes down on mine yet again. My toes curl just as my fingers curl into the front of his shirt. A noise escapes me, a sigh torn between longing and pleasure.

"Dec." I bite my lip.

He raises a single brow at me.

"I mean, you screwed Selene."

His eyes narrow, his mouth becoming a hard line.

"Haven, you look pissed, but you did it."

"I did, and from this point forward, I never want to hear about it, think about it, or remember it." A shudder rips through his torso.

"So, you're not... I mean, you aren't in love?"

He laughs like I have just told him the funniest joke in the universe. He tries to kiss me while still chortling. "You are too damn cute."

I roll my eyes, having no idea what I said that is so funny. "I'm not cute."

He tucks loose hair back from my face behind my ear. "Sex isn't love, but I suppose someone like you would never understand that."

"Sure, I guess."

He grins. "You'd never touch someone you do not care for."

I look away, considering. There are few I could think willing to fornicate with me. Erac would be willing. I think about having sex with Erac and grimace, giving in to a full-body shiver.

Declan lets out a bark of laughter, pulling my face to his. I get a brief taste of his tongue before he pulls back. On his feet, he takes my hands in his, pulling me from the bed to my feet. The cool air kisses my naked flesh as his eyes drop to my uncovered body. My face flames. He smirks as I attempt to cover myself.

"Dec," I whine.

He prevents me from grabbing a blanket from the bed, pressing me against him. He kisses me, his hands sliding down my back to grip my butt. He pulls back and spins me around. The sensation of his fingers running along my spine gives me goosebumps.

"I noticed when I brought you here, got you out of those bloody clothes. What happened to you?"

I glance over my shoulder. "The spirits. Sordello had them take them."

His eyes trail down my back. He spins me, fingers brushing against my skin where scars long gone ought to be. He lifts my leg, his fingers cupping the back of my thigh as his thumb runs down the smooth skin on top. "There's nothing left."

I hold my forearm between us. "Nothing but this one."

He grabs my forearm, caressing me with his thumbs. "Which? This?" He brushes over it, lifting curious eyes to mine.

"You gave me that one. Well..." I flip the arm over, showing the remainder of the exit wound. "Both. I wouldn't let them take it. I thought it was the only thing I had left of you."

His eyes glitter as silver does in the sun. "Get dressed. We're getting married."

"What?"

His eyebrows lift. "Marry me."

"Um?"

"Marry me, please?" His brows furrowing together.

"Now?"

"Now."

With the use of elements, I create a dress of cream fabric that shimmers gold as I move. Then Declan takes me by the hand, and cold seeps through me. I sigh, giving in to his control over my elements.

We are in a massive tent. Seth stares at us, stopping midsentence with his mouth open next to Malik. I glance around at the other surprised faces, some I know, others foreign. Legia wrinkles her nose at me.

Declan clears his throat. "Sordello?"

I point at my father in the middle of the room. The man next to him surprises me. "Marx?"

Marx gives me a closed-lip smile. "Ella. A pleasant surprise, given your current predicament."

I give him a rude gesture with my hand, drawing a booming laugh.

"It's always a pleasure, young queen."

I grin at him. "Likewise, old king."

Declan gives me a look, then his eyes travel around the room. "Sordello? You're a king of sorts."

My father turns, his arms dropping from across his chest to hang by his sides. "Yes, boy, I am."

"Marry us."

"Now?" The hooded face flips between Declan and me.

"Now," Declan and I say in unison.

He nods, coming over to us. "You exchange rings, yes?"

Declan produces the old engagement ring. I stare. "Haven, Dec, you cannot be serious. How did you even find that?"

"You do not know how long I worked on creating this bloody thing!"

I laugh and then get an idea. I pull on the chain around his neck, breaking the sapphire away. He scowls at me. I roll my eyes, compressing the gem between both of my hands. I close my eyes, compacting the elements, rounding the jewel, and hollowing it out.

I pant a bit but smile as I hold it up to him. "See if that fits."

He takes the ring. His pupils dilate. "Damnatus," he breathes, "that's stronger."

"Does it fit?"

He slides it onto the second to last finger of his left hand. He flexes his fingers. "Yes."

He grips my left hand to worm my engagement ring over the knuckle. Once on, he pushes it to his lips. "Still fit?" I nod. "Good."

He looks at Sordello, who waves a hand between us. "Is this all? Do I need to say words or something?"

We look at each other. My eyes cut left and then right at those around us. "You know—" I sigh.

"We have no idea," Declan finishes for me.

"You need to agree to maintain a bond," Legia shouts. I glance over my shoulder toward her. Chase stands with an arm around her. They are both smiling ear to ear.

"And agree to commit to each other," Chase adds.

I smirk. "I agree to commit to a bond."

Declan's eyes sparkle, but Sordello sighs. "I believe the words were—"

"No, I agree to commit to a bond," he repeats. "That's it."

"Then, consider yourselves married."

There are cheers and clapping from around the tent. Declan grabs my face. "Mine," he growls softly, probably so low only I can hear.

I kiss him, arching into him as he leans over, tipping me back. I shriek with laughter and sheer happiness. Then the cold rushes through me.

When I open my eyes, I gasp. We are in a cavern with dancing, glittering green water. The light reflects off the water's jewel surface and casts around the white marble walls. I look around, trying to figure out where the light is coming from. It appears the water itself is the shimmering source.

Declan begins to tug at my dress. He curses, and it disappears. Swinging me in his arms, he steps toward the water.

"Declan, don't you dare."

He tosses me into the water. I yelp, expecting it to be cold, but the spring is warm. I wipe water from my face, treading the surface, watching him peel his shirt off over his head. I grin up at him with my tongue between my teeth.

Naked, he plunges in next to me. He pulls me to him, kissing me. We bob under the water, breaching the surface and laughing like idiots. He shoves me toward the edge.

My eyes sweep around us. "What is this place?"

"I found it looking for the runes."

I grimace. "Under Marx?" I fold my arms on the edge and rest against the wall. "It's beautiful."

"I wanted to wash any remaining blood or demon pus from you."

"Mmm," I hum, looking at him, clinging to the wall next to me. "And a shower wouldn't do?"

"I didn't want to be interrupted." He grins. "I really want to sink my cock and teeth into you, and Selene is going to be out for blood."

I roll my eyes and rest my chin on my forearms, the warm water lapping around me. "We're going to have to deal with her sooner or later unless we decide to move in here."

"Yes, and I will, but she is coming for your head. You left the palace and destroyed a legion of demons." He tilts his head and narrows his eyes. "Which you did with magic, by the way." He grabs the ledge. "How did you manage that when not even the spirits can?"

My eyes wander about the cavern's marble walls. "I don't know. I kinda figured out I could do that a while ago, though."

"Yeah? We'll talk about *that* later." His tone is cranky. He reaches out, water trickling from his fingers and over my shoulder, but his voice shifts to tender. "I liked your wording."

I smile. "I thought you might think I just screwed it up."

"No, I understood." He adjusts and looks away. "Ella." The muscles in his jaw jump and his nostrils flare. "You have a choice."

"I already chose, Dec." I reach out, putting a hand on his arm. "I choose you. I choose the bond with you." His eyes lock on mine with a ravenous hunger. I move from clinging to the wall to clinging to him. "I will always choose you."

# CHAPTER 36

*S* *he's beautiful.*

    I can hear him, lying on my stomach, head on his shoulder, watching the way the light dances on the marble walls. I am floating somewhere between ecstasy and disbelief as his fingers trail over my spine. My head is throbbing in time with my heart, and I wish it would stop. It is the only thing keeping me from bliss.

*"It's your own damn fault, lover."* He chuckles and kisses my shoulder. "If you ever break our bond again, though, I'll break your neck to give me a reason to have to go through this again."

I snort and snuggle in closer to him, relieved when he wraps me in his arms and pulls me close. *I bet he's thought about breaking my neck anyway.*

"No. Not you, never you. I won't hurt you," he murmurs and kisses my temple. He growls in my ear and squeezes tighter. *"You are mine. It has taken me too long and too much work to fix what you did. Mine. I had to make you mine again. My head hurts, and I've been worried half to death about what is going on with you. You're mine. Mine. All mine. I must protect you."*

I roll over in his arms, wiggling against him. "I'm sorry." My heart hurts. "For everything. For always missing sessions and leaving you to deal with the crown on your own. For... I didn't know what to do, I guess, so I just did nothing."

He kisses the round of my shoulder. There are no judgments coming through our link, only support and love. I groan and squeeze my eyes shut.

"Dec, you should be furious with me."

He chuckles. "I was. I wanted to slaughter the court and drown you in their blood for what you—what I... After that fight, after you let that prick Erac break our fucking bond." He sighs. "That was... Fuck, that was low. I charged Marcus with the court and got the fuck out of there before I hurt someone. I thought you'd hate me if I did."

I snuggle into him, and his hand lands on my hip. "I don't think I could ever hate you."

He nips my earlobe. "And when I came back—when Marcus told me you wanted to see me..." His face buries against my neck. "I lost it when I saw the estate. Nothing mattered to me but finding you. I spent two days searching for you before Seth said what I wouldn't, couldn't." His arms wrap around me and squeeze me tight enough to crush my lungs and force the air from my chest. He lets up.

"Fuck." His voice is constricted with emotions. "I didn't care about Erac or our bond, or all the times you missed session. I didn't give a flying fuck about anything other than wanting to hold you, hear you laugh."

The pain leaking from him into me pricks my eyes with tears. I smile at his overwhelming love. "I know what you mean." I recall times in Medius, thinking about him and the tumultuous aftermath of seeing him with Selene.

A snarl curls in the back of his throat. "I came to that spot every chance I could. That bitch got a hold of me on my way there that day, and I was too drunk to care if she was there or not." A wretched, dark chuckle escapes him. "I should have pushed her off Shadow on the way there. I should have known you weren't dead."

"There's absolutely no way," I chortle, "no way you could have known. What elemental in their right mind would think, hmm, she probably dissipated to Medius and just blew up the estate by accident in the power release it took to move between the dimensions?"

He grumbles deep in his chest and runs his hand down my body. "I blamed myself."

"I thought you were better off with Selene."

"Haven," he groans and presses his face against me. "Do not mention that to me ever again. I am erasing those memories and never want to hear about it again."

I snicker. "No, really, she—"

He rolls over, forcing me facedown, his body covering mine. "Lover, you're not dead. You're naked, in my arms—I just fucked you—we are not talking about this."

One of his hands collects my hair in a fist, dragging it away to expose my neck. The other is wrapped around the front of my neck as he bites my shoulder. I twitch at the sharp sting, but it is not hard enough to puncture through skin.

I grin. "Then what are we talking about?"

"How fucking happy I am to have you back—that you aren't dead—that you'd still choose me."

I do my best to cut my eyes to him. "I'll always choose you. I like you." He angles his face and lifts his brows at me. "Yeah, I do. I like you, who you are. You're my best friend. You're good for me and to me." I bite my lower lip and smile. "I love you, Declan Dean Bard."

A soft whimper releases from him as he stares at me with an expression I have never seen before. I am on my back. His mouth is on mine. His fingers are digging into my flesh as he grips me, pressing himself to me.

"Declan Dean Byron," he pulls back to murmur against my lips.

I snort through my nose with laughter. "Oh, right. Hmm. Are you sure about being a Byron?"

"Fuck no, but," he murmurs against my lips. "I don't ever want to not be able to feel you, hear you, ever again. I felt so empty without you." His face pulls away from me. "Promise me."

I open my eyes to see silver orbs staring at me. "Promise what?"

"Promise me, you and me, no matter what, that we will figure it out together. Promise me we can make this work, that you'll stay here with me, that this is the last beginning. Promise me you'll love me even at the worst of times and especially at the best. Promise me that you'll always be my wife."

I smile at him in bliss. "I promise."

# CHAPTER 37

*I* dissipate Declan and myself back to Byron Palace. We stand in front of the window seat in my room. I blink, my eyes focusing on the individual lounging in my window seat.

"Seth?"

He grins. "Ell." He stands, wrapping me in a giant hug. "Congratulations." He lets go of me, offering a hand to Declan.

"Thank you." Declan looks pleased, but he is fuming that his brother is here. He wanted to drag me to the bed and continue ignoring the world.

I grin, wrapping my arms around his waist and tucking myself under his arm. He kisses the top of my head.

"You two probably want to be left alone..." Seth rubs the back of his neck. "But, I am under strict orders to deliver you to the dining hall as soon as you arrive."

I raise my eyebrows, peeking at him. "Why?"

He squirms. "Can't tell you that."

Neither Declan nor I believe he is incapable of telling us. Declan laughs. "Under threat of bodily harm, if you drag Ella and me out of here for something, it had better be worth it."

Seth kicks at the ground and winces. "Damned if I do and damned if I don't." He smirks. "Follow me."

I roll my eyes. "You said, dining hall?" I hold my hand out, one arm still clinging to Declan.

Seth takes my offered hand. "Dining hall."

I rip the three of us apart and build us back together in front of the doors. Seth shudders. "I don't think I am ever going to get used to that feeling."

Declan hums at him. "Why are we here?"

Seth sighs and opens the door. He waves a hand, ushering us inside. I glance at Declan in time to watch his nostrils flare, then he takes my hand and drags me forward.

As we enter, there is applause. Declan starts to fume, but my head tips back, and I laugh.

*"This is not what I had in mind for tonight."*

I laugh harder. Legia and Cannamore come bouncing forward. They wrap themselves around me, pushing Declan away. They squeal in unison, ensuring I will hear a ringing in my ears for the next minute.

*"Haven, I think I'd rather get hit by the bell in Clemm again."*

*"And I would rather you hit me with a wave of fire again than be here right now."*

I laugh harder. They let go, Cannmore dragging me along, Legia leading the way. I glance over my shoulder at Declan with his hands in his jean's pockets, rocking on the balls of his feet.

Cannamore and Legia giggle as they shove me back into the kitchens. "Haven, Ella, this is what you wear to your reception?"

"Reception?"

"Black, Ella? Whose funeral is it?"

I glance around, then toward the dining hall. "Don't know yet, but give me a minute. I might kill Selene if I see her." I grin.

The girls snicker. Legia snaps her fingers at me. "Dress, now."

I roll my eyes but comply.

"*Marx is here. And Erac. And Selene. And everyone in all of Caleum.*" Declan is far from pleased.

I sigh. "Legia, what did you do?"

Cannamore is busy running her fingers through my hair, brushing it out to twist it in a pretty fashion. She giggles. "She's throwing you your wedding reception."

"Much more grand fashion than your ball. So, hold still." Legia taps the end of my nose with a makeup brush.

When they are done preening over me, they drag me back into the hall. Declan is leaning against the wall, one leg bent up as he stares at the floor. As we burst through the door, he looks to us. His eyes train on me, and his thoughts sink toward dissipating us back to the cave where we could be alone without interruption.

I grin at him. He offers me his hand. "I was instructed that we are to dance whenever you were ready."

I glare at his hand, then at my friends. "Dance?" I throw my hands up in the air. "I'll take the dress, the hair, the makeup, the shoes." I lift my skirt showing the heels adorning my feet, only to throw it down in a huff. "But dancing?"

Declan wiggles his fingers at me. "*Come on, let's get this over with.*"

I roll my eyes and take his hand. I glare at the two women over my shoulder. "This is ridiculous."

Declan leads me to the middle of the dining hall, where tables have been cleared to create space. He squares up to me, watching me down his thin nose. I make a face of disgust at him. He smirks.

"Just follow." He grins. "And avoid my feet."

I narrow my eyes. I consider sticking my feet between his if I could find my feet under this dress. The music starts. He pulls me forward as he steps back.

"*I hate dancing.*"

"*Have you ever considered it as a fight? I've watched you dance around a pole swinging and stepping in time.*"

I peer at him with admiration. "*You know, I've never considered it that way.*"

He nods curtly and twirls me. "*Each step is away or toward an opponent.*"

"*Yet you never land a punch.*"

He smirks. "*Alas, there you have the problem with dancing.*"

I snicker as he dips me, and the music dies. I reach up, tugging his face to mine, kissing him. He rights us, pulling away from me with a grin smeared across his face.

I look around the room, spying Selene standing next to Skylar. They are scowling. "*This must be killing them.*"

"*What do I care?*"

"*Two jilted women watching you with your wife? They have both tried to hurt me in various ways throughout my life, and one is seriously trying to kill me.*"

Declan plants a kiss on my temple, leading me away from them to our closest friends. Marcus beams at me as we approach.

There are smiles all around, and remarks of congratulations and joy abound. I cannot keep the smile from my face, nor the welling in my chest at bay. Declan keeps a firm grip on me. Despite his grins and shared happiness, his thoughts are only half focused on the present. He is dwelling on what I said about Skylar and Selene.

"*Ten more minutes, lover, then we are leaving.*"

I nod, watching Erac approach. Declan stiffens next to me. Erac ignores me, extending a hand to Declan.

"Congratulations." His tone is flat. He is smiling, but the expression does not touch his violet eyes. They remain dark.

Declan takes his hand. "Thank you." He drops his hand.

Erac turns to me. "May I have a dance, Ella?"

"No, you may not," Declan answers for me.

"Perhaps another time," I say quietly. I do not want to incur a fight right now.

Erac grimaces. "Of course. There will be plenty of time. You will outlive your weak and fragile husband." He turns on his heel and saunters away.

I gape after him with wide eyes. *"Did he really just say that?"*

*"We're leaving."* Declan's fingers lace in mine. *"Now."*

I nod. "Legia."

She looks to me. "No." She points a finger at me. "No, you will not leave. You just got here. And I went through all this trouble." She looks around.

*"And we never asked for this."* Declan is losing his temper. Outwardly, he sighs. "We are appreciative, Legia, but neither of us is overly fond of dances."

She pouts. "Five more minutes." She lifts her glass. "I need a drink. I want to make a toast to my king and queen."

Confusion blooms between Declan and me. We share sideways glances, and I frown. "I don't think either of us is royalty at this point."

"Not entirely true."

I raise my brows at Declan. "What?"

"Sordello has been perfectly clear that you are his daughter. As king of the spirits, that makes you royalty, a princess, in fact."

I roll my shoulders. *"I was fine without a title."*

He kisses my temple. "Get a drink, Legia, and make your toast, and then we are leaving."

She sticks her lower lip out. She huffs, then spins. Cannamore grabs me. "Come on, Ella, come with us."

Declan lets go of me, and the three of us head to the servants distributing drinks. I stand at the end of them and wait for a servant to finish with the others who came before us. I look around at the faces of everyone present.

I get the feeling of disgust. My eyes scan for my husband and the source. I find Selene speaking with Declan. I frown, watching her laugh. She holds a tray of glasses, handing them out. Marcus meets my gaze and grimaces.

"Hello, Ella."

I look to see Skylar standing next to me. She offers me a flute of champagne. I nearly snarl at her. "Hello."

A deep feeling of uneasiness settles like a rock in my stomach. I exhale. Skylar shoves the glass further in my face. "A congratulatory toast to you, Morella."

The sound of my full name feels like spiders crawling down my spine. I take the glass, down it, and offer it back to her. "Thank you, Skylar, you are too generous."

She sneers. "You deserve this, that's for sure."

She turns on her heel and strides away with her head held high. My gut clenches, my stomach churning. I exhale the aftertaste of alcohol on my tongue. I look back at Legia and Cannamore.

They are gaping at me. "Why in Haven's name did you just drink something from Skylar?"

My eyes shift between them. "She didn't just get that from the bar?"

The girls give each other looks of shock. "No." Legia shakes her head. "No, she just walked over with it."

I wince. "Well, even if I die, it won't stick."

I expect a growl from Declan or for him to come storming over. Neither happens. He stands with the others, holding an empty flute.

I look back at Legia. "I should go," I breathe, "before something happens."

The women nod in unison. "Yes, that is a good idea."

We get four steps from the bar when Elizabeth cuts between us and the group of men. She grabs my shoulders, leaning in and kissing one cheek and then the other. "You look adorable! How cute of your little friends to throw this party for you."

Next to her, Wyatt inclines his head. "Very beautiful, Ella." He looks to be in pain. Still, he offers a hand to me. "Come dance with me."

Elizabeth smacks his hand away. "Never mind that now! She has a husband to attend."

On cue, we all look toward Declan. He is hunched over, sideways, and twisted wrongly, mouth to mouth with Selene. I feel a flicker of anger, but Selene's eyes are open, cut toward me. In the back of my mind, I know she is trying to make me jealous.

I sigh. Shaking my head, I look to Elizabeth. She grins, showing off her too-big teeth. "Oh my." She fakes surprise, covering her mouth with a hand. "Maybe the happy couple isn't all that happy."

I should feel the rage of my inner demon unfurling, but the world feels sluggish. I look back to Declan, who has my sister at arm's length. He is giving her a look of disgust, saying something.

"Ella," Wyatt takes a step forward.

Elizabeth clamps a hand on his arm, jerking him back. "Stop right there, Wyatt."

His gaze flickers around the room. He is pale, his eyes dilated. I frown, feeling Legia link her arm in mine.

"What is going on?" she demands. "What have you done to my brother?"

"Legia," Wyatt shakes his head.

"You're afraid." The words blurt out of my mouth before I can even register it as a thought. My tongue feels too large in my mouth. I try to shake off the feeling.

"He has no reason to be afraid." Elizabeth wraps her arm through his, pulling him close to her. "We have an understanding."

Legia lets go of me, stepping forward. She may be in a dress, but the stone expression of her face lets me know she is a hunter right now, not a fashionable young woman. "Let go of him and leave us."

Elizabeth laughs. "No can do, little one." She taps a finger against Legia's nose. "You'll know soon enough."

Shrill screams come from further away in the room. My head pivots toward the source of the commotion. I do not know why I feel so sluggish. Demons are cutting through the crowd, and my heart should skip a beat, but it rolls over evenly.

I take a step and falter, my knees buckling under the weight. Cannamore and Legia try to help me back to my feet. I stand, shaking. "What's going on? What did you do to me?"

Elizabeth's grin claims her whole face. "Right on time."

"Time?" Cannamore squeaks.

I look to Declan, sure he is going to come to me. My eyes take seconds to focus from close to far. I blink, realizing the duchess is standing next to Declan. Marcus and Chase stand, frozen in time.

"No." I try to take another step, and my friends struggle to keep me on my feet. "No." I slur. Breathing and moving are taking far too much energy. "Dec."

I watch as the duchess speaks. I cannot hear her, only see her lips moving. Declan drops to his knees. A blade glints in the duchess' hand, her other a fist gripping the hair at the top of his head. My eyes lock on Declan's. I cannot breathe. I blink, seeing the tip of a blade pressed against his neck.

I lift a hand, watching the limb shake. My arm is like marble, heavy, detached, and cold. I try to make a fist, gripping at the air in front of me. I open my fingers, trying to focus enough to pull the blade from the duchess. Nothing happens, my head is too thick and foggy. I cannot concentrate enough to bend the elements to my will.

Tears burn my eyes in confusion and fear. I reach for him through our link but only feel a blistering cold. The sensation is familiar, the same as when I believed he was dead. It is wrong, an interruption in our bond, but not a removal.

The blade drags across his throat, a red line forming behind it as it moves like a tracer. I blink, the line thickening until blood is pouring forth. It rushes down his neck, staining the front of his shirt. His head bobs, even under the duchess' grip. His body is shaking and jerking, and then she lets go, and he falls forward.

"No!"

My scream kickstarts the room into full-blown chaos. Everyone moves, running around as everything blurs. Elizabeth stands, grinning, holding Wyatt to her side. She turns, pulling him away. Legia lets go of me, going after her.

Cannamore tries to move me, but I stumble. She lets go of me, throwing her hands up at a progressing demon. It barely slows, then swings an arm in a backstroke, knocking her legs from under her. She lands with a sickening crunch.

I stare at the demon, holding a hand up toward it. The elements fail me as it swings an arm at me. The contact burns, the force of the hit knocking air from my lungs. I blink, realizing I am on my back, staring at the ceiling. The world is spinning around me.

"Ella?" Hands grab me.

"Marc?"

"Haven, Ella, what are you doing? Snap out of it. Come on, fight, get to Dec and heal him."

Another pair of hands latch onto me. Marcus glares at the other. My head rolls on my neck. Erac is helping to support me.

"What are you doing? Go help them." Marcus waves around the room. "I'll get Ella out of here."

Erac chuckles. "No. I will get Ella out of here."

"I'm not as useful as you are. I can barely control the elements at all."

I try to get my feet to work. One step and I falter again. I curse, the words slurring from my lips. I need to get to Declan.

"I know." Erac pulls a blade from thin air. "You're a disgrace to the name mage."

Marcus throws a hand up, but Erac grabs hold of it with his free hand. He stabs the blade into Marcus' gut.

The world is growing gray around my field of vision. Erac shoves my brother, who stumbles back. I feel his hand on my bare shoulder. I feel something warm and wet between our flesh. Blood. Marcus' blood. I feel sick, and I make a fist, twisting to spin and punch Erac.

The blow glances off his stomach. He grins at me. "It's alright, Ella. Everything is going to be alright."

I feel the cold spreading through my chest. I try to protest, but the world goes black around me.

# CHAPTER 38

*I* find myself in a familiar room. It is large, open, and round. I sway on my feet, and Erac catches me as I begin to fall. He lowers me to the ground, leaving me to stare out a large open window. Gauzy curtains billow in a breeze.

"Easy there," he tells me in a hushed tone. "Just breathe. Don't do anything stupid. You've taken a strong paralytic."

"What?"

"We needed you to be weakened, to be unable to control the elements."

His face disappears from above me. The world is spinning beneath me. My head falls to the right, and I watch him kneel next to me. A small wooden chest is set in front of my face.

"These are your bearings, Ella. The very ones given to you by Viktor. You never used them." His tone is quiet but steady. "They need only be marked and applied. Viktor wanted me to use these bearings specifically, his gift to you. He said that it would only be fitting, as this is all a gift to you."

I try to speak, but all that escapes me is a gurgle.

"Hush, my love." One of his fingers runs down my cheek. "You need only relax. Breathe. I will do the rest."

*"What is he going to do to me?"*

Fear clogs my throat. My breathing pitches, beginning to quicken. I take short pants, barely feeling the air in my lungs now.

*"Haven, what is happening to me? What have they done to me? Oh, Haven, Declan?"*

Water is leaking from my eyes, my vision narrowing. I feel the stinging pain of something sharp against my fingertip. I manage to focus on Erac. He lifts a small metal ball from the chest, drawing against the surface with a small, thin piece of metal.

"Memories are an easy thing to trap within a bearing." His even, low tone is relaxing.

*No,* I scream at myself, *don't relax. Fight. Fight back.*

"The thought would never have occurred to me if Marx had not given me the idea. It was brilliant, what he did to remove Declan's real memories and implant false ones."

Panic is causing my mind to thrash. The demon in me is starting to trash out of sheer will to survive. Another gurgle escapes the back of my throat. I try to swallow, air wheezing past the drool collecting in the back of my throat when I fail.

"Now, I am going to remove your memories." My arm lifts, his hand gripping my wrist. "Memories are powerful. They're our experiences, the personal connections we share, and the lessons we learn. They make us who we are, and without those? You'll be an empty vessel for me to shape and mold as you always should have been."

He shoves the metal ball against my skin. There is a burning sensation, like the flame of a candle against my skin. The pressure behind the bearing increases, the ball glowing bright blue. I watch in a haze. My right arm twitches in his grasp as I try to command my body to move away.

The burning sensation lingers as the bearing dims from the glowing bright blue to a burned discolored metal. Heat is discharging away, but the throbbing burning remains. Another sharp sting against my finger occurs, then Erac draws on a bearing again. He repeats the process. The bearing is suctioned to my arm next to the previous one.

I want to ask what he is doing to me, but the words fade in my mind. I blink. There is a man next to me. He looks familiar, his violet eyes burning in the dim light of the room. His name lingers unknown on the tip of my tongue. I watch, confused, as he takes a small, thin piece of metal in one hand. I feel a sting in my fingertip.

*What is happening?*

He touches the thin piece of metal to a small metal ball. I watch him draw on the surface, then press the ball to my wrist. It burns. My arm twitches.

My head is swimming. *Where am I? What is happening to me?*

I try to ask who the man is, but there is a sting in my fingertip. The pain distracts me. He presses a thin piece of metal against a metal ball.

*What is he doing?*

The metal ball presses against my wrist. There is a blistering pain. I cannot fathom how to describe the pain. It feels too hot.

My head swims. Every thought in my head is like smoke. The tendrils curl, but when I think there is a solid thought, it disappears.

I stare, blinking away wetness. Drops roll down my cheeks as he releases my arm. It lands on the floor without resistance. Free from his grip, I try to move. My left leg twitches.

"Breathe, Morella, and relax. It is over."

*What is over? Morella? Is that my name?*

# CHAPTER 39

## DECLAN

*I*'m thirsty. Not a desire to drink, but a need. My throat is tight. Every draw of air splinters pain down my esophagus. There's a burning pain down the front of my neck. Mid-range is the worst. I try to swallow, making the muscles work. I snarl in pain.

The pain is only doubled by the demanding urge to consume. I need to wet my tongue, get liquid down my pharynx. The tangy metallic taste of life-giving blood is all I want. I growl, my thoughts bathed in a red haze, a desire for blood.

There is an echo to my heartbeat. The thunk-clunk is reverberating in my ears. I sniff the air, tasting with my tongue. Someone is close. I hear panicked breathing, a source for what I crave. I twist to a crouch, my eyes focusing. Gray everywhere, my vision focusing in and out in time with my heartbeat.

There's something else here, the source of the heartbeat. I grin, my dry lips cracking as they pull. I lunge, tackling the vessel, emitting a guttural growl. I bite the nearest part, feeling flesh and bone give way under my jaws as I clamp down. The deeper I pierce my victim, the more it will bleed.

A purr of pleasure escapes me as the first taste of sweet

blood teases the tip of my tongue. I clamp down harder, trying to push my teeth further. There are noises. Ones of pain and fear. They tantalize my senses. With a grin, I swallow the first mouthful of blood. Pain and fear are my friends. They make a heart beat faster, increasing the blood flowing into me.

The vessel squirms. I move my grip, feeling blindly for a softer area, something that will bleed more. I find that patch of softness, the skin feels so delicate.

I swallow again, my throat aching with heat. Growling, I latch onto the spot, biting down and ripping the flesh with my teeth. There is a scream. It is louder. I must be closer to the mouth. I drink blissfully as the thing flails.

The flailing becomes twitching. The twitching stops. As do the noises. I growl, ripping at the flesh, having to suck harder to draw blood forth. It is not enough. I need more. I pull at the body, sinking teeth into different areas to reach pools of blood remaining. The vessel is dead; even I can tell that now. The blood is growing colder, hardly any left to draw out.

A deafening metal against metal grating draws my attention, my head snapping toward the source. My ears ring. My head hurts, pounding in time with the throb in my neck. I want quiet. I'll kill whatever is making the noise. I glance about wildly for the source.

There are gray walls all around. A door is open, a man standing there. Bright blue orbs watch me from its head. I hate those eyes. I want to rip them out.

I jerk toward it, fumbling and stumbling over the empty vessel. The man shoves something else, someone else toward me. The grating screech is back. I blink. The door is closed, there is another heartbeat. A woman. She turns, banging and screaming on the door. It is loud, so loud.

I need more. The burn in the throat is pulsating with sharp jolts of pain and what feels like flies dancing across my skin. I stalk toward her, listening to the steady strumming from within her center. She turns her back to the door. The stance is perfect. I can already see the neck, the most vulnerable, softest part. The skin is thin. It breaks and tears beneath my teeth.

~

*I* am crouched in the corner of the cell. The only light coming in is from the window with bars. Holding my head in my hands, I try not to look too hard at the blood congealing on the floor. I gorged myself so much the sight of the stuff is making me queasy.

There are bodies strewn about. I count five. Five lives I have just taken to save my own. I drop my head between my knees, trying to breathe. My neck is easing up, the last lingering itch of the skin pinching together diminishing. I grab at my hair on the back of my head.

*That damn woman and her bleeding heart are going to hate me for murdering five innocent elementals.* I look up, dropping my hands to rest my elbows on my knees. *Then again, she may just be happy I survived.*

I stand, stretching. I roll my shoulders, forcing my head this way and that. With a sigh, I step through the bodies. I knock on the door.

No answer. I try again. This time a voice answers me. "Are you civilized again?"

"Open this damn door, Marx." The door swings open. He stares at me with those disturbing, bright eyes. I glance over my shoulder at the mess. "How long have I been locked in here?"

"Less than a full day." He crosses his arms. "You recovered quite a bit faster than I expected." His eyes shift to the cell behind me.

Silently I snarl at him. "Does Ella know what it cost to keep me alive?"

Marx shakes his head. "No."

I sigh and reach for her through our link. I get a sharp pain in my temple. I rub it absent-mindedly. "Where is Ella?"

"Clean yourself up." He drops his arms. "There is going to be a handful of us meeting to discuss."

There is something off about his answer. I narrow my eyes. "Legia threw a reception for Ella and me, which Viktor and his allies used to catch us when our guards were down. My mother slit my throat, and I sat there like a fucking puppet and let her because she has a set of spirit runes." My voice is steadily escalating. I pinch the bridge of my nose, taking a deep breath. "I don't want to discuss. I want my wife."

I use the word without thought. It echoes around the stone surrounding us. *Wife. I married her, made her mine in every way possible. She promised me.* My throat constricts as I wait for him to answer. I clench my fists, still waiting.

Something in his expression tells me I am not going to like what I hear. He nods, rubbing a hand over his scalp and looking down. "Ella's whereabouts are currently unknown." A growl rips from me. "In the commotion, Erac stabbed Marcus as he was trying to get her to safety and dissipated with her."

My mind is cloudy, hazed. I feel a splinter in my chest. I cannot think, cannot add the pieces in my mind. There is something in me keeping me from thinking, like a drug. Rage. My head is swimming. My body feels foreign to me. I cannot focus.

*Ella.*

My limbs feel heavy, and my body sways, the ground like sand beneath my feet. I am unstable, my legs weak. My knees give away, and I sink down. I need to breathe. I need air. I focus on breathing.

My palms are sweating, but my fingers feel thick and numb as I try to make a fist. I cannot draw strength to squeeze hard. My hands shake. I stare at them, willing this feeling to go away. I need to focus, to think. I am screaming at myself to think, but the haze in my mind will not let me.

The air filling my lungs isn't enough. I stare up at Marx. He is standing there, watching me. He looks to be at ease while everything in me is disintegrating. I bare my teeth at him, hating him.

I push myself to my feet. The world sways. I inhale, deep and slow. Blinking, the world comes into relief around me. The feeling is wearing off, and my head is clearing. I still feel too hot inside while my body shivers, my skin crawling with goosebumps.

"Pull yourself together. We need a plan of attack. I'll meet you in Marcus' private library. The others are already there waiting."

He disappears from my sight. I snarl at the empty hallway. My instinct is to find Viktor and rip his limbs off until he tells me where Ella is. He wears the runes, though, and so does my mother. Rushing in would be foolish, not to mention my mother's insistent desire to kill me.

I squeeze my fists, shivering. I need more blood. I glance down at myself. The white button-up is stained with blood. It looks more like a red shirt with white stains. The scent is making me crazy. I rip it off, tossing it into the cell to rot with the bodies. I'll figure out what to do with them later. Right now, Marx was right.

I need a shower. I need more blood. I need facts.

# CHAPTER 40

*A*fter a shower, I dissipate in clean clothes to Marcus'
study. I have tried to reach Ella several times, but
anytime I do, I feel pain. I assemble myself, looking around the
room. Leo Wyndam offers me a glass of bourbon. I throw it
down my throat and go looking for more.

I grab the carafe from the middle of the desk, filling the
glass. I drink it down. There are the usual suspects. Leo
Wyndam. Marcus. Seth. Marx. A spirit I suspect is Sordello.

At the far end of the room, a man sits with his fingers
shoved through hair, head in his hands, elbows on knees,
staring at the ground. Next to him is Selene. Her hands are
bound in front of her, her face red and patchy from crying.

There are others, Aron, Samuel, and slumped on the floor,
curled into a ball, a girl with bright orange hair, sobbing into her
hands. My eyes flicker over the others. I do not recall their
names. I do not care to right now.

I set the tumbler down on the desk to fill it again. Alcohol
may not be the best thing for my rattled brain right now, but it
may help me keep my temper in check.

"Declan?" I look toward the sound of my name and the man on the couch. It is Wyatt. "How the hell did you survive?"

I take a sip, feeling the muscles in my neck protesting mildly. They are newly healed, and I have overworked them already. I look toward Marx.

"Shades heal quickly; it was just a matter of providing blood."

"She slit his throat. He was bleeding out for minutes." Wyatt says in response.

Marx crosses his arms. I know he doesn't deal well with being challenged. "I did what was necessary to save his life."

I raise an eyebrow at him. I am not even sure how he managed to keep me alive long enough to feed servants to me. Marx remains silent, so I focus on Marcus. How I survived is not relevant information.

"Erac stabbed you and took Ella?" My voice is hoarse.

His eyes flicker away from me. "I tried. I tried to stop him."

I grip the glass tighter. "What happened?"

He sits up in the chair, wincing and groaning. "After the duchess told Chase and me to run away, I went straight for Ella. She was..." he scrubs a hand over his face, "Something was wrong with her. She could barely stand."

"Shock," Aron says. "It must have been. It's the only explanation on why she didn't manipulate the elements to save Declan."

I roll my shoulders. I recall her lifting a hand toward me. I take a drink. "Something had to have been wrong before I had my throat slit for her to have let it happen in the first place."

"Skylar." My head pivots toward the broken girl on the floor. Legia's voice is small. It is weird. She is always too loud, always annoying with that squeal.

"What?"

"Before all of it. Ella drank something from Skylar. She thought Skylar had just got it from the bar because we were all standing there, but..." Legia's voice cracks. She dissolves into silent tears.

"What the fuck is wrong with you," I ask her.

A throat clears, and Marx frowns. "Her husband, the blond man, he did not survive."

My fist clenches in time with my jaw. I liked Chase. He was as much a pompous ass as I am. We understood each other.

Wyatt stirs. "Skylar and Selene were to drug you and Ella." He pushes fingers through his hair and stands. "They slipped paralytics and some herb that interrupts a bond into drinks for you."

Marx chuckles. "Flower of dreamwort."

Everyone but me looks at Marx. He would know what the herb was. He used it to dose me every day I was under his control. I return my attention to Wyatt. "And you know this how?"

"Because I..." He winces, holding hands up defensively, "I was privy to this plan before it started."

I grip the glass hard enough to shatter it. Legia is miles ahead of me, an orange blur on her way to her brother. She is screaming, that shrill squeal that makes my ears want to bleed.

"You bastard! You fucking prick!"

She is beating against him, pounding tiny fists against his chest. Wyatt flinches. When I hit him, he'll feel it. I will break him. I step forward, but Leo cuts off my direct path.

Legia is screaming, her voice shrill. It makes me wince. "Chase is dead! Dead! You fucking bastard!"

I look around Leo to see Legia sobbing against Wyatt's chest. She is no longer attempting to hurt him. I will. I won't give up. I meet Leo's gaze. "Move."

"My son was coerced. He made the choice to keep Legia safe by keeping his mouth shut."

"I knew what was coming. I thought if I just kept my mouth

shut until the last second, that I could save them both. I tried to get to Ella, but Elizabeth prevented it."

I force myself to exhale and flex my hands. He had known, allowed this disaster, and chosen Legia over Ella. I step back for now. There will be time later for me to collect my pound of flesh from Wyatt for his part.

I focus on Marcus. "She was drugged. You tried to get her to run away, and then what?"

Marcus shakes his head. "Not run. Fight. I told her to fight back. I thought it was shock too." He scrubs a hand over his face. "Erac helped me get her up. I told him to go fight back too. He told me he was going to get Ella out of there. When I told him no, he made a blade. I wasn't strong enough to force the elements against him." He rests back, panting, on the verge of tears.

*Tears. As if that is going to do me any good.*

"To summarize, Chase is dead. Ella has been taken. Wyatt knew about this beforehand. Skylar and Selene..." I pause just long enough to lock my eyes on the latter, "drugged me and Ella." My words trail away. I am going to break that face she loves so much, and I am going to deal with Skylar the way I should have the first time around.

Seth comes over, helping himself to the bourbon straight from the decanter. "Marcus was stabbed. Elizabeth was involved. Mom has a set of spirit runes and keeps trying to kill you." He drains the glass, then sets it down. "This is a shit show."

"Exactly how does Mother have a set of spirit runes?" I look from my brother to the spirit present.

It's shoulders slump. "Erac knew about the wedding. He was furious."

"My brother was with Orso when Orso disappeared from the collective." Aron hangs his head. "I believed him when he said he was not responsible, that it was a coincidence that they disappeared from the collective together."

"Hold up." My brother lifts a hand in the air. "I thought anyone in the collective had a set of spirit runes, so don't you and Erac already have runes?"

Aron looks from Seth to me. I curl my lip. "Don't be a fucking idiot. He killed Orso, and he did it for the runes, but not for himself. He has runes, and Viktor had runes. You know who didn't have runes? Mom."

Seth stares into his drink and then throws it back with a shudder. "Erac killed another spirit for runes and gave them to Mom?"

I don't waste my breath, trying to explain it to him. I bare my teeth at Aron. "You knew what happened, that Erac had a set of spirit runes, and no one said anything to me?" I whip my accusing glare from Aron to Sordello. "Both of you? He already had runes. The only logical explanation was he was taking them to Viktor. He's working with Viktor. Viktor mentioned he has a teacher, someone who knows more than Ella about magic."

"He told me it was a coincidence," Aron yells, his round face beat red. "He is my brother, and I trusted him. No one is more furious with Erac than I!" Aron points at his chest.

I laugh, my chest hollow with fury. "I doubt that."

"He is my brother and my oldest friend. He betrayed me. He went against me." Aron thrusts his finger toward himself once more. "I believe in you and Ella. I was filled with happiness that you two had found each other once more. He has destroyed much in this madness and is far beyond help. I see that now, but do not blame me for his actions and do not blame me for believing in my own blood."

I look at Seth, judging if I would hesitate to break his neck if I believed him on the verge of betrayal.

Seth lifts his glass to me. "If I thought for one second that you'd hurt Ella, I'd figure out a way to kill you."

The left side of my mouth twitches before I can control the reaction. Sometimes I like my brother. Shrugging and crossing my arms, I focus on Selene. *She gave me the drugs. She knew the plan.* I grin. *She is going to tell me everything we do not already know.*

"What are you grinning about?" Aron asks. "I see nothing humorous."

I glance over at Marx. He grimaces. "If there ever was a time for them to know the truth about you..."

"I really don't care." I step around Leo, moving toward the couch. "I don't care if I am king. I don't care what the court knows or doesn't know anymore. I don't really care about much beyond getting Ella back."

"What's going on?" Marcus asks. "The truth about what?"

"So many secrets and so little time," I breathe, tangling my fingers in blonde curls. I want to rip them from Selene's scalp. I want Ella. That damned woman had pretty hair. It was different, purple or red or brown. It changed colors in different lights. I liked it.

I tighten my grip around the bland, curly strands and drag the bitch Selene off the couch by the roots of her hair. She cries out, grabbing at my wrist with both her hands. I smirk. "I am going to get answers. I suggest none of you interfere with me."

"Dec," Seth sighs. "Wait."

I glare at him. "Don't fucking get in my way."

Seth takes another drink. "I was going to say I will help."

I laugh. "I don't need help. Find out what you can. Maybe torture this one." I jerk my head toward Wyatt.

"I cannot accept—" Leo starts, stepping toward me.

I hold my hand out, forcing him back with energy. "Until now, everything has been about threat management. Until now, it has been chasing packs of demons and forcing Viktor's forces to one corner of Caleum."

Leo picks himself up off the floor across the room. "You are King of Byron and—"

I ignore whatever he is blathering on about. "Up to this very point, it has all been about setting the chessboard. But now...?" I grin. "This is war. I don't care if Wyatt is your son; he betrayed us."

"He saved his sister!"

"And Ella?"

"Ella is not the only life," Leo snaps. "We all know you care for her, but she is not the only life that matters because the King of Byron fancies her."

I snarl at him, bearing teeth, but Sordello cuts me off. "Ella is the main concern because of what she brings to the table. Feelings aside, her power is greater than any other. If Viktor has her, we are all doomed. She is far more powerful than any of us, and I fear the day she is persuaded into fighting us. No single life is worth the price of my daughter for that fact."

The room is quiet. I hear Legia still sobbing. It makes me want to rip her throat out. She is clinging and sobbing to the man who could have prevented it. I have a strong urge to shake her until her neck snaps.

Instead, I grip Selene hard enough to cause her to cry out. I look to Seth. "Get what answers you can."

Marcus is on his feet, Samuel helping to support him. "What are you going to do? If Ella is dead, Selene is the only Byron heir."

I laugh, finding it oddly humorous that Marcus would consider Selene fit to be queen. "I am going to get answers, to find out who was involved and what the plan was."

"How?" he asks.

"Any way I possibly can." The thought draws my lips upward.

Done with this mess, I dissipate myself and Selene to that old, familiar room in Marx's estate by the black sea. The room is freezing cold, but it only helps to clear my head. I shove her against the iron door, the only way in or out of the room.

She cries out, struggling as I listen to the iron burning her bare shoulders and arms. I like the sound, enjoy watching her writhe in pain. It was such a simple thing, to force her pale white skin against the iron, but effective.

"Please," she sobs. "Please, Dec, stop!"

I pull her away from the door, throwing her to the floor by that bloodstained mattress. I had laid there so many times after punishment for failure or an act of disrespect, thinking I might die. I never begged like she just did, and I am only getting started.

She leans back on her hands, staring up at me with glassy eyes. She crawls a few paces further away from me. I watch her, contemplating what to start with. My eyes travel over the tools on the table.

"Dec," she whispers, drawing my eyes back. "Please, please don't hurt me." She sits up, moving to kneel before me, sitting back on her heels. "Please," she reaches out to me. "I know you care for Ella, but you care for me too. Do you really want to lose both of us?"

"Care for you?" My words come out as a strangled whisper. "Are you really so stupid?"

She shakes her head, popping to her knees. "Don't do that, baby. I know you're scared, probably a little upset, but don't push me away." Her words are a breathless whisper.

Rage slithers through me. The feeling is euphoric, a bitter taste lingering on my tongue. *The bitch thinks I care. I'll show her just how much I care. I'll start with flesh and blood.*

I take her hand in mine. It is dainty, delicate, soft. Ella's hands were always rough, the skin battered, and calloused from physical activities and beating a practice post to perfect her punch. She was never so beautiful to me as she was when she was lost in thought, dancing around a wood post. Her hair was a mess, the way it was when I had her on her back underneath me.

I grin inwardly at the memories of Ella, then blink, focusing on the girl in front of me. She bats her lashes, her eyes glassy orbs in a pretty face. I run a finger over her cheek, aching to know how easy her face will break.

Her face is shaped like a heart, Ella's is more angular, her features strong, not dainty and frail like the ones before me. Selene might have more curves to her body, bigger assets. So many differences down to their heart and height.

"Push you away?" I pull her to her feet. "Why would I push you away?" I take her hand between the two of mine. It is going to break with minimal effort. I smile at her knowing she is going to cry and beg and break.

"Dec, I know you, baby, and I knew you wouldn't hurt me." There is relief in her voice. She breathes easier, panting a bit and trying to smile.

I snap her wrist with a flick of my own. She shrieks, trying to pull away from me. "What do you know about me?" I jerk the broken wrist, pushing her hand back so far that bones are crackling. She is screaming and sobbing. "Ella knows me. Ella knows what I am capable of."

I grab Selene's hand, forcing it in the other direction. She wails, the cries echoing around us. I hold her thrashing body by her forearm as I twist her hand, rotating the broken bones against each other. I can hear them grinding, sweet music to my ears.

I grin at her ugly, crying face. "You don't know me at all, and I do not care about you."

"Please, please stop," she begs, falling to her knees. For now, I allow her to kneel before me. She drags air into herself in annoying gasps. She shakes as she draws in a breath, staring up at me with wide eyes. They're too far apart in her head, like a bug.

*How did I ever manage to fuck this thing?* I smirk at my own jest.

"Please, Dec, don't do this. I know you're mad, but you'll see, this way, everyone is happy."

I tilt my head, confused by her words. "I'm not happy."

"You will be." Her words are too loud, too fast, like the beat of her heart wildly pulsating in my ears. "I promise, baby, you will be. We'll be happy again like we were before she came back." The bitch's voice slowly dies away with her words.

I raise my eyebrows. "You think I was happy?" I drop her hand, tipping my head back to laugh wholeheartedly. Getting control of myself, I drop to one knee. I lift her face toward mine with two fingers under her chin. "I was out of my mind with grief. I was drunk all the time. You were convenient, an easy whore to fuck and play with for entertainment. If I had not been so broken and drunk, I might have gone to find a toy that wasn't so lackluster, someone who might have offered me a decent fuck."

Her lower lip trembles. Her eyes well up. All I do is grin. I grab her by her hair, lifting her to her feet. She yelps, reaching up as if she may drag my hands from her. I force her back against the wall, closing an iron collar around her neck.

She howls, clawing at it. I tug on the chain, holding the collar to the wall to make sure it is still attached. This is going to be more fun if I know she isn't going to crawl away.

I turn to the table amidst her pleas echoing around the stone walls. I have stopped listening, tired of her words. I choose a blade, thinking of cutting her tongue out.

I set the blade down again. I need her to talk. I need to know what happened, what the plan was, where my wife is. I growl, the memory of Ella in this very room, hugging herself, looking lost and scared as she looked around. She had felt sorry for me, had wanted to take my pain away.

I pick up a pair of plyers. "Tell me what I want to know." I smirk. "If you cry, if you beg, or if you refuse to answer my questions, I am going to show you who I truly am, and you aren't going to like it."

# CHAPTER 41

## MORELLA

*A* man enters the room, the heavy wood door dragging along the polished floor. The space is luxurious, vast with gilded furniture and silk pillows. The bed is massive, dead center in the room, and I am perched in the middle. I am cross-legged and watching him.

The man stops just inside. The door closes with a soft thud as he looks at me. I narrow my eyes back at him. I woke in this room and have been sitting here waiting for something, although I don't know what. I don't recall anything, not where I am or how I got here. I have sat here, waiting, trying to remember anything at all before I opened my eyes, but there's nothing.

He is tall and thin. He wears a clean white shirt with buttons in the front and dark jeans. I eye him, unmoving.

"Morella?"

"Is that me? Who are you? Where am I? Is that my name?"

"I know you're probably confused, maybe even a little scared, but you don't need to be." I sit straight, waiting for him to say something else. "We tried..." He sighs. "We've been trying to save you for a while now."

I look away and around the room. I feel a sensation slithering through my veins like fury. *Why would I be angry about being
saved?*

"This is going to be difficult for you to understand, hard for
me to explain, but there's a war going on. One that involved
you, and for a while, you were held on the other side. They
poisoned you. We finally got you back, but their poison, it is—
was—in your brain. It made you crazy. We couldn't remove their
poison. The only thing we could do was pull everything out of
your head. It was the only way to remove the poison."

I grunt as he sits on the edge of the bed. He looks at me,
almost with pity. There's something soft in his violet eyes even
as they appear to glow in the dim light of dusk through the
windows. I have an uneasy feeling as he puts a hand on my
thigh.

"What are you telling me?" I wheeze. My voice is hoarse, and
forcing those words out hurts like sand scratching the back of
my mouth.

He smiles. The expression is tight like he had forgotten how
to. He stares at me, and I stare back. He has sandy-blond hair
that kind of curls at the ends. I cannot take in all his features,
just keep circling back to those indigo eyes. "I'm trying to tell
you I'm sorry. It wasn't supposed to be like this."

"Like what?" My voice is a deep croak.

"Your father and I made the proper sort of arrangement for
your hand in marriage."

I lean away from him, weary. I have an odd sensation in my
chest. Discontentment? Dishonesty? Dis-something feels right,
but I cannot put a word to the feeling that starts with dis. He is
watching me.

"I gave up everything for you. I gave him what he needed,
and..." The man stops, staring at me. I don't know if he is
expecting me to say something. "It's what you want," he begins
again. "To be loved." Something about those words resonates

within me. "And I love you more than Caleum itself. I love you more than I love my brother, more than anything, Morella." He is choking on words and quits talking.

I flex my hands, curling fists and releasing. I make circles with my shoulders, then pull my knees to my chest, snuggling into myself. If I do want love, it wouldn't be that kind of love. There's something sick in what he is saying.

He swallows and tries to grin again. He moves closer, so he is sitting next to me. "You might not remember, but I do. I'll teach you everything." His fingers trail down my arm. I squirm, a sick knot sinking in my stomach. "You're so beautiful."

Those fingertips brush along my exposed shoulder. His hand slides against my neck then pushes my hair away. He flips it over my shoulder to expose more of me. I cannot look at him. I swallow hard.

"So very, very beautiful," he whispers.

I feel his lips against my ear. I shift and move away. The strapless black dress I wear is negligent against him. I feel naked under his eyes. His touch makes me feel grotesque. I want something more to cover myself with.

"Do you want out of this room?"

That catches my attention, and I look at him, nodding with apprehension. He shifts closer, pressing up against me. His hand slips under the hem of my dress. I jerk, but he grabs my thigh and holds tight. His fingers dig into my flesh with brutal force even as he nuzzles against the hollow connection of my jaw and ear.

"You're hurting me," I whisper, swallowing my nerves.

"Don't fight me, and it won't hurt."

Suddenly, I have to pee. There's tightness in my body, and it's hard to breathe. "I'm not fighting."

He grins, those thin lips parting. I jerk to my feet, just trying to take a step away. He grabs at me, ripping the skirt of my dress.

"I don't understand," I manage, holding hands out between us. Standing on my feet at the edge of the bed isn't making me feel any safer. My voice is warbling, and my throat feels constricted. "Why did you ask if I wanted to leave this room?"

He stares at me with suspicious humor, as if my warding is enticing. "Because if you behave, you can. I'll let you out."

He holds a small metal key. My eyes drop to the cuff around my ankle, attached to the chain tying me to one of the bed's supports. I watch him tuck the key back into his pocket.

"Come here," he whispers. I don't move. "Come here," he repeats a little firmer.

I shuffle forward about a step. His eyes close, and he sighs. He smirks while shaking his head, and when he fixes his eyes on me once more, there's nothing soft in them. I watch, half horrified, half curious, as he moves toward me.

I move a few steps back away from the bed. He leans over, grabbing the chain lying against the floor. I remember he put the key away, and the horror overtakes me. "I said," he grunts and yanks, "come here."

My leg is whipped from under me. I cry out in shock as I start to topple. I land on my back, and my head cracks loudly against the floor. I stare at the ceiling, dazed, and seeing spots. I am only partially conscious as he drags me back to him. I blink, realizing he is kneeling over me. His hands are pulling up my skirt. The tulle and massive amounts of fabric cause him to fumble. I hear cloth ripping in his furious endeavor.

"I'm trying to remind you of our love."

"No," I beg. "No, stop." I start to squirm. I try pushing at him.

He grabs my wrists, squeezing hard enough to make my eyes prickle with tears. He stares down into my face. "Stop fighting this. You're mine."

"But I don't know who you are," I whisper. I blink, and tears push out. They roll down the side of my face into my filthy hair. "Who are you? Where am I? Who am I?"

"I am Erac. You are in your home, in Asperheim, in my room where you're safe. Your name is Morella." He collects my wrists together in one hand. He gets off me, and I sob in gratuity.

He wrenches me to my feet by my wrists. My left shoulder pops, but at least we are both standing on our feet. I lean my head against his chest, taking a deep breath. I almost relax, but he yanks me around, so he is behind me. My arms are bent behind me, and he holds them there with one hand. I draw in shaky breaths, not sure of what is going on. His other hand pulls my hair together and off to one side.

"So beautiful," he whispers again, his lips trickling over the thin skin of my neck.

I try not to cringe, but my body shudders. "Erac, please, stop. I don't know what's going on. I don't love you. I don't even know you."

"You will. You'll know me, and you'll love me."

The feeling in my chest of nausea and horror returns. *No. I won't. I don't. I can't.* I shake my head, pressing my lips together tight as my eyes prickle with tears.

"Fine," he snarls in my ear. "You won't behave?"

He whips us around so fast I am dizzy. The room sways, and he kicks me in the back of my knees. I buckle, hitting the stone floor hard, and pain rips through my knees, up my thighs.

I try to move my arms, but his grip tightens like metal around them, making me cry out. His lips press against the side of my face, curved as he sneers in a low whisper, "Know that I am going to enjoy this, feeling you after waiting so long."

He's tearing at the skirt of my dress again, using his body weight to force me into a bent-over position. I squirm as I feel cool air against the bare skin of my backside and thighs.

"No, please," I sob, trying to wriggle my way into freedom.

My eyes water and I'm trembling. It hurts. He hurts. A pain

like I am being split in two as he thrust in and out. I sob, and he pushes me flat with pressure on my wrists against my back as he lifts his body off mine to move faster behind me. In agony, my hands pinned by his ferocious grip, all I can do is squeeze my eyes shut and try to breathe even as I tremble and cry.

His rocking drags my face against the bedding. The friction burning the side of my face. I try to focus on that. It hurts less. I close my eyes, sobbing and praying this is over soon.

# TO BE CONTINUED...

## DEAR READER, YOU HAVE MY SINCERE APOLOGIES FOR SHOVING YOU OFF THAT CLIFF...MY BAD...

To my fellow sexual assault survivors, you aren't alone. As powerless and demoralizing as the experience makes you feel, there are people who can help.

**Sexual Assault & Abuse Help**

https://www.nsvrc.org/find-help

https://www.rainn.org

National Sexual Assault Telephone Hotline
1-800-656-4673

# ELLA AND DECLAN'S STORY WILL CONTINUE IN...

## POISON

### The Spirit Runes Book Three

#### Morella

I wake up in an unfamiliar room, tended to by a strange man who watches me with dark indigo eyes. He says he's Erac, my betrothed, that I'm safe now with him and my father. A pair of brothers poisoned me, he says, turned me against those I love, and the only way to remove their poison was to strip me of my memories. Without them, I am empty, lost in a sea of confusion with no concept of myself, and a hollowness inside that leaves me bitter and full of questions.

Erac teaches me magic, and my father teaches me chess, while I must fight for answers about my past. Isolated with only Erac's cruelty and my father's aloofness, I find friendship in a servant boy, George, who hints at the life I yearn to recall. Even as I try to help my father reclaim what is rightfully ours, I begin to unravel the mystery that left me shattered, but the truth may be far from what I've been told.

#### Declan

Ella's gone. Again. There's not enough liquor in all of Caleum for me to handle this hell. I need to find my strength and a way to get my wife back. Experiencing Erac raping my wife as she pleads for it to stop damn near destroys me, but they've tried to kill me before and failed.

Selene is furious with my marriage, and jealousy drives her to condemn me if I don't refute my vows.

I fight to keep the crown and my mind as I work to find a way to bring Ella home. This might kill me, but I can't give up. I don't know when all of Caleum became my responsibility, but someone has to kill Viktor or die trying.

Order Poison today!

Learn more at cjwallingsford.com

# THANK YOU

**Thank you for reading Unravel!**
**Please leave a review!**
Write a customer review
You, my dear reader, control the success of my humble story. By leaving a review you help others discover a story they can enjoy.

**I love hearing from my readers!**
Send me an email at cjwallingsford@outlook.com or find me on Facebook or Instagram to chat.

# ACKNOWLEDGMENTS

The voices in my head get about seventy-five percent credit for this story. Most writers will tell you that characters have a mind of their own, and in this case it's true. Twenty precent of credit is owed to my husband. He has indulged this obsession, withstood hours of me reviewing plot and character development, and given me ample time and resources to pursue this little project. The last five percent is split between hard work, resulting in headaches, and Brittany.

To Eric Wallingsford, thank you. I am beyond grateful to you for your support.

To Brittany Santagato, you helped make this story what it is. You have provided notes, spent hours talking about this book, and provided invaluable insight that tightened characters and removed plot holes.

Thank you to my beta readers, Sue Hayes and Natalie Davidson.

Thank you to KillingItWrite for the editing and feedback that helped to create this story.

Thank you to Storywrappers for the beautiful cover.

As always, music is a major influence to provide mood and tone to my writing. There are so many artists that I can thank, but too many for me to list. I'll limit to specific artists whose albums I listened to on repeat: Slipknot, Taylor Swift, Bring Me The Horizon, and The Beautiful Monument.

A nod to Dan Hermeyer who liked to read snippets of this

story over my shoulder as I wrote at work. Every line he read he managed to twist into something incredibly inappropriate as an innuendo. Thank you for that.

# ABOUT THE AUTHOR

C J Wallingsford is a lover of writing and traveling. When not exploring new places and tracing down history, she lives in St Louis with her husband and two dogs, Jovina and Rat. This is CJ's second book in her first trilogy.